TIN SOLDIERS

A DCI ROBERT KETT NOVEL

ALEX SMITH

RELENTLESS
MEDIA

TIN SOLDIERS

Published Worldwide by Relentless Media.
This edition published in 2026.

Edited by Hanna Elizabeth and Jacqueline Beard MBE

ISBN: 978-1-913877-22-4

2.19.5

www.alexsmithbooks.com

ALSO BY ALEX SMITH

The DCI Robert Kett Thrillers

Paper Girls

Bad Dog

Three Little Pigs

Whip Crack

Run Rabbit Run

Stone Cold Dead

Every Mother's Son

Sweet Briar Rose

Jaw Breaker

Knock Knock

King Rat

Knuckle Bones

Lucky Number Seven

Unholy Saints

Truly Madly Deadly

Every Last Devil

Red Line

Cold Iron Kills

Tin Soldiers

Until Death

ALSO BY ALEX SMITH

The DI Harrison Baird Thrillers

A Long-Dead Thing

Open Wounds

Mad Dogs

Other Books

Six Days, Six Hours, Six Minutes

The Harder They Fall

For Grub and Midge,
Long gone, and much missed.

PROLOGUE

Friday

If Helen Coulter could pick her least favourite time of the day, it would be this: the godforsaken evening.

Evenings were afterthoughts, unwanted and undesired. They were pegged onto the back of the afternoon as if nobody knew what to do with them, sandwiched uncomfortably between daylight and night-time like a runt sibling between its favoured brothers. They were the time of day when you said goodbye, or goodnight, and surrendered yourself to the dark. Quiet times. Lonely, too—even now, as she walked down the dark-drenched street with Roger Sexton on her heels.

"You're not saying much, pet," said Roger, wheeling his bike beside him like a cowboy leading a horse. The clickety-clack of his wheels was strangely comforting, the same way his soft voice and his Geordie accent were. Familiar sounds, even here in the unfamiliar dark.

Helen crossed the deserted road, ducking beneath the damson trees that overhung the gardens. It wasn't far from the stop where the bus dropped her off for her flat in the city, but a day in the hospital had filled her legs with nails and needles, every bone grinding.

Roger stayed on the road, scratching at the feathery down that clung to his almost-bald scalp. He wasn't a bad-looking man for sixty-three, she knew, his jawline still relatively firm and his waist slim thanks to the hours he spent on that bloody bike of his. He dressed older, like he'd borrowed his dad's wardrobe, and his dentures didn't really fit him, but it was nothing she couldn't fix if she had the time and the patience to do so.

And it wasn't like she was still a looker, was it? She was three years older than Roger, and it looked like she'd borrowed her mother's *face*. She couldn't quite believe how hard age had hit her in the last couple of years, an invisible mallet that had stretched her jowls and hollowed her cheeks and pitted her face with wrinkles. She'd done her best to dye the grey, but her job didn't leave much money for the good stuff, or much time to apply it properly, so now she looked like a badger to boot.

That was one good thing about the evening, of course. It was dark enough to hide the imperfections.

"Hel," said Roger. "You alright, love?"

"I'm okay," she replied. "Always okay, Rog, you know me. Just tired. Long shift."

Fourteen hours, to be precise, and it hadn't been an easy one. Not that being a nurse was *ever* easy, but there seemed to have been even more vomit, piss, shit and blood than usual on the wards today.

More death, too, and not quiet ones.

"Just tired," she said again. "Hate this time of day, don't you?"

"Night?" said Roger. "Dunno, pet, I quite like my sleep."

"Evening," she said, cutting across a triangle of dry grass as she headed towards the main road. There wasn't much traffic about, most people long home from work. "I hate them. They do nothing but let you know how little time you've got."

"How so?"

"That's all the evening ever is for me, the walk home before you go to sleep and then do it all over again. The only free time I get, and if I blink, I miss it."

Roger nodded, looking a little uncomfortable. He thumbed the bell on the handlebar of his bike, the ring filling the quiet street. Every time she saw him, he seemed to have another bike, all of them new. She didn't know how he afforded it on a porter's wage.

"Make more of it, then," he said. "You don't have to rush home. There's a... a poem, I think. Isn't there?"

She gave him a look that asked how the hell she would know the answer to that. Roger cleared his throat, staring at the houses that lined the side of the road.

"Fall in love with the vibrant mornings," he said. "Uh, and caress the quiet of the afternoons."

"I'm just going to stop you there, Roger," she said. "Because one, that's not a poem, that's the ramblings of a sixty-three-year-old hospital porter who's obviously been sniffing too much floor polish. And two, who the hell gets a quiet afternoon? I had an old bastard try and stab me with his catheter at half past three."

Roger laughed, but carried on regardless as they made

their way towards the underpass that connected this side of the road to the park.

"Take the warmth of the evening in a wild embrace, and put your lips to it."

A giggle fell out of Helen's mouth like she was a schoolgirl again, and she felt the warmth creep into her cheeks. She set off down the slope and into the dark mouth of the underpass, where the lights never seemed to burn bright enough. Roger glided down beside her, his head tucked in like he was racing the Tour de France. Graffiti stared at her from the walls, twisted figures and angry faces and the endless gang tags that made her feel uneasy. She wouldn't normally go this way, she'd use the crossing further up by the roundabout, but when Roger was there, he made her feel a little braver.

Not that Roger would be much cop if a bunch of thugs was walking the other way. Wasn't like you could use bike clips as a weapon.

"That it?" she asked, entering the tunnel. "The poem?"

There was enough light to see the drifts of litter piled up like shovelled snow, the puddles of what couldn't be rainwater, seeing as how the weather had been glorious for days. The smell was worse down here than it was at work, and that was saying something.

"Well, no," he said, clearing his throat again. The soft click of his wheels followed her down. "There's another couple of lines, but I'm not sure it's suitable."

"I'm over eighteen, I'll be okay."

He cleared his throat again.

"Then get naked with the soft, glowing nights."

It wasn't a giggle this time, it was a snort that echoed off the tunnel walls, and Helen had to cover her face with her hand to hide it.

"Roger! That's filthy!"

He roared a laugh in reply, ringing the bell again as they emerged from the arse end of the underpass. Helen started the gentle climb into Chapelfield Gardens, hearing no sound at all other than the rumble of traffic on the main road.

"I didn't write it," said Roger. "Can't even remember if those are the right words. But it's true, isn't it? I think that's what the poem is saying. You... Ah, I don't know, I haven't got the gift of the gab. You have to grasp the moment. Make the most of every time of day. Make the most of... of every time in your life. The morning, the afternoon."

He blew out a sigh.

"The evenings, too."

Helen reached the top of the slope and stopped walking. So did Roger, rocking his bike awkwardly from side to side while they both tried to fumble a way back into the conversation. Some of the park lights were on, while others had been broken, leaving immense pockets of darkness in every direction. They could have been in the middle of nowhere here, but she didn't feel afraid. This was the city, the pubs and clubs all around them and the police station close enough to hear her yell if something jumped out of the trees.

"I hope that isn't your poetic way of calling me old," she said after a moment. "Because I'm only sixty..."

She mumbled the *six* so quietly he didn't pick up on it.

"I'm still very much in my afternoon," she finished. "Thank you very much."

Roger had the good grace to bow his head in agreement.

"That's one of the many reasons I like you, Hel," he said. "You make it feel like the sun is always shining."

"Oh bloody hell, Roger," she said, her cheeks on fire

now. She took a couple of steps into the park, then stopped again, turning back. "You shouldn't lead a girl on like that, you know. Goodness knows what people will think."

"What people?" he said, still standing there with his bike like a bashful teenager. "And I mean it. You must know it by now. I walk you home after every shift, and I don't even live on this side of town."

"I just figured you enjoyed riding your bike," she said.

"Well, I do," he told her, giving the bell another ring, like he was a game-show contestant trying to answer a question. "But I enjoy *you* too."

"Oh, you do, do you?" she said, hearing the words coming out of her mouth even though she had no idea why she'd spoken them. It was a ludicrous thing to say, completely without substance, so unlike anything she might have said if she'd had a little time to prepare. She tried to finish with something that was halfway coherent, and ended up adding, "Do you, do?"

"Yes," he said. "I do do."

For a while, they stood there in the quiet dark, just looking at each other. Then a little black and white dog trotted past, taking a second to sniff at Helen's shoes before thundering onto the lawn, erased by the dark. Its owner followed, too busy with her phone to bother looking up.

"Look, Roger, I like you too," said Helen when they were alone again. "It's just, you know, I..."

I'm not sure I've got it in me anymore. I'm not sure I can remember how to do it, any of it, the dates, the romance, the jokes, the kissing, the stuff that happens after the kissing. I'm not sure there's enough here to keep you interested for more than a day or two, because my head's full of stuffing and so's my body. I'm like a scarecrow, Roger, and if something starts between us and then you end it, you'll pull out the rest of my stuffing, and I'm going to be empty again, and I'm not sure I can take that, I'm not sure I've got enough years left to fill myself up again, I...

"I've got an early start," she said. "I'm sorry."

He thumbed the bell, but not hard enough to make it ring.

"You don't have to be sorry, pet," he said. "You never have to be sorry. I'm the one who should be apologising. Old farts like me should know better."

He huffed out a tired breath.

"But if you change your mind, uh..."

This was hard for him, she saw, but she didn't know how to make it any easier.

"Maybe we could go away? When's the last time you had a break? A proper holiday?"

Helen laughed, and she hated the way it made him seem to doubt himself.

"Who's going on holiday on a nurse's salary, Rog?" she said. "And most of the time these days I'm volunteering."

"I've got a bit stashed away," he said. "More than you might think. Been working on something new. I could, you know..."

He lost steam, fiddling with his bell.

"Maybe," she said, and the lack of conviction in her voice wasn't anything to do with how she felt about Roger.

It seemed to sting him, though, because he fell awfully quiet.

"I'll see you tomorrow, though, won't I?" said Helen, trying to repair the damage.

"Aye," he said. "I'll be there. Come on, I'll walk you the rest of the way."

"Don't," she said, feeling like there was a wildcat in her

chest trying to scratch its way free. "I'm fine, it's not far. I'll be okay."

"If you're sure?" he said. "It's no bother."

"I'll be fine," she told him, although she felt the exact opposite.

"Goodnight, then, Hel."

He wheeled his bike in a sad little circle, walking it back down the slope. Helen watched him for as long as it took her to understand he wasn't going to look back, until he was swallowed by the dark underpass, then she turned on her worn heels and headed into the park. Her cheeks were still burning, but it wasn't embarrassment she felt now, it was anger. She was furious at herself, at the part of her brain that had locked the door as soon as Roger Sexton had begun to knock. That bastard voice in her head had scuppered every shot at romance she'd had since Dominic had left her, nearly forty bloody years ago.

See that, Helen? it said. *See that little shot of happiness? You like it? You want it? Well, tough. You can't have that. Goodness gracious no. A happy Helen? That won't do anyone any good now, will it?*

The voice even sounded like her ex-husband, as if Dominic hadn't just won the house and the car and the dog in the divorce, but had given himself a part ownership of her skull, too. A free room from which he could watch her life slowly circle the toilet year after year after year. She could hear him laughing at her the way he always had, like she was a walking joke, the court jester to his kingly throne.

The evening seemed to laugh at her, too, and she stopped walking again, scuffing her old shoe on the path. For some reason, even though she hadn't smoked in decades, she desperately wanted a cigarette.

The same little black and white dog ran past, heading

the other way, no sign of its owner this time. Helen found herself doubling back too, walking as fast as her aching knees would let her towards the underpass. Roger would be on his bike now, speeding through the city, probably calling his daughter in New Zealand the way he often did on his rides. There wasn't a hope in hell of catching him.

Maybe, though, he wouldn't be. Maybe he'd be on the other side of the pass, *umm*-ing and *ah*-ing and ready to turn back and come after her. That's how they worked, wasn't it? These love stories. Two people, both realising the same thing at the same time, running into each other's arms.

Well, *walking*. She doubted either of them was capable of a sprint.

She made her way down the slope, everything from her ankles to her hips burning like she was a witch on a pyre. And she was so busy searching the end of the tunnel for any sign of Roger that she didn't see the body that lay on the filthy ground until she'd almost tripped on it.

She stopped, taking a couple of lurching steps back. The heel of her foot caught a loose bottle, and the sound of it rolling away dragged a scream up her throat. She clamped her teeth around it, turning it into a grunt.

It was definitely a person. Even with the flickering lights, she could see that much. They lay across the width of the tunnel, dirty trainers pressed against one wall, the head almost reaching the other. She couldn't make out any details because they were covered with something, a dirty great tarpaulin, maybe, or a blanket. Whatever it was, it was filthy, streaked with grime. There was no sign of movement there at all, not even the gentle rise and fall of breath.

But they couldn't be dead, because how was that possible? She'd literally walked through here five minutes ago, and even though her eyes weren't as good as they used to be, and she probably should be wearing glasses, there was no way she'd have missed a dead man. She'd have had to step over him, for one thing, and Roger would have had to lift his—

Roger.

It was like she'd been kicked in the chest by a mule, the idea that this could be him. Had he been attacked? Had somebody thumped him one as he'd run back into the underpass to find her?

But if that was the case, where was his bike? Stolen?

And now that the drumming pulse of adrenaline had cleared, how had he found time to change his shoes?

It had to be a homeless person, then. Unhoused? Was that the word they used now? She'd seen more than her fair share of them at the hospital—men like this one with dirty coats and old shoes—not that she was judging, of course, because nobody deserved to be out on the streets. She treated them the same as she treated everyone else.

And if anyone needed to be treated, it was this man. He still hadn't shown any sign of movement, not a twitch, not a tremor. If he'd crawled in here to die, then she didn't have a lot of time.

"Hello?" she said, taking a couple of steps towards the person. "Can you hear me? Do you need help?"

She opened her bag and found her phone, holding it in one hand as she reached for the tarpaulin with the other. It was greasy to the touch, as warm as human skin, and she almost let go immediately.

Then she pulled, and the coat—it was a wax jacket, she realised—slid away from the man's head.

He didn't have a face. Or rather, she couldn't see a face, because he was wearing some kind of mask. It was made of a dull black metal, no features except for two perfectly round holes for the eyes, glazed with dark glass. He looked like an insect, like a spider, no emotion in those lifeless black holes at all.

"Hello?" she said again, pulling the rest of the jacket away to reveal a set of black overalls, a neck damp with sweat. She didn't need to put her fingers to it because she could see the pulse in his throat, she could see the rise and fall of his Adam's apple as he swallowed.

The head tilted, those eyes finding her.

"Thank you," said a quiet voice, muffled by the mask.

If she'd even known what to say to that, she didn't have time to speak. A gloved hand grabbed her arm, yanking her down, pulling her into the stinking mass of him. He rose to meet her, that helmet thumping into the bridge of her nose, as heavy as a sledgehammer. She fell onto her back, the phone slipping from her fingers. She couldn't see anything, just flashes of black light as the pain roared inside her face.

He's broken me, she thought.

And he had, he'd broken something inside her that stopped her from screaming, stopped her from fighting back as he crawled over her, pinning her beneath him.

Her vision ebbed back, and she saw herself reflected in the glass circles of his eyes, or at least a pale, frightened spectre that might have been her.

"Please," she said, the word made of blood.

The man stroked her hair, his hand moving down her face, over her broken nose.

Tightening around her throat.

"Thank you," he said again.

He squeezed, and the effect was instantaneous. For a moment, her head swelled, ballooning with blood and a rush of sound. She tried to lift a hand, tried to fight him off the way she'd done so many times with the drunks and the crazies at work—with Dominic, too, when things had started to get nasty.

But something had been severed. Nothing worked, not even her voice.

Roger, she thought. But he wouldn't hear her. Not now.

Not ever.

"Thank you," said the mask. The last thing she'd ever hear.

The pressure in her head grew too much, and just like a light being switched off—as simply as that, so different to how she'd imagined death might be—she dropped away, into the evil bastard evening.

CHAPTER ONE

Saturday

What on earth are you doing, Robbie?

DCI Robert Kett hadn't known the answer to that question for most of his life, and the mystery had only deepened in the years since he'd arrived in Norwich. Right now, sitting in his car, blinded by the sunlight that streamed through the windscreen, listening to his children screaming at each other outside the window and his wife trying to quiet them, he seemed further away from an answer than ever.

It had been over six months since he'd faced off against John Maynard and the last of his psychopathic soldiers in the brutal Cold Iron Kills case. But Kett had been back there every night since, lost in the dark tunnels beneath the sugar factory, chased by an army of madmen with sharp knives in their hands and cruel grins beneath their masks.

Every night following that one, his dreams had been full of death—his own, Billie's, Kate and Pete and Aaron.

His daughters, too, swallowed alive by the horror of Hollenbeck.

He'd escaped physically, but he knew he'd be a prisoner of that night until the day he died.

And he'd only *just* escaped. He carried the scars of their violence the way he carried the memories, a constant reminder that those tunnels had almost been his grave. Once upon a time, he and Billie had looked at each other's battle-worn bodies and told themselves they were a testament to their strength, to their ability to survive. They had been a tapestry of hope, a message written in flesh that no matter what happened, no matter how much pain and hurt they'd been through, they were still here, for each other and for their children.

Now, though, those half-healed wounds felt like an autobiography of madness—the madness of continuing to do the job even when it had tried so hard to kill him.

And here he was, about to descend into insanity again.

"What on earth are you doing, Robbie?" he asked himself, aloud this time.

He was answered by a squeak from the car window, Moira's face smushed against the outside of the glass, blowing wet raspberries. Evie squeezed in next to her. They looked like a couple of Cabbage Patch Dolls as they gurned at him.

Billie stood behind them, a welcome glimpse of calm. She'd let her honey-coloured hair grow out in the last year or so, and with her cornflower blue summer dress, she looked just like the woman he'd first fallen in love with. He gave her a smile, but she didn't see.

He knocked on the glass, and when Evie and Moira

didn't stop, he started to wind down the window. They pulled back, laughing wildly as they rubbed the saliva from their mouths.

"You should be careful pulling faces," he told them. "If the wind changes, they'll stay like that forever. Wait..."

He gasped in mock horror.

"Oh no," he said.

"What?" said Evie, suddenly serious. She turned to Billie. "What?"

"Oh no," Billie echoed, her eyes wide. "It's too late!"

Kett opened the door, trying not to let the pain show on his face as he climbed out. His back had been worse than ever recently, although the doctors couldn't find anything wrong with him—other than being a copper well into his forties. A welcome breeze nipped up his shorts and down the sleeves of his T-shirt.

"*What*?" said Evie, almost a screech.

"The wind must have changed," he told them. "You're going to look like that forever."

"No!" wailed Moira, squishing her face with both hands. "I don't want to look like a marshmallow."

"I'll still love you," he told them. "Even if your faces now look like bums."

"You're joking," said Evie, prodding the worry lines on her face. "That's not true."

"He's joking," said Billie with a laugh.

Kett pulled them both into a hug, and Billie bookended it.

"You're doughnuts, for sure," he said. "But not because you look like them."

Alice got out of the car, slamming her door behind her. She was glued to her phone, her face lit by the screen that she seemed to hold permanently six inches in front of her.

"Alice, wanna get in on the hug?" he asked.

She ignored him, her thumb working double time as she scrolled through whatever idiocy she'd found on TikTok.

"Alice!" said Evie, her muffled voice hot through his T-shirt. "Huggy time!"

"Huggy time!" echoed Moira. And then they were both chanting it.

"She can't hear us," said Billie. "She's got her ear things in."

"I can hear you," said Alice, without looking up.

"She's a loser," said Moira, as the hug ended.

Alice shot a middle finger at her sister, and Moira shot two right back. Evie, who had an aversion to breaking the rules in any way, lifted both pinkie fingers instead, jiggling them up and down.

"Hey!" said Kett. "That's enough, girls. There are people here. Can you all just try to act normal?"

The car park was absolutely mobbed, the crowd making its way towards the enormous sports complex that was hosting the *East Anglian Constabulary's Annual Dodgeball Tournament*. Most of them were coppers, easily identifiable even when they weren't in suits or uniforms. Like Kett, they'd all thought that bringing their families was a good idea.

Like him, they all looked like they regretted it.

"Robbie!" came a booming shout, cutting through the noise of the crowd.

Kett turned to see DI Peter Porter jogging over, wearing a blue and gold patterned outfit that could surely only be pyjamas. He stopped beside them, plopping a leather sports bag on the bonnet of Kett's Volvo and beaming at the girls.

"Did I just see huggy time? Is it too late to get in on that?"

"Yes," said Evie, matter-of-factly. "Huggy time has now ended."

"Oh," he said, crestfallen.

"You forget to get dressed this morning, Pete?" Kett asked, looking at Porter's clothes. The patterns on the silky material were tigers, all with their tongues out.

"This is Gucci, mate," he replied, giving his neckline a tug. "You up for this, sir?"

"Dodgeball?" said Kett. "Christ no. I can barely walk. I don't even know why the Super wanted me for the team."

"He told me it's because you're scary," said Porter. "Everyone knows who you are, so they won't want to hit you with a ball. In case you, you know, come after them with a..."

He made the motion of somebody hammering a nail.

"Daddy's not scary!" said Moira, pointing through the parked cars and swarming people. "*He's* scary."

Kett turned to see Superintendent Clare stomping towards them like a horror movie Frankenstein. He was wearing a brown tracksuit that was as ugly as Porter's was ridiculous, and he had an open Bounty in each hand.

"The Bounties are out," said Porter, shuffling around so that he was sheltering behind Kett. "He must be stressed."

"Kett!" roared Clare. "You're late!"

"I literally got here before you, sir," he protested, gesturing to his car.

Clare turned his attention to Kett's legs, staring at them like they were giant spiders.

"Why are your knees so knobbly?"

"What?" said Kett. "They're not!"

"Pete," the Super growled, spraying a fine mist of shredded coconut in Porter's direction. "If the dress code for this was 1920s Parisian prostitute, I'd have told you. What the hell are you wearing?"

"Gucci, sir," muttered Porter. "It's my lucky tracksuit."

"Well, I don't feel very lucky," said Clare, devouring the last chunk of Bounty. He stared at them awkwardly for the twenty seconds it took him to chew it, nobody quite knowing what to say. "Where's Savage and Duke?"

"Inside, sir," said Porter. "Kate texted me. Did you find a sixth player? Spalding wasn't interested?"

"Only if she could play for the other team," said Clare. "And if she could throw spanners instead of balls. I got somebody; he's waiting for us. *Move*!"

They all jumped to attention, including Billie and the girls. Kett grabbed his bag and led them to the Sportspark, inhaling his way through a mob of smokers as he entered the lobby. It was so busy in here that he could barely move, the heat of the day amplified by the countless bodies, making him feel like he'd stepped into an oven.

Clare took over, ploughing through the crowd like a wild-eyed, Bounty-wielding ice-breaker. Kett did his best to corral his girls, although with Evie and Moira trying to get to the vending machines, and Alice bumping into everyone like a shambling zombie, it was practically impossible—even with Billie's help. That was the trouble with having three of them, they were always outnumbered and usually outgunned.

Luckily, the mob thinned as they passed the enormous queue for the café, and Kett spotted Savage and Duke. They were dressed in matching black tracksuits and were both chugging Red Bulls.

"Kate!" cried Evie and Moira together, running to Savage and squeezing her in a hug. She laughed as she pulled them in, and Duke completed the sandwich.

"Hey!" moaned Porter. "You said huggy time was over!"

"This is a new huggy time," said Evie.

"Can I get in on this one, then?"

"No."

"Well, if it isn't Detective *Sergeant* Savage," said Kett, waiting for the girls to let go of her before offering a hand. "Congratulations, Kate. You deserve it."

After the events of last October, Savage had run for a promotion. And a few days ago, she'd got the news that she'd aced the exams. If there hadn't been rules in place, Kett was pretty sure she'd have been promoted above the rest of them, straight to Chief Superintendent.

"Thanks, sir," she said, giving his hand a firm pump. "It's brilliant, mainly because I'm now Aaron's senior officer."

"It's horrible," said Duke, although he was smiling through his beard as he said it. "You're so bossy."

Savage looked at him expectantly, one eyebrow arched.

"You're so bossy, *Sarge*," he finished, with the weary tone of a man who'd been made to say it far too many times. "See?"

"Sergeant Savage is a great name, though," said Kett, and Savage laughed.

"I sound like a wrestler from the 80s," she said.

"Stop gibbering like a bunch of horny baboons," said Clare, pushing into the middle of the group. "Has anyone seen Balls?"

Duke checked his trousers.

"Balls?" said Porter. "I think they'll be on the courts."

"No, *Norman* Balls, you bollock," spat Clare. "He's our sixth man."

"Balls?" said Kett, horrified. "Why?"

"Probably because he looks like a ball," said Duke.

"Same shape. He can go undercover with all the other dodgeballs, surprise the enemy teams when they're..."

He tailed off when he saw the look Clare was giving him.

"Is that him?" said Billie, nodding to the front of the building.

They all turned to see a short, round man waddling towards them, dressed like he was about to play cricket. As well as his white trousers and woolly jumper, he had leg pads, an enormous box over his crotch, and a helmet with protective bars that concealed his face. The only thing that gave him away was the homemade badge he'd pinned to his chest that stated: 'Official Deputy, Norfolk Constabulary'.

"You're late, Balls!" roared Clare.

"Actually, I've been here for two hours," said Balls, adjusting his helmet. He held up a notepad. "I've been studying the tournament schedule and making notes on each team. I have a full game plan here, outlining the best tactics with which to beat the other constabularies. I can almost guarantee that victory will go to our team of *official* police officers."

"You're not a police officer, Norman," said Kett.

Balls tapped his badge to prove him wrong.

"Now, our first opponents are from Wisbech. I suggest that our tactics involve—"

He stopped speaking when a Bounty bounced off the front of his helmet.

"Shut it, Balls," said Clare, opening yet another one. "If I'd wanted to spend the morning with a short person who can barely squeeze their meat patties into a cardigan and who loves telling me what to do, I'd have brought my wife. We're on in ten. *Move!*"

They all jumped again—as did half of the people in the lobby—before following Clare down a crowded corridor. Kett passed one open door to see a game of dodgeball already taking place, a team of enormous coppers dressed in black tracksuits with red sweatbands absolutely demolishing their opponents. Clare had disappeared through the next door along, and Kett waited there for his girls to catch up.

"Best behaviour, okay?" he told them. "There are a lot of scary people here, and those balls look hard. Please stay with Mummy, and don't touch anything."

"But I want to play!" said Moira. "I like throwing things!"

Telling her no would be like telling the tide it couldn't come in, and Kett half thought about asking around to see if anyone had brought any cuffs.

"Just try," he told her.

He entered the second room, the noise of the crowd close to crushing him. Luckily, his kids weren't the only ones tearing around. Half a dozen lads Evie's age were running laps of the court, a couple more hurling their water bottles at the basketball hoops. Nobody was playing, but five or six teams were warming up in the middle of the room, and two referees in striped outfits were chatting to one another.

"I'm starting to feel nervous," said Porter by his side.

"Why have we never taken part before?" asked Kett. "This thing happens every year, doesn't it?"

"Yeah, but the Norfolk Brass put the kibosh on it after the castration thing in 2020."

"Hang on," said Kett. "The *what*?"

"You don't want to know, sir," said Porter, heading for the stands.

"I kind of do," said Kett, following.

His girls overtook him, Alice dropping into a seat in the front row, still staring at her phone. Billie sat next to her, looking a little nervous at the size of the crowd. Evie clung to his hand, the way she always did, her fingers gripping tight enough to hurt. He'd managed to lose Moira in the rush, but he could hear the cackle of her laughter, so she couldn't have gone far.

He dropped his bag, then pulled free of Evie in order to take off his hoodie. Even that hurt, his spine full of nails, and he turned to Clare to ask him if he really needed to do this.

"Yes," said the Super, reading his tortured expression like a book. "You're playing. You see them all looking at you?"

Kett surveyed the room, but nobody seemed to be paying him any attention.

"You're our dark horse, Kett. Our not-so-secret weapon."

Clare pulled another Bounty from his pocket, which had to be as deep as Mary Poppins' carpet bag. He unwrapped it like he was ripping the cap off an EpiPen in a medical emergency, then jabbed the chocolate bar at Kett's face.

"They all know what happened to Joseph Maynard last year," he said, his eyes wild. "Dead. They all heard about Carmichael, too. Dead."

"Neither of those were me," said Kett, his stomach contracting as the memories leaked back in—Maynard drowning in blood in his hospital bed after being stabbed in the throat.

Carmichael's fate far, far worse.

"*I* know that," said Clare, his bushy eyebrows wiggling.

"But *they* don't. Not for sure. They're more scared of you than they are of the castration thing."

The idea of it made Kett feel like he'd swallowed a brick, but Clare didn't seem to notice. He turned to the others, using his lanky arms to round them into a huddle. He chewed off a hunk of Bounty before speaking, spraying them like champagne after a victory.

"Now listen up. Norfolk Constabulary used to be the kings of this tournament. We won it five years in a row, before the whole sausage-on-a-string debacle."

"Can somebody just explain this castration thing?" said Kett. "Because I'm starting to—"

"It's our time again," Clare went on. "No mercy. No quarter. I want to see you tossing your balls into the faces of your enemies! I want to see them choking on those mighty tosses! I want you to toss so hard that your balls literally explode over those poor bastards."

"Oh God," said Kett. "I want to go home."

"Well, tough," said Clare. "Lose this, and you'll never go home again, I can promise you that. I will bury you and your useless balls in the middle of the running track outside."

He glared at them all in turn, then practically screamed. "*Move!*"

They jumped again, although there was nowhere to move to. Teams were still pouring through the doors, families trying to find their seats. Kett felt a tug on his T-shirt and saw Evie. Her hair had come loose, and he dropped onto one knee in order to redo her ponytail.

"What does castration mean, Dadda?" she asked.

"I'm hoping none of us find out," he said, wrapping the bobble around one more time before smoothing down the loose hairs. "Go sit with Alice. Can you see Moira anywhere?"

He was answered by a drumming of feet and another cackling laugh as his youngest daughter sprinted into sight. She'd found a dodgeball, and she hurled it into the stands. There was no time to be impressed with her aim. The ball hit Alice's arm with an audible thump, sending her phone sailing into the row behind.

Kett saw the scream coming, but there was nothing he could do to stop it. Alice's shriek was so loud that, for a second, the entire auditorium fell silent.

"Stop being a twat!" Alice yelled at Moira, whose wide-eyes and tight lips made it perfectly clear she hadn't expected the ball to hit its target.

"Hey!" said Kett. "Alice, that's enough."

"She is, though!"

Billie tried to calm her, but Alice dropped to the floor, scrabbling for her phone beneath the chair.

The chatter had resumed, the gym drowning once again in sound. Moira ran to him, clinging onto his legs, still looking at Alice like she expected the girl to come after her. Evie joined in, never one to miss a cuddle. When Alice popped up again, Kett beckoned her. She didn't look like she wanted to, but after a moment or two she sloped over, and he pulled her in for the hug too.

"You're sisters," he said. "Literally, your only job is to look after each other, keep each other safe. Please, girls, do it for me."

There were no objections, so he planted a kiss on each of their foreheads.

"And if not for me, do it for Colin. Otherwise, he might throw a Bounty at you."

They laughed as they drifted away.

A moment of calm, at last.

Then, for a reason he couldn't quite fathom, a sixth sense that made his scalp shrivel, Kett looked at the auditorium door.

And saw a man staring right back at him.

It was like he'd been kicked in the stomach. He couldn't get a breath in. The man was in his thirties, his brown hair tousled, his serious face shaded with stubble. He wore tracksuit trousers and a T-shirt, a pair of old trainers on his feet. But none of this was why Kett had such a bad feeling.

It was the way the man was looking at him, the intensity of his stare.

It was the hatred that seemed to be etched into every line of his face.

Kett stood as straight as his aching back would let him, puffing himself up like a dog that's seen a rival. His heart was clattering, his skin drenched in cold sweat. The man at the door was *still* looking at him, he hadn't even blinked.

It was a look he'd seen so many times, and one he'd hoped never to see again.

It was the same look he'd got from Joe Carmichael, and from every other Hollenbeck soldier he'd met—the look of somebody who wanted him dead.

Kett dropped his head, frowning. Had he really been that stupid? To think that Maynard's death would be the end of it? How many people had the old bastard recruited over the years? How many disaffected young men were desperate to prove their worth with bloodshed and butchery? How many people had he spoken to about Kett? Knowing him, he'd made a sport of it.

Keep going after him until he's dead.

He felt a hand on his arm, and the touch was like an electric shock. It was Norman Balls, the little man leaning in and speaking quietly through the bars of his cricket helmet. His eyes were on the door.

"You know that guy?" he asked.

"No," said Kett.

"He's a police officer," Balls said. "His name's Harrison Baird. He's Scottish, but he's been working in Suffolk. I met him a couple of weeks ago, on official business, and he was asking a lot of questions about you."

"What kind of questions?"

"Weird ones," said Balls. "He asked me because he knew I was your best friend. He wanted to know about your past. About your family."

It was that last word that pushed Kett forward, the engine of his anger driving him across the gym. He picked up speed as he went, heading right for the door, right for the arsehole who was still staring at him.

Baird staggered away, vanishing like he was ready to make a run for it. But when Kett pushed through the door, he saw him backing into the wall of the corridor, uncertain. The guy was a few inches shorter than he was, and Kett made the most of the size difference, looming over him.

"I hear you've been asking about me," said Kett, a low growl through gritted teeth.

The man called Baird was struggling, a dozen emotions passing over his face before he erased them all with a hollow grin.

"Ach, dinnae flatter yourself, pal," he said, his Aberdonian accent so broad Kett almost didn't catch what he was saying. "I'm in a happy relationship with my Diana."

The smile widened, like it was painted on. It wasn't quite the shit-eating grin he'd got from other members of Hollenbeck, but it was close enough for him to be sure.

Baird seemed to find his courage, pushing away from the wall, putting Kett on the back foot.

"I am curious, though, Robert," he said. "Because I think you kent my father, back in London. Dougie Baird. Used to work for a fella called Nigel Topper, back when you were under John Cooper in the Met. Ring any bells?"

The bell it rang could have belonged to a cathedral; the sound of it loud enough to shatter every bone in Kett's body. He couldn't remember a man called Baird—although the name was familiar—but the mention of John Cooper dragged him right down into the nightmare of his past. Cooper had been the worst kind of copper, the worst kind of man. For decades, when Kett and Porter were newly fledged constables in the Met, Cooper and Barry 'Bingo' Benson and a handful of others had been in the pockets of every monster in London.

Including Hollenbeck.

If he'd needed confirmation, this was it. It was all he could do not to rip the man's head off right here in the corridor, to hurl it across the court like a dodgeball.

Instead, he leaned in, the fury radiating from him.

"Did you not get the message?" he said, his voice low and dangerous. "You lot are done. You come at me again, I'll fucking bury you."

"*What?*" said Baird.

"You heard me," said Kett. "And I'm going to say this once, Harrison."

It was like he'd slapped the other man around the face.

"Just once. You've been asking questions about me, so you've probably got some answers, too. And if even a fraction of what you've learned about me is true, then do you really think you should keep pushing?"

Baird shook his head, that smile long gone.

"Tread carefully," said Kett. "Understood? Or you're a fucking dead man."

He jabbed a finger into the man's shoulder to emphasise his point, and he must have done it harder than he'd intended because Baird fell back against the wall with a cry of pain. He looked like he was about to pass out, and Kett didn't feel much better. His eyes were pulsing with every frantic beat of his heart, his head a mess of white noise.

He walked back into the gym, clamping his teeth around the scream that wanted to tear up his throat.

He'd thought it was over, but it wasn't.

It was *never* going to be over.

"Dadda!" said a voice, and Evie was right there, grabbing his hand. "I was scared. Where did you go?"

He clung to his daughter's fingers like she was a rope on a mountain. It took him a few breaths to remember how to speak.

"Nowhere, beautiful," he said.

"What's wrong?" she asked, her brow furrowing. Of all his children, she was the one who was able to read him like a book.

He did his best to smile.

"I'm fine, Evie. Better than fine."

It took a few seconds for her to accept the lie. She wrapped her arms around him, and Moira flew in for what was probably supposed to be a hug, but which felt like a tackle.

He glanced over their heads, expecting to see Baird in the open door, grinning. Or running at him, a knife in his hand.

But the other man had gone.

"Jesus Christ," bellowed Clare when Kett had rejoined

the group. "You're as pale as bog roll, Robert. Don't tell me there's been a castration already."

"What? No, sir, I..."

He looked back again, even though he didn't want to. The noise and the heat of the room were overwhelming; it made him feel like he was being buried alive. Clare must have noticed his panic because he moved closer, suddenly alert.

"What's going on?" he asked.

"Nothing," said Kett, wiping his dry lips with his free hand. Evie stared up at the Superintendent, squeezing Kett's hand with her little fingers. "I'm good. I'm ready."

Beside the court, he saw Savage pick up her bag and kiss Duke on the lips. She started towards them.

"The game's off," said Clare. "For you, anyway."

"Sir?" said Kett. "I'm good, honestly. I'm fit enough to play."

"As much as I want your strong hands on my balls, Robbie, something's happened. A body's turned up in the middle of the city. A nasty one."

"Oh," said Kett, who didn't know whether to be disappointed or relieved.

"I need you and Kate to take a look. We'll handle the game."

"Does that mean you're not playing, Dadda?" said Evie.

"I guess not," he told her. "You guys can stay, though."

"We'll need your cheering to help us win," said Clare, ruffling Evie's hair the way she hated him doing.

"Ready, sir?" said Savage as she walked up.

Kett nodded, giving Evie's hand one last squeeze before pulling free.

"Stay with Mummy," he told her. "Tell her I need to go.

And don't let your little sister join in any of the games. You're in charge, okay?"

Evie trotted over to the stands, sliding onto Billie's knee. Billie glanced up, and Kett offered an apologetic wave that she met with a resigned nod. He set off after Savage, feeling that awful churn of adrenaline inside him.

Because, despite everything he'd done, there were still monsters out there.

There always would be.

CHAPTER TWO

Despite the presence of over a hundred coppers at the tournament, there were no IRVs anywhere on site. Kett took his Volvo, finding himself snarled in traffic the second he pulled out of the Sportspark. The Spring heat was unseasonably awful, blazing through the windscreen and covering him like a sweaty blanket. He ramped up the air conditioning and wound down the windows in the hope of a breeze.

"Probably better just one or the other, sir," said Savage from the passenger seat. She fanned herself with both hands, her face beaded with sweat.

"Huh?" he said, putting his foot on the accelerator for a second or two until he caught up with the car in front. The queue went the way down the road, the hot air full of honking horns.

"The blowers won't work with the windows open," Savage said.

"I know," he told her. "I'm just desperate. What on earth is going on?"

He leaned out the window for a better view. There was

no sign of an accident, so he crashed back into his chair, releasing a huffing breath.

"You want to tell me what all that was about back there?" said Savage. She pulled a bottle of water from her bag, pressing it to her forehead. "That man you were talking to. Who was he?"

Kett didn't answer straight away, because he didn't know how.

"Because I haven't seen you look like that for a long time," she went on. "Not since last year, not since... You know."

He knew.

"It's that kind of intuition that's going to make you a great DS, Kate," he told her.

He realised she was watching him, still waiting for an answer.

"It was nobody," he said. "Mistaken identity. Hang on."

He pulled the Volvo out of the line of traffic, accelerating down the wrong side of the road. There were cars coming the other way, but they must have seen the look on his face through the sun-bleached windscreen because they all pulled onto the grassy verge to let him roar past. He reached the roundabout to see that there *had* been an accident, a BMW with its nose in the side of an Amazon Prime van. The two drivers were arguing, and Kett rolled down the window.

"Oi!" he yelled, and when they didn't pay him any attention, he laid on the horn. "There's about a million police officers up the road, and unless you want them all turning up, calm down and sort it out."

Neither of them seemed to know what to say, and Kett didn't wait for them to figure it out. He nosed the Volvo past the van and crossed the roundabout, the road on the other side clear.

"Can you call that in, Kate?" he said, seeing that she already was.

He stayed quiet while she was on the phone, watching the city roll past. The morning streets were quiet, but the few pedestrians he saw looked bug-eyed and short-tempered. The heat did that. As soon as the thermostat crossed twenty-five, people seemed to lose their minds. Arguments broke out, fists were thrown, cars crashed.

And sometimes, people died.

There was another queue of traffic on the inner ringroad, but this one was being held up by an IRV, its blue lights rolling. There was no way of getting past, so Kett bumped the Volvo onto the kerb and parked it. He and Savage walked the rest of the way, a uniformed officer barring their path for the second or two it took the penny to drop.

"Sorry, sir," he said to Kett. "Didn't recognise you in your PE kit. You guys win?"

"Kate and I are winners," Kett told him. "But only because we didn't have to play."

The constable lifted a line of police tape, allowing Kett and Savage to duck beneath it. The wide pavement was sandwiched on one side by a four-storey block of flats and a taller office building covered in scaffolding, and on the other by the four lanes of the main road. Past the cars lay Chapelfield Gardens, the park that served the city centre. They were connected by an underpass, and it was here that most of the PCs had assembled.

"Where's the body?" Kett asked as he walked down the slope.

"Other side," said a young PC, fanning herself with her hat. "In the park. Nice shorts, sir."

Kett nodded his thanks, heading towards the square of darkness that made up the entrance to the underpass. He hesitated for a moment before entering the cold tunnel, the same way he always did now—with underpasses, with car parks and lifts, with basements.

With anywhere underground.

It still felt too familiar: the fug of damp and piss, the rancid air as warm as breath, the shadows like a long-forgotten tomb.

He scrubbed the sweat from his brow, glancing at Savage to see her looking at him. *Everyone* was looking at him, he realised, and it was this that goaded him back into motion. He walked into the narrow tunnel, the ceiling so low he thought he felt it scraping the top of his head. The colourful walls were tattooed with graffiti, pressing in from both sides, crushing him. Part of the floor had been taped off, forensic markers scattered in the mess. There was no air down here, just that stench, and he doubled his speed, pushing between another two constables until the underpass spat him out on the other side.

Here, he stopped again, the sweat running down his face, pooling around his collar. Savage was still in the tunnel, talking to the constables—all of them still watching him. She beckoned for him to come back, and he chose to ignore her.

Ahead, the sloping footpath rose into the park, where more police officers waited, holding back a smattering of curious onlookers and their dogs. To his left was a patch of scrubby woodland that led up to the road, and it was here that most of the activity seemed to be taking place. As well as two more uniformed coppers, Kett could see a couple of people in white forensic overalls.

The last thing he wanted was to walk up that path. Whatever lay there—*who*ever lay there, in the dirt and the litter and the dog shit—it would only be the start of something awful. The thought of another case felt like a noose around his neck, and once more he found he could barely breathe.

You've done enough, Robbie, he told himself. *You've done more than enough.*

One of the technicians peeled free from the crowd and walked over. It was Cara Hay, the lead forensic officer, and she used a gloved hand to pull the hood away from her face. She wore the same serious expression she always did, one part worry to two parts determination.

"Who is it?" asked Kett.

"A woman," she replied in her Trinidadian accent.

Kett took a long breath, then released it as a groaning sigh.

"Murdered?" he asked.

Hay nodded, running her hand over the smooth skin of her scalp.

"Most definitely murdered," she said.

She retreated into the woods, motioning for him to join her. As much as he loved Hay, he couldn't help but picture a witch luring him into the woods, like a lost child—because he knew only bad things lay that way.

Bad things, and monsters.

Still, what choice did he have?

It was the job.

He climbed onto the low retaining wall and struggled up the slope, the dry, powdery earth giving way beneath his trainers. Hay offered him a hand, and he took it, the woman using surprising strength to haul him into the shade.

"Cheers," he said.

"Do not thank me yet," she told him, walking off. "It's over here."

The tangled plants tried to stop him, but the vegetation here was stunted by years of traffic fumes, sickly and thin. He could see right through it to a little hollow where the police had congregated, five of them. They stood in a circle like mourners around a grave, and when he walked over, he realised the comparison was spot on.

A woman lay on a bed of dirt, as perfectly positioned as if they'd found her in a coffin. She rested on her back, her legs straight, her arms crossed over her chest. Whoever had left her here had attempted to cover her with a blanket of sticks and leaves, but they hadn't done a very good job. Kett could see black trousers and a navy coat. Her shoes were scuffed almost to oblivion.

Only her face was hidden, a square cloth napkin resting over it—perfectly white, except for two red circles where her eyes would be. Strands of jet-black hair fanned out from the makeshift shroud, like she was floating in water. It made him think of a Renaissance painting. Ophelia, was it? Perfectly serene in death.

"You've looked at her face?" said Kett.

Hay nodded, her jaw bulging as she clenched her teeth.

"I covered her up again," she said. "I..."

She didn't seem to know how to finish, turning to the motionless canopies overhead.

"There's something wrong with her eyes," she went on.

A rush of cold passed through Kett, enough to make him shiver despite the warmth of the day. He had the feeling, as he so often did, that he was dreaming, that he was caught in a nightmare, full of heat and fever.

No dream could be as awful as this, though.

Cara Hay squatted, one gloved hand on the ground to steady herself, the other reaching for the napkin. She pulled it away like a magician performing a trick, revealing the face of a woman much older than Kett had been expecting. Late sixties, maybe early seventies. Her skin was a geological map of wrinkles, her cheeks pale, the blusher all but rubbed away. The nose was swollen, the skin split down the middle like somebody had tried to unzip her face. The nostrils were plugged with blood, but it seemed like the rest of her face had been wiped clean. Her lips bore a trace of colour, a faint purple that might have been lipstick, or death, he wasn't sure. Her hair was grey at the roots, and he realised she'd dyed it; not very well, and he felt bad for thinking it.

He couldn't get a good look at her eyes, because there was something in them—two discs of dull silver, one tucked beneath each swollen lid. They could have been coins, but he couldn't make out markings of any kind. There was a thick crust of blood around each one, making it look like she was wearing a carnival mask.

"Christ," he said.

He didn't think the woman had been here long, but the body was starting to lose itself to the heat, the smell of her like a broken fridge in a butcher shop. The insects had already made her their own, burrowing into her clothes, into her skin, laying eggs in her ears and her nose, gorging themselves on the blood that leaked from her eyes, oblivious to everything that had been lost.

"You know what they are?" he asked, looking at the silver discs.

"No," said Hay. "I'm waiting for Emily. I thought they might be coins, but they're not flat. And..."

She struggled again to find the words she needed.

"They're *deep*."

"Deep?" said Kett. "How do you mean?"

"Just that," she said, crossing her arms over her chest like she was trying to mirror the woman at her feet. "She was strangled."

Kett turned his attention to the victim's neck, seeing the bruises that mottled her throat. It had been done with some violence, the front of her thorax caved in from the force of the attack. He looked at her hands, laid so neatly over her chest. They were dirty, but there was no blood on her fingertips, no nails pulled loose. It didn't look as if she'd fought back.

"Cover her up again, Cara," he said.

Let her rest.

Hay did as she was asked, draping the napkin over the woman's face. Kett wished he could erase the image from his mind so easily.

"Any ID?" he asked.

"No," said Hay, standing up. "Pockets are empty. No bag, no phone."

"There haven't been any missing person reports matching her description," added one of the constables, who looked like he was three seconds away from unloading his breakfast. He had the back of his hand pressed against his mouth, his fingers muffling the words. "Nobody's asked about her."

"She hasn't been here long, though," said Kett, looking at his watch to see that it was a little past ten. "A few hours?"

"I'll leave the exact time to Emily," said Hay, but she was nodding. "I'd guess last night."

"Nobody saw her?"

"No," said Savage as she climbed the slope. She stopped next to him, and even though she had the good grace not to gasp, he saw the grief fill her face when she saw the body. "No witnesses yet, and there's no CCTV in the underpass. There's a camera in the park, but it's on the other side."

"You think she was killed here?" asked Kett, looking at Hay.

"In the trees? No. There's some blood in the tunnel, and a lot of trampled vegetation on the route up here. I'm guessing, and it's just a guess, that she was attacked in the underpass. Her nose is broken; you saw the swelling?"

Kett nodded.

"Looks like a pretty hefty blow to the face, which probably would have knocked her out. It would have been easy enough to strangle her."

"That explains why her hands are so clean," said Kett. "She couldn't struggle."

"At least she wouldn't have known it was happening," said Savage. "Hopefully."

It was a nice thought, but not an easy one to believe.

"She might have come in off the road, though," Hay went on, looking behind her to the line of traffic that stewed in its own fumes. There were chunks of the old city wall here, big gaps between the ancient flint fortifications. "It's easy enough to enter the woods that way. Somebody could have stopped their car, dragged her down here, then left. It would take less than a minute."

"Do we know who found her?" asked Kett.

"Guy called Keith," said the same constable, still

covering his mouth. "He's in the park, over by the café. He was a little shaken."

"What was he doing in here?"

"Walking his dog, sir," the guy said. "Although… it's not really a dog."

Kett gave him a look.

"You kind of have to see it for yourself, sir."

"How long ago?" he asked.

The constable checked his watch.

"Nearly an hour."

Kett licked his lips, tasting the sweat that had accumulated there.

"You alright here, Cara?"

She nodded, although her expression said otherwise.

"Then let's go see Keith and his dog."

CHAPTER THREE

It was early, but the park was mobbed. Dogs bounded across the open space, chasing wild rabbits and oblivious to the horrors that lay in the bushes. Lycra-clad joggers and cyclists clogged the paths, battling with parents and their pushchairs. In the small playpark, kids went wild, the sound of their shouts and screams and laughter carrying effortlessly through the hot air. Teenagers congregated in the bandstand, the smell of weed catching in the back of Kett's throat as he walked past. He couldn't even summon the energy to glare at them.

"Can we not clear the park, sir?" said Savage.

"Only if you want a riot," he told her. "Where else are they all going to hang out?"

There was a small group of PCs hanging around in the shade of an enormous tree next to the park's small café, and he made his way over to them. Three were devouring ice lollies, he noticed, the fruity smell making his mouth water. Another guy sat on a chair between them, somewhere in his late forties. He had a lolly as well, which had given him a beard of orange syrup. There was no sign of a dog.

"First things first," said Kett as he stepped out of the sun. "Where did you get them?"

"Caf," said a PC, mid-lick. "You want one, sir?"

"Orange, if they've got them. Kate?"

"I'm fine, sir," she said.

The PC headed off, and Kett took his place in the huddle.

"I'm guessing you're Keith," he said to the man on the chair. "Got another name that goes with that?"

"The," said Keith, a dull mutter.

He used the back of his hand to wipe the mess on his face. It wasn't just the lolly juice, Kett saw. He looked like he had half his breakfast caught in his stubble. The rest of him wasn't in much better condition, his white shirt a tapestry of stains and his green cords crumpled. His grey trainers were so dirty that it took Kett a moment to notice that one was a Nike and one was a New Balance. Only his puffer jacket looked brand new.

"I'm sorry?" said Kett, leaning in. "Your name is Keith The?"

"Are you an idiot? *The* Keith."

"The Keith?"

The Keith nodded.

"As in, the only Keith?"

He nodded again, his lolly dripping onto his trousers as he took another lick.

"What's wrong with your knees?" he asked, staring at Kett's bare legs.

"Nothing," said Kett, who was starting to feel a little self-conscious. "Any ID?"

"You'd love that, wouldn't you?" said Keith. "I give you that, and next you'll be after my fingerprints, my DNA, my saliva and sperm and everything."

"Nope," said Kett. "I absolutely will not be after any of that. Can you tell me what you were doing in the park this morning?"

"Walking the dog," said Keith, biting off a hunk of ice lolly and obviously struggling with how cold it was. He swallowed painfully, his eyes bulging.

"The dog," said Kett, looking around in case he'd somehow missed it.

The constable who'd gone to the café reappeared, handing Kett a Coke-flavoured lolly.

"All out of orange," he said.

"You can have a lick of mine if you want," said Keith, holding it out.

"No thanks," Kett replied, taking the Calippo from the PC and peeling off the top. It felt perfectly cool in his hands, and when he nibbled the top he felt his inner thermostat drop a couple of degrees. "Keith, where—"

"*The* Keith," he corrected.

"Keith, where is your dog?"

"It's in his pocket," said another constable.

Keith patted his coat with sticky fingers to confirm this. Kett stared at him until he got the message, clamping his lolly between his teeth as he fished something out of his coat. It looked like a bundle of matted fur, and it was completely motionless. If it had ever been a dog, it had shuffled off the mortal coil a long time ago.

"Keith," said Kett, keeping his lolly close to his face to mask the smell of the thing. "What is—"

"*The* Keith," the man said, planting the furry abomination on his lap. It had limbs, Kett saw, four of them, each maybe five inches long, and a tail, too. "And this is Miranda."

"Miranda?" said Kett. "Your dog?"

"Uh-huh."

Kett looked at Savage to see if she understood, but she was equally mystified.

"Your dog is a teddy?" said Kett.

"Fuck off," said the man, outraged. "She's a dog. *Look*. With your *eyes*."

"It is way too hot for this," said Kett, giving up. "So, you were walking your... dog, in the park this morning. Why were you up in the trees by the underpass?"

"She needed to piss," said Keith, pursing his lips around the lolly and sucking off the last of it. He offered the stick to Kett the way a child would to a parent. "She's a little bashful, is Miranda, so we often do our toilets up there, away from prying eyes."

Keith was still holding out the stick, and Kett continued to ignore it. He bit off a chunk of frozen Coke, sucking the flavour out of it.

"I didn't see nowt until she started growling. Like, proper nasty, haven't heard her growl like that for a while. Usually she does it with other dogs, big dogs, so I was looking about trying to see one. Don't like big dogs, I like little ones, like Miranda. You know, even if they bite you, they're not going to do much."

He jiggled the stick, looking at Kett expectantly.

"I'm not touching that," said Kett. "There's a bin right there."

"Fuck's sake," said Keith, dropping his hand. "Call yourself a public servant."

"Miranda was growling?" said Kett, prompting him.

"Yeah, growling, and I was so busy looking for this other dog that I stepped on something. Tripped. Landed on my arse, twig right in the hole. You ever had a twig up your hole?"

Kett shook his head.

"Hurts! I about screamed. Went right through my trousers. And I was so busy trying to remove it, I didn't even notice what was next to me."

His eyes glazed over, and he seemed to run out of words.

"You saw the body," said Savage, her tone much softer than Kett's.

Keith rested his hand on the back of the not-dog, stroking gently. There was blood on his fingers, Kett noticed, where he'd chewed his nails to shreds.

"Ain't the first deado I've seen, mind. Not even recently. Get a lot of them when you live where I do."

"You're unhoused?" asked Savage.

He didn't answer the question, still staring across the park.

"Sometimes you give your neighbour a shake and they're cold as anything. Stiff, like they... Like they stopped being real, or never were real. I don't know. Rest of the world don't even know, because you lot turn up and take 'em away before anyone sees. Don't want those deados ruining your trip into town, scaring your kids. Gave her a shake n'all, that woman there. Cold and stiff. Proper deado."

"Did you see anyone else in the woods?" asked Kett. "Anyone nearby?"

"Loads of folk," he said. "That's why we were pissing in the bushes."

"Anyone near the body?"

Keith shook his head.

"You called us?"

"Yeah, with my magic phone," he said, finally meeting Kett's eye again. "I told her in the caf, and she did it."

"You gave the woman a shake, but did you touch her in any other way?" Kett asked.

Keith pulled a face.

"What are you saying, mate?"

"Not like that. You didn't move her, or try to cover her, or put something in her eyes?"

The man answered with a shrug.

"I'm going to need a yes or a no, Keith."

"*The* Keith," he spat. "I didn't touch her, but I can't vouch for Miranda. She roots in everything, can't keep her nose out of the shit. She might have had a sniff and a scratch, I can't tell you, I was too busy trying to get the twig out of my arse."

"Keith," said Kett. His mouth was so full of Calippo that the man's name dripped over his chin. He slapped his hand to his lips to cover the mess. "You do realise that's not a dog, right?"

He felt Savage's hand on his arm.

"She *used* to be your dog, didn't she?" she said.

Keith lifted the animal from his lap, holding it up so that Savage could get a closer look. Kett caught another whiff of it—not the stench of a dead thing, but the whiff of unwashed fabric and old fur coats and something else that he couldn't place.

"She's still mine," he said. "That's her pelt. Bit of it, anyway. And her ashes. She was the best girl, couldn't bear to lose her when she went. Fixed her."

"She's beautiful," said Savage, earning a smile from the man. "You did it yourself?"

"Had a bit of help," he said. "But yeah, did all the stitching, mended her little face."

He turned the animal upside down, and for the first time Kett saw its face: a drooping mouth, a plastic teddy bear's nose.

And two gleaming eyes.

"Wait," he said, as Keith went to pull the animal back. "What are they? The eyes?"

"Nothing," he said, clamping the dog to his chest. "Just buttons."

"Metal ones?"

"Yeah, so what?"

"Why metal?" Kett asked. "Why not plastic? Seems like a weird choice for a toy dog."

"She's not a fucking toy," he said, and the expression on his face was so full of sorrow that Kett felt bad for saying it.

"Sorry," he said. "Seems like a weird choice for your Miranda. Why metal?"

"Better to see the men with," he said. "Metal eyes, metal men. She'll let me know when they're coming."

"What does that mean?" Kett asked him.

Keith didn't reply, pushing the mangled pelt against his sticky face, breathing it in.

"We're going to take you to the station, The Keith," said Savage. "But only so we can sort you out some clothes and a cuppa. Maybe a bowl of water for Miranda. How does that sound?"

Keith shrugged, his face still buried in whatever remained of the dog.

"Can one of you drive him over?" Savage said to the constables. "Make him comfortable?"

"We arresting him, Sarge?" said the PC who'd got the ice lollies.

Savage glanced to Kett for confirmation.

"No," said Kett. He took another look at the dog, its eyes glinting in the sun—far too similar to what they'd found in the woods. His next words were quieter, spoken into the PC's ear. "But watch yourselves."

He walked away, lifting the Calippo to take another bite

only to find that the entire thing had melted. Liquid coke sloshed over his chin and down his neck, freezing cold.

"Bloody hell," he said. He tried to mop it up, but it was the stickiest thing in existence, coating his fingers, running down his arms. "Help."

Savage took the Calippo wrapper from him with a motherly eye-roll, throwing it into the nearest bin. Kett angled for the café, feeling the cold fingers of coke meander down his chest.

There was a woman behind the counter of the café, and she gave Kett a knowing look as he walked up.

"Another Calippo-related catastrophe, I see," she said. "You need a PhD to operate one of them."

She studied the stain on his T-shirt, which was spreading fast.

"Coke, too. Not sure you'll be able to save that."

She handed him a couple of napkins anyway, as if they might help. Kett patted his chin and his neck, the juice so sticky that the tissue started to rip.

"Look at the state of him," said the woman, turning to Savage. "Always the men who get themselves in a mess, eh?"

"It melted!" said Kett.

She passed him another few napkins, but he didn't take them.

"Don't suppose I could borrow your sink?"

She laughed, unbolting the door next to the counter and letting him inside. He turned on the tap, giving his hands a good wash, then used some wet napkins to clean his face and neck.

"You know that man out there?" he asked her.

"The Keith? Yeah, I know him."

She didn't look overly happy about it.

"Him and his dog. Quiet little thing."

"Because it's dead?" said Kett, using some kitchen roll to dry himself.

"I mean even when it was alive. Terrified of everything, that dog. Was a Pomeranian, I think. Used to be in the park all the time. He never had it on a lead. He tell you that?"

Kett shook his head.

"That's why it died. Spooked at something and ran out the gate, hit by a bus."

"Ouch," he said.

"Yeah. Ouch. Nearly caused a bloody pile-up. This was about a year ago, and he hasn't been right in the head since. Not that he *ever* was, to be honest."

She seemed to consider something, and Kett gave her the time she needed.

"You get a lot of weirdos here. Park's a magnet for them, *in't it*? Most are harmless, they've got their ways, and you learn to live with them. Give 'em a wide berth, sometimes, if you know they're unpredictable. But The Keith?"

She glanced out of the door, as if to make sure the man wasn't there.

"He's one of the ones you tell your kids not to go near, not ever. You start walking the other way when you see him."

"He's dangerous?" said Kett.

"He's just... wrong," she said. "Weird vibes. Always hanging about in the underpass. You know it?"

"I know it," said Kett.

"I'm not just saying it because he's down on his luck," said the woman. "I'm not like that. Plenty of homeless come here, and I'll always give 'em a cuppa, sandwiches too, if it's later in the day. But him..."

She shuddered so hard she almost came off the ground.

"Don't even know why, sorry."

"You happy to answer some more questions, if we need you to?" Kett said.

"Yeah, I guess."

He nodded his thanks as he made his way out of the door.

"Hey," she called out behind him.

He turned to see her standing there, a wicked smile on her face.

"You want another Calippo to take with you?"

CHAPTER FOUR

Kett didn't regret not taking another Calippo, but he did wish he'd asked for a bottle of water as he made his way back across the park. The syrupy lolly had lined his throat and his stomach like wallpaper paste, making him feel nauseous.

By the time they'd got back to the underpass, it was busier than ever. Alongside the dog walkers and the joggers was a group of five teenage lads, all wearing expensive grey tracksuit trousers and black jumpers, the hoods pulled up. Four of them had scarves around their faces, despite the sweltering heat, and all had bumbags strapped diagonally across their torsos. They were staring at the uniformed coppers who stood on the other side of the barricade, muttering quiet words and cold laughter. To their credit, the bobbies weren't rising to the bait.

"Who let you lot out of the crèche, then?" Kett shouted as he walked up.

The boys turned to him, jiffling the way all the wannabe gangsters did—their hands hovering by their sagging waistlines like they had guns tucked there.

"You asking for directions to the toilets?" he said. "Because you're fidgeting like you're about to shit yourselves."

"Says the geezer who *already* shit himself," said one of the kids through his scarf. He was looking at Kett's T-shirt.

"It's not shit, it's Calippo. What do you want?"

"Want access," said another of the lads, his voice muffled by the scarf. "Want to go home, innit, and your boys is in the way."

Kett glanced into the underpass, then back to the young men, hoiking a thumb over his shoulder.

"So go a different way. There's a crossing about a minute in that direction."

"Fuck that," said another of the lads, although Kett couldn't tell which one. He closed the gap between them.

"Why are you so desperate to get in there, eh? You know something?"

"Know you're a pussio," said another lad, and the rest of them laughed—all except for the one kid without a mask. He was in his late teens or very early twenties, his sculpted jawline set. His blue eyes were bright against his dark skin. He had to have been roasting like a turkey in all those layers of clothes, but he didn't have a bead of sweat on him.

"You want to hang around and answer a few questions?" Kett asked him.

The kid seemed to think about it for a moment, then he hawked up a ball of phlegm and spat it into the dirt.

"No time, bruv," he said. "Got *tings* to do."

"Then go do them," Kett told him. "*That* way."

The boys sloped off, all limping like they had one shoe too big and one too small. Their laughter carried back, scratching at Kett's patience like sandpaper.

"Is it just me, or are those guys multiplying?" he asked.

"Wannabe roadmen," said Savage. "Seems to be all the rage right now. Most of them are harmless."

"Most," said Kett, turning to the Uniforms. "They say anything weird?"

"They told me I had a tiny helmet, sir," said one of the PCs, touching the helmet that perched on his head. "That was a bit weird."

"About the body," said Kett.

"Oh, right. Then no."

The man lifted the police tape so that Kett and Savage could get through. Kett took a couple of steps, then looked back.

"Your helmet *is* a little small," he told the PC.

"Yeah, I had to borrow it," he said. "Lost mine."

As they neared the woods, Kett heard Emily Franklin's voice. The young pathologist was standing at the top of the slope, talking to Cara Hay with more than a little enthusiasm.

"Alright, Emily," Kett called up to her.

"I am now," she said, looking back. "Yikes."

"Yikes is right. You've seen our dead woman?"

"The yikes was for you," she said. "How did you manage to get... *that*... all over yourself?"

"It's Calippo," he explained. "Long story."

"It's not a long story," said Savage. "He had a Calippo, he spilled it all over himself."

Kett glared at her.

"This is amazing," Franklin said. "Have you ever seen a body like this before?"

"No," he told her.

He didn't want to have to climb over the retaining wall

again, partly because of the effort, and partly because he didn't want to see the woman's body, so he stayed on the footpath.

"You've had a look?"

"I have," said Franklin. "Severe laryngeal trauma. Somebody crushed her throat."

"You think they used a weapon?"

"I think they used their hands," said Franklin, wafting away a fly. "The pattern of bruising suggests the killer had both hands around her throat. He either had all his weight on her, or he must have been immensely strong—maybe both—because the compression was enough to cause the entire structure of the larynx and the trachea to crumple. You remember that submarine that sank last year, on its way to the Titanic?"

"Yeah," said Kett. "I think so. Why?"

Franklin smacked her hands together, imitating the sound of something blowing up.

"Complete implosion," she said.

"That's awful," said Savage.

"Yes and no," said Franklin. "Usually, strangulation is a protracted and painful affair. You know it's happening, you feel every second of it, and death creeps in slowly but inevitably."

Kett rubbed his throat as Franklin gleefully carried on.

"But this happened quick. Wham, bam, goodbye ma'am. She'd have been dead in seconds, and she wouldn't have felt much. If the injury to her nose happened before the strangulation, then she wouldn't have felt it at all."

"So the killer wanted her to die quickly?" asked Savage.

Franklin shrugged.

"Cara and I were just asking that very question," she said.

"I think he got carried away," said Hay. "Like a child that breaks a new toy."

"Whereas I think he wanted the job done as efficiently as possible," added Franklin.

"You're saying 'he' a lot, considering we know absolutely nothing about our killer," said Kett.

Both Franklin and Hay stared at him until he lifted his hands in surrender.

"You're right," he told them. "This feels like a man."

"It was quick," said Franklin. "A blow to the face to knock her out, then another thirty seconds, max, to crush the throat. This is why I think he was working to a deadline, because he needed to leave as much time as possible for something else."

"The eyes," said Kett.

"The eyes," echoed Franklin, and her own seemed to gleam.

"What's on them?" he asked.

"Not *on*," said Franklin. "The victim no longer has her eyes at all."

It was a good job that he was propped up against the low wall, because he felt a sudden wave of vertigo. He braced his fingers on the bricks, leaning closer.

"What?"

"They've been removed entirely," said Franklin. "As far as I can see, anyway."

She made a motion that might have been somebody using an ice cream scoop.

"The orbits seem to have been hollowed out, the eyes replaced with two metal balls equivalent in size."

"What?" he croaked again.

"Not an easy feat," said Franklin, who was enjoying herself far too much. "Given the limited space afforded by the cranium. It's like those sets you get for kids, where you have to fit the blocks into the right holes. The balls are dented, which means the killer probably used a hammer to get them into place."

"What?"

"He needed to be quick," Franklin explained, mimicking somebody using a hammer. "Ball on the eye, smack. Ball on the other eye, smack. All in, from the first blow to the final insertion, he could have been done in as little as three minutes."

The images paraded in front of Kett, working with the heat to churn the sickness in his stomach. If he wasn't careful, he was going to see the Calippo again.

"Why?" he grunted.

"Now that's something I can't tell you," said Franklin.

"But if it makes a difference," added Hay, "the killer used tin to make the balls."

Kett nodded, trying to digest it.

"You need any help up there?" he asked.

Both women shook their heads.

"Thank God for that," he muttered.

He staggered away, belching Coke scent into his hand. He was so desperate to escape the body that he barely noticed he'd walked into the underpass. The claustrophobia crushed him as though the ceiling had dropped, and he rushed past the forensic team, running to the other end like a cartoon elephant who's seen a mouse.

"Are you sure you're okay, sir?" said Savage as she followed him out. "You seem like you're losing it a bit."

Not just a bit, he thought.

"It's the heat," he told her, fanning his face. "I'm fine."

They climbed the slope together, the sun wrapping

them in a sweaty hug like it had missed them. The IRV had moved, freeing up traffic on the main road, but a couple of television vans were blocking cars in the other direction. Kett heard his name yelled more than once by the men and women who huddled behind the tape, but he didn't even look over.

"Did I hear that right?" he asked, setting off towards the flats along the side of the road. "She had her eyes *taken out*?"

Savage nodded miserably.

"*Why*?" he asked again.

"If I knew the answer to that, sir, then the job would be a lot easier. But it's weird, right, that we've seen two sets of metal eyes today?"

"The Keith's dead dog," said Kett, nodding. "He said something, didn't he? That the dog's eyes helped her see better."

"Helped her see the metal men," said Savage, adding a shrug.

"You know anything about tin?" he asked.

"Not much," she said, frowning. "I mean, it's a pure metal, quite rare, very soft and malleable. You can bend it by hand. People have used it for centuries."

"Not much," said Kett with a soft laugh. "Encyclopaedia Jones."

Savage smiled, although it didn't last long.

"I can only think of tin cans," said Kett.

"Which aren't really tin," Savage explained. "They're stainless steel, with a very, very fine coating of tin. Steel provides the strength, the tin stops them from rusting."

"How do you know all this?" said Kett.

Savage shrugged.

"Granddad, mainly. He was full of facts. He knew everything. He would quiz me on it all when I was a kid. I guess that made it stick."

Kett stepped into the shade of the first block of flats, and there he stopped.

"So the killer made his eyeballs out of tin because they wouldn't rust?" said Kett.

Savage chewed on it.

"I think tin probably has some other significance. You get people tin gifts for their tenth wedding anniversary. Gran got a little tin box for hers from Granddad. She kept her pills in it, until it got nicked when their bungalow got broken into."

"Helpful," said Kett.

"Hey, you asked. Tin's also used to make bronze as well, as you know."

"I definitely knew that," said Kett, who definitely hadn't.

"I vaguely remember from my bell-ringing days that bronze bells with high quantities of tin make the best sound," she went on.

"Now you're just showing off."

"I would never do that, sir," said Savage. "If I *was* showing off, I'd add that the atomic number for tin is fifty, and the symbol is Sn, which comes from the Latin *stannum*, which means an alloy of silver and lead. Even though it's not an alloy."

He gave her a look, and she laughed.

"Sorry," she said.

"Never be sorry," he told her.

He looked around, studying the blocks of flats that crowded the wide pavement. There were five or six of them, each four stories tall and all looking pretty sorry for themselves. Even though it was only getting hotter, there were barely any windows open—probably because of the proximity of the busy road. Pulled curtains and half a dozen England flags made it impossible to see much through the dark glass. A bunch of kids kicked a ball off the walls of the closest one, the echo like a heartbeat. More people had gathered by the police tape, chatting to the uniformed coppers that stood there.

Towering over the flats was the office building, this one made of bright blue glass and almost hidden inside a cage of scaffolding. The name above the door was Norvic House, and the billboard mounted at the gate announced *Offices To Let*.

"You want the crowd or the flats?" Kett asked Savage.

"I'm happy to tackle the crowd, sir, if you want to get out of the sun? You're looking a little crispy."

She leaned in, scrutinising his face.

"Or maybe that's just the Calippo."

Kett was more than happy to escape the heat, so he set off towards the nearest block of flats. He was about to call for a constable to come with him when he spotted Porter's Mondeo pulling up a little way down the road, right outside the blue office building. By the time he'd walked over to it, Porter and Duke had climbed out. Both were back in their work clothes, and both were sporting a couple of nasty bruises on their faces.

"Don't tell me you've been knocked out already?" said Kett.

"It was a massacre, sir," said Duke, rubbing his eye. It might have been the light, but it looked a little swollen.

"It was rigged, is what it was," said Porter, wobbling one of his front teeth. "Our balls weren't inflated properly."

"Doesn't everyone use the same balls?" asked Kett.

Porter shrugged.

"I think they greased our side of the court, then."

"Greased your shoes, more like," muttered Duke. "I was playing fine until you knocked me over."

"I didn't knock you over, *Constable*," Porter shot back. "You tripped me up with your size bloody sixteen elephant feet."

"Where's Clare?" asked Kett, before they started trading blows.

"He's riding in the ambulance with Norman Balls," said Duke.

"What? Why?"

"Cricket box malfunction," said Porter. "Something to do with the elastic strap."

"You should have heard the snap," said Duke. "I thought somebody had been shot."

"Christ," said Kett.

There was a moment of silence as they all tried not to picture it.

"So what have we got here?" Porter asked.

"Nothing good," Kett replied, setting off. "Aaron, go help Kate, will you? Pete, come with me. I'll tell you everything on the way."

They were walking off when Kett heard a crunch, and a hoarse voice calling out to them. A man was walking out of the main door of the blue office building, somewhere in his early fifties, with a solid foundation of muscle beneath a decade of fat. His head was the shape and colour of a baked ham, his eyes like an unsharpened tool. Even if he hadn't been wearing a fluorescent yellow vest over his black jacket, Kett would have guessed that he was a security guard.

"What's all the commotion?" said the man as he hobbled up. His accent put him somewhere around Essex.

He held a mug in one hand, the scent one part coffee to nine parts scotch.

"Somebody was attacked in the park last night," said Kett. "You work here?"

The man nodded as he came to a halt, bracing one hand on his hip with a grimace. He was wearing gloves that looked like they'd been used to muck out a stable, and in the gap between them and the sleeves of his jacket, Kett saw a hint of black ink.

"You weren't working last night, were you?"

"I was," he said. "Do the nights here, and the days sometimes too. Not much to do, if I'm honest, other than chase away the vermin."

"Rats?" asked Kett.

"Teenagers," he said. He put a gloved thumb to one side of his nose, turned away, and ejected a gust of snot over the pavement. "They're always trying to get in. Climb the fire escape and the scaffolding up to the roof, making videos and all sorts. Graffitied the shit out of it before they brought me in."

"It's empty?" asked Porter.

The man nodded.

"Used to be a wine place or something, they all moved out. Nobody wants it, too bloody expensive to run. Too cheap to pay me properly as well, I only do it for the beer money."

"Did you happen to see anything strange on the road last night?" said Kett. "Down near the underpass. You must have a good view."

"Heard a few screams," he said, loosing a spray from his other nostril. "Went on for ages, wouldn't bloody shut up."

"Screams?" said Kett. "What time was this?"

"Midnight, maybe? Little before."

"And you didn't think to go and check?" said Kett. "Or call us?"

"Why?" said the man. "What would you have done? Come out with a fucking net?"

Kett shook his head, confused.

"Cats will be cats," the man went on. "Can't bloody stop 'em shagging and fighting."

"They were cats?" said Kett.

"I said it, I heard cats screaming. Foxes, too. Hear it every night, and that's about all you hear, other than the traffic, and the pricks taking a piss on the doors."

"Right," said Kett. "That's very helpful. What's your name?"

"Terry," said the man, rubbing his nose with his encrusted glove before offering the same hand to Kett. "Prince."

"Prince or no prince, I'm not touching that," said Kett.

The man's face hardened, his chin jutting, his lips drawing back to reveal small, yellow teeth. He pulled his hand back slowly, like he thought Kett might change his mind, his body swaying slightly from side to side. He was doing a good job of hiding it, but he was pissed.

"Won't tell you what happened to the last person who wouldn't shake my hand," he said.

"He didn't die from diphtheria?" muttered Kett, walking off.

"Hey, I did see something strange, thinking about it," said Terry. "Around ten. Maybe earlier. Or later?"

"Yeah?" said Kett, turning back.

The man took a sip from his mug.

"Yeah. Was on my rounds, top floor. Happened to look out the window, saw somebody walking by them bushes over there."

"What's strange about that?" asked Porter.

"Could have been the light," said Terry. "Could have been the distance, or all the scaffolding. Could have been the fact I can't see for shit anymore."

He took another long drink.

"But it looked like he was wearing a mask."

CHAPTER FIVE

The flats were every bit as run-down inside as they were out; so neglected, in fact, that there wasn't even a lock on the communal door. Porter opened it for Kett, and they walked into the cool interior, assaulted by the smell of joss sticks. It was surprisingly bright in the foyer, the walls covered with children's artwork and posters for community events. The plant basking by the window obviously hadn't been watered in some time, its leaves scattered across the tiled floor. Several bikes were chained together on the far side of the space, two of which didn't have their front wheels.

"A mask," said Porter. "You think he's full of shit?"

"He's full of something, alright," said Kett.

They'd asked Terry to elaborate, of course, but the security guard hadn't been able to give them anything else. When pressed, he wasn't even sure if it had been midnight, dusk, or dawn.

"If I put that much whisky in my coffee, I'd be seeing stuff too."

They walked into a dark, narrow corridor. There were

doors on either side, but Kett was only interested in those on the right, because of the view they'd have of the park. He knocked on the closest one and stood back, waiting.

"Still, worth looking into," he said, pressing his ear to the wood. There wasn't a hint of sound from inside.

Porter was already at the next door, and he rapped his hand delicately on it, wincing in pain.

"You alright?" Kett asked him.

"Took a fall," he said. "It was Aaron's fault. Clumsy git wasn't looking where he was going."

"What was the score?" Kett asked.

"You don't really get a score in dodgeball, sir. But they had all their players still in the game, and we had four out, one on the floor screaming about his strap, and one choking on a Bounty. Nobody home here."

They pushed through the door at the far end of the corridor, taking the stairs.

"I'm sorry I missed it," said Kett, who wasn't sorry in the slightest. "You'd have won if I'd been there, though."

"Obviously," said Porter. "Although it was Kate we really missed."

They chuffed their way up the concrete steps and entered an identical corridor, which felt too high up. They must have been maisonettes, Kett realised, two-storey apartments. Porter knocked on the first door.

"Clare was actually choking?" Kett asked.

"He was blue," said Porter. "Luckily, he took a ball to the solar plexus, and he spat it back up. Honestly, it was pure carnage. I'm amazed we made it out alive."

From deeper in the building came an angry shout, echoing off the stark walls. Porter knocked again, but it wasn't this door that opened, it was the next one along. A man stepped out of it, dressed in nothing but his pants and a

Blondie T-shirt. He was holding a frying pan over his head, and the expression on his face made it clear he wasn't planning on using it for cooking.

"I'm not going to tell you again, you cunts, pack it..."

He stopped when he saw Kett and Porter, his expression morphing from anger to shock in less than a second. He was in his early forties, although his hair and his stubble were almost completely silver. He lowered the pan, and reversed into his flat.

"Sorry!" he shouted as the door slammed shut.

Kett walked over, giving it a gentle tap.

"You want to try that again?" he shouted. He held his warrant card in front of the spyhole. "Police."

He heard a faint grumbling from inside, and the door opened again. The man stood there, still in his pants and still holding the frying pan. He was a good few inches shorter than Kett.

"Police?" he asked, staring at Kett's knees. "Is the budget so bad you've run out of trousers?"

"Something like that," said Kett. He offered the man a closer look at his warrant card, but he didn't bother.

"It's not as bad as it looks," the man said, lifting the pan. He had an accent, but Kett couldn't place it. "You here about those little pricks?"

Kett was about to ask which little pricks he meant when he heard another shout from somewhere else in the building. This time it was followed by the hammer of footsteps from the stairwell they'd just left, an echo of wild laughter. The man's face tightened, his jaw set.

"Kids?" asked Kett, remembering the lads he'd seen in the park.

"Kids?" scoffed the man. "Nah, these aren't kids, as

much as they act like it. They're all grown up. Making life miserable for all of us. You been knocking on doors?"

Kett nodded.

"How many folk answered?"

"Just you," said Kett.

"Because they're all scared shitless. Mostly old folk around here, and families. What are we gonna do? They got knives and all sorts. About time you lot actually did something."

Kett didn't have the heart to tell him otherwise.

"Can we come in, Mr...?"

"Short," he said, gesturing to his diminutive frame. "Just like it says on the tin. Call me Junior."

"Junior?" said Kett.

"It's what's on my passport."

There wasn't much room in the entrance hall of the maisonette, but the man did his best to stand back so Kett could walk through the door. Porter followed him in, making the place feel half as big as it had a moment ago. A set of stairs led up to the top floor, a cramped kitchen on the right.

"Go through," said Junior.

The living room felt too large and too bright to be possible in such a small home. Morning sun poured through two windows, washing over a couple of sofas, a large TV, and a rug that looked like a dead zebra. The walls were covered in framed photos of Junior with a woman and two kids, a boy and a girl, as well as countless pieces of children's art. Kett recognised a few of the misshapen animals.

"Your kids do the artwork in the lobby downstairs?" he asked.

"Yeah," said Junior. "Luke's a little Picasso, although Cora does her best. She's younger. We always try to make it look nice, and *they* always ruin it. You see the plant down there? Bastards pulled all the leaves off. Why do that?"

"You from South Africa?" asked Porter, perching on the edge of the sofa.

"That obvious?" said Junior. "Jo-Berg. Been here thirty-two years and I still can't shift the accent."

Kett walked to the window, seeing the road below. Police and pedestrians still swarmed over the pavement, the sound of their voices muffled. He would have had a perfect view of the underpass from here if it weren't for the tree that barred the way.

"So," said Junior. "What are you gonna do about them? Because no word of a lie, if things carry on the way they are, somebody's gonna end up dead."

Kett gave him a look, and he chucked the frying pan onto the sofa, holding his hands up.

"I'm not gonna do anything, obviously, but somebody will. Those pricks'll put a knife in you as soon as look at you, and they know you lot won't do anything. No offence."

"None taken," said Kett.

"They've done it already, haven't they?" Junior went on. "That's why you're all here. They've killed somebody."

"Just so we're clear," said Kett, "can you tell me exactly who you're talking about?"

"Yeah, sure, sorry," said Junior. "I thought you would have known. They're... I mean, I know I said they weren't kids, but they're young. Late teens. I don't know, exactly. Old enough to know better. They hang around in a pack of about six or seven, sometimes less, sometimes more. Montirex tracksuits, hoods up, masks and stuff over their faces."

"Walk like they've had an accident?" said Kett, and the man nodded.

"What's with that?" he asked. "Like, why act all hard and flash your knife and be the big, tough man, and then walk like a geriatric?"

"We saw them on the way over," Kett said, speaking as much to Porter as to Junior. "They were trying to get into the underpass. Not exactly pleasant to talk to."

"At least you got to talk," said Junior. "Most of the time, they just stare at you like they want to hurt you. They do it to everyone, do it to my kids, too. Who does that to a couple of children?"

"They around?" asked Kett. "Your kids?"

Junior shook his head, his expression darkening.

"Their mum has them most of the time now. Got too much for Luke here, with the noise and stuff. She doesn't want them with me, she wants them tucked up in her nice little semi-detached palace in the Golden Triangle. Don't even blame her. At least it's safe there."

He picked up the pan again, his knuckles white around the handle.

"So you gonna do something?" he asked. "You gonna do your job?"

"Yeah," said Kett. "We'll do something. Do you know if the lads live around here?"

"I don't think they come here for fun," he shot back. "Yeah, they live on the estate, no idea where, though. Ask the scagheads that come round looking for drugs, they know where to find them."

"They're dealing?"

"Well, they don't have jobs, I can tell you that much, and something's paying for those shiny trainers. Yeah, they're dealing. You see them in the park all the time, needles fucking everywhere. Another reason Luke and Cora couldn't stay here. Who wants their kid stepping on some junky's fucking hepatitis stick? Bad enough, all the dog shit, all the rubbish."

He hung his head, his body slouching.

"They're supposed to be coming here tomorrow, but Emma's already said she's trying to find somebody else to look after them. I'm their bloody dad, can't even give them a home."

"You think those lads are capable of killing somebody?" Kett asked.

"Just said, didn't I?" Junior replied. "They've got knives on them. Not always, they're not stupid, but I've seen them. Seen them in the bushes, too, where they dump them."

"Carrying a knife is one thing," said Kett. "Using it is another."

Junior thought about it for a second or two.

"All I know is that I'm scared," he said. "And I can't escape it. Can't sell this place for love or money. Can't rent it out. Probably couldn't get rid of it if I offered it for free. What are we supposed to do? *You* need to do something."

He met Kett's eyes, utterly miserable.

"*Please*."

"Let me look into it," Kett said.

Junior spluttered out a bitter laugh.

"Great," he said. "I'll rest easy now, then."

There was an awkward silence, broken only by the sound of a door slamming somewhere in the building. Junior flinched so hard he almost dropped the frying pan.

"Look," said Kett, taking a breath. "A body was found this morning, right across the road from here. In the park. An older woman."

Junior paled, his head shaking.

"They actually killed somebody?" he said. "I fucking knew it."

"We don't know for sure. It might not have anything to do with them. We're trying to work out what happened, and we're looking for anyone who might have seen something."

He pointed to the window.

"You've got a perfect view from here. Did you notice anything unusual last night?"

"When?" said Junior, still shaking his head.

"After dark."

"No," said the man. "You think I want to remind myself where I live? I don't stare out the windows, especially at night."

"You didn't hear anything?"

"I heard plenty," said Junior. "All those pricks running around, same thing they do every night."

"Do you know if any of your neighbours might have seen anything?" Kett asked. "Next door? Or downstairs?"

"Maybe. I don't talk to them. Drunk off their faces most of the time."

He lifted the frying pan, staring at it.

"I might have something that can help, though," he said. "As long as you don't break my balls about it."

He walked out of the room and up the stairs, almost tripping on a toy ambulance that had been left on the landing. Figures scattered out of it, some tumbling down the stairs.

"Bloody hell," he said. "How does their shit get everywhere?"

There was barely enough room up here for all three of them, but Junior opened a door into a microscopic bedroom at the back of the maisonette. It must have been right over the living room, because Kett could see the park through the window, the view even better. There was just about enough space for the bunk beds and the chest of drawers.

"I know you're not supposed to have these," he said, pulling a plug out of the socket with his free hand, then lifting something off the windowsill. "But they were keeping the kids awake every night. I thought it was better to have some kind of record."

He walked back, handing a small security camera to Kett.

"It's just for the pavement," he explained. "Because they sometimes hang out there, slinging shit. Had one outside my front door too, but they kept nicking it. You gonna arrest me for that?"

"For having a camera?" said Kett, turning it over in his hands. "No. There's nothing illegal about it."

"Oh," said Junior, genuinely surprised.

"Was this recording last night?" Kett asked.

"Should have been. I don't check it much. It's a cheap one, so the quality is shit. No Wi-Fi or anything. There's a memory card thing in it. No idea if it's full or not. Think it overwrites itself after a few days."

He shrugged, the frying pan clattering against the wall.

"You got a computer we can check it on?"

"Laptop, yeah, but the kids have it when they stay with Emma. I can call her, ask her to bring it over?"

"No need," said Kett. "You mind if we take this with us?"

Junior shook his head, a strand of white hair falling in front of his eyes. He brushed it away with the hand holding the pan, almost braining himself. He rested his other arm against the top bunk like he needed it to hold him up. Kett could see how close to breaking he was, but only because he'd been there himself, so many times.

"If you think of anything else, call me," he said, pulling a business card from his wallet and handing it to him. "And I mean anything, Junior. I've got kids, I know what it's like when you feel like you can't keep them safe. But we can help. We *will* help. Okay?"

Junior nodded, breathing out slowly.

"Call me," Kett said again. "You're not on your own."

"Nothing worse than being on your own," said Junior, nodding. "Thanks."

For a second, Kett thought the man was coming in for a hug, but he must have changed his mind, retreating so fast he hit the wall. Kett squeezed past him before it could get any more awkward, almost tripping on the discarded toys as he walked down the stairs. There were more noises from somewhere close by, the hammer of running feet in the corridors. They were so loud that he opened the front door expecting to see somebody barrelling past, but the hallway was empty, the building playing tricks.

He waited for Porter to walk out, then he stepped back, seeing Junior at the top of the stairs.

"I meant to ask: this group of kids, they got a name?"

"I don't know their names," Junior replied.

"I mean a gang name. They always have one."

"The Pant Shitter Crew," suggested Porter. "The Vauxhall Bedwetters. Something like that."

"Oh, right," said Junior. "I don't know, sorry. But the fuckers are always spraying on the walls, tagging shit. There's one right out there. Might help."

Kett spotted it, a splodge of graffiti halfway to the fire door.

"Thanks," he said.

He pulled the door closed behind him, walking to the tag that had been left on the wall. Even though it was huge, he still needed to put his glasses on to see it properly. Two words had been spray-painted in red and yellow and black, but they were so stylistically done he couldn't make much sense of them.

"Can you read that, Pete?" he said, winding the cord around the little security camera.

"Casey likes cocks in her arse?" said Porter, nodding to a line of writing further down the corridor.

"Not that."

Porter's brow furrowed as he studied the graffiti.

"Sausages?" he said, pointing to the word at the bottom. "That's an S, I think. Sausages. Wait, *soldiers*. That makes more sense. No idea about the top one, though."

Kett tilted his head, and the tag suddenly made sense—like one of those 3D images you have to squint at. The word had been folded into a yellow crown, studded with red gems.

"Iron," he said. "Right?"

"That's it, sir," said Porter, nodding. "Iron Soldiers. Not as catchy as the Vauxhall Bedwetters, is it?"

"But a little more relevant," said Kett, thinking of the dead woman and her tin eyes—thinking of The Keith and his metal men. He took out his phone, snapping a photograph. "Something tells me we need to pay these guys a visit."

CHAPTER SIX

"It was Porter's bloody fault!" said Duke, for what had to be the tenth time since he'd turned up. He was back in uniform, and he cut an even more imposing figure than usual because of the bruise around his eye. "He's the reason we didn't win."

Savage ducked beneath the police tape, pushing into the crowd that had formed on the other side of it. More people seemed to be arriving by the second as word of the police presence spread. So far, Norfolk Constabulary had managed to keep a lid on what they'd found in the park. But it was a small city with plenty of big mouths, and she knew it wouldn't be long before the news broke.

"I heard you the first hundred times, Aaron," she replied. "It was Porter's fault."

"He ran into me. I was about to throw a kill-shot, and he lumbered right into the back of me like some kind of..." Duke threw up his hands like he was trying to catch the word as it flew overhead. "He's an oaf."

"Poor widdle Aaron," said Savage, pouting dramatically at him. "I'm sorry you lost at sportsball."

"*I* didn't lose," Duke said. "*Porter* did."

He winced.

"And Norman. Judging by the scream he let out, he definitely lost... something."

Savage tuned him out, searching the faces of the crowd. On the surface, the atmosphere felt like a carnival, the way crime scenes often did before the horror of them got out. Parents shared ice creams with their kids, chatting to the uniformed police, their laughter drifting over the slow-moving traffic. A couple of older men sheltered in the shade of the trees, sipping from cans of beer and smoking roll-ups. There were more teenagers here than she could count, pouring from the shopping centre further down the road. She could see the coppers asking them to stop taking photos, but nobody was listening.

She wondered what the poor woman in the woods would have made of it all, of this circus that seemed to revel in her death.

There was something else in the air, too, something that simmered beneath the laughter and the smiles. Savage could feel it, the same tension you sometimes sensed before a fight, or a riot. It was the heat. It burrowed into your head and lit a fire there, and it didn't take much for the flames to spread. It was happening right now: two teenage lads, toe to toe, a girl trying to separate them as they yelled at each other. An older couple arguing with another police officer, gesturing to the underpass like they owned it. The line of constables by the underpass, losing their patience as the crowd edged closer, the hot air full of angry voices.

In this weather, any city come become a tinderbox.

"Step back, please," Savage told one group of onlookers, doing her best to help. "Or better still, move on."

She ushered them away down the street, still searching

the sea of faces. It was Detective 101, proven time and time again: killers came back to the scene of the crime.

Judging by the anger she saw on so many faces, though, any one of these people could have done it.

"Back off," Duke hollered to the mob, one hand on his Taser. "If you're not police, you shouldn't be here."

He growled at a group of younger kids and they scattered like tenpins, laughing their way towards the city.

"See," he said. "I'm a winner. People see me and run."

"Every time I see you, *I* feel like running," she said beneath her breath.

"What?"

She gave him a stern look, and he rolled his eyes.

"What, Sarge?"

"Nothing, Aaron. Just try to focus, will you?"

"I am focus," he said, narrowing his eyes at the crowd. "Laser focus."

She left him to it, climbing onto one of the raised concrete flowerbeds that dotted the courtyard outside the flats. Whatever was growing in them wasn't doing well, the leaves browning. It was no surprise. The soil was buried beneath a mountain of litter, including half a dozen upended energy drinks. If there had been anything left inside the cans when they'd been dumped, then these plants would soon be pulling themselves out of the dry soil and walking off on their own.

At least she had a better view from up here, though.

If only she knew what she was looking for.

"Any luck?" said a croaky voice from behind her.

She glanced over her shoulder to see a woman walking down the pavement. She was somewhere in her eighties, although she seemed sprightly enough. Her face was crinkled like a leather purse, probably something to do with the cigarette in her hand. Her eyes were bright, and she winked at Savage as she walked up. She was wearing a lacy black dress that would have been better suited to a Victorian ghost story. All it was missing was the veil.

"Sorry?" said Savage.

"I said, any luck?" the woman repeated. Her voice was like a piano full of gravel, and there was an accent there, something European, maybe. "With whoever you're looking for."

"Not yet," said Savage. "Maybe you can help?"

The woman eased herself down onto the low wall of the flower bed, the dress pooling beneath her like oil. She rested one elbow on her knee, taking another drag on her cigarette. She held it in for a count of five before releasing it.

"Not sure how a *babushka* like me could help," she said.

"You live around here?"

The woman nodded, jabbing her cigarette towards the flats.

"For my sins," she said.

Savage hopped down, stepping back so she wouldn't have to breathe in the smoke.

"You didn't happen to see anything weird around here last night? Near the underpass, or the park? Mrs..."

"Heathen," said the woman. "Enid."

Savage frowned.

"Real name," she croaked, like she'd said it a million times before. "Look it up."

"It's not that. I'm a Savage. Kate Savage. Heathen and Savage, it was a strange combination, sorry."

The woman smiled, but there was something else there, a flicker of recognition.

"Savage," she said. "You aren't related to Jeff?"

Another laugh fell out of Savage's mouth, this one full of surprise.

"He was my granddad," she said. "Don't tell me you knew him?"

"Oh, I knew him," said Enid. "Knew him well, him and Betsy. She still with us?"

"Yeah," said Savage. "Hanging on. How on earth do you know them?"

"Oh, this and that," she said, that glint back in her eye. "He looked after me when I came over from the old country."

"Which old country is that?"

"Birmingham," she said with a snort. "It was Georgia, before that. I can tell you how he looked after me, but then you'll have to arrest me."

"Wait, you and Granddad weren't, like, together?"

The woman hacked out a laugh, taking another drag even though she was coughing.

"No," she managed after a moment, tears rolling down her powdered cheeks. "He only had eyes for his wife, that one. He hauled me in a couple of times, back in the day."

"Seriously?" said Savage, with another laugh. "What for?"

"That would be telling," said Enid. "Nothing awful, just the usual Saturday night stuff. He always joked about my name, too. Savage and Heathen, he'd say. Quite the team."

Savage shook her head. She had no idea what to make of this strange little coincidence.

"One of the good ones, was Big Jeff," said Enid. "Didn't matter that you were on opposite sides, he treated you right, treated you fair. It was different back then. More honour. Less of this shit."

She gestured to the crowd with her cigarette.

"Less death, too, although maybe I'm remembering it wrong."

"Maybe," said Savage. "Maybe not. It's definitely getting worse."

They stared at the entrance to the underpass for a moment, listening to the murmur of voices.

"You didn't see anything?" Savage asked again. "Yesterday evening, or into the night. Somebody stopping their car, maybe? Or somebody dragging something into the tunnel?"

Enid took another long drag, holding it in her lungs like she was about to dive beneath the water. She crushed the butt beneath her heel, shook her head, and only then did she breathe out again.

"I don't go out after dark," she said. "Too many bad spirits."

"Bad spirits?" asked Savage. "What do you mean?"

"Just that. You got your good spirits, like Jeff, like you. You shine."

She scratched at her wrinkled neck with yellow nails.

"But you got your bad spirits too. You got to know what you're looking for, but you can see them plain as day when you do."

Enid was watching the crowd like a bird of prey, making soft noises in her throat. Before Savage could ask her what she was talking about, she jutted her chin towards a family that was standing at the back of the crowd. A tall man stood with his arm around a woman, both in their mid-twenties. One kid stood on the buggy board at the back of a pushchair, the other was fast asleep in a swaddle of blankets.

"Like him," she said.

"Who?" asked Savage.

"Him," said Enid. "Bad spirit. Peel off that pretty face, and you can't *not* see it."

The guy looked about as normal as it was possible to be. A slim build, a handful of tattoos poking out of the sleeves of his yellow and green Norwich City football shirt, straight, blond hair swept back, a dusting of stubble, the glint of an earring.

"I don't know what you mean," said Savage. "Sorry."

"Just wait," said Enid.

Savage waited, watching the man pull his wife closer, his arm around her neck like he was going to noogie her. He planted a kiss on her cheek, and there was no denying the way she tried to pull away from it. He held onto her for a few seconds, the muscles in his arms like steel wires, then he released her. There was a smile on his face, but it wasn't a kind one.

"How did you..." Savage started, watching the young woman take a few steps away from the man, pulling the buggy with her. He closed the gap instantly, picking up the young boy from the buggy board and holding him to his chest, never taking his eyes off his wife. He was every bit the loving father, but she'd seen it—for a fraction of a second, she'd seen what lay beneath the mask. "How did you know?"

"Just do," said Enid, nodding at the crowd. "Bad spirit there. Bad spirit there. There. There. Never used to be so many, but now you can't spit for hitting one. Thought maybe I was getting better at seeing them, but sometimes I wonder if there's just more of them to be seen."

Enid rummaged inside her dress, pulling a packet of Mayfairs from a hidden pocket. She slid another cigarette into her mouth before pulling something else from the box.

It was a business card, Savage realised when she handed it over.

"You're a psychic?" she said, trying to read the garish pink letters that were scattered over a photograph of a starry sky.

"I am." Enid lit the cigarette, inhaling deeply. "Read your cards, read your tea leaves, read anything you like. I'm never wrong. Come see me one day, have a chat with your granddad."

Savage pocketed the card, feeling a sudden sting of anger at the suggestion.

"I'm not really a believer," she said.

"You sure?" asked Enid. "Because of all the people here, something led me right to you."

Savage had no idea what to say to that.

"Help me up, Kate," said Enid, holding out her free hand.

Savage took it, marvelling at how soft the woman's skin was. She gently heaved her to her feet, but when she tried to let go, Enid clung on. The woman leaned in, craning her neck so that she could meet Savage's eye. There was something in the intensity of her stare that made it impossible to look away.

"Bad spirits," she said. "Learn how to see them, because if you don't, then nothing's going to save you."

"What?" said Savage.

Enid let go, Savage's hand smarting from the force of the woman's grip.

"Come see me. Maybe I can help."

She breathed out a lungful of smoke as she turned away, thick enough to punch the air from Savage's lungs. The day was too hot, the sweat rolling down the neck of her tracksuit.

"You look just like him, you know," Enid called back as she walked away. "Your grandfather. Be safe, Savage. Us heathens have to look out for one another."

Savage watched until she'd walked out of sight, then she let go of the breath she'd been holding. The encounter had left her feeling so giddy she may as well have been drunk, and she rubbed her face with both hands.

"What the heck was that?" she asked herself.

"What the what was what?" said Duke, walking up.

"Did you see her?" she asked him. "The woman?"

"Woman?" he said, shaking his head.

"Laser focus, my arse," Savage muttered. She pulled out Enid's business card just to make sure it was real, then slid it into her wallet to keep it safe.

"See anything?" Duke asked.

Savage turned to the crowd again, holding back her answer. The man with the wife and kids had gone, but there were more people here now than ever. She studied them in turn: the woman standing in the shadows of a doorway texting on her phone, the reporters who fought to get past the police tape, the tall, balding man who straddled his bike, watching the underpass with dark eyes.

"Bad spirits," said Savage, wondering just how many there were.

CHAPTER SEVEN

The day seemed to have grown twice as hot in the time that Kett had spent inside. Even though he was only wearing his shorts and T-shirt, he was drenched in sweat as he reached the underpass. Savage and Duke were already there, chatting to members of the crowd. Porter had run to the line of IRVs to look for a laptop, taking the camera with him.

"Alright, Kate," said Kett when Savage had finished talking. "Anything?"

"Not yet, sir," she said, running the back of her hand over her damp brow. "No witnesses. People say it's quiet here at night, because of the gangs."

"I heard that too," said Kett. "And it's not like the gangs are going to report anything suspicious. We found a camera in that flat up there, covers the street. Might get lucky."

Duke wandered over, his eye swollen.

"You should probably get that looked at, Aaron," said Kett.

"I'm fine," the big PC replied. "Head's made of concrete."

"Doesn't he always look like that?" said Porter, walking back. He was struggling to hold the laptop and the camera, the cord trailing behind him. "Like Quasimodo's uglier brother."

"Least I don't look like Quasimodo's ballsack," muttered Duke, earning a stern glare from Kett.

"What was that?" said Porter.

"Nothing, sir," said Duke, seeing the camera. "What you got there?"

"Hopefully some answers," said Kett. He went to put on his glasses before realising he was already wearing them.

"That's how it starts, sir," said Porter, who had obviously noticed.

Kett took the laptop from the DI a little more forcefully than he needed to. The glare of the day was too bright for the cheap screen, and he didn't fancy sitting inside the oven of an IRV, so he carried it towards the underpass. They were halfway there when Savage was hailed by a passerby, a young woman asking too many questions to be anything other than a reporter.

Kett left her to it, walking down the slope. It was much darker at the bottom, the temperature plummeting thanks to the stagnant air that poured out of the tunnel. He had to fight a surge of claustrophobia—those same awful memories entering his head like knives.

It was still busy down here, Cara Hay offering a weary nod from where she squatted beside a heap of rubbish. Kett handed the laptop to Duke and opened the back of the camera. The memory card inside was a standard one, and there was a slot for it in the old computer. They crowded together in the damp as Kett found the right folder, then the right file.

"Last night," he said, double-clicking it. "Jackpot."

Not quite. The angle of the camera meant that only a small section of the pavement was in shot, and it was blurred by the window and dimmed by the night. Kett could just about see the slope they were currently standing on, and a sliver of darkness that was the underpass tunnel.

The timestamp read 19:00, and he let it play. A handful of people walked by, most heading out of the city, just the tops of their heads visible. Smudges moved behind the railings of the underpass, impossible to make out. He couldn't see the road from this angle, but the constant movement of headlights meant it had been busy.

"Do we know when she was killed, sir?" asked Duke.

"No," answered Kett. "We don't even know if she was murdered here. The killer might have just dumped the body."

The PC leaned a little closer, earning a grunt of annoyance from Porter.

"Can you move?" Porter said. "We can't see through you."

"Maybe if you were a little taller, sir," said Duke.

"I'm plenty tall enough, Aaron."

"In your high heels, maybe."

"Can you pack it in?" Kett said. "Both of you."

Both men grumbled an apology, and they watched on in silence. Each file was exactly an hour long, and Kett scrubbed through them, stopping any time somebody entered the frame. There were too many people, though, it was impossible to watch them all. On a couple of occasions, he spotted the gang of youths strutting past, their hoods up. At just after nine, one of them seemed to throw something at the window of a flat, but Kett couldn't see what it was.

As the evening grew into night, the number of people on the pavement thinned, and it was only because of this that he noticed the cyclist. He began as a dark shape moving up the slope of the underpass, vanishing out of frame for a few seconds before reappearing. It looked like a man, and either he was wearing a helmet or he was bald, the top of his head gleaming in the streetlights. He climbed on his bike and started pedalling, only to stop again almost immediately.

"What's he doing?" asked Porter.

The man stood there on his bike, then turned his head to the underpass. Kett counted twenty seconds before he moved again, sweeping the bike in a wide circle and heading back towards the slope. But here he stopped again, still looking down into the underpass, like he was waiting for something.

Or like he'd heard something.

"Nine twenty-one," said Kett, looking at the timestamp.

There was nobody else about, no lights on the road, either. The man waited for almost a minute more, never taking his eyes off the slope that led underground. Then he turned his bike back the way it had been facing before. He put both hands to his face like a mourner at a funeral, holding them there, then he pedalled out of sight.

"That was weird, right?" said Kett.

He rewound to the start of the clip, and they watched it again.

"Really weird," said Duke. "It's like he wants to go back down, but he doesn't dare. Maybe he saw something."

"If he'd seen something, though, he'd have called the police," said Kett. "Surely."

"I don't know," said Duke. "The way he's got his head in his hands there, he looks guilty. Looks like somebody who's done something they shouldn't have."

"Porter?" said Kett, when the DI didn't contribute.

"How the hell would I know, sir? All I can see is this gorilla's sweaty armpit."

"You want me to get you a box, sir?" said Duke.

"I'm bloody tall enough!"

"Would you both quit it!" barked Kett, in the tone of voice he usually reserved for his children. "It is too hot for your nonsense."

He rewound the clip a little, freezing it on the cyclist just as he pulled his hands away from his face. The resolution scrubbed away his features, erasing his nose, turning his eyes into two pockets of darkness. There was something monstrous about the image, the tunnel colder than ever.

"We need to find this man," he said. "Can one of you get a copy of this to HQ so we can put the word out? Then lift every stone on this street, find cameras, see which way he went."

"Who, sir?" asked Savage as she clattered down the slope.

Duke flipped the laptop so she could see the screen.

"This guy, Sarge," said the PC.

Savage leaned in, her face scrunching up.

"The man on the bike," Duke explained.

"I can see that, mate," said Savage. "Since he's the only one in shot. I think..."

Her frown deepened.

"I think he's here," she said. "Up there. I saw a man on a bike, an older guy, bald. Looked just like him."

They walked up the slope together, hovering near the top and peering through the railings.

"Is that him?" Savage said, pointing.

Kett followed her finger through the crowd, spotting the man almost immediately. He was standing right at the back, far enough away that Kett couldn't make out his face in any detail. He looked like he was in his fifties, maybe early sixties, and he was definitely bald, or near enough. He had both hands on the handlebars of a sleek, expensive-looking, bright red bike, which leaned against him. He was dressed like he was about to cycle the Tour de France, his black and yellow Lycra practically painted on.

"I can't tell," said Kett. "Duke."

Duke held up the laptop, although once again the glare of the sun rendered everything practically invisible. Kett angled the screen down, focussing on the bike instead of the man. The night vision camera had turned everything grey.

"What colour do you think that is?" he asked.

"Grey?" said Duke. "Looks like the same bike, though. It's got two wheels."

Kett glanced at him to see if he was joking. He looked deadly serious.

"It's got a water bottle right there under the saddle," said Porter, who had joined them. "And the D-lock. Same as his."

They all peeked over the lip of the slope together. If anyone had seen them, they must have looked like whack-a-moles.

"Bad spirit," said Savage.

"What?" asked Kett.

"Nothing, sir," she said. "But if that's our killer, it makes sense that he's here. He wants to be a part of it, he wants to relive the murder, experience it through the eyes of other people. It's not enough for them to take a life once, they want to take it again and again, even if it's just through the memory of it."

"Then let's go and speak with him," said Kett. "But don't spook him, that bike looks fast."

"Pft," said Duke. "He's about a hundred years old. Even Porter could catch him."

"You are about four words away from getting a shoe in your arse, Duke," said Porter, red-faced from the heat and from his anger.

"Enough!" Kett roared. "If you two can't play nicely, then you can both go away. No more, understood?"

They didn't look happy about it, but they both nodded.

"I get enough of this at home," said Kett. "Spread out, get around the back of him in case he splits."

Kett climbed to the top of the slope, moving around the bushes that grew next to the underpass. Porter and Duke walked ahead, trying to race each other without actually breaking into a run. Savage split off to the right, edging the road. Kett walked slowly, passing under the line of police tape and using the crowd to cover his movements. The closer he got to the man, the more he doubted that it was the one in the video. He was older than he'd first guessed, somewhere in his sixties, and skinny—the bodysuit he wore made him look like a walking rake draped in hi-vis. He didn't seem like somebody who was capable of overpowering a woman and crushing her throat.

But he had been wrong before.

He closed in, seeing Savage on the right, Porter and Duke on the left. They were still squabbling; he could hear them over the noise of the crowd.

The man with the bike could hear them too. He lifted his head, watching Duke and Porter as they moved towards him. His expression changed to one of alarm, and he started to wheel his bike in a circle.

"Oi!" yelled Porter. "Stop!"

But it was far too late for that.

CHAPTER EIGHT

"Which part of 'don't spook him' wasn't clear?" yelled Kett.

The bald man was climbing onto his bike, struggling for balance as his feet slipped on the pedals. Porter had started running, Duke too, the PC taking the lead with long, powerful strides. A constable further up the road had tuned into the shouts, charging towards the cyclist from the other direction. The man was panicking, turning the bike back towards Savage as he fought to get going.

"Stop!" she yelled.

He wasn't going to. He turned sharply again, one foot on the floor to stop the bike toppling. He pedalled hard, Savage almost getting a hand on his arm before he picked up speed. He cut towards the flats where there weren't many police, passing Duke with feet to spare. Duke whirled around, colliding with Porter, who was right behind him, both of them landing on the ground in a tangle of limbs.

"Get up, you muppets!" Kett roared as he passed them.

He broke into a sprint, chasing the man past the towering buildings. The guy was fit, powering through a flock of pigeons that had congregated next to some garages, sailing effortlessly past a pub on the corner. Kett battled past the panicked birds, every bone grinding against its neighbour, every tendon as tight as a harp string. It was useless. The man was already fifty yards away, and there were a dozen roads he could turn down. This side of the city was a maze of streets and alleyways.

They'd lost him.

"Fuck's sake," he said, and he'd almost given up when the man on the bike made the mistake of glancing over his shoulder. His front wheel skimmed the kerb, and it was like he'd been launched out of a catapult, sailing off his saddle and landing hard on the road. The bike meandered on for a little while without him, as if it was trying to escape. Then it collapsed, the back wheel spinning.

Kett jogged up to where the man lay on the road, curled into a ball, both hands to his face the same way they had been in the footage from last night.

"Stay down," Kett told him, although he didn't seem capable of getting up. His right leg had been chewed to pieces by the asphalt, his elbow too. When he peeked through his fingers, Kett saw that the entire bottom of his face was a mask of blood. "Christ," he said. "Stay there, I'll get an ambulance."

The man replied, but it sounded like he was chewing toffee.

"Hang on," said Kett.

There was a drum of footsteps behind him, and he turned to see Savage, Porter and Duke running up.

"How on earth did you catch him, sir?" said Porter. "He was flying."

"I'm faster than I look," said Kett. "Duke, get an ambulance over here, will you?"

The PC nodded, speaking into his radio. Savage dropped down beside the man, gently pulling his hands away from his face. There was a nasty graze on his cheek, but the blood seemed to be coming from his mouth. When he spoke again, Kett saw that his two top teeth were missing.

"Easy," said Savage, helping him sit up. She looked at Kett like *he* might have done this.

"He hit the kerb," Kett explained. "Went flying."

The man spoke again, something that sounded like: "It's my own fault." It was hard to tell, partly because of his injuries, and partly because he had an accent. Without his teeth, he looked closer to a hundred years old.

"What's your name?" Savage asked. "If you're okay to speak."

"Roger," he mumbled, blood leaking over his chin. "Sexton."

"Sex what?" said Kett, moving closer to hear him.

"Ton," he said. "*Sexton*."

"Roger," said Kett. "What were you thinking, trying to get away from the police like that?"

"I don't know," he said, wiping away a tear and leaving a streak of blood instead.

"I'm sorry about your teeth," said Savage.

Incredibly, a laugh bubbled out of the man's bloody mouth.

"Dentures," he tried to say. "They're only dentures. I bit my tongue."

He stuck it out as if to prove it, blood pattering to the ground. Kett winced, his own tongue curling up in sympathy inside his mouth. A car passed, bathing them in exhaust fumes as it headed for the main road.

"Let us help you off the street," said Savage.

"Bring my bike too, will you, pet?" he mumbled. "Don't want to lose her."

Savage took one of the man's arms, and Kett took the other. He was as light as a feather, and they practically carried him to a low garden wall. He sat there, doubled up, the blood dripping onto the pavement like spilled paint. Duke scooped up the bike and rested it against the gate, fiddling with the front wheel, which had been bent out of shape.

"What a bloody idiot," Roger muttered. "You probably think I'm guilty, don't you?"

His accent was a Geordie one, although it had been softened.

"That depends," said Kett, sitting next to him. "Guilty of what?"

Roger's eyes were bloodshot, the lines on his face so deep they could have been scars. Most of his hair had gone, just a few grey wisps stewing in a coating of sweat.

"I don't know," he said. "You found something in the park, didn't you?"

Kett nodded.

"Some*one*?"

"Yeah," said Kett.

The man sucked on his tongue, his face full of pain. Kett gave him a moment to find the question.

"A woman?"

"Yeah," said Kett. "You mind telling me how you know that?"

Roger dropped his head between his knees, groaning.

"I don't," he said. "Just had a feeling. How old is she?"

"Tell me who you're missing, first," said Kett.

"A friend," he said. "Helen."

"Helen what?" asked Savage.

"Coulter."

She walked off, typing something into her phone.

"Hel never showed up at work this morning, and she won't answer her phone," Roger went on. "Not like her."

"What makes you think this has anything to do with Helen?" asked Kett.

The man squirmed on the wall, his mouth gurning as he tried to find an answer.

"Just a feeling," he said. "I left work to come and see if she was okay, got here and saw all the police. Just gave me a weird feeling, you know?"

"There must be more of a reason than that," said Kett. "You were here last night, weren't you? Just after nine."

Roger's head jerked up so fast that a dewlet of blood spun off his lips, landing on Kett's trainer.

"How do you know that?" he said.

"You were caught on a security camera, coming out of the underpass with your bike. You're acting weird."

He shook his head, confused.

"That's why you all came at me just now?" he said.

"It *was* you?"

"Yeah," said the man, tonguing the gap between his teeth.

"You want me to show you the footage, or do you remember what you were doing?"

"I remember," said Roger. "I was with Helen."

"Hang on," said Kett. "You were with her? In the footage, you're on your own."

"I can't be," said Roger. He looked down as if he were trying to remember. "No, she was there. I was walking her home. You must have seen her. I didn't bloody imagine it."

Kett glanced at Porter, who opened the laptop and brought it over. He sat on the other side of Roger, the three of them watching the sun-washed screen as the footage started to play. There was the top of Roger's bald head as he walked up the underpass, vanishing for a moment before he reappeared on the pavement.

"That's you," said Kett.

"Yeah," said Roger, brushing a hand over the top of his wrinkled head. "Didn't realise I'd lost so much hair."

The man on screen dallied for a while, wheeling his bike back and forth, putting his face in his hands before pedalling away.

"Where's Helen?"

"I'd just left her," he said. "Rewind a bit."

Kett did as the man asked, starting the video a few minutes earlier.

"There," he said, jabbing the screen almost hard enough to knock it out of Porter's fingers. The DI caught it before it fell.

"That's us," said Roger.

Kett had to lean right in, staring through his glasses at the section of slope that was visible. He could barely see anything through the railings, but there was a definite smudge of shadow heading down to the tunnel. He paused it.

"That's only one person," he said.

"I was riding the bike," said Roger. "The hill's the best part. Had my head down."

It didn't seem a very likely story. Kett watched the shadow vanish beneath street level.

"Tell me what's happening now," he said. "You were walking her home?"

"Yeah. We both work at the N&N. She's a nurse. I'm retired, officially, but I work a couple of shifts a week. Portering. Cash comes in handy. Bus drops us off round the back here, and she lives in town. One of the flats in the shopping centre."

He craned his head down the street.

"Just over there. If I'm with her, she cuts through the park, otherwise she uses the crossing."

"You live around here too?"

"No, I'm over Drayton way. But I'm always happy to see her home."

There was something he wasn't saying, but again, Kett didn't press it.

"So you both walk into the underpass at..." He checked the timestamp. "Nine seventeen. How far did you walk her?"

"Literally through the tunnel," he said. "Made it into the park, but she didn't want me to go any further."

"Why not?" asked Kett.

There it was again, that unsaid thing. It was written all over his bloodied face. He didn't have time to answer, anyway, before Savage walked back over. The expression on her face was as easy to read as a book, and Kett sighed at the inevitability of what was about to happen.

"Is this Helen?" Savage asked, holding her phone out.

On the screen was a photograph of an attractive woman in her late sixties, a giant smile on her face, her eyes full of kindness. Her hair was pulled back into a ponytail and kept in place with a rainbow headband that was topped with a plastic unicorn. She stood in a line of four women, all of them wearing identical scrubs.

Kett almost didn't recognise her, because there was so much life in the woman here, so much joy, so much pride. She was nothing like the silver-eyed corpse they'd found in the woods.

And yet there was no denying it was her.

Kett put a hand to his mouth, breathing a long, quiet sigh through his fingers.

"Roger?" Savage prompted.

The man didn't answer, and Savage zoomed in on Helen's face.

"Oh, yes," Roger said, wearing a smile of his own despite his injuries. "That's her."

Savage walked away again, the phone to her ear.

"You and Helen, you're a thing?" Kett asked. "In a relationship?"

Roger squirmed a little more.

"You want to be," said Kett. "That's why you walk her home?"

"Come on," Roger protested. "Can't a man walk a lady home without wanting to get into her bed? It's common decency."

"Bit of an effort, though, isn't it? Getting your bike on the bus, then cycling back from town?"

Roger smiled again, scuffing his shoes on the pavement like a bashful schoolboy.

"Can't blame me, can you?" he said. "She's bloody gorgeous, Hel. Most beautiful woman I know, inside and out, but she don't know it. I tell her all the time, and she don't believe me. How can she not believe me, when she looks in the mirror every day? I love her."

He jumped, like he'd given himself a fright.

"Don't be telling her that, though. Made a big enough cock of myself already."

"Is that what you were doing in the underpass?" Kett asked. "Telling Helen how you felt?"

Roger put his fingers to his injured elbow, grimacing.

"Too chicken to do it properly," he said. "I told her this stupid poem, and she told me to bugger off. Not like that, because she's far too nice. But that was the gist of it. If I wasn't such a fanny, I'd have just come out and said it."

"You told her you liked her, and she rejected you?" said Kett.

"Not like that," Roger replied. "It was just awkward. I went off on me bike, came up there just like you saw. And I had a feeling, right here."

He rubbed his stomach.

"Just thought maybe I should go back, catch her up, and tell her. 'Be a man,' Roger. 'Tell her how you feel.' That's what I'm doing, pissing about there like an old fart, no idea if I'm coming or going. Bottled it, went home."

"Hang on," said Kett. "You say you walked Helen as far as the park, which meant she was out of the underpass."

Roger nodded.

"But we think Helen might have been attacked *inside* the underpass," said Kett.

"She was dragged in?" said the man, the horror of the thought all over his face.

"I don't think so. Is there any reason she would have retraced her steps? Any reason she'd have walked back through?"

Roger frowned, and Kett thought he saw the man's heart break right there and then.

"She came after me?"

"I don't know," said Kett.

"I was right there," he said, groaning. "Right there."

If his grief was a performance, it was an impressive one.

"In the video, you grabbed your face before leaving the scene," said Kett. "Why?"

"Why what? Why'd I grab my face? I don't know. Why do we do anything?"

"It's the sort of thing people do when they've made a

mistake," said Porter. "When they've done something wrong."

Roger looked at Porter for a second, then back at Kett.

"Can you do me a favour?" he asked. "Tell me what happened. Is it Hel?"

He was shaking, his jaw trembling as the shock of his injuries set in. Kett looked up to see if the ambulance was coming, but there was no sign of it.

"I think so, Roger," he said. "We found a woman's body in the park this morning, in the trees on the other side of the underpass. The description matches what we know about Helen."

Roger shook his head the way people always did when they got bad news, that awful belief that if you denied something, it wouldn't be true. Blood was still leaking from his mouth, dripping off the end of his chin.

"Please don't," he said, like Kett had a choice.

"Somebody killed her, Roger," he said. "Brutally and violently. And we think it happened right around the time you left her."

"Why would somebody do that?" he said, seemingly oblivious to the accusation. "She would never hurt a fly, she was golden, was Hel. Why would somebody hurt her?"

"I don't know," said Kett.

The wall was making Kett's backside numb, so he stood up, cricking his neck. Porter did too, closing the laptop and standing over Roger. It was this that made the man suddenly understand, and he gasped like somebody had spoken it aloud.

"*I* didn't do it!" he said. "Is that what this is? You think I could do something like that? To somebody like her? Never."

The man struggled to his feet, gasping again, but this

time in pain. He staggered a little on his injured leg, shaking off Kett's hand when he tried to help him.

"Never! I swear to the Almighty, and I'll suffer an eternity in Hell if I'm lying. I never touched her."

He snorted a sob, smearing more blood from his mouth over his cheeks.

"I *love* her."

There was every chance he was lying, but Kett had been in the job long enough to bet that he wasn't.

"What did you do after you left Helen, Roger?"

"Went home," he said. "Rode, and spoke to my daughter on the way. Lou can tell you. She's in New Zealand. I call her after work sometimes."

"Can anyone verify that you got home? Anyone else in the house?"

"No," he said. "But I've got one of them cameras, the Ring ones. You'll see me get back. I didn't do this. I swear to God."

Kett nodded.

"All the same, we're going to need you to answer some questions," he said. "That okay?"

Roger nodded.

"Anything you need," he said. "Anything to catch the bastard who did this to her."

Kett looked at Porter.

"Make sure somebody gets him to the hospital, Pete."

"You want me to go with?"

"No, I need you and Duke here. Keep speaking to the locals, somebody must have seen something."

"I'm not under arrest, am I?" said Roger.

"No," said Kett. "And you won't be, as long as you do exactly what they say."

He left them to it, meeting Savage as she walked back along the street. She blew out a sigh.

"It's her, isn't it?" she asked.

"Looks like it," said Kett. He remembered the spot of blood on his trainer, and he tried to scrub it off with his other shoe. "We've got a name, that's the main thing. You've found her address? Roger said she lives in the flats on the other side of the park."

Savage nodded.

"She does. You think he did it?"

"I have no idea, Kate. My gut's saying no. What about you?"

She chewed on it for a moment.

"He's not giving off bad spirit vibes, sir. But it's not always easy to tell."

"What is it with you and bad spirits today?"

Savage offered a tight smile.

"Not sure you'd believe me if I told you. But my gut's not feeling it either."

They both looked up the road, seeing Roger staring back at them. In the light of the sun, the blood on his face looked too bright to be real.

"I hope you catch him," he slurred, his choked voice carrying through the warm air. "I hope you fucking kill him. That's how it should work, isn't it? A death for a death."

He fixed Kett with a glare.

"An eye for an eye."

The man turned away, lifting his head to the sky, putting his hands over his face again.

"You know something, Kate?" said Kett. "My gut might have just changed its mind."

CHAPTER NINE

There was no need to take a car. Kett and Savage walked the long way back to Chapelfield Gardens, crossing further up the main road so they didn't have to use the underpass again.

The park was busier than ever, the children's play area full to bursting, and a bunch of what might have been university students kicking a ball about on the largest section of grass. Nobody seemed bothered at all by the huge swathe of the gardens that had been cordoned off, or the dozen or so uniformed police who guarded it.

They were halfway to the gate on the other side when Kett's phone rang. Clare's name was on the screen, and the only thing he wanted to do with it was hurl it into a bin.

"Sir," he said when he answered. "How are Norman's balls?"

"Swollen like you wouldn't believe," said Clare.

"Oh, God. I didn't actually want an answer."

"Then why did you ask? We've got a name, Helen Coulter, am I right?"

"Yes, sir. She's..."

"Sixty-six," said Savage when Kett glanced at her.

"Sixty-six years old, works..."

He looked at Savage again, and she took the phone from him, putting it on speaker.

"Works at the hospital, sir, as a nurse. Part-time, but volunteers too. She's never been on our radar. Walked into the underpass at seventeen minutes past nine, as far as we can tell. Possibly with a man called Roger Sexton."

"Sex tape?"

"Ton, sir. Sexton. He's a little dodgy. We're bringing him in, after he's got the all clear from the hospital. His face got in a fight with the floor."

"Which one of you numbskulls did that?"

"Kett, sir," she said, with a guilty look in his direction.

"I didn't touch him!" Kett protested.

"We're heading to Helen's flat now," Savage went on.

"That's what I was calling about," Clare said. "There's somebody waiting for you there, a DS."

"Who?" said Kett, taking the phone back and switching off the speaker mode.

"I can't remember her name," said Clare. "Cromarty, something like that. She works over in Lincolnshire. Heard about the death this morning and offered to help. She's got some experience with this sort of thing."

"Fair enough," said Kett. "She's here already? That was quick."

"She was supporting the Boston team at the dodgeball," said Clare. "Drove right over. Just try and behave, will you? It's bad enough that you Kett everything up in front of our own constabulary, but I'd rather you just did the job the way you're supposed to do it when we've got company."

"I am doing the job the way I'm supposed to do it, sir," he said, a little indignantly.

"Tell that to Roger Sex Tape and his broken face!"

"I didn't touch him!" Kett said again, but Clare had hung up.

He grumbled his way across the rest of the park, ignoring Savage's questions. Sure enough, when he walked through the gate on the far side, he saw a woman leaning on the bonnet of a Peugeot. Her trouser suit was exactly the same shade of metallic grey as the car, and she wore a bright yellow pocket square in her jacket. She was somewhere in her early thirties, he guessed, although with her short hair and big smile, it was hard to tell.

"DCI Kett," she called out as she pushed herself off the car. "I don't need any introductions, sir, that's for sure."

"DS... Cromarty?" he tried, offering a hand when she was close enough. He was surprised to find she was an inch or so taller than him.

"Not a hugger, then?" she said, giving him a couple of hefty pumps. "It's Cafferty, not Cromarty, as much as I do look like a picturesque Scottish fishing village."

She turned to Savage.

"You must be DC Savage?"

"It's, uh, DS now," she replied, a little bashfully. "I'm still getting used to it. But yes. Kate."

"Snap!" said Cafferty as she shook her hand. "Congratulations, Sergeant. How long until you're running the place?"

"She already is," said Kett, who, despite everything, was starting to warm to the woman. "Look, I don't know exactly why you're here, but—"

"I'm going to stop you right there, sir," said Cafferty, holding up a hand. "I'm not here to poo in your porridge. I was up the road watching my team get absolutely trounced in the quarterfinals, and a little bird told me there was something better to do with my time. I've got a background in psychology and a weird fetish for serial killers. I can help, and you'll barely notice I'm here."

She turned to Savage and winked.

"You, on the other hand, will notice, because you'll be taking me dancing."

Savage laughed.

"I'm kidding," said Cafferty. "Just do your thing, I'll stay out of your way."

"Thanks, uh..." said Kett, leaving the word hanging long enough for her to get the hint.

"Stephanie," she said. "Steph."

"Stephanie Cafferty," said Kett. "That's a mouthful."

"It's worse when you know my middle name is Melanie," she said, laughing. "Thanks for the welcome."

"You're from Boston?" asked Savage.

"The cabbage one, not the *Cheers* one," said Cafferty. "Like I said, my background's in psychology, did my degree at Oxford and a stint as a psychotherapist before I joined the Service. Nothing better than being locked inside the head of a psychopath."

"I can think of a few things," said Kett.

Cafferty clapped her hands together loud enough to startle the pigeons from the trees.

"So, who wants to fill me in?"

"I will," said Savage. "I'm interested in psychology too. You've heard about the body? The eyes?"

"Can we walk and talk?" said Kett, ushering them forward like a couple of children.

"I have," said Cafferty. "Lead balls?"

"Tin," said Savage. "Inserted in the sockets. Her real eyes were removed."

"How?" said Cafferty, a little too gleefully for Kett's liking.

"We don't know yet," Savage went on. "But it happened quick. Helen, we think that's her name, was killed with force. The killer needed her dead so he could..."

"Operate," said Cafferty, when she saw Savage struggling for the right word.

"Yes, operate on her. It's a busy park, and a busy road. He'd have needed to work quickly. He knocked her out, or knocked her senseless, anyway, then crushed her throat."

"Efficient," said Cafferty. "Minimal blood loss, guaranteed death. Do you know how long it took him to finish the job?"

"You're both saying 'he' a lot for two people who still don't know anything about the killer," said Kett.

Cafferty and Savage turned around to give him identical looks of disdain.

"I'm just saying, it's better not to assume."

"Pronouns aside," said Cafferty, "how long?"

"We don't know," said Savage. "Emily Franklin's our pathologist; she's working on it."

"I met her a minute ago. Great style."

"The best," said Savage. "You should see her car."

They were coming up to the communal door that led into the flats that flanked the enormous shopping centre, and Kett stepped into the shade. He pressed every single button on the panel, rubbing his eyes while he waited for an answer. It didn't take long, the door buzzing like a trapped wasp. Cafferty grabbed it before he could, gesturing for him to go first.

"Age before beauty, right?" he said.

"Well I wasn't going to be the one to say it, sir," said the young woman.

He walked in, but stopped inside the door, looking back past Savage and Cafferty. The park was right there, basking in sunlight.

"She was so close," he said. "She was almost back."

Savage followed his line of sight.

"How many times have we seen it, sir? She was just walking home."

"She was just walking home," echoed Cafferty.

They stood in silence for a little while, then Kett set off again, entering the cool foyer of the building. These flats were a lot newer than the ones he and Porter had visited earlier, but they weren't as welcoming—even without the patrolling gangs. The floor was grey, the walls painted white, not a scrap of decoration. The place stank of cleaning products, and there wasn't a noise from anywhere in the building.

"First floor," said Savage.

A lift waited for them, but Kett found the stairwell instead. He clattered up as fast as his aching joints would let him, trying to tune out the conversation happening behind him.

"The eyes are what make this interesting," said Cafferty. "You've heard about Charles Albright, haven't you?"

"The Eyeball Killer," said Savage. "Of course. He murdered three women, didn't he, back in the Nineties?"

"Four, as far as they know. Probably more. But he only removed the eyes from three."

"He was a doctor," said Savage.

Kett opened the door, walking into another windowless corridor.

"Pre-med," said Cafferty. "Never completed his training. How clean were the cuts on your victim? Did it look like a surgical job, or an amateur?"

"I didn't actually see," said Savage. "Her face was covered with a handkerchief. A white one."

"It was messy," said Kett. "A lot of blood, and some damage to the sockets."

"An amateur, then. There are plenty more killers without medical training who liked to take the eyes of their victims. Ramirez was one, the Night Stalker. Richard Chase. Uh..."

"Chikatilo," said Savage.

"Oh, boy, how could I forget about him?" Cafferty actually shuddered. "Actually, he's a good example, because he only took out the eyes of his victims because he thought they contained a snapshot of the last thing they saw. He was worried they could use it to catch him."

"Right," said Savage. "He stopped doing it when he found out that wasn't true. Maybe our killer is worried about being found? Maybe the tin balls are meant to blind them in a more... I don't know."

"Permanent way," finished Cafferty. "In this life, and the next. Worth thinking about."

Kett stopped outside a door, a fist to his mouth as he belched acid.

"You alright, sir?" asked Savage.

"Little queasy," he said. "Probably just the heat. This is the one?"

"Yep," said Savage.

Kett tried the handle, but it was locked. He knocked anyway, in case they were wrong.

"Shall I get an enforcer, sir?" asked Savage.

"Actually, I've got a pry bar in the car," said Cafferty, snapping her fingers. "I should have thought. Shall I get it?"

"Sure," said Kett.

She bolted like a startled giraffe, the sound of her galloping down the stairs echoing back along the corridor.

"I like her," said Savage.

"Then she's all yours," Kett replied.

He walked to the next flat along, pounding on the door. Before anyone could answer, he moved to the one after that and knocked there too. He stood between them until he heard the key turn in the flat next to Helen's. The door opened to reveal a teenage girl, not much older than Alice. She was wearing her pyjamas, her ears covered with a set of giant headphones.

"You knock?" she said, giving him the same insolent stare that his own oldest daughter often did.

"I did," said Kett, walking up to her. "You on your own?"

The girl pulled a face.

"Why do you need to know that? Just give it to me and go away."

"Give what to you?" said Kett.

She performed an award-winning eye roll.

"Whatever you're delivering, obviously."

"Oh, right," he said, reaching into the pocket of his shorts and pulling out his warrant card. He opened it up. "I'm delivering this. Police."

It took her a moment or two of squinting at his photograph before it hit home.

"Oh, shit," she said. "The *actual* police?"

Kett nodded, and the girl leaned into the flat.

"Mum, you'd better get this."

The girl gave Kett another scathing look before disappearing. She was replaced by a woman who didn't look an awful lot older, mainly because she was wearing an identical set of pyjamas. She pulled them protectively around her neck when she saw Kett standing there.

"Police," said Kett, offering her his warrant card.

"You sure about that?" she replied, looking at his shorts and his T-shirt. "What's wrong with your knees?"

"Nothing," he said, glancing down. "They're just... knees. Does a woman called Helen Coulter live next door to you?"

The woman nodded, peering out of the door to where Savage was standing. In her black tracksuit and her hoodie, she looked more like she was about to rob the place than save it.

"Hi," said Savage. "Sorry to bother you."

"No bother," said the woman. "Miss Coulter? Yeah, she lives next door. Why? She okay?"

"You don't happen to have a key to her place, do you?"

"We used to," she said. "Until Frankie decided to invite a few friends over while Hel was at work. It's a whole thing. Why?"

"We just need to take a look," said Kett. "You know her well?"

"Well as anyone knows their neighbours these days," said the woman. "She's nice. Quiet. Doesn't complain about our music or the screaming matches. Didn't even make a lot of fuss about the whole party in her flat thing."

She shrugged, not sure what else to say.

"When was the last time you saw her?"

"Yesterday morning, maybe? I think?"

"You didn't hear her get home from work last night?"

The woman shook her head.

"Is she okay?" she asked again.

He was saved from having to answer when Cafferty reappeared, strolling down the corridor with a crowbar over her shoulder. She offered the woman a friendly wave, then proceeded to jam the tool into the door of Helen's flat.

"What are you doing?" the woman said.

"Please don't worry," Kett replied.

There was a crunch as Cafferty wrenched the door open with almost superhuman strength, splinters of wood flying into the corridor.

"This is all... perfectly normal," Kett told the shocked neighbour. "Thanks for your help."

Cafferty stood to the side, the heavy pry bar back over her shoulder.

"You've done that before," said Kett.

"Few times," she said. "They don't call me Crowbar Cafferty for nothing."

Kett entered the flat, finding himself in a short, dark corridor. The air was perfectly still, no hint of life, but he called out anyway.

"Helen? If you're here, can you let us know? It's the police."

He used an elbow to switch on the lights as he went, finding a small kitchen cluttered with equipment, a single plate and bowl drying in the rack by the sink. There were a few illustrated pictures hanging against the floral wallpaper, all showing kittens, and most of them with motivational quotes.

A stack of opened mail sat on the table, everything in Helen's name. A glance at the bills made it clear she was a long way from being wealthy, but not in any trouble. She was halfway through writing a letter to somebody called Maureen, her handwriting neat but not perfect. Kett scanned it, seeing talk of work and of the weather, but little else.

Savage was in the living room by the time he got there,

but there wasn't a lot for her to do. The small space had been made as cosy as possible, crocheted blankets over the sofa and the chair, thick rugs on the floor and woollen tapestries hanging from the walls. A small forest of spider plants had congregated on the coffee table by the window. A pile of books sat by the armchair, topped with a ball of wool and some knitting needles.

"Cosy," he said.

"You're not kidding," said Savage. "It's like my gran's house, right down to those."

She nodded to a glass cabinet in the corner, where a bunch of porcelain figurines were on display, almost all of them cats. There were some framed photographs too, one showing Helen with another woman, who was so similar that she had to be a sister. Helen was a good decade younger here, her hair jet black. The next photo showed her at work, in a ward full of kids, all of them wrapped in tinsel and snapped mid-laugh. Behind that was a child's illustration of a happy face, painted in every colour of the rainbow. Two were photographs of a distinctive ginger cat, one taken when he was a kitten, the other when he was an old boy with a torn ear and a snaggletooth.

"She doesn't seem like the kind of person who would be targeted," said Savage. "You think she was just unlucky? A random attack?"

"Wrong place, wrong time," said Kett. "Maybe."

He ducked down to see the last photo, which was tucked away on the lowest shelf and faded with age. The Helen who sat there was in her twenties, a giant smile on her face. There was a little dog on her lap, some kind of terrier, and she had her arms wrapped around it. Somebody was sitting next to her, Kett could see a hand on her knee, but the photo had been folded to exclude them.

"You want these, sir?" asked Savage, and he turned to see her holding out a pair of gloves.

"Thanks," he said, cramming his fingers into the holes.

He picked up the frame, unfastening the clasps and gently pushing out the photograph. When he unfolded it, he saw a man on the sofa beside Helen. At least, he assumed it was a man. Somebody had scratched his eyes out. It had been done with some fury, leaving two ragged holes that took up most of his face. Beneath that, covering his entire body, somebody had etched the word CUNT.

"Maybe not so cosy after all," said Kett.

"Ex, probably," said Savage. "We've all got them. Strange coincidence about the eyes, though."

"Not as strange as what's in here," said Cafferty, peeking out of a door.

Kett joined her in the only bedroom, which was as twee as the rest of the flat. The bed was almost hidden beneath a woolly blanket, and the picture that hung over the headboard was an enormous piece of embroidery showing the same ginger cat sitting on a sunny doorstep. Cafferty stood next to a dark wooden dresser that was topped with a jumble sale's worth of stuff, her hands in her pockets. It took Kett a moment to see what she was referring to, amidst the lotions and hairbrushes, the sewing kits and fabric samples and endless balls of wool.

"The hell?" he said, leaning in. "Are those *eyes*?"

Nobody needed to answer his question. It was clear enough. A dozen or so glass eyes sat in a small metal box on the dresser. They were all shapes and sizes, a couple as big as ping-pong balls, some like marbles. Most weren't spherical at all, they were flat—more like large contact lenses than anything—but each one was made with incredible detail. When Kett put his glasses on, he could see the patterns in the irises, dozens of intricate bands and whorls that looked far too real. Most were blue, but there were some green and brown ones, plus a couple that were almost golden.

He looked at Cafferty, then at Savage.

"Who keeps a box full of eyes?" he asked.

"Not a box, sir," said Savage. "A *tin*."

He turned his attention to the container, noticing the same dull sheen he'd seen in Helen's eyes. The sickness was back, his stomach doing a full loop-the-loop at the memory. He stood straight, his fist to his mouth again.

"That's enough," he said. "Let's clear out, let forensics do their thing. Can you wait here for them, Kate?"

He followed Cafferty and Savage out of the flat, then stopped in the doorway for a moment, looking back. He pictured the eyes that were missing from the dead woman, and the ones they'd found here.

"What are you thinking, sir?" said Savage.

"I'm thinking maybe this isn't so random after all."

CHAPTER TEN

He spent the next hour or so knocking on doors, with little to show for it other than bruised knuckles. Most of the people in the building were aware of Helen's existence, but few had ever had any meaningful conversations with her, and none had any inkling of why she might have been attacked. The consensus was that the woman was perfectly lovely, but practically invisible.

Sometime after one, just as Kett was showing two members of Cara Hay's forensic team into the flat, he got another call from Clare.

"Body. Morgue. You. There. Now."

Kett gathered Savage and Cafferty, the three of them riding out of the city in Kett's car. The two women sat in the back, swapping serial killer theories for the entire twenty-minute journey to HQ. As much as he tried not to listen, his stomach was churning by the time they walked up to the front door of the morgue.

And he knew it was only going to get worse from there.

Helen Coulter's body lay on the steel slab in Franklin's lab, the unforgiving lights making it look like some kind of

Halloween decoration. Her eyes were open, the dull metal sheen making her appear more alive than she should have.

She looked so human, thought Kett, and yet so inhuman, the way the dead always did. It seemed impossible to think that the vastness of this woman's life lay behind her, countless days severed like a cut rope. All of that joy, all of that sadness, all of that *everything*, only to end up here.

The gravity of the situation was only slightly dampened by the fact that Franklin had her radio on, and the song that was coming out of it sounded suspiciously like it was being sung by the Muppets.

The young pathologist welcomed them in with a wave and a smile, like they'd turned up at a children's party, not an autopsy.

"Gather round," she said, gesturing to Savage and then Cafferty. "Kate, you come this side. Stephanie Melanie Cafferty, you get over here. My two favourites."

"Hey," said Kett, who was happy enough to remain at the foot of the table. "I thought I was your favourite."

"You are... my favourite DCI, whose first name is Robert."

She cocked her head, thinking.

"And whose last name is Kett."

"Thanks," he muttered, trying not to listen to the insane music that was coming out of the speakers. "Emily, are you listening to the Muppets?"

"Yes," she said, with no further explanation.

"You've got something for us?"

"Not exactly," said Franklin. "I just thought you'd like to be here for the extraction."

Franklin cupped her hand to Helen's face, her thumb hovering over one of the metal eyes.

"Oh," said Kett.

"Oh indeed," said Franklin. "You're welcome to sit it out, if you don't fancy it?"

He would have liked nothing better, but he owed the victim more than that. He nodded for her to continue, and she did a little hop of happiness.

"Sorry," she said. "It's not often you get to investigate something this exciting."

"That's exactly what I was saying," said Cafferty, both hands gripping the metal table. "This is one for the textbooks. It's an honour just to be here."

Franklin clicked on a video camera that was mounted on a tripod beside the corpse, then she picked up a set of tongs from a tray of surgical equipment.

"I'm going to try to extract the replacement eyeball," she said. "But it might need something stronger to get it past the orbital sockets, especially if they were hammered in."

Kett belched into his hand again.

"I've cleaned up the wounds and had a closer look at the injuries to our victim's eyes. There is damage to the entire structure. See here, where the upper eyelid has been partially torn away, and this tear along the lower lid, severe enough to expose the orbicularis oculi. There is damage to the tarsal plate on both sides, and here, on the left, the tear duct has been crushed."

Franklin looked up.

"Are you okay, Robbie?" she asked. "You look a little green."

"The heat," he croaked.

"It's freezing in here, sir," said Savage.

"The cold, then," he snapped. "Get on with it, Emily."

"All this is reinforcing what we already know—that the enucleation was done with a lot of force and not much care."

"Enucleation?" said Kett. "It's got a name?"

"It does indeed," said Franklin. "It sounds a little better than 'gouged out'. But in this case, I think that's what happened. The killer drove something sharp directly into each socket, then scooped the eyes out."

Kett was sweating, his face prickling. There were tears in his own eyes, and he had no idea why. He wiped them away, earning a kindly look from Savage.

"I'm not crying," he said. "My eyes are just..."

"Crying," said Franklin when he didn't finish. "Mine too. It's a sympathetic response to assumed danger, we all do it."

"I don't," said Cafferty, who seemed as happy as ever.

Franklin returned to the corpse, pointing the handle of her scalpel at a pattern of marks around the edge of the eyes.

"See these, notice the curve in them?"

Kett would have had to put on his glasses to see what she was getting at, and he didn't want to.

"Remind you of anything?" Franklin asked.

"A spoon," said Savage, a fraction of a second before Cafferty blurted out the same thing.

"Dammit," said Cafferty. "You win."

"A spoon?" Kett said weakly.

"I'm guessing a slim dessert spoon," said Franklin. "Almost certainly sharpened, because they're not exactly designed to cut through flesh. Stainless steel, most likely, for strength. The killer must have used quite a bit of force to get the spoon in, and he wasn't exactly precise."

She held the tongs in her fist, driving them down towards Helen's face like they were a knife, but not making contact.

"He hit the wrong target three, maybe four times. There's even a mark on her cheek, there, where he was way out. They're deep cuts, he wasn't holding back, he just wasn't a good aim. But eventually, he got it right. A solid driving motion with the spoon, sliding into the socket, parting the eyeball from the fatty tissue and possibly the muscle, then... Pop! Out it comes."

The Muppets were singing a Christmas song now, which only made Kett's nausea worse.

"So..." he said, swallowing bile. "Uh..."

"I can get you a chair, sir?" said Savage.

He shook his head, whirling his hand in the air in the hope of speeding things up.

"Once the eye is out, the killer would have had to detach it from the muscles at the back, and the nerve. A sharp knife would do the trick. Any loose fibres and flappy bits can be poked back inside before the prosthetics are inserted."

Kett covered another belch with his fist, this time leaving it there.

"She was definitely dead when this happened, wasn't she?" asked Savage.

"Oh, yes," said Franklin. "Dead or unconscious. Almost certainly dead. She wouldn't have felt it."

It was a small mercy.

"Right," said Franklin. "Are you happy for me to proceed?"

"Happy isn't the word I'd use," said Kett, still speaking through his hand.

He had to look away while Franklin worked, but he could still hear the clink of the tongs as they connected with the eye, the squelch as the pathologist tried to yank it free, the way Helen's head thumped on the table. He never imagined he'd think it, but he wished the music was louder.

"Can you just hold her there, Kate?" said Franklin. "She's a wriggly one."

More clinks, more wet noises, a series of grunts that rose over the chorus of a Muppet's *Christmas Carol*.

Then, finally, the sound of something coming free.

"Got you!" said Franklin. "Steph, grab that dish for me."

Kett turned back just as Franklin dropped her prize into a steel kidney dish. She placed it on the table next to Helen's head, the three women leaning in together to get a better look. With a heavy sigh, Kett shuffled over to join them, trying not to look at the gaping hole that had been left in the victim's face.

He put on his glasses and turned his attention instead to the object that lay inside the dish.

It was a lump of metal the size of a jawbreaker, and it was nowhere near as spherical as Kett had assumed it would be. It was more of an oval in shape, covered in lumps and dents and looking almost organic—an illusion that wasn't helped by the scraps of flesh and smears of blood that clung to it. The metal had a soft, silky sheen that was accentuated by the bright lights, silver in colour, but too dull to actually be silver. There were scuffs and scratches over the surface, as well as an indentation that almost looked like a finger.

Franklin picked it up in a gloved hand, turning it back and forth.

"It's definitely tin," she said. "Although there's every chance it could be an alloy. The dullness of it suggests lead, maybe. Or a more modern pewter. Either way, it's fairly light, and quite soft. It looks as if it has been hammered into shape, but this mark here."

She lifted the ball to show the finger-shaped dent.

"Somebody has held it, and I don't think you'd get a

mark like that unless the tin had been melted, and was cooling."

"You think the killer made this himself?" said Savage. "Melted it down into a ball?"

"Makes sense," said Cafferty. "He needed something that would fit, and it's not like you can go into an antique shop and say, 'Hey, I need a tin ball that will fit in an eye socket.'"

"How easy is it to melt tin?" asked Kett, thinking of the foundries he'd seen on TV, the furnaces needed to shape metal. "Surely you need specialist equipment to do that."

"Not really, sir," said Savage. "Tin's got a very low melting point. 231.9 degrees."

"There is no way you knew that, Kate," he said.

"I looked it up on the way over. Had a hunch. But that's cool enough for somebody to be able to melt it at home."

"At home?" said Kett.

"All he'd need is a gas hob," said Cafferty, nodding sagely. "A camping stove, maybe, if they want to work outside. A stainless steel pan would be enough, maybe a crucible, and a mould, obviously."

"Although it's not exactly a perfect sphere," said Savage. "He might have tried to roll it out, hence the fingerprint."

"That's my guess," said Franklin. "He probably poured it into an egg cup or something to get the rough shape, then rolled it into a ball by hand. With some seriously thick gloves, obviously. It's definitely homemade, see the marks on it?"

She held it out for everyone to look at.

"Tin scuffs very easily. Some of these look like they're the result of the melting process, but others seem to have been scratched in afterwards. And these dents are probably from a hammer, where he tapped it into place."

"Would they have been hot when he did that?" Kett asked.

"No," said all three women at once. Franklin did the explaining.

"There's no sign of burnt skin in or around the sockets, and if he'd inserted molten tin into the victim's face, it would have been impossible to remove it. They'd have fused. Tin cools pretty quickly once it's been removed from the heating process. He'd have needed to bring his stove and his equipment with him to do that, which would have taken a lot of time."

"So he made them up in advance," said Kett. "Two tin balls the exact size of a person's eyes."

"Smaller," said Franklin. "He wouldn't have been able to get them in if they were identical in size. Eyes are bigger than you think."

"So making sure they fit was more important than making sure they were realistic," said Savage.

"It's not the objects themselves that hold power," added Cafferty, "it's the positioning of them that's important."

"I like her," said Franklin, looking at Kett.

"You can have her," he replied, a little more unkindly than he'd intended. The music was unbearable, the smell of the woman's gaping eye socket making him feel like he could scream himself into lunacy.

"Anything else?" he asked. "Because if not, I'm going to—"

"Hang on," said Franklin, looking at the ball. "Is that..."

She snatched up a magnifying glass from her equipment tray.

"There's something written on it," she said, twisting the object in her fingers. "Letters. An L, maybe, and a B. That looks like an O."

She held it up, but even with his glasses on, Kett couldn't see what she was talking about. The letters must have been tiny. Franklin dropped the ball gently back into the dish, spinning it until she found the right place. She pulled down one of the flexible lights so that it was almost touching it. Savage leaned in, and so did Cafferty, all traces of a smile gone from her face.

"I see them," said Savage. "LBO. Or an I, maybe?"

Kett was still struggling, and Savage took pity on him. She used her phone to photograph the ball, then passed it over. Kett zoomed in on the image, finally seeing what they were all talking about. The letters were barely there, partially erased as if somebody had tried to sand them away.

"It says OBI from this angle," he said. "That's what it looks like to me, anyway. You think it's a signature?"

"Initials, maybe," said Savage.

Kett nodded.

"Good spot, Emily. Can you take some photos for us?"

"I'll scan it," she said. "See if I can pick up anything that we can't see with the naked eye. I'm going to drill it, too, at some point, in case there's anything in the middle."

"Thanks," he said, turning away from the ball, and the dish, and the dead woman, content to stare at the wall. "You okay on your own now?"

"I am," said Franklin. "But you're welcome to stay. I'm about to take the second ball out."

Kett shook his head, practically running from the room.

CHAPTER ELEVEN

"You've got to admit it, Aaron," said Porter. "You've got literally no spatial awareness."

Porter and Duke walked between two of the blocks of flats that made up the estate, clinging to the meagre shade like mountain goats on a ledge. They'd knocked on as many doors as they could, but nobody had been very friendly—apart from one woman who seemed to have mistaken them for some kind of cabaret act, and wouldn't let them leave—and fewer still had told them anything useful. It seemed that people here didn't make a habit of looking out of their windows after dark, which wasn't exactly news.

He was nursing a sore elbow from where Duke had knocked him over chasing the cyclist, on top of the sore leg where he'd knocked him over during the tournament, although he would never have admitted it to the constable.

"I'm *aware* that you're in my *space*, sir," said Duke, stroking his beard. "My personal space."

"Clever," said Porter. "I can see why it took you thirty seconds to think of it."

"Wasn't thirty seconds," he said. "And I only ran into you because you're so bloody slow. If you didn't run like a two-legged kangaroo, I wouldn't have crashed into you."

"Kangaroos have two legs, you dunce," said Porter. "And they don't run, they jump."

"Exactly, they don't run. Like you."

They emerged from the shade into the full force of the sun, the temperature doubling in an instant. Porter loosened his tie, tugging at his collar. He could feel the sweat running down the back of his neck, and was intensely annoyed that Duke didn't seem flustered at all, even in his full kit.

"You do realise, Aaron, that I could write you up for insubordination," he said, holding his hand over his eyes to stop himself from being blinded. "I can talk to you like that, but you're not allowed to do it back. I'm your senior officer."

"Senior in weight," mumbled Duke.

Porter stopped, pointing a finger at the tall PC. Duke lifted his hands in surrender.

"Sorry, sir," he said. "You're right. I just get irritable in the heat."

Porter left his finger there for a few more seconds, then dropped his hand.

"It is really bloody hot," he said.

They rounded a corner, seeing a small courtyard ahead. Somebody had hung their sheets out to dry on a communal washing line, but they'd been tugged off and strewn over the ground. Duke wandered over, collecting the nearest one and giving it a shake. Porter scanned the buildings, trying to remember which ones they'd already been inside. The place was a labyrinth, the tall walls blocking out the rest of the city and making him feel like he'd left the real world altogether.

"Give me a hand, sir, if you like?" said Duke, who was pegging the sheets back onto the line.

"Nah," said Porter. "You're doing a grand job, mate."

Close by, somebody shouted something, their voice echoing off the walls. It was followed by laughter, the kind of loud, abrasive, male laughter that instantly got Porter's hackles up. The voices grew louder, and a group of young men spilled through an archway on the left side of the courtyard. They were dressed like they were auditioning for a London gangster movie, grey Montirex trackies, bumbags strapped diagonally over their torsos like ammunition belts. Three of the four lads had their hoods up, scarves wrapped around their mouths and noses. The last didn't. They were so busy laughing like hyenas that they didn't spot Porter until they'd almost reached him.

"Oioi," said one of the lads with a scarf around his mouth. "New boy."

The lads formed a tight line, fidgeting like distressed animals, their hands tucked beneath the front of their jumpers as if they were reaching for a gun. They glared at Porter like they'd happily shank him just for being in their way. The one without the scarf was particularly intense, his blue eyes boring into Porter's skull.

"Afternoon, lads," said Porter. "You mind keeping your hands where I can see them? We all know you've got nothing down there but your todgers, tucked into your little Spider-Man pants."

"The fuck?" said another of the lads, looking to his friends. "This Mickey Mouse, man."

Porter glanced back to see that Duke was still hanging the washing on the line, invisible behind the sheet.

"You wet?" said one of the young men. "Wet gets got around here, man. You get me?"

"Not really," said Porter, looking back.

"Man's not trouble, man's a narc," said the kid with the bright eyes. "Am I right?"

"I have no idea," said Porter. "You lot the ones who've been causing so much trouble around here?"

The lads laughed, all except for the kid without a scarf. He kept his fierce eyes on Porter, barely blinking. The rest of the gang were kids, Porter knew he could floor any of them if it came to it, and that was only if they didn't run away crying first. But there was something about this last lad that made him wary.

"Any of you out last night?" Porter said, trying his luck. "Near the park, around nine?"

"You wish," said one. "Batty."

"You happen to see a woman using the underpass. Older, in her sixties, black hair, dyed. She might have been with a man on a bike."

One of the lads started to reply, but the kid with the intense eyes touched his arm. The lad instantly fell quiet, stepping back, his hand still tucked into his waistband.

"Why you asking?" said the intense kid.

"Because somebody killed her," Porter told him. "You lot know anything about that?"

The young man still didn't break eye contact—not until there was a clatter from the middle of the courtyard, that was. They all stared past Porter to see Duke standing there in full uniform, one hand on his Taser.

"Boo," said the PC.

It was like he'd thrown a live grenade into the middle of the pack. The boys turned and bolted with a chorus of shouts, their trainers skidding as they headed for the archway.

"Fuck's sake, Duke!" said Porter. "I was talking to them!"

He went after them, but only made it a couple of steps before he tripped on a loose flagstone and almost fell. Duke ran past him, chuffing like a train, his arms and legs moving like pistons.

"Twat," grumbled Porter, as if it was the PC's fault.

He picked up speed, chasing Duke through the archway into a narrow alley. Duke was halfway down it, and Porter couldn't see anything past his annoyingly broad shoulders. He plodded on, already knackered, watching Duke spin left at the end of the passage.

"Careful," he yelled after him.

He reached the road a few seconds later, turning the corner so fast that he thumped into the back of Duke. He bounced off, skittering until he'd found his feet.

"Jesus Christ," he said, rubbing his face where it had connected with the PC. The impact had winded him, snipping the fuse of his patience down to the last inch. "What are you doing?"

He walked around Duke to see an empty street ahead, no sign of the lads anywhere.

"Great work, mate," said Porter. "You lost them."

"I don't know where they went," said Duke.

"Yeah, that's what 'lost them' means. They were right in front of you!"

Porter rubbed his nose, checking for blood.

"At least you've finally found your calling," he said. "You'd make a great wall."

The PC didn't reply, setting off again. They'd left the bigger blocks behind them, the street lined with terraced houses on one side and newer flats on the other. Up ahead,

Porter knew, was a parade of shops, and past that another little park. He could hear the sound of kids playing, but there weren't many people around, and nobody close enough to have seen where the lads had run off to.

"Bloody hell," he said, fed up with the heat and the job. "They were about to tell me something."

"They really weren't, sir," said Duke.

They passed a wire fence that had been erected around an old pub, the building drowning in vegetation, its windows boarded. Porter couldn't remember the name of it, but he knew it had shut last year after the owners had bolted, leaving unpaid bills and a big debt to the taxman. He was surprised nobody had taken it over, being so close to the city centre.

Duke kept moving, but Porter stopped, holding his breath to try to hear anything.

"Kids like that don't ever talk," Duke went on, oblivious. "Snitches get stitches and all that."

"Would you shut up for a second?" said Porter.

He stared into the pub's overgrown gardens, seeing the remains of a play area—a giant red elephant with bulging eyes, its trunk flattened into a slide. The rusted swings were now a support system for an enormous creeper that looked like it belonged inside a fairy tale. There would be no golden harp at the top of that thing, though. Just tetanus.

He thought, for a second, he heard the ring of metal against metal, then Duke started yabbering again.

"Maybe I could have a chat with them. They might recognise me from Britain's Bravest Copper. People still talk about it, you know."

"Aaron," said Porter, turning to see that the PC had come to a standstill. "Shut up."

There was the noise again: a hollow clank from the pub garden.

"You think they went in there?" said Duke, his hand on his Taser.

"One way of finding out," said Porter. He walked along the front of the site, looking for a way in, but the fence was intact. "I'll give you a foot up."

"You'll never be able to get me over there, sir," said Duke. "I'll give you a lift."

"You're not strong enough. I'll do it."

Duke gave him a look, and Porter flapped his hands.

"Fine," he said. "I'll go. But if you strain those puny arms, then don't blame me."

Duke laced his fingers together, his distinctly *not* puny arms bulging beneath the sleeves of his polo shirt. Porter grabbed a handful of fence, and stepped into the cradle.

"Just a little," he said. "You don't—"

Duke straightened, lifting his arms with a bear-like grunt. Porter rose like he was strapped to a rocket, a scream escaping his lips with the unexpected terror of it. He had to let go of the fence or risk losing his fingers, and with nothing else to grab on to, he flopped over the top of it like a tossed caber. There was time for another scream on the way down before he landed hard on his back in an overgrown flowerbed.

"Shit!" said Duke, his face to the wire fence. "Sir?"

Porter sat up, trying not to let the pain show even though he felt it from the base of his skull to his hips.

"I'm fine," he said, little more than a whisper.

"Don't know my own strength," said Duke, staring at his hands as though they'd betrayed him.

"Wasn't you," said Porter, standing up. He braced his

hands on his knees until he felt like he could straighten his back. "I jumped. Like a ninja. You barely did anything."

Duke was still too shocked to argue with him.

"I'll go take a look," said Porter, limping off.

"I'll find another way in, sir," said Duke.

The ground was treacherous, the thick weeds hiding divots and rubble and even an uncapped manhole, which might have been the end of him. He made his way towards the play area first, giving the sad little elephant a reassuring pat as he passed it. There was plenty of litter here, empty bottles smashed or scattered around a merry-go-round, cigarette butts and used joints everywhere. There were syringes, too, planted in the dirt with their needles pointing to the sky.

"Fuckers," growled Porter, giving them a wide berth.

As he walked past the swings, a couple of pigeons took flight, and he was grateful that Duke wasn't there to see his reaction. They settled on the top of the slide with the same metallic thunk he'd heard before, their claws scratching. He gave them the finger as he passed, heading for the main building. It stood naked, all the signage taken down, the paint peeling off the bricks. The door was open. Porter was surprised to find Duke standing there.

"Found a gate," said the PC, slinging his thumb over his shoulder.

Porter gave him the finger too, although he was too busy staring into the pub to notice.

"Bit dark in there," he said.

Porter pulled out his torch and clicked it on, pushing past Duke into a corridor that stank of old piss.

"Oi," he called out, his voice barely making it through the door. "If any of you little twerps have run in here, then now's the time to tell me, because I'm going to call somebody over in a minute to nail this door shut."

He cocked his head to listen for a reply.

"I think I came here for a drink once," said Duke. "It was called the Walpole or something."

Porter hung his head, taking a deep breath and counting to five.

"Last chance," he called out.

Any reply there might have been was drowned out by the PC once again.

"It was a date. Before me and Kate got together, obviously. She was a little odd."

"She must have been, if she went on a date with you."

Porter walked a little deeper into the pub, the temperature dropping and the smell getting worse. There was a door to the right and one to the left, both leading into toilets that were crammed full of more rubbish.

"Watch your feet," he told Duke when he heard the PC lumber in. "Bastards have left needles everywhere."

He entered the bar, which was relatively intact. Only the stools seemed to have suffered any damage, smashed into pieces. He aimed the torch at the blackboard on the wall to see that the specials were still written there, and he felt a stab of pity for the poor pub. The booze had all gone, obviously, but at least in here the smell was of stale beer and old age.

"I had that," said Duke, nodding to the board. "The steak pie was delicious. Apple crumble for pudding, too. Extra custard."

"How are you not the size of a house?" asked Porter.

The bar curved around the front of the pub, and he followed it into a corridor where a set of stairs led up into an even deeper darkness.

"Check upstairs, would you, Aaron?" said Porter.

Duke aimed his torch skyward.

"By myself, sir?"

"If you run into those kids, just remind them that you were Britain's Bravest Copper."

Duke creaked his way up the old stairs, the light from his torch gradually fading. Porter heard him call "Police!" a handful of times before he reappeared.

"Nothing up there but squirrels," he said.

There was only one door left to try, and Porter opened it. He never thought he'd be nostalgic for the smell of piss, but when the stench rolled out, he would happily have run to those toilets with his nostrils wide open. He reeled back, making a sound in his throat like he'd tried to swallow a chicken whole.

"Shit a brick," said Duke, pinching his nose. "What is that?"

It was a redundant question, because only one thing smelled like that.

Death.

Porter pushed through the half-open door, clamping one hand to his face as he swept his torch from left to right. The room was a forest of old furniture, with stacks of mouldering chairs and wooden tables and not much else. The walls had a few scraps of old posters clinging to them, and the floor was stencilled to look like a chessboard. Other than that, he couldn't see a thing.

"Probably a squirrel, sir," said Duke, far too close. He was leaning through the door behind him, blocking the way out.

"They're rats, Aaron."

"I know, but they probably fought the squirrels and left them in there, to scare the other squirrels away."

Porter turned to him.

"What?"

Duke shook his head, as if he was confused at Porter's confusion. Porter turned back to the room, taking a few steps just to give himself space. Unfortunately, Duke closed the gap almost immediately. The PC was probably right, though; what they were smelling was most likely an animal that had crawled in here to die. Hopefully, it had found an old keg and happily drunk itself to death.

With Duke breathing down his neck, the idea seemed quite tempting.

"Just back off," he snapped. "Go look over there or something."

Duke did as he was asked, pushing past a stack of chairs hard enough to knock them over. Spores of black mould exploded upwards, hanging in the torchlight, and Porter held his breath.

"Nothing back here," said Duke.

"You sure?" said Porter.

"Just an old tarp or something," said the PC.

"Anything under it?"

Duke shone his torch back, sending a supernova of light into Porter's brain.

"You want me to touch it?"

"Unless you've developed the power of telekinesis, then yes," he said, blinking blotches of fire. He couldn't see a bloody thing.

"Yuck," the PC moaned. Porter heard the rustle of fabric moving.

Then a gasp.

"Oh," Duke said, stumbling backwards into another stack of chairs.

"What?" said Porter, his heart clattering as he made his way over.

"It's not a squirrel, sir."

Porter rounded the chairs, aiming his torch at the floor. He still couldn't see much past the afterburn, but there was no missing what lay there. The body rested on its back, its hands crossed over its chest, its mouth open in an unheard scream.

Only the eyes held any brightness. Twin metal orbs that glowed like quicksilver in the torchlight.

CHAPTER TWELVE

Kett was at home when he got the call, fastening the buttons on his shirt. As awful as it was to have to put a suit on in this weather, he was tired of having to explain his shorts and trainers to everyone he spoke to.

"You're kidding," he said when Porter told him what they'd found inside the pub. "A body? You're sure?"

"Yeah, and get this, sir." Porter's breath rattled the line. "It's got no eyes, same as the last one."

"What?" he said, grabbing a tie from the back of his chair and heading out of the bedroom. "You're sure?"

"I'm sure, sir. Metal balls in the sockets, just like the woman in the park. I didn't get a closer look, thought forensics should do it first. Cara's just arrived."

Kett clattered down the stairs, finding Moira and Evie waiting for him at the bottom. Evie was wearing his boots.

"I'm on my way," he said.

"I'm on my way," Evie imitated in a surprisingly deep voice, stomping around in his boots. "My name is Robert Kett, and I'm a policeman."

"I know, sir," said Porter on the phone.

"That wasn't me," said Kett. "Evie, my boots."

"I wear sensible shoes for my sensible job," said Evie.

"What?" said Porter. "You're breaking up. What about shoes?"

"My name is Robert, and I eat farts for breakfast," said Moira, and the pair of them doubled over with laughter.

"I don't understand, sir," said Porter. "Why are you eating far—"

Kett hung up on him, giving his girls *the look*. Evie stepped out of his boots and Moira picked them up, handing them to him. He tugged them on, tying his laces, then he ruffled their hair the way they hated.

"Don't go," said Evie, smoothing her bob back into place. "Watch Moana with us."

"And eat popcorn," added Moira. "And farts."

"As tempting as that sounds, I can't," he said. "Sorry."

He walked past the living room, seeing Billie lying on the sun-drenched sofa in her blue dress, hearing the dull chatter of the TV. He knew that if he really wanted to, he could kick off his boots again and do exactly what his girls had asked. Forever. The job would be fine without him, and everything he loved was right here.

When he closed the front door behind him, he felt like somebody had taken his spirit in their fist and crushed it.

He had to fight the traffic to get back into the city, and thanks to the ongoing investigation, the inner ringroad was still gridlocked. By the time he pulled up to the old Walpole pub, it was mobbed with police, a troop of forensic technicians filing through the door. He parked the Volvo down the road and got out, trying to find a way through the wire fence.

"Round the back, sir," came a shout from the overgrown bushes. He couldn't see who it was past the foliage, but he thought he recognised Savage's voice. He traipsed around the perimeter of the site, finding an open gate at the back guarded by two constables.

"Afternoon, sir," said one, doffing his hat as Kett passed.

Savage was waiting for him by the door, DS Cafferty towering over her. They both looked like they were close to overheating, Cafferty wiping her brow with her bright yellow handkerchief before folding it into a square and returning it to her pocket.

"This way," said Savage, walking into the open mouth of the building.

Temporary lights had been rigged up, and Kett battled through the blinding glow into a fog of god-awful stench. They seemed to do a full lap of the derelict building before arriving at the crime scene. Cara Hay and Emily Franklin crouched on the floor of a room between towering piles of furniture. When they turned to look at him, the lights made their faces look like masks.

Lying on the ground between them was a body, half covered with a filthy tarpaulin. Kett felt lucky that he couldn't see the corpse's face past Hay's legs. The smell here was worse, catching in his throat like he'd tried to swallow a spoonful of rotting meat. His stomach churned in protest.

"Not another one," he said.

"Yep," said Franklin. "You can come in."

"I'm fine out here," he said. "Another woman?"

"A man," said the young pathologist. "Young adult. Maybe a teenager. This body's been here a while. He definitely died before our park woman."

"How long?"

"Two, three days," said Franklin. "The heat has absolutely battered him, and somebody's been having a nibble."

"Christ," said Kett. "Not the killer?"

"No. Rats, I think. We've seen a few since we got here."

"Nasty things," said Hay, her forehead creased with worry. She looked exhausted.

"Was this guy strangled?" asked Kett.

"Yes," Franklin answered. "But it wasn't so violent. The throat hasn't been crushed."

"The kid fought back," added Hay. "He must have got a couple of good scratches in, because one of his nails has torn free."

Kett put a hand to his mouth as the boy's last moments waltzed through his imagination. He never knew whether it made it better or worse if they'd had a chance to fight back. Sometimes, it was kinder not to know what was happening.

"I'll see if we can get some samples," Hay went on. "If the killer left anything else for us, it's lost in the misery of this place."

"You think he was killed here?" Kett asked.

"It looks like it," said Hay, and Franklin nodded too. "Not much for us to go on, but enough to make me think he died in this room."

She bowed her head, and Kett knew she was thinking of her own teenage sons.

"Of all the places to meet your end," she said. "Here in the dark, in the cold. To lose your..."

She stood up, and the boy's face appeared. Even though Kett had been warned, the sight of him was still a shock. He looked young, maybe seventeen or eighteen, with dark skin and a pillow of black hair. His eyes burned with cold light, staring sightlessly at the ceiling.

"To lose your eyes," Hay finished. "It's unbearable."

"If it makes you feel any better," said Franklin, "and I

know it probably won't, he died before his eyes were removed."

"How do you know?" said Kett.

Franklin stood up as well, arching her back.

"I don't for sure, but there are no scratches on his face, just the injuries to the eye sockets. If somebody's coming for your eyes, you fight tooth and nail to stop them. You're going to be twisting your head every which way. He wasn't tied up, that's for sure, there's no bruising or swelling to suggest he was being held down. The cuts here are fairly precise, and there are only a couple of them. It was a clean job, cleaner than our other victim."

"He had more time," said Savage. "Both victims were unconscious or dead when he started the procedure, but here he could go slow, remove the eyes carefully. In the park, he was rushing, because anyone could have walked past."

Franklin nodded.

"We've got two metal balls in the sockets, just like before," she said. "I'll have to take them back to the lab to be sure, but it looks like tin."

"Right," said Kett. "Does this mean what I think it means?"

Nobody answered, so he did it himself.

"A serial killer."

"Another one," said Savage. "It's getting worse, sir."

"Bad spirits," he said, and she replied with a grim nod. "Any ID?"

"No," said Hay. "He's wearing braces, though. They're expensive ones."

"Spalding's looking into it," said Savage. "She's checking MISPERS too. This is a kid. Two, three days, somebody will be missing him."

Kett stared at the boy's face for a moment longer, ignoring the urge to stop looking. He was a child, and he deserved more than to be dismissed like that. But the metal in his eyes seemed to gleam, it gave him the illusion of a terrible kind of life, as if he might suddenly twist his head and look right back. It was this that made Kett turn away, the sickness still sitting on the back of his tongue. He swallowed hard before speaking.

"What I don't understand is why the killer murdered his first victim here, where he's unlikely to be caught, then attack his second victim in the underpass, where anyone could have seen him. Why not bring Helen back here? It's tried and tested."

"Maybe he couldn't bring her back, sir," said Savage. "Maybe he attempted it, but she wouldn't come. Or maybe he only attacked Helen because he saw her walking home. If this is random, then he might have seized the opportunity last night."

"Typical escalation," said Cafferty. "His first kill was controlled, it showed him he could do it, gave him the confidence to attack again. Killers like this often have inflated egos, they think they're superhuman."

"Or gods," said Savage.

"It means he's more dangerous now than ever. It's shown him he can attack anyone and get away with it."

"He's not going to get away with it," said Kett, but something else had occurred to him. "This might not be his first victim. Helen might not be the second."

"Right, sir," said Savage, nodding. "He could have been building up to this for a while."

Kett swore again.

"Who found him?" he asked after a minute.

"Porter, sir," said Savage. "He's around somewhere."

Kett set off, holding his breath as he returned through the bar and passed the toilets, close to fainting by the time he walked outside. He took in a lungful of relatively fresh air, giving his cheeks a slap to try to scare away the nausea. When his ears had stopped ringing, he heard familiar voices from the other side of the bushes. Pushing through the tangled leaves, he spotted Porter and Duke sitting on either side of a decrepit seesaw, using their legs to stay perfectly balanced. The sight was so surreal that it stopped him in his tracks.

"What on earth are you doing?" he said when he'd found his voice.

Duke shot bolt upright, and Porter's side of the seesaw crashed to the ground with an ear-shredding shriek. The DI rolled backwards, almost doing a full somersault.

"The fuck!" said Porter, scrabbling up. "Little bloody warning, Duke. There's needles all over the place."

"There was nowhere else to sit, sir," Duke said to Kett.

"Unbelievable," Kett said, walking over. He didn't have the heart, or the stomach, to lay into them. He leaned against a plastic elephant slide, rubbing his mouth. "Tell me what happened."

"That wally stood up without telling me," said Porter, trying to check his back.

"With the body," said Kett.

Porter walked over, turning away.

"Is there anything in me?"

"There's about to be a size eleven boot in you," said Kett. "But no, you're fine. How did you end up here?"

"We were chasing a bunch of lads," explained Porter. "The arseholes in trackies."

"Black and grey, scarves over their mouths?"

"Yeah. I'm not sure, but I'm guessing they must be the

ones causing all the trouble, tagging the flats. The Iron Sausages, or whatever they're called. Followed them down an alleyway, and then Lurch managed to lose them."

Duke grumbled something that Kett couldn't hear.

"Figured this was the only place they could have hidden. Took a look, and we found..."

Porter fell silent, staring into the distance.

"Emily says he's been there a few days," the DI said after a moment. "Same killer."

"Has to be, right?" said Duke. "The eyes."

Kett nodded, glancing at the pub to see Savage and Cafferty walking out the door. They were still chatting like a couple of teenagers who'd decided to be best friends.

"You think those lads have anything to do with this?" Kett asked. "They led you here, right?"

"Kind of," said Porter. "They might not have. We never saw them in the pub. They could have gone anywhere, plenty of houses around, lots of places to hide. But yeah, it's weird they came this way and vanished."

"These roadmen wannabes aren't exactly natural born killers, though," said Duke. "They think they are, but they're never going to hurt anyone, not outside of the actual gangs in London."

"Agreed," said Kett.

"I don't know," said Porter. "There was one kid who had a hell of a stare on him. Gave me the creeps."

"Blue eyes?" said Kett, remembering the boy from that morning in the park.

"Yeah," said Porter. "Had a bit of a psycho feel about him."

"Agreed," Kett said again.

He waited for Savage and Cafferty to join them.

"Someone has definitely been dealing here. Looks like

people have been shooting up all over the place. Maybe we're looking for one of them. Somebody has a psychotic break, they know the pub, they bring their first victim back here. The dead kid could have been using. I doubt anyone ever goes in that back room, and even if they did, they'd be off their faces. The killer could have done whatever they wanted in there."

"There are sometimes dealers down in the underpass too, sir," said Savage. "And in the park. It's a link."

"But Helen Coulter doesn't exactly seem like your typical baghead," said Porter.

"He's moving up to the next level," Kett said. "Like you were saying, Kate. He's gone from killing a kid who might be using, to targeting an adult in a public place. Makes it feel more like it's random."

"Apart from the eyes," said Cafferty. "The ones we found in Helen's flat."

"Eyes?" said Porter.

"Fake ones," Kett told him. "Glass. I don't know what they are. It could be a weird coincidence. Is there anything else that could link our two victims? A black teenage boy, and an older white woman."

Nobody answered, because there was nothing to say.

"Let's focus on the gang for now," said Kett. "They call themselves the Iron Soldiers, that might not be a coincidence. They might be sending a message that we're not reading right. Do we know anything about them?"

"I can go back to HQ, sir, dig up any reports," said Savage. "There are bound to be hundreds of complaints."

"I'll do it," said Kett. "I need all of you going door to door, see if you can get some answers out of the locals."

"But it's so *hot*," said Duke, fanning his face.

Kett ignored him.

"Kate, Stephanie, can you two work up a profile on the killer as you go? Since you seem to be enjoying it so much."

Both women jiggled with barely contained excitement.

"If you can bring those lads in, do it," he said. "But be careful."

He looked at each of them in turn.

"That means all of you," he said. "I've got a bad feeling about this guy. We don't know much, but one thing's guaranteed."

They had to know what he was going to say, but he said it anyway.

"If you get in his way, he'll kill you."

CHAPTER THIRTEEN

Norfolk Constabulary HQ was a furnace.

The building was only a quarter of a century old, but it conducted itself like an elderly man with a myriad of health problems, and temperature regulation seemed to be the main one. As so often happened when the heat climbed, the air conditioning had broken. Kett walked through the door ready for a blast of Arctic cool and instead felt like he'd stumbled into a buffalo's crotch.

"Not again," he said to Shelley on the front desk.

"They're working on it," she said with an apologetic shrug.

Like the circles of hell, it grew warmer with every fire door he walked through, culminating in the pit of despair that was the Major Investigation Team bullpen. He approached Clare's office with some trepidation, well aware from experience that he could be sitting at his desk in his underwear. When he knocked and entered, though, he saw that the Superintendent was still wearing his heavy brown tracksuit. He was slumped in front of a feeble fan, the sweat rolling off him.

"Sir," said Kett, and then he stopped, because it was painfully obvious that Clare had an enormous bulge in the front of his trousers. "Uh... Do you need me to come back?"

"I don't need you to do anything, Kett," Clare shot back, rubbing the sleeve of his tracksuit over his face. "Except maybe deal with this."

He gave the bulge a squeeze, and Kett almost screamed.

"What? I'm not... I don't even... *What*?"

"It'll only take you a second," said Clare, reaching into his trousers. "I need it."

Kett's mouth hung open, but he'd run out of words. He could only watch as the Superintendent grappled inside the crotch of his sweaty tracksuit, red-faced and gurning. It seemed like a thousand years later that he pulled out a green plastic bag, throwing it onto his desk. They were peas, Kett saw to his immense relief. A super-sized bag of Green Giant.

"I think I just aged about twenty years, sir," he said. "What, exactly, are you asking me to do?"

"Grab me another bag out of the freezer, obviously," Clare barked, scrubbing the damp patch on his trousers. "I'm dying in here, and I'm not allowed to disrobe anymore, thanks to whatever perverted bastard put in the complaint."

He eyeballed Kett.

"Wasn't me, sir."

By which he meant it hadn't *only* been him. The entire department had signed their names on that particular email to the Chief Constable.

"You've heard about the second body?" Kett said, trying to change the subject. "Or first body, that is. Young lad, killed a few days ago. Same MO, eyes replaced with tin."

"I heard," said Clare. "I'm not going to use the term

serial killer, because we all know you need three deaths for that particular accolade."

"I think it's only a matter of time, sir. And that's only if we're not missing another corpse. This doesn't feel like a personal thing, or a vendetta. The victims are on the opposite ends of pretty much every spectrum."

"Not every one," said Clare. "We don't know anything about the lad yet. If he's local, if he's from the estate, that's a connection."

"True," said Kett. "Any luck with an ID?"

"Go ask Spalding," said Clare, putting his face so close to the fan that he was in danger of being shredded. His nose hairs wafted in the breeze, almost hypnotic. "And get me my tossing peas."

Kett ignored the order, heading for the Incident Room. DS Alison Spalding was there, pinning photographs to an evidence wall that looked more battered with every passing month. She glanced over her shoulder, and the look she gave him wasn't exactly friendly. Luckily, she had a pen in her mouth, so she kept whatever she was thinking to herself.

"Alison," said Kett, walking over. "Hot enough for you?"

She'd taken off her jacket, but she still looked like she was suffering. She picked up another photograph and added it to the collection. It was Helen Coulter, he saw, the same photo that Savage had found on the NHS website.

"Any luck with our second victim?" he asked.

Spalding's reply was muffled into nonsense by her pen. Kett was too scared to ask her to repeat it, but luckily, she wagged her finger at a stack of files on the desk. He picked them up, finding half a dozen missing person reports, already narrowed down to young men.

"Thanks," he said, carrying the files to the nearest desk.

He dismissed the first three because they were white, spreading out the rest.

He saw him immediately, the boy from the pub. He looked up at Kett from a photograph that had been taken outside the gates of City College, the building behind him instantly recognisable. He wore jeans and a white shirt that was so new Kett could still see the folds from the packaging. He had his hands in his pockets, his stance a little awkward, like he didn't know what to do with himself. But the smile on his face was genuine, wide enough to show off a set of slim braces. His wide eyes were full of joy, and Kett had to take a second to compose himself as the horror of what had happened to them passed through his head.

He lowered the file to the desk, resting his hands on it, taking a deep breath.

I'm sorry.

He picked it up again, his hand trembling a little as he scanned the information. The boy's name was Idris Mellor, and it turned out he wasn't a boy at all, but a man. He was twenty-two, so much older than he looked. It didn't make his death any less tragic, of course, but it was a little easier knowing they hadn't found the body of a child.

He took a photo of the picture, sending it to Emily Franklin with the message, *Is this him?*

Spalding wandered over, standing behind him.

"That the kid you found?" she asked.

"Yeah," said Kett. "I think so."

"The call only came in this morning," she said. "Parents were worried because he didn't show up for his dad's birthday breakfast. Nobody's heard from him since Wednesday morning."

"That fits with what Franklin told me about the body," he said.

He checked for an address.

"Trory Street. That's right down the road from where he was found."

"And a stone's throw from the park," said Spalding.

"Clare was right, that's a connection. Two victims living less than a mile apart; he's targeting locals."

"There's another connection, sir," said Spalding, turning over the first sheet of the file and tapping the paper. "He was doing a Health and Social Care diploma at college, and he'd applied for a nursing degree at UEA."

"Like Helen," said Kett. "Good spot, Alison."

His phone buzzed with Franklin's reply:

100% :(

"You think our killer has a grudge against healthcare workers?" Spalding asked, returning to the wall.

"If he does, he's an even bigger arsehole than I thought," said Kett.

He stood up, collecting Idris' file. He could call Savage, he knew, or Porter. He could ask them to do it, the knock on the door. But it hardly seemed fair.

"Can you find a FLO for me?" he said. "Get them over to Idris' house."

Spalding nodded.

Taking as deep a breath as his lungs would allow, Kett headed for the door.

THE ADDRESS LED him to a row of neat little terraced houses that sat across the road from the enormous Winchester Tower block, the sixteen-storey monolith throwing its shadow over them like a supportive arm. He struggled to open the gate because it only came up to his knees and the clasp was rusted solid, but it felt a little disrespectful to step over it. He was so busy shooting daggers at the stubborn thing that by the time he reached the front door, he was surprised to find it open.

"Oh," he said. "Hi."

A man and a woman stood there, both wearing glasses and neither of them tall enough to reach Kett's shoulder. They were in their sixties, and they were both white. Kett had to check the number on the door to make sure he was in the right place.

"Sorry," he said, opening his warrant card. "My name is DCI Kett, from the police. I'm looking for the Mellors?"

"That's us," said the woman. She was clinging to her husband's arm so hard that it looked like it was causing him pain, but he didn't try to shake her away.

"You're Idris'... uh..."

"Parents," the woman confirmed, nodding. "Have you found him?"

"Do you mind if I come in?" said Kett.

"Goodness, yes," said Mrs Mellor, steering her husband out of the way, still not letting go of his arm. "Let's get you out of the sun. Can I fetch you a drink?"

"No, thank you," said Kett, although he was gasping for one.

He stepped into a narrow entrance hall, the tiles on the floor doing a good job of keeping the temperature down. There was barely any room to move thanks to the dozens of coats and bags that hung on the wall, and the sea of shoes beneath them. The Mellors had already made their way into the closest room, walking in tandem like they were afraid to let go of each other.

Kett closed the front door behind him and followed them into a living room that swam in golden light. The alcoves around the fireplace groaned beneath the weight of hundreds of books, the air full of the dusty smell of them. Oil paintings hung on two of the walls, neither of them straight, while a dozen or so framed photographs crowded the oak mantelpiece. Idris was in most of them, as well as a girl who could have been his sister.

There was a smattering of cards on the windowsill, but Kett didn't feel like wishing Mr Mellor a happy birthday.

The couple finally parted, the man tugging the curtains halfway across the pole to dull the blade of daylight. The woman hovered by the sofa, wringing her hands together.

"Are you sure I can't get you anything?" she asked.

"I'm fine, Mrs Mellor. Thank you. Would you both take a seat for me?"

They did as he asked, Mrs Mellor clutching her husband's arm again. She was already crying, quiet little sobs that made her whole body vibrate. Mr Mellor was tapping his hand on her arm, gently, the way you might comfort a child.

Kett didn't want to make them suffer any longer than they already had.

"I want to start by saying that we don't know anything for certain," he said. "But the body of a young man who matches your son's description was found today."

The couple seemed to deflate into themselves, the woman folding her body against her husband. He continued to pat her, harder now, making soft shushing noises.

"I'm sorry," said Kett. "We won't know for sure until somebody formally identifies him."

He would have done anything to spare them the horror of that.

"But everything points to it being Idris."

On the street outside, a car door slammed, and Mr

Mellor flinched. It seemed to shake him out of whatever trance he'd been in, and he met Kett's eye for the first time since he'd arrived.

"What happened to him?" he asked, his voice so soft it was almost inaudible.

"We're not sure yet. But we're treating it as suspicious."

"Somebody did this to him?" the man went on. "Somebody killed him?"

Mrs Mellor's quiet sobs became a cry of grief. She burrowed her head into her husband's chest. His hand bounced on her arm, faster and harder now, *tap tap tap*.

"We think so," said Kett. "I need to ask you, did Idris have any enemies? Anyone he'd argued with, or anyone new in his life? Was he involved with anything dangerous, or illegal, maybe?"

The man nodded, leaning forward on the sofa so urgently that he risked crushing his wife's head.

"It was them that did it, I'm telling you. Those bastard dealers. They wouldn't leave him alone."

"Drug dealers?" said Kett. "You know any names?"

"I know they're all wankers," he spat, waving his arm through the air like he was wielding a machete. "Idris was a good kid, always was, ever since he got here. Him and his sister both, good as gold. Small miracle, when you know what they went through."

"You fostered them?" said Kett. "Adopted?"

"Weren't planning to. But we never had kids of our own. Then Idris and Zahra fell into our laps. Been caring for them ever since."

"Zahra's his sister? Where is she?"

"Dubai," he said. "She moved there after she graduated, but she still calls every week, comes back for the holidays. She's going to be... She's going to..."

The cracks were starting to show, his eyes filling.

"What do we say to her?" he asked.

"We can help," said Kett. "You're not on your own. We can help with everything."

"Can't bring him back, though, can you?"

The man asked the question like there might actually be a positive answer, and Kett shook his head.

"But we can find out what happened to him, and we can catch the person who did it. Can you tell me which dealers Idris was speaking to? Did you see them?"

"No," said Mr Mellor, sitting back. "Maybe. I don't know. You see the little worms around here all the time, no manners, no respect."

"What makes you think they were speaking with Idris?" asked Kett. "He was at college, wasn't he?"

"Wanted to be a nurse," said the man, sniffing.

He was still tapping his wife's arm, and she'd stopped crying. She'd stopped doing anything, Kett realised, her eyes closed and her mouth open. It was almost like she'd gone to sleep.

"He'd have made a wonderful nurse," Mr Mellor went on. "Heart of gold. He was always helping out, spent half his life at the little church up the road, looking after the neighbours and their kids, working over at St Martin's. He ran clubs for the little ones, did you know that?"

Kett shook his head.

"Football. He was so good at it. Never charged, although some of the parents gave donations. Had dozens of kids on the estate join in. Bloody waiting list for it, he was so popular. He always glowed, Idris, and never brighter than when he was helping people. But he was soft. He wasn't all there, in some respects. Gullible. I don't know the best word for what he was."

"Easily led," said Kett, and he nodded.

"Didn't know how to say no to people. Folk like him don't, do they? You give so much of yourself to the world that you forget to hold anything back. And then it eats you alive."

"Do you know what these dealers were asking your son to do?"

"He never said. All he ever told me was they kept harassing him, kept turning up at the clubs. We spoke to you about it. One of you. Somebody on the phone. Sandra called the non-emergency number."

"Yeah?" said Kett, knowing exactly what they'd have been told.

"Yeah. They said there was nothing they could do unless a crime had been committed."

He coughed out a bitter laugh.

"I guess I can call them now, eh?"

"I'm sorry," said Kett. "I really am. We should have done a better job."

For a few seconds, the only sound was those percussive slaps as Mr Mellor tapped his wife's arm. She *had* gone to sleep, Kett saw, her breathing steady, her snores as soft as velvet.

"Is she okay?" he asked.

"It happens," he said. "It's alright now, but when she wakes up, she'll have to go through it all again."

The man sniffed, his eyes on the carpet as he considered something.

"He's got money," the man said. "In his room. Couple of hundred, in cash. I asked him where he got it, and he couldn't tell me. No good at lying, is Idris."

"When was this?" asked Kett.

"Wednesday. After lunch, although he didn't eat with

us. I asked him about it, and he got upset, flew out the house. Was the last time we saw him."

"You didn't worry when he ran away? He lives here, right?"

"He does, but he has a room in a friend's house, a shared place. We pay for it. He usually tells us if he's not coming back, but after an argument..."

He shrugged, the guilt written all over his face.

"I never checked in."

"The money, do you think he got it from the dealers?" asked Kett.

"He wouldn't have done anything bad; he wouldn't have sold drugs. These kids came from hell, and I mean *hell*. Both parents dead, whole country killing each other. He never wanted any of that. He wanted love, and laughter, and peace. He wanted everyone to be kind. Not much to ask, is it?"

"No," said Kett. "It's not. The gang might have given him the cash as an incentive. It doesn't mean he did anything for them. It's a common trick. They give kids money and tell them it's a gift, then they ask for it back, with interest. Kids can't pay, so they have to work instead."

"And Idris wouldn't do it," said his father. "So they killed him?"

"We don't know that for sure," said Kett. "Do you know if your son ever hung out in the pub up the road, the derelict one?"

"The Walpole?" he said. "No. Why would he..."

He swallowed hard as it dawned on him.

"That's where you found him?"

"Yes," said Kett.

"In that shithole?"

The man's glare was so full of hatred that Kett had to

turn away. He looked out of the window to see that an IRV had pulled up, no sign of the driver.

"That's your answer then, isn't it?" said the man. "People only go in there to sell drugs or take them. We called you about that, too. So many times. Everyone on the bloody street called you about that."

"I know," said Kett. "I'm sorry."

There's only so much we can do, he didn't add.

There was a knock on the door, then the rattle of the letterbox. Mr Mellor made to get up, his wife snorting. Kett waved him back down.

"It'll be our Family Liaison Officer," he said. "I'll get it. You mind if I take a quick look in Idris' room?"

"Upstairs," said Mr Mellor. "On the right."

Kett opened the door to a friendly older constable in uniform, letting her in.

"You've been briefed?" he asked quietly, and she nodded. "The mum's asleep. Maybe get the kettle on for when she wakes up."

The FLO walked into the living room, her hat in her hands. Kett climbed the stairs, poking his head into the young man's room. The wall above the bed was a tapestry of Polaroid photographs, a snapshot of Idris' short life. He was as young as four or five in some, standing with his sister and a woman who wasn't his adoptive mother. The more recent pictures showed him with college friends in the pub, playing football with a bunch of younger kids, hanging out in the church, working the line at what looked like a soup kitchen. In every single one, he was smiling.

There was no sign of the money that Mr Mellor had been talking about. No sign of anything illegal.

Kett stood by the door for a moment longer, then he turned to leave, Idris Mellor's joyful eyes watching him go.

CHAPTER FOURTEEN

SAVAGE HAD NEVER KNOWN A HOTTER SPRING, AND SHE was loving it. While everyone else seemed to be sweating themselves into a miserable stupor, she soaked up the sun like she was a solar battery. It was easy to forget that she was walking down a street in the middle of the city, going from door to door in search of answers. When she closed her eyes, she could have been strolling along the beach in Tenerife, the cool sea foaming to her left, the palm trees swaying—

"Watch the shit!" yelled Cafferty.

Savage opened her eyes just in time, performing an athletic sidestep to avoid a dog poop the size of a chair leg. She almost dropped the hoodie that she had slung over her shoulder, and it took her a second or two to compose herself.

"How did you not see that?" asked Cafferty, incredulous. Unlike Savage, she looked like she was struggling, her shirt unbuttoned and the sleeves of her jacket rolled up. There were a couple of tattoos on her forearms, but Savage couldn't make them out. "I thought we were going to have to climb over it. I was going to call for air support."

"Miles away, sorry," said Savage. "What were you saying?"

"I was saying, where next?"

They'd reached the end of the road. A scrubby green sat in front of them, bookended by yet more blocks of flats. They were three streets away from the main road and the underpass. Nobody would have seen anything from this far away, even if they'd been standing on the roof of the highest building.

As predicted, they'd learned absolutely nothing from any of the people they'd spoken to—other than the fact that the dealers were a persistent blight on the entire neighbourhood. There was a real anger here, a simmering rage that things had been allowed to get so bad. No small part of that was directed at the police, and Savage didn't blame them. Budgets had been cut, salaries frozen, recruitment was at an all-time low, and more often than not arrests didn't lead to anything but a slap on the wrist.

And the criminals knew it.

"Head back, I guess," said Savage, doing a military turn and walking the way they'd just come. She gave the turd a wide berth. She wasn't even sure it had come from a dog, but that didn't bear thinking about. "So what have we got for our profile so far?"

"The killer doesn't feel like a missionary killer," said Cafferty.

"Right. He's not trying to eliminate a certain group. His victims couldn't be more different, there's no real sense of prejudice. It doesn't feel hedonistic, either. No evidence that he's got any pleasure from it. No sexual assault, anyway."

Although they hadn't had confirmation of that yet.

Cafferty nodded, swiping her damp forehead with her pocket square, which looked in bad shape.

"So it's likely to be a power thing," said the visiting sergeant. "He's trying to get some kind of control over them. Killers will sometimes blind their victims to stop them escaping, or to ensure they're somehow reliant on them."

Savage put a hand to her stomach, feeling like she'd been kicked.

"It's my worst fear," she said. "The horror of it, of somebody doing that to you."

"It's unthinkable," said Cafferty, nodding. "Monstrous. But sadly real."

"He's not blinding them when they're alive, though," said Savage. She checked for traffic before crossing the road into the meagre shade. "He's doing it after they're dead, which means there has to be some kind of psychosis there."

"He's a visionary," said Cafferty.

"Exactly. He believes that something happens to his victims after death. It's like he's staking some kind of claim to them in the afterlife."

"Why metal, though?" said Cafferty. "I'm inside his head right now: I've just strangled a young man, I'm removing his eyes and replacing them with tin balls that I've probably just forged myself. What am I thinking?"

"See what I see," said Savage, spitting out the words as soon as they entered her head. "See the world the way I see it. This world or the next one. You'll only see what I want you to see."

"I control you," added Cafferty. "I own you. That feels right."

"Or maybe it's you only see me," Savage said. "You only have eyes for me. I won't let you look at anyone else. A jealousy thing, maybe?"

"Maybe, but usually the victims would all fit the same profile. Young women, or young men, in most cases."

They turned the corner, nodding to a couple of constables who were walking the other way. Even though there weren't many coppers to spare, because of the football match taking place on the other side of the city, Clare had put at least twenty officers on patrol to try to reassure residents.

Not that any of the residents seemed happy about it.

"What does the strangulation tell you?" asked Savage.

Cafferty thought about it for a moment.

"Okay, so strangling is intimate, yeah? You have to be right there, and usually you're face-to-face. There's absolutely no getting away from the truth of what you're doing."

"It takes time," added Savage. "It's not like shooting somebody, it's not even like stabbing someone. It can take, what, a minute to properly choke somebody?"

"Longer," said Cafferty. "Unless you're cutting off the blood supply too."

"You have to really want them dead," said Savage.

There were two more coppers walking towards them, still some distance away, and she had to put her hand to her brow before she recognised Porter and Duke.

"But you also want them to know they're dying," said Cafferty. "Our killer is prepared, he's made his tin eyes, he's planned enough to buy the equipment. If he wanted, he could bring a knife or a hammer, he could source a gun, he could get some hypodermics and fill them with whatever. But he's chosen to kill his victims by hand. He wants them to know it's happening. He wants them to feel it."

"Except Helen didn't feel it," said Savage, waving to the men ahead. Duke waved back, smiling. Porter looked like a pug that was unhappy about being walked around the block. "He knocked her out first."

"Shit, yeah," said Cafferty. "Good point. He didn't want her to feel it, but he still wanted it to be personal. Or he would have just slit her throat."

"Maybe he wants them intact," said Savage. "He doesn't want their injuries to be too severe. It goes back to what we were saying about the afterlife."

"Good, Kate," said Cafferty. "So, let's get back into his head."

They stopped walking when they reached Porter and Duke.

"I'm standing over my victim," Cafferty went on, acting it out. "I've got my hands around their throat and I'm squeezing. Hard. I want them to die, I don't want them to make a sound, I'm happy to crush their windpipe if I need to. It doesn't matter how long it takes, I'm going to see the lights go out, and I want them to feel it happening. I want them to know that death is here."

Both Porter and Duke looked horrified.

"Please tell me this isn't a personal anecdote," said Porter.

Cafferty laughed.

"God, sorry, sir. That must have sounded awful. We're just trying to figure out who we're dealing with."

"And it's not looking good," said Savage. "Any luck with the neighbours?"

"Nothing," said Porter. "Half of them won't speak to us at all. Gang must have its claws in deep. Anyone heard from Kett?"

"He's back in the city," said Savage. "They ID'd the lad in the pub. He's with his parents."

"Shit," said Porter, both hands in his hair. "He's local?"

Savage nodded past the DI's shoulder.

"About three streets that way, sir."

Porter set off in that direction, everyone else following. Duke moved to Savage's side, taking her hand in his.

"Missed you," he said, earning a grin from Cafferty. As much as Savage liked it, she pulled free—a little too forcefully.

"I wondered who gave you the ring, Kate," said Cafferty. "When's the big day?"

"Oh, we haven't quite got around to planning it yet," said Savage. She felt rather than saw the look that Duke gave her. "Well, *he* has, but I'm... I've been busy. It's a lot to do, you know, and..."

She was starting to feel the heat after all.

"What about you, Steph?" she said, deflecting. "How come you're so interested in serial killers?"

"Always have been," she said. "How could you not be? I used to get the magazines when I was a kid, the crime ones. All I ever talked about, everyone thought I was a massive weirdo."

She lifted her hands.

"And they were right!"

Savage laughed. There was something in the woman's easy-going nature and her geeky excitability that made her infinitely likeable.

"My first case as a DC was the Randolph murders, back in 2017. Did you hear about them?"

"The Mini Cooper guy?" said Savage.

"Yeah, killed his wife and her sister, put them in his cars. He had five Minis, and he said he wanted somebody in each one."

"I remember that," said Porter. "Somebody figured out they were in the engine compartments."

Cafferty put up a hand.

"Me! He was a mechanic, obsessed with how things worked, vehicles and people. I just put two and two together."

"Nice one," said Porter.

"I might not be able to help," Cafferty said, using the pocket square on her face again. "But I'm here to try."

Savage was about to reply when she heard somebody yell her surname from the other side of the road. There was a line of red-brick houses there, as narrow as books on a shelf, and somebody was standing in the open door of one of them. Savage had to narrow her eyes against the sun before she recognised the woman she'd spoken to earlier, the medium.

"Enid?" she said.

She waited for a car to trundle past before she crossed the road, walking up to the house. There was a horseshoe over the door, turned upside down so all the luck would drain out. Enid Heathen was still wearing her enormous black dress, although she didn't look any hotter for it. She gestured for Savage to come inside.

"Get in here," she said. "Too hot today, even for heathens and savages like us."

Savage laughed politely, although the joke was starting to wear thin. It reminded her too much of being at school, the taunts and the jeers and the endless calls for her to go back to where she came from—even though the place she'd come from was right up the road.

"I can't," she said. "I'm working."

She heard the others saunter up, and Enid welcomed them all with a smile. She paid extra attention to Duke, craning her neck up to better see him.

"How about the rest of you? Fancy a cold drink?"

"We really shouldn't," Savage started, but Duke was already moving down the short path.

"Wouldn't say no to a juice," he said.

Enid beamed.

"You're a strapping lad, aren't you?" she said as she ushered him through the door. Porter was next.

"I'm strapping too," he said.

Enid slapped her hand on the DI's stomach loud enough for it to echo down the street.

"You *need* a strap," she bellowed to his shocked face. "To hold all that in."

Duke's laugh exploded out of the door. Porter vanished inside, and Enid waited.

"Five minutes," she said. "Maybe I'll make it worth your while."

"In what way?" Savage asked, but the woman had waddled inside, leaving the door open behind her.

"And I thought folk in Boston were weird," said Cafferty. "Come on. I always say, never turn down an invitation, it might be the universe telling you something."

"Oh, it's telling me something alright," said Savage, heading into the house.

It wasn't much cooler here than it was outside, and the kitchen was so small that it was a struggle for them all to fit inside it—mainly because there was already a young woman sitting at the table. She was in her early twenties, and she looked rough, her skin pasty and her hair lank. She wore a purple tracksuit, the hood up. The room stank of cigarette smoke, although nobody was smoking. The kitchen wasn't what Savage had been expecting from the strange older woman at all, the units and countertops bright white and an awful grey laminate on the floor, the corners peeling.

"Right," said Enid, moving to the fridge. "Let's see what we've got."

She opened it up, but there wasn't a lot inside.

"Milk?" she asked.

"I'll take a milk," said Duke.

"He likes it in a baby bottle, if you've got one," added Porter.

"Or water," said Enid, carrying the bottle of milk to the sink. She opened a couple of cupboards before she found the cups. "Or I can make tea."

"We don't have time for tea," said Savage. "Sorry, Enid. It's been a crazy day."

"I know," she said.

She filled a cup with milk and handed it to Duke. He downed it like he hadn't drunk in a month, milk dripping from his beard. He wiped it away with a sleeve, and Savage resisted the urge to chide him for it. Enid was filling more cups from the tap, and she passed one to Porter and one to Cafferty.

"A woman," she said. "Right?"

"Me?" said Cafferty.

"No, the person you found in the park."

Savage didn't commit to an answer, shaking her head when Enid tried to pass her a cup. The older woman drank from it instead, a delicate sip, before putting it in the sink. The girl watched from her chair, her dark eyes trying to make sense of the visitors.

"Who's your friend?" Savage asked.

"Dascha," Enid replied. "My granddaughter. Comes for the weekend sometimes, and you can see how happy that makes her. Old grandmothers are no fun, when you are used to the TikTok and the Facebook. She's thick with cold, so maybe don't get too close."

The girl rolled her eyes, pulling the hood down over her face.

"Get out of here, *zajka*," she said, still waving. "Let these people have a seat."

The girl got out of her chair, squeezing between them. Savage heard her sneeze as she walked up the stairs. Duke planted himself in the chair that had just been vacated, as casually as somebody who was in his own house. Porter took the next one over, chugging his water.

"We should probably go," said Savage. "Thanks for the drinks, Enid."

"It's no trouble, Kate," she replied. "Did she tell you, I used to know her granddad?"

"No way," said Duke. "Big Jeff Savage?"

Enid nodded, throwing Savage a wink.

"Nicest man on the Force, he was. And his granddaughter's not fallen far from the tree, I can tell you that for free. Sit down, Kate, let me help you."

All eyes were on Savage, so she took a chair. Cafferty looked like she was going to sit in the last one, but Enid beat her to it, lowering herself with a groan of discomfort.

"I'm cool standing," said Cafferty, doing an awkward jig. "Don't mind me."

Enid rummaged inside her dress, and Savage thought she was pulling out her cigarettes. What appeared in her hand, though, was a pack of cards—tarot cards, she realised, when the woman shook them out of their box and placed them on the table.

"Just give me a chance," said Enid, seeing the look on her face. "I know you all think it's codswallop, but let me have a go. I knew it was a woman who died, yes? Didn't get that from a newspaper."

Savage looked at Porter, who shrugged.

"Fine," said Savage. "But we really don't have long."

"It will only take a jiffy," said Enid. "Who here is closest to the case?"

Nobody answered, and Enid closed her eyes, holding one trembling hand out in front of her. She aimed it at Porter, who was finishing his drink.

"I'm sensing... a child," she said. "A young boy. He's yours?"

Porter's eyes widened, and it looked for a second like he was about to spit out a mouthful of water. He swallowed noisily.

"How did you know that?"

"I'm sensing something frozen," Enid went on, shivering. "There is no warmth in your house."

"Well, the heating's off, if that's what you mean."

"I sense a terrible coldness between you and the boy's mother."

Porter sat forward, a few shades paler.

"What?" he said.

"But this severance can be mended. Find your warmth, or lose it forever."

"Get out of my head," said Porter.

Enid had already swung her hand towards Duke. She frowned.

"Um..." she said, twisting her fingers like she was trying to tune a TV. Duke waited patiently, rapt. "I'm not seeing much," Enid went on. "Just an empty space. Wait..."

Everyone leaned forward, including Savage.

"Nope," said Enid. "There's nothing there, just a gaping void."

Duke put both hands to his head. Enid, meanwhile, had turned her wrinkled fingers towards Savage. Her eyes were still closed.

"I'm really fine," said Savage. "I'd rather you didn't—"

"I sense a great outpouring of grief," she said. "A woman, lying in the dirt."

Enid frowned, shaking her head at the horror of whatever she was seeing.

"Somebody has killed her, recently. She died a terrible death. I see her, I see her pain. Quick."

She opened her eyes and slammed her hand on the table hard enough to make everybody jump.

"Cut the deck, Kate. Now."

"I—"

"Now!"

Flustered, Savage picked up the top half of the deck of cards, putting it down next to the original. Enid lifted the top card in the bottom stack and flipped it over. The picture on it was so intricate that Savage had to lean in. It showed a woman in a blue dress with a serious face, a crown on her head and a crescent moon at her feet. The words underneath were in Cyrillic.

"The High Priestess," said Enid, speaking quickly. "The divine feminine. Our victim? Perhaps, but I think this is you, Kate."

She pushed her finger into Savage's chest hard enough to hurt, rocking her back in the chair.

"Ow!"

"The High Priestess teaches us to trust our inner wisdom, listen to our subconscious, find the hidden knowledge that lies within us all. Do not doubt yourself."

She flipped the next card over before Savage could reply, or before she could tell her to stop. This one showed a body on the ground, pierced by ten swords that jutted upwards like crucifixes. Three men stood behind the swords, their faces covered by hoods, their hands stained with what had to be blood.

The card was upside down.

"No way," said Duke, leaning in. Porter put a hand on his arm to hush him. The room felt like a gunpowder keg right before the fuse burned down.

"The Ten of Swords," said Enid, her eyes wild as she studied the card. "Deep wounds and painful endings. Betrayal, loss, crisis. Three men watch on, their hands red, their identities shrouded."

"It's upside down," said Duke, and Enid smiled knowingly.

"Reversed," she said. "Which tells us we must resist the inevitable conclusion. Things are not always as they seem."

"I've had enough," said Savage, getting up. "I'm done."

"One more," Enid told her, and the severity of the woman's voice was enough to root her in place.

She flipped a third card and laid it next to the others. Even here, in the hot, claustrophobic room, Savage felt a chill run right through her. The card showed a tower, like a lighthouse, only the thing at the top wasn't a light.

It was an eye.

It stared out of the card, full of fury, full of terror, a lightning strike carving right through it. Beneath the tower was a churning black sea, the waves big enough to wash the whole world away.

"The hell?" said Porter, leaning over the table so fast that he knocked over his mug.

"The Tower," said Enid, studying Porter's reaction. "A sudden, destructive revelation. A terrible, irreversible change. Misery."

She clapped her hand to the table with this word and every one that followed.

"Distress. Calamity. Disgrace. Ruin."

And there she fell silent, breathing hard.

"Well," said Cafferty after a moment or two. "That was cheery."

Savage moved to the door, her head swimming.

"We'd better crack on, sir," she said to Porter.

The DI nodded, stretching as he got out of his chair. Duke lifted a hand.

"Help me up, sir."

"Get yourself up," Porter replied. "Thanks, Miss, uh..."

"Heathen," said Enid.

"Ha," said Porter, grinning. "Heathen and Savage. Good team."

Savage felt her entire body bristle.

Porter and Cafferty left the room together. Duke waited a moment longer, seeing the uncertainty on Savage's face and asking an unspoken question. She nodded to show him that she was okay. And she *was* okay. The kitchen was bright, Enid was just a crazy old lady, and Tarot was as real as horoscopes.

"Sorry," she said. "Little on edge."

"I just want to help," said the woman, pushing herself out of her chair. "Take it or leave it, *zajka*, it's up to you."

Enid looked to the door and back again, speaking quietly.

"But what those cards are really telling me, is that you need to be very careful, Kate. Somebody close to you is a bad spirit."

She placed a soft hand on Savage's cheek.

"And they're hiding something terrible."

CHAPTER FIFTEEN

Kett was sitting in his Volvo outside the Mellor house when he saw Porter's name light up his phone.

"Pete, any news?"

"I don't even know where to start, sir," he said. "Where are you?"

"Trory Street, I'm about to head back to HQ."

"Can you pick us up on the way? We're right by Winchester Tower."

"Sure, now?" said Kett, but Porter was speaking over him, his voice fainter.

"Hey, do you think that's what the crazy lady meant? That tower?"

"What?" said Kett, but the call ended.

He started the car, making it to the tower block in less than a minute. The Winchester was enormous, a sixteen-storey 1960s monolith that dwarfed every other building on the estate. Porter and Duke were sitting on the low wall of a garden, Savage and Cafferty standing next to them, chatting. Savage looked like she was about to cry.

Kett wound down his window, calling out.

"It's going to be cosy. Should I call for an IRV?"

Duke and Porter both propelled themselves off the wall, running to the car and jostling for the passenger seat. Duke won, diving through the door so clumsily that the Volvo rocked on its wheels.

"Hey!" Kett yelled. "Pack it in!"

"Out," said Porter from outside, looking like a bear with a mouthful of bees. "I'm your senior officer, Aaron, and I'm ordering you to give me that seat."

Duke grumbled into the back with Savage and Cafferty. Porter replaced him, wearing an expression of hollow victory.

"What's happened?" Kett said, seeing Savage's expression in the mirror.

"Nothing, sir," said Porter. "Some friend of Kate's—"

"Not a friend," Savage said. "I only met her this morning. Enid Heathen. She knew Granddad, back in the day. She's a fortune teller."

"She did the Tarot thing," said Duke, leaning between the seats. "Three cards. One with a woman, one with a dead person and a gang of killers, one with a tower and an eye."

"What?" said Kett, turning around. He had to push Duke out of the way so he could see Savage. "Seriously? That's like a confession. Do you think she's our killer?"

"It *was* weird, sir," she said, frowning. "But I cut the cards, not her. It had to have been a coincidence."

"Honestly, with tarot, you can read into whatever card you turn over," said Cafferty, squashed against the window. "The Devil, a killer. Death, that's obvious. The Hermit, some psychotic junkie killing people because he thinks they're looking at him weirdly, the Three of Cups, because..."

She shrugged.

"I can't think of anything for that, but you get the idea. Whatever card you picked, we'd have connected it to the case somehow."

Savage nodded, although she didn't look sure.

"I just hate it," she said. "Gran used to read Tarot cards when I was a kid, she was obsessed with it for a while. Drew a Hanged Man on the day my dad died, and she never went back to it. I know it's not real, but..."

"I didn't know that," said Duke. Savage shrugged.

"Just hate it," she said again.

"The dead guy card was strange," said Porter. "All those hooded figures looking at him."

"Hooded figures?" said Kett.

"Like the gang. With their hoods up. Not that I believe it."

"She said your wife was frosty," said Duke. "I believe that."

Porter spun around, pointing his finger at the PC. Duke pressed himself into his seat like he was trying to escape a rabid dog.

"Just saying, sir," he muttered. "We've all met her."

"Can we forget about the bloody fortune teller for a minute?" said Kett, losing his patience in the suffocating heat. "I've got some *actual* information, from the *real* world. Idris Mellor, the young man in the pub, was in contact with one of the gangs. Probably the Iron Soldiers. They were trying to recruit him; his parents think he turned them down."

"That's something," said Porter.

"Wait," said Savage, leaning forward. "That *is* something. What if they tried to recruit Helen too? We know the gangs target NHS workers. Low salaries, and loads of them are mobile, they travel all over the place. It makes them great mules. What if they approached her, offered her a job, and she turned them down?"

"What if they don't like to hear the word no?" said Porter.

"Good thinking," said Kett. "Let's take it back to HQ. I've just got to make a quick stop at the supermarket first."

"For snacks?" asked Duke.

"For frozen peas."

IN THE END, the peas were a lifesaver.

The Extreme Crime Task Force sat inside the oven of the Incident Room, everyone—including DS Cafferty—hugging their own family-size bag of Birds Eye Petits Pois. Clare had restrained himself from sticking them down his trousers this time, probably because of the official warning he'd been given from the Top Brass. Instead, he sat on them like a proud mother hen perched on her eggs, cooing with pleasure every time he adjusted his backside.

Kett had his tucked underneath his shirt, and he did his best to ignore the trickles of icy water that probed beneath his belt.

"What is up with this weather?" said Spalding as she walked in, fanning her face with a sheaf of documents.

"Global warming," barked Clare, spreading his arms to the room. "Which is your bloody fault, you bunch of tossers. First, you lose the tournament. Next, you fail to solve this case. And now you're destroying the world with all your steaming toss."

"We're really not, sir," said Kett, moving the peas up a little.

"If I say you're to blame for global warming, Kett, then you're to blame for global warming. Understood?"

"Understood."

"Now, where are we? Because everything you've shown me so far points to the gang being responsible for our two murders, and I'm finding that hard to believe, because I've spent my life dealing with tracksuit-wearing toerags like this lot and I don't think they're capable of finding their own private parts in a public urinal, let alone orchestrating two horrific murders."

He had to stop in order to suck in a breath, and Kett jumped in while the opportunity was there.

"Agreed, sir. The kids we've met on the estate don't seem like the type to do this, but what if they're the foot soldiers? What if somebody else is calling the shots? We've seen so much trouble pushing up from London these last few years, all the County Lines stuff, and those guys mean business. The two beheadings down in Colchester last year were young men who tried to get away from the Hoxton lot. They killed them to send a message."

"Essex Police never confirmed that," said Clare. "They never caught the people who did it."

"It just fits," said Kett. "Like Kate was saying in the car, crimes like this are designed to scare people, and there is literally nothing more terrifying than somebody carving out your eyes."

"Pete?" said Clare. "What do you think?"

"I'm with Robbie," Porter said, holding his peas to his neck. "Two victims living in the same area, it just doesn't track with a serial killer. They leave more time between their victims. Months, maybe. Years. This feels different. It feels like somebody's trying to send a message to a community. And these guys call themselves the Iron Soldiers, they've got metal in their name. They make a point of scaring people. This feels like an escalation of that, something to strike terror. It's like they're saying, 'Stop looking,' or 'Don't watch us.' 'Don't snitch,' maybe."

"That makes sense," said Kett. "Maybe they were snitches. A lot of people have called us about the gangs, maybe Helen and Idris were on that list."

"It's what the cartels do in Mexico," said Porter.

"This is Norwich, Pete, not Juarez," said Clare. He wiggled his buttocks on the chair, shivering with pleasure. "Kate, I can tell by your face that you don't believe a word of what you're hearing. Anything you'd like to contribute?"

Savage was curled over her desk, her arms resting on her peas. She picked them up, turning the bag in her hands and glancing at Cafferty, who sat on the desk next to her.

"I hear what you're saying, sir," she said to Kett. "The gang feels like a good fit, especially if they're getting their orders from somebody else."

"And it's what the Tarot lady said," added Duke.

"Shut your hairy tosshole, Aaron," said Clare. "Kate?"

"It's the eyes, sir. It just requires so much work. The killer had to melt down the tin and mould it into the exact shape, they had to extract the eyes from the orbital sockets and then replace them. You can scare people a hundred different ways. They could have hung Helen and Idris from a lamppost, they could have decapitated them, they could have cut their throats and given them a Mexican necktie. They could have done anything, and pretty much anything would have been easier. This feels..."

"Personal," said Cafferty, taking over like they'd rehearsed it. "It feels symbolic. Our killer is obsessive, he's trying to do everything the same way each time. The strangulation, the enucleation, the metal prosthetics. This is a ritual for him, it holds meaning."

"He's psychotic?" asked Clare.

Savage bit her lip, thinking.

"I don't know," she said. "This feels too controlled for psychosis. But he's certainly got visionary traits. He's not just decorating a corpse, and I don't think he's leaving a signature. He thinks he's doing something else, something more important."

She spoke so elegantly, and with such conviction, that Kett found himself changing his mind about the gang.

"And what you were saying about timing, sir," she said to Porter. "It's true that generally serial killers space out their kills. That's what differentiates them from mass murderers. But think of it like a craving. Some of these guys get a thrill, or a closure, from murder that will keep them going for years. Others feel the urge to do it again almost immediately."

She faltered, as if doubting herself.

"Go on," said Kett. "This is great."

"Steph and I, we—"

"Who?" barked Clare.

"Steph," said Savage, pointing. "DS Cafferty."

"Oh, right," said Clare. "I forgot you were here."

"Rude," muttered Cafferty.

"We were asking ourselves what sort of person would feel the need to do this."

"What sort of man," said Cafferty.

"Yeah. If we're going by the standard model for a serial killer, we're looking for a guy. White, most likely. He's probably local, but not on the estate. Helen lived in a different place from Idris, she was on the other side of the park. I don't think the location where they lived had anything to do with it, other than the fact that he's obviously picked this side of the city to be his hunting ground."

"So why did he choose those two people to kill?" said Clare.

"The victims have some sort of symbolic value to him," said Savage. "We just don't know what."

She looked at Cafferty again, and so did Kett. The visiting DS had opened her bag of peas and was eating them like crisps.

"Oh," she said, swallowing hard. "Right. Symbolism. We wondered if these were people who'd maybe looked at him the wrong way, or mistreated him. Serial killers often have very fragile egos, it's why they're so easy to bait. It could be something as simple as Idris giving him a sideways glance on the street one day, or not apologising for some kind of grievance."

"And Helen?" said Kett.

"Maybe she was his nurse, and she didn't give him the respect he thought he deserved."

"He wants to be viewed as something more than he is," said Savage. "And because nobody sees him like that in real life, he forces them to do it in death."

"And this helps us how?" asked Clare.

"Because we're probably looking for somebody with low self-esteem," said Savage. "Somebody who struggles to talk to women, maybe. They might have a repetitive job where they don't get a lot of credit, something like that. They might have a record, too; it'll be some sort of intimidation or abuse. Domestic. A mother or a sister, a girlfriend, somebody who insulted them, in their eyes, anyway."

She drummed her hands on her bag of peas.

"I know it doesn't narrow it down much, sorry. And it might be completely wrong."

"But it's probably not," said Cafferty. "The Mini Cooper killer was a nasty piece of work, a serial abuser with a deep-rooted hatred of women. He had a record as big as Aaron's arm for assaulting sex workers, beating them, uh... yes, sir?"

Porter had a hand up.

"I just want to say that my arm is easily as big as his," he said.

"You can shut your tosshole too, Pete," said Clare. "And put those tiny arms down."

"I, uh, I've lost my train of thought, sorry," said Cafferty.

"It happens a lot around here," Kett told her. "Mini Coopers."

"Oh, yeah, so I worked up a psych profile for the killer based on the first body we found. The, uh, damage that had been done to her. Martin Randolph was pretty close to the top of the list. I'm just saying, these things work. You should listen to Kate."

She put another handful of peas in her mouth, crunching them like ice cubes. Clare was suspiciously quiet, his eyes moving between everyone in the room like he was judging a game of musical statues.

"I can't figure out which theory I hate more," he said.

"Rude," Cafferty said again.

"For what it's worth, Kate's feels like a more likely scenario," said Kett. "This has all the hallmarks of a serial predator."

"It does," said Clare. "But we also have to consider that this is what the gang wants us to think. It might be a distraction."

There was a muttering of disagreement that the Super chose to ignore.

"It could be the little old lady," said Duke. "The fortune teller. Enid."

"She's a hundred years old," said Porter. "But it is weird how much she knew."

"I've added her to the list," said Clare.

"And Roger," said Kett. "What's happening with him?"

"Sex Tape? He's still in the hospital. I'll deal with him when he comes out, but phone records, CCTV and his Ring camera corroborate his story. He went straight home, and he didn't leave the house again. Not that we can see, anyway. Oh, and that weird Keith down at the park has an alibi too. Any luck with Idris Mellor's housemate?"

"No," said Kett, who'd made the call as soon as he'd arrived at HQ. "Another guy, and he's out of town. Has been since last weekend."

Clare leaned forward in his chair.

"Then we start looking for somebody who matches the profile, Kate, and..."

He clicked his fingers at Cafferty.

"*You*," he said.

"Rude!" said Cafferty.

"Kett, Porter, you're on the gang."

"After today, they're going to go underground," said Kett.

"So get a spade and dig the bastards up," said Clare, baring his yellow teeth. "I want them in my interview room by tomorrow. Understood?"

Everyone nodded.

"Then get to bloody work!" he roared, crashing back with enough force to detonate his pack of petits pois like a landmine.

CHAPTER SIXTEEN

THE AFTERNOON WAS A BLUR OF MUGSHOTS.

Kett sat at his computer, clicking through every booking photograph he could find for young men between fourteen and twenty-five. After the first fifty, the kids started to blend together—all wearing the same expressions of arrogance and defiance, with the occasional look of terror thrown in. After two hundred, he was losing the ability to interpret faces altogether, as well as his will to live.

The trouble was, he'd only seen one of the boys without his mask. That lad's face had been pretty distinctive, because darker skin and bright blue eyes weren't exactly a common combination. But that guy didn't seem to have a record here or anywhere else, and Kett didn't know what any of the others looked like. He could have scrolled past all of them already and not have had the faintest clue.

He growled like a trapped dog, sitting back in his chair. When he checked his watch, he saw to his surprise that it had gone six. He looked around to see what everyone else was up to, and realised he was on his own.

"Oh," he said, his voice reverberating around the empty bullpen. "Hello?"

He made his way to Clare's office to see that he'd vanished as well, his fan still blowing. It was eerie, like the start of a zombie movie. He half hoped it *was* the start of a zombie movie. At least it would mean he could go home.

He headed to the kitchen instead and popped the kettle on. He sent Billie a text while it boiled, explaining that it was going to be a long night. She fired one right back.

We're all in bed, watching Moana for the 300th time.

It was followed almost immediately by another one.

Stay safe. Don't do anything stupid.

"As if," he told her.

He made a round of teas, even though there was nobody to drink them, carrying his mug back through the bullpen and out into the corridor. Here, he finally heard the chatter of voices. Clare appeared first, lurching around the corner like a wind-up monkey who's furious that it's lost its cymbals. Porter and Duke followed, and Savage and Cafferty brought up the rear.

"Where have you all been?" said Kett.

"In the morgue," spat Clare. "I bloody told you that when I walked past your desk."

"Huh?" said Kett. "When?"

"Half an hour ago, but you were too busy ogling naughty young boys on the internet."

"I wasn't ogling naughty young boys!" he protested as Clare barged past. "You can't say that, sir. They were mugshots. I didn't hear you."

"You were pretty zoned out," said Savage as they all walked into the bullpen. "I don't blame you. It's been a day."

"It's been a day," he echoed, following them in. "There are some teas in the kitchen, if anyone wants one."

The answer must have been yes, because everyone except for Savage made a beeline for the far door. She turned to him, stretching her hands above her head and flexing her neck.

"Idris?" asked Kett.

She nodded, letting her arms flop to her sides.

"Emily's still there, if you want her to walk you through it?"

The mere thought of being back down in Franklin's workshop while she pried the metal balls from a young man's eyes was too much.

"Can you give me the bullet points?" he asked.

"Sure," she said, crossing the room. "Definitely strangled by hand, the bruises left by the killer's fingers are very prominent. There's no serious damage to the structure of the throat, like we saw with Helen, so he went slower this time. Franklin says the position of the bruises over the arteries suggests Idris probably passed out pretty quickly, long before he asphyxiated anyway. He definitely fought back, there are grazes on his knuckles and that missing nail. But he was just a kid. Skinny thing. He never stood a chance."

She reached her desk, slumping into her chair.

"Eyes were removed in the same way, with a sharpened implement, probably a spoon. The balls are made of tin, although the lab's taken a look at the ones from Helen's eyes and they think they're more likely to be some kind of alloy. Pewter, but an older kind. It's lead, not antimony or copper. The ones in Idris' eyes looked like they were smelted and shaped by an amateur as well, the same lumps and bumps and dents. No numbers or letters this time."

There was a file waiting on Savage's desk, and she picked it up, talking and reading at the same time.

"Uh, Hay says death definitely took place in the pub, there's skin tissue and blood on the walls. Probably from Idris, but she's taken samples in case the killer scraped himself."

She frowned.

"What?" Kett asked, moving behind her so he could peek at the file in her hands.

"Spalding left this. Said she tried calling them earlier, but they were all at the dodgeball. Suffolk Constabulary had a case recently, bodies with silver coins in their eyes. Look. Happened in Southwold."

"Southwold?"

It was like a chisel to his heart. He thought back to the morning, which felt like a lifetime ago, the man who'd come at him in the Sportspark, who'd acted just like one of Hollenbeck's soldiers.

Harrison Baird.

Norman Balls had mentioned Southwold, he was sure of it. Baird had been seconded there, just a few weeks ago.

He took the file from Savage and scanned it. A fishing boat had dredged a long-dead man from the sea, and there had been a silver coin in his eye. Another coin had been found in a second victim just a day later.

"Timeline matches ours," he said. "Give or take. Two victims in a matter of days. A coin in their eyes. That's some coincidence, Kate."

"I know," she said. "But coins in the eyes is a little different than tin balls."

"You said it yourself. Maybe he's escalating. He starts with the coins. Kills two men. But it's not enough for him. The thrill wears off, he has to push to new extremes. When that doesn't do it for him anymore, he moves to a new place, goes one step further."

Like Baird, he thought. From Scotland to Southwold, where two corpses showed up.

From Southwold to Norwich, just in time for two more.

"Number's here," she said. "Shall I give them a ring?"

"I'll do it," he said. "It's your turn to ogle those naughty boys."

He ignored Savage's expression of disgust, heading to his desk. He picked up his phone, dialling all but the last digit, then hesitating.

If he called now, and Baird answered, what was he supposed to say?

Remember me?

In all the drama of the day, the man's words had partially dissolved. He'd said something about John Cooper, hadn't he? The arsehole DCI he'd worked with back at the Met.

The man who'd tried to kill him during the Cry Baby case in London, the same day that Billie had been kidnapped by the Pig Man.

Cooper was dead; the coward had hanged himself in Belmarsh rather than face up to what he'd done. But Baird had mentioned more names, hadn't he? Somebody called Topper. Something about a dog? It was all nonsense, the ramblings of a madman.

So why was it stirring a feeling of sickness deep inside him? The memory of something awful that had happened decades ago. He reached for it, but like two negative magnets, it moved away from his grasp. The more he tried to find it, the further away it slid.

"Fuck's sake," he muttered, finally pressing the last digit.

He rubbed his dry lips as the phone rang, his heart doing ten to the dozen. There was a click, then something that sounded like a slurp, and finally a voice, spoken through what sounded like a mouthful of food.

"Hello? Southwold Major Investigation Team, DC Constance Connell on duty."

It wasn't a Scottish accent, or a man, and for that, Kett was infinitely grateful.

"Hi," he said. "I'm calling from—"

"Brain freeze," said the woman on the end of the line. "Give me a second."

Kett waited, hearing a low groan that went on for a good ten seconds.

"Look," Connell said when she'd bounced back. "I know what this is about, and I'm not going to say sorry. Rules are rules, the referee said it herself. Any and all groin shots are *legal*."

She took great care to emphasise the last word.

"It's on *your* players to ensure they have adequate protection. Frankly, leaving your danglies dangling behind a couple of layers of fabric is insane when you've got balls flying around at ninety miles an hour."

"I'm not calling about..." he started. "Hang on, ninety miles an hour? You're talking about a *dodgeball*?"

"That's the record," said Connell. "A heavyweight ball weighs four hundred grams. At that speed, it's going to break bones, let alone... balls. My advice, wear a cup."

"I'm not sure that would help," said Kett, thinking of Norman Balls and his malfunctioning strap. "Look, this isn't about the tournament. I'm calling from Norfolk Constabulary. You had a case a few weeks ago, dead bodies with coins in their eyes."

"Oh, gosh, yes. That was exciting."

"You found out who did it?"

"We did," said Connell. "They're behind bars waiting for a court date. Job done."

"You're sure it was them?"

"One hundred per cent, uh, should I call you sir? Sorry, I don't know your rank. Or your name."

"DCI... Peter Porter," said Kett.

"I appreciate a nice bit of alliteration, sir, good job. Yes, it was them. Full confession, a pile of evidence, solid motive. No doubt. Can I ask why?"

"We've just got some stuff going on up here," said Kett. "There are no other 'metal in the eye' cases that you can think of?"

"Barney Arnupp across town got a splinter in his eye once," she said. "Metal shaving from his tractor. It was nasty. Does that help?"

"No," said Kett. "Thanks, though. Listen..."

He hesitated for a moment, popping his lips.

"That's a nice tune, sir," said Connell.

"What?"

"You said listen, and then started... popping? I don't know what it was, sorry. I'm confused."

That made two of them.

"You've got a guy working with you, a Scottish copper," he went on.

"Oh, yes! Harrison."

"Can you tell me what he's like?" said Kett.

"Intense," she replied. "So intense."

"Has he mentioned anything to you about anyone up here in NorCon? Somebody by the name of Robert Kett?"

The pause on the other end went on for too long.

"I don't think so," said Connell, who didn't sound sure.

"Maybe? Kett's a bit of a legend, lots of people ask about him."

This almost brought a smile to Kett's face, until he remembered what he was legendary for.

"Does he seem *okay*, though?" asked Kett.

"Okay's a strong word," said Connell. "He did try to throw a guy off the pier, and he's been shot at a few times since he got here, took an arrow in the shoulder, and nobody can really understand what he's saying. I don't know what else to say. He's got a dog."

"Right," said Kett. "You know if he's planning on hanging around?"

"That, sir, is the question of the hour."

Kett felt a presence behind him, and he turned to see Savage standing there, watching him like a hawk.

"Thanks for your help," he blurted out, and he hung up the phone.

"What was that?" Savage asked.

"Nothing," he replied, a little too quickly. "Suffolk closed that case, they've got their killer. It's nothing to do with us."

"Scottish man?" said Savage, who didn't miss a thing. "That doesn't have anything to do with this morning, does it, sir? The guy at the dodgeball?"

He shook his head and picked up his tea, although it was still too hot to drink. After a few seconds, Savage let it go.

"Boss wants us in his office," she said.

Kett took his mug with him, finding Porter, Duke and DS Cafferty already inside. Clare sat in front of his fan, looking like a melted snowman that somebody had tried to shovel back into shape.

"Right," he said. "We've got a plan. Porter, you tell him. My lips are too hot."

"We're going to set up a honeypot, sir," Porter told Kett. "Plant a junky on the estate and see if the gang bites. Soon as they turn up, we grab them."

"Who's the junky?" said Kett. "Because Aaron's too fit, Kate's too put together, and you're a little... round to be an addict."

Porter gasped, sucking in his gut.

The only person who looked like they were six minutes away from a catastrophic overdose was Clare, but Kett didn't mention it.

"We're using Jonesy," said Duke.

"That makes sense," said Kett. "When?"

"Now," said Porter. "You in?"

"No, he's not," said Clare, puckering his lips in front of the fan, his words vibrating. "Anyone who's watched the news will know his face from a mile away. He's going home."

"He is?" said Kett, feeling a glimmer of hope.

"We won't learn any more about our killer until Hay and Franklin get their full reports back in the morning. I need bodies here early, so go home, Kett. Get some rest. You too, Kate, and your... friend. But leave your phones on and your shoes laced up. If anything kicks off in the night, I want you back quicker than a gnat's toss."

Cafferty raised her hand.

"I don't suppose there's a spare bunk in the station, sir? I haven't got anywhere to stay."

"You can stay with me," said Savage. "If you don't mind dogs? The neighbours will keep hold of her for the night if you do."

"I love dogs."

"Have you got enough clothes?" asked Savage.

"I always pack heavy," said Cafferty. "Got a suitcase full of stuff in the car."

They grinned at each other.

"Whoop-de-doo," said Clare, slumping even further into himself. "A sleepover."

"You sure you'll be okay?" Kett asked Porter.

"We're big boys, sir," the DI replied.

"Some of us are bigger than others," said Duke, and Porter glared at him.

"There's more chance of you killing each other than the gangs doing it," said Kett. "Be safe, okay? You do *not* want to risk this guy getting you on your own."

"I'll have tactical around the corner," said Clare. "They'll be fine."

Famous last words, thought Kett.

"Be safe," he said again, before walking away.

CHAPTER SEVENTEEN

AT LONG LAST, THE HOT, BASTARD DAY WAS DYING.

Porter stood in the car park of Police HQ, enjoying the cool breeze that had picked up in the last twenty minutes or so. The sun had tucked itself in beneath the roof, the evening settling with a chorus of birdsong that was the most annoying thing he'd heard all day.

Correction, thought Porter, *the second most annoying thing*. Because Duke was leaning against the unmarked BMW next to him, humming what sounded like the theme tune to *Bonanza*.

The tune broke off as the PC spoke.

"Here he comes."

A man was shuffling across the car park in their direction, dressed in a filthy red tracksuit and battered trainers. His prominent bald spot was surrounded by a swamp of yellow hair, looking like an egg in a nest.

"Jonesy," said Porter, nodding a welcome. "How are you?"

Sergeant Gavin Jones, known to everyone at the station

as Jonesy, was a rare example of somebody who fit their name perfectly. The man permanently looked like a heroin addict going through withdrawal: as skinny as a rake, with a sheen of sweat and eyes so red he could have been a werewolf. Admittedly, most of these things were the result of the fact that he had a chlorine allergy and went swimming every morning before work. But it still made a convincing impression.

Until he opened his mouth, that was.

"Alright, old chap," said Jonesy, sounding like a member of the landed gentry. "How are things? How's Bobby doing? He must be getting on a bit now. Time flies!"

"He's good," said Porter. "He's a little chunk."

"Like his dad," said Duke. "Evening, Sarge."

"Good evening, Aaron. Been hitting the gym, I see. That beard of yours must bench two hundred kilograms."

He snorted a laugh at his own joke. Duke grinned, and even though Porter had no idea how he did it, the constable flexed his beard.

"You ready for this?" Porter asked the sergeant. "All you have to do is stand there until the lads show up. Then you ask for some drugs, give them some money, job's a good'un."

Jonesy's smile wavered, and he wiped a bead of snot from his nose.

"This isn't anything to do with the eyeball thing, is it?" he said. "I'm not sure I want to mess with that."

"It's a gang thing," said Porter, skirting around the truth. "We just need to lure them out. Me and Aaron will be right there, and tactical will be around the corner."

"Safe as houses, sir," said Duke.

"Right-o," said Jonesy. "Don't let me out of your sight, though, okay?"

"I'm going to be on you like a rash," said Porter, opening the back door of the BMW. He looked at Jonesy's mottled neck as the man climbed in. "*Another* rash. Let's go, we'll be back here in time for supper."

FOUR HOURS LATER, there was still no sign of the Iron Soldiers.

Porter sat behind the wheel of the Beemer, halfway down the street from the derelict pub where they'd found the second body. Duke sat in the passenger seat, fast asleep in his uniform. His snores were slightly less irritating than his voice, so Porter hadn't bothered to wake him up. The air temperature had plummeted, the car as cold as a fridge, but he couldn't turn the engine on without everyone knowing they were inside it. He wrapped his arms around his chest, tucking his hands into his armpits, comforting himself with the knowledge that, however bad it was for him, it was significantly worse for Jonesy.

The sergeant had been outside the derelict Walpole Arms since they'd got here, pacing back and forth, fidgeting and jiffling and muttering like a true junkie. Every now and then, he'd stagger up the street and back again, always returning to the same spot. A few people had walked past, all crossing the road as soon as they'd seen him. One of them had phoned in a non-emergency call about a man who needed help, which went a small way to restoring Porter's faith in humanity.

But there had been no sign at all of anyone remotely suspicious.

Duke snorted, muttering something. Porter regretted

not bringing a Sharpie with him. He could have given the PC a pair of glasses and a few freckles, maybe a cock on his forehead too. He was wondering whether he'd get the same satisfaction from trying to stick the constable's baton up his nose when he heard voices from outside.

He ducked down, glancing through the steamy side window to see a couple of people walking up the pavement behind the car. It was too dark to make out their faces, and when they walked past, he realised they had their hoods up. Both wore the roadman uniform, grey tracksuit trousers and black hoodies. One had a bumbag strapped diagonally over his body.

"Shit," said Porter. "Aaron, wake up."

He gave Duke a solid elbow, and the PC moaned.

"Go weewee," said Duke, and Porter smacked him around the back of the head. Duke sat up with a Frankenstein-like groan, rubbing his scalp. "Ow, sir, I wasn't asleep."

"They're here," said Porter. He picked up his radio. "Ed, we've got two scrotes approaching, over."

A fizz of static, then a gruff voice that belonged to Ed Proctor, the new lead tactical officer. Julia Gorski hadn't quite retired after the events of the Cold Iron Kills case, but with a bullet wound in her shoulder—not to mention a baby in her belly—she wasn't going to be back anytime soon.

"Received. We're ready."

The two lads in tracksuits were on the opposite side of the road to where Jonesy was lurking in the shadows, and Porter wasn't sure they'd seen him. They were talking loudly about something, their laughter echoing off the buildings like a couple of hyenas.

Jonesy watched them pass by, chewing on his thumbnail. Then he stepped into the road and called out to them.

The two men spun around, their faces pools of shadow

beneath their hoods and scarves. The one without the bumbag stuck his hand into the pocket of his trousers, leaving it there. The other was already halfway across the road, walking with an arrogant swagger, his arms out to his sides in a challenge. Jonesy had gone full Jonesy, hunched over like Quasimodo, his hands clasped together like he was praying. The roadman walked right up to him, leaning in. Porter could hear the guy shouting, but he couldn't work out what he was saying.

"I don't like this," he said, his thumb on the radio button.

"Hang on, sir," said Duke. "He knows what he's doing."

Jonesy was almost bent double, grovelling to the kid in the tracksuit. The other one had walked over, his hand still in his pocket. There was every chance he had a knife in there.

The first roadman grabbed Jonesy by what was left of his hair, screaming at him.

"Nah," said Porter. "I've seen enough."

He lifted the radio.

"They're armed, Ed. Move in."

Porter opened his door, making it halfway out of the car before he sensed a shape rising up beside him. He looked around to see another lad right there.

There was no time to say anything before the kid hit him, the impact too hard to be a fist. A grenade of white light detonated inside his skull, and he tumbled back through the open door.

Duke roared, his voice lost inside the thunder of Porter's panic.

More shouts, but he couldn't make sense of them. Adrenaline pulled him free of his shock, the fear that whoever had hit him would be coming in for another go. He sat up, blinking away stars to see Duke legging it down the street, chasing two men—one of them still holding the hammer that he'd hit Porter with. The original roadmen were right there, too, and sure enough, they both had knives in their hands.

There was no sign of Jonesy. He'd bolted.

"Fuck," Porter grunted, grabbing the door frame and hauling himself out of the car. The world swam, a fist of nausea pushing up from his gut. "Aaron!"

He started walking, holding onto the parked cars along the road for support. He could hear a siren, Proctor's van close enough for the roar of its engine to fill the street. But there was still no sign of them. Up ahead, everyone was shouting, the guy with the hammer turning to face Duke.

"Put it down!" Porter yelled.

Duke had his Taser out, thank God, and he fired a shot into the hammer man's chest. The guy dropped hard, fitting on the street. His mate wasn't happy about it, swinging a fist at Duke and catching him squarely in the jaw. The PC's head snapped back, and he staggered away, the Taser clattering to the street.

The two original lads had scarpered around the side of the pub, probably chasing Jonesy.

"Fuck's sake," said Porter.

He skirted around the guy on the ground, throwing himself at the one who'd hit Duke and driving him into the wire fence. He was a big guy, older than Porter had been expecting. Stronger, too, because when he threw an elbow back into his cheek, he felt like he'd been hit by the hammer again.

The man tore free before Porter could recover, legging it around the side of the pub.

"You alright?" said Duke. He was on his knees, cuffing

the man who'd been Tasered. This guy was older too, wearing jeans and a leather jacket.

"I'm fine," said Porter, rubbing his face, feeling where it was already starting to swell. "Where the hell is Jonesy?"

"Ran that way, sir," said Duke, collecting his Taser and pointing it at the pub. "They've all gone after him."

"Christ," said Porter. He looked down the street to see red and blue lights turning the buildings into a disco. Not close enough. "Give me your baton, Aaron, and tell Ed where to go."

Duke didn't argue, sliding the baton free and handing it over.

Porter snapped it out to its full length as he ran around the fence that surrounded the pub. He could have waited for tactical, he knew, but when there was a copper being chased by three armed men, every second counted.

"Jonesy!" he yelled, his voice making his injured head ring.

The street was deserted, but the gate that led into the pub gardens flapped on its hinges, squealing. The line of police tape had been torn free, trampled into the dirt.

Porter made his way into the impenetrable darkness of the overgrown gardens. He pulled out his torch, clicking it on, but he didn't need to see where the men had run. He could hear them inside the building, more shouts, then a cry of alarm.

"Jonesy?" he said again, approaching the open door. He walked in, yelling at the top of his voice. "Armed police!"

He hoped nobody would call his bluff.

The corridor was deserted, and so were the toilets. He pushed into the bar, hearing more shouts from upstairs, the thump of feet making dust rain from the ruined ceiling.

"Come on," he told himself, the fear like a live wire

clamped between his teeth. He glanced back, praying he'd see Proctor and his team run through the door, seeing nothing but the night. "Fuck's sake."

He turned the corner, passing the room where Idris Mellor had been found. The stairs were slick with rot, almost too slippery to walk on. The landing was deserted, every door open. The voices had fallen quiet, but they had to be up here, there was nowhere else to go.

"Armed police," he said again, his voice sinking into the dark without a trace. "Make yourself known."

A hiss from the nearest room. Porter walked in, seeing a handful of tables and chairs and another bar in the far corner. The hiss came again.

"Jonesy?" he whispered. "That you?"

A head peeked over the bar. It was the sergeant, his nose bloody.

"What are you doing?" said Jonesy. "They're right there."

A thunder of feet, somebody running behind him. Porter whirled around, only to see one of the roadmen flying down the stairs.

"Oi!" he yelled, chasing him onto the landing. "Get—"

Something thumped into his back, shunting him forwards. He put out a foot to stop himself, but there was no floor, the stairwell opening up to catch him. He tumbled, managing to grab the handrail only to feel it explode out of the wall.

He landed hard where the stairs doubled back on themselves, his head banging like a bomb had gone off inside it. Somebody was coming down the stairs after him, he could hear their footsteps, he could feel the tremor of their approach.

A hand in his hair, lifting his head. He glanced up, not enough light to see who held him.

"Leave it alone, pussio," said a voice. "None of this is what you think it is."

The hand let go of him, his head cracking into the stairs.

And all that was left was the sound of the lads fleeing into the night.

CHAPTER EIGHTEEN

Sunday

Kett should have known not to bother trying to sleep.

It was after one when he got the call. He'd barely managed any rest at all, his head full of dark thoughts and his blood full of adrenaline. Billie watched him get dressed with one part worry to two parts relief that she wouldn't have to share the bed with her restless husband for the rest of the night.

"Make sure the door's locked," she said.

"I will," he replied, knowing full well that she would come down after he'd gone and check every lock, every light. Her OCD was one of the many unwanted gifts that the Pig Man had left her with. He kissed her on the forehead. "I love you."

He checked in on the girls as he went, because Hollenbeck had given him obsessive tendencies too. Then he made the drive back into the city. The street where the Walpole Arms sat was bathed in light like it had forgotten the time of day, the portable LEDs so bright that the birds had started singing. A handful of neighbours stood in the doors and windows of their houses, wearing pyjamas and frowns. Some were probably curious about why there were a dozen police officers and an armed tactical unit inside the grounds of the pub.

Most had probably gathered to listen to Superintendent Clare, whose shouts of rage were so loud that Kett could hear him before he'd even got out of the car.

"And then what would have happened?" he roared as Kett walked up. He was directing his fury at Porter, who sat in the back seat of an IRV with an ice pack held to the top of his head. The DI looked utterly miserable. Duke was chatting with Ed Proctor on the other side of the street, the tactical unit loitering with their weapons stowed. "They'd be scraping you off the floor of the toilets like a crust of old toss. Is that what you want to be? A crust of old toss?"

Porter shook his head.

"What happened?" asked Kett. "You okay, Pete?"

"Oh, look who it is," said Clare. "DCI Kett. How was your beauty sleep, Robert? How comfortable was your duvet? How silky was your negligée?"

"You literally told me to go home, sir," Kett protested.

"Badger toss," said Clare. "I never said anything of the sort. What happened, Detective, is that your bosom buddy here fell down the stairs and nearly lost poor Jonesy to a bunch of thugs."

"Not *exactly* what happened," muttered Porter, shifting the ice pack to the side of his head.

"Well, let me put it another way," Clare said, baring his teeth. "He Ketted up."

Porter didn't argue with that.

"It was the lads?" asked Kett. "The Iron Soldiers?"

"Yeah," said the DI. "Four of them. They chased Jonesy into the pub. I went after them. Somebody gave me a shove down the stairs. I think it was the kid with the blue eyes, because he said something to me. He said this wasn't what it looked like."

"Pushing you down the stairs wasn't what it looked like?" said Kett. "Seems pretty self-explanatory to me."

"As does being hit with a hammer," said Clare.

"You got hit with a hammer?" said Kett.

Clare nodded, a glimmer of concern creasing his face.

"They weren't holding back. They could have killed him."

"Probably would have," said Porter. "Except Ed's team were running down the street. They scarpered."

"Jonesy's alright?" asked Kett.

"He's fine," said Porter. "Busted his nose running into a door in the dark. He managed to hide from them."

"This doesn't make any sense," Kett said. "Why would they go after Jonesy like that? He asked them for drugs?"

"Yeah, he said as soon as he mentioned drugs, they turned on him, like they were trying to scare him off. Probably suspected he was a copper."

"You sure you're okay?" said Kett.

"I'm fine," said Porter. "Hammer only scuffed me. Duke Tasered the twat; he had a bunch of gear on him. He's not talking."

"Oh, he'll be talking," said Clare. "Porter, go get that melon you call a head seen to. Kett, with me."

Clare marched away on his heron-like legs, heading for Duke. Kett jogged after him.

"Alright, sirs," said Duke.

"Oh yes, Aaron," said Clare. "I've never been so all right. I haven't been this alright since Fiona and I had our last string bikinis and string cheese night. How are you?"

"I'm fine, sir," said Duke. "Got off lightly, I—"

"I don't care," said Clare. "Where is he?"

"The suspect? Over there."

Duke pointed to an IRV a little way down the street. The man who sat in the back was in his thirties, his shaved head almost hiding the evidence of his male-pattern baldness. He was staring through the window with such intensity that the glass kept steaming up.

"He say anything, Aaron?" asked Kett.

"He said 'argh, aaah, stop Tasering me, it hurts,' a fair bit," said Duke, a smirk on his face. "That was about it. He had six baggies on him, probably heroin. A bunch of pills."

The constable standing by the car opened the door as Kett and Clare walked over. The man inside held his position, acting as tough as it was possible to act when your hands were cuffed behind your back.

"What's your name?" said Clare, leaning in.

The guy spat a reply, *literally*, a gob of foamy saliva hitting the ground by Clare's feet.

"That was your first and only mistake," said the Superintendent. "I'm going to ask again, and this time I want you to consider something. The average width of a male urethra is... You do know what a urethra is, don't you, before I carry on?"

The man licked his lips.

"Good," said Clare. "The average width of one, including yours, is about nine millimetres."

He demonstrated the size of it with his yellow fingernails, then significantly widened the gap.

"The average width of a police-issue extendable baton is twenty-five millimetres, although they get wider at the base. Can you see where this is going?"

The man's eyes bulged.

"Name," said Clare.

When the man still didn't answer, the Superintendent walked away, heading for the nearest cluster of constables.

"He's not joking," said Kett. "I've seen him do it. His nickname in the department is the Surgeon."

"No, it isn't," said the guy, just a whisper.

Kett checked over his shoulder to see Clare trying to wrestle a constable's baton out of its holster.

"Just start with your name," he said. "Before he comes back."

"Craig," he said, swallowing hard. His eyes were locked on Clare, full of fear. "Capper."

"You ever been arrested before, Craig?" said Kett.

He shook his head.

"We found some drugs on you. What were you going to do with them?"

"Nothing," said Craig. "Personal use."

"Craig, the only reason you'd need six bags of heroin for personal use is for pain relief after some kind of horrific physical trauma to your..."

He glanced back. Clare was returning, the baton extended. His expression of insane, wide-eyed joy made him look like Nosferatu right before a feeding frenzy.

"Never mind," said Kett, taking a step back. "I'm sorry for what's about to happen."

"Wait," said Craig, sliding along the seat in an effort to

get away. "Look, it was hardly anything. Couple of bags, only for the regulars."

"What happened? Why did you chase the guy who asked you for drugs? He wasn't a regular?"

The man shrugged, flinching at every one of Clare's approaching footsteps.

"I don't know if he was or not," he said. "He legged it."

"He'd just seen you wallop a police officer with a hammer."

"I didn't know he was a copper," the man said. "Honest. I thought he was..."

"Who?" said Kett. "Who did you think he was?"

"Nobody," said Craig, his eyes like moons. "Just keep that mad prick away from me."

"I will, but you have to answer one more question. You and your mates. Who are you working for?"

"Nobody, I..."

He stared in horror as Clare reached the car, the baton gripped tight. Kett put a hand to the Superintendent's chest, holding him back.

"I can't keep you safe, Craig, unless you tell me."

"I don't know," he whined. "We don't get told anything. Just where to pick up the stash and where to drop off the cash. We never see anyone."

"Likely story," said Clare. "Go get me some gloves, Kett. The last time I did this, I couldn't get the juices out of my suit for weeks."

"I *swear*! That's all I know."

"Iron Soldiers, right?" said Kett.

"Yeah, the Soldiers," said Craig, tripping over his own words. "This is all them."

"You're going to write us a list of names, just as soon as you get to the station. Understood?"

The man nodded furiously.

"Go," Kett told him. "You're safer in a cell."

Kett slammed the door shut, one hand still on Clare's chest. The constable started the engine, navigating the IRV down the cluttered street. Only when it had turned out of sight did Kett let go of the Superintendent.

"Poor bastard actually believed you were going to stick that baton up his knob, sir," said Kett. "Nice ruse."

"Ruse?" growled Clare, folding the baton away with what looked like disappointment. "What are you talking about?"

"Uh... nothing," he said. "I'll head over to HQ, grill him while he's still terrified."

"I'll do it. That twat struck one of my officers, he's going to regret that for the rest of his life." He flashed Kett a wicked smile. "And I am the Surgeon, after all."

He walked off, calling back.

"I want answers, Kett. None of you are leaving until you've got them."

"Right, sir."

"And find those other dealers."

Kett turned to the pub, breathing out a long sigh that filled the air like smoke. His cravings were back the way they always were on a bad case, especially in the middle of the night, and he chewed on a fingernail to take his mind off them.

"You want me to show you where it all happened?" asked Duke, walking over.

Kett shook his head.

"I just don't get how they knew Jonesy was one of us," said Kett. "Did he say anything? Do anything to give himself away?"

"No, sir. The first guy went for him as soon as he saw

him, grabbed him by the hair. He was screaming at him. We got out to help, and that's when it all kicked off."

"What do you think that guy meant when he pushed Pete down the stairs?" Kett asked. "None of this is what it looks like?"

Duke thought about it for a second as another IRV peeled away, this one containing Porter. He gave them a sad little wave from the back seat.

"Maybe they meant it wasn't a drug thing," said Duke. "Maybe they were going to do to Jonesy what they did to their other victims."

"You think they're all involved?" said Kett. "The entire gang? That makes it infinitely more complicated. You see which way they ran?"

The PC nodded to the open gate that led into the pub gardens.

"I was there, needed to show Ed where to go. Tactical ran in that door, and the lads had already gone, so they must have legged it the other way. Back towards the city."

Back towards the city, back towards the underpass and the park.

"Let's check it out," said Kett. "Grab a couple of Uniforms, will you?"

He set off, passing the empty tactical van as he headed around the front of the pub. The street here was pretty much deserted, darkness gathering between the small houses and beneath the bulk of the apartment blocks. By the time he'd figured out which way to go, Duke had bounded over with three constables at his heels. They walked in silence, not wanting to disturb the people who slept behind the curtained windows. It was well after two, the city deserted, no sound at all other than a couple of distant sirens from the other side of the river.

After a few minutes, Kett emerged from a narrow street onto the main road. This, too, was empty. On the far side of it, Chapelfield Gardens slept deeply. Only the underpass seemed awake, still marked off with police tape. Soft lights watched him over a mouth of pure darkness. It reminded him of one of those trapdoor spiders, ready to strike.

Anything could have been in there, waiting. Hollenbeck's soldiers, their knives glinting. The guy from the Sportspark, Harrison Baird. A bunch of wannabe gangsters.

A serial killer.

"Aaron, can you lot go check the park?" he said, nodding to the underpass. "Go that way. Stick together. If you see them, radio for tactical."

Duke nodded, leading his pack towards the slope with a drum of footsteps. Kett watched as the underpass swallowed them all, then he turned his attention to the rest of the street. Some of the lights were broken, probably smashed by the gangs. The rest did a poor job of holding off the darkness, the weight of the night smothering everything. Only Norvic House, the glass office building, showed any sign of life, the lobby lit up. In the dark, it had lost its colour—its windows black rather than blue through its cage of scaffolding.

With no better ideas, Kett headed over to it, tapping the top of each bollard as he walked up to the door. He cupped a hand to the tinted glass, peering through to see a small reception area filled with boxes. The white walls had been covered by a tapestry of graffiti, the brown carpet pulled up like somebody had been looking for treasure.

He rapped his knuckles on the glass, the sound barely making it through the heavy door. He waited a minute or so, then thumped again, using his fist this time. Another minute passed before Terry Prince limped down the stairs in his black jeans and jacket, his round, red face knuckled with anger. He was still wearing those gloves. In one hand, he held a torch, shining it at the door even though all the lights were on.

In the other, he held what looked like a short truncheon.

"Who's there?" he yelled, his voice muffled by the glass. "Piss off, this is private property."

"It's the police, Terry," said Kett, one hand to his face against the glare of the torch. "Can you let me in?"

Terry didn't seem to trust him, keeping the torch in his face until he was on the other side of the glass. There, he clicked it off, sliding the truncheon through his belt before using a heavy set of keys to unlock the door. He pulled it open with no small effort, waving Kett inside with the torch. The man stank so strongly of alcohol that Kett felt drunk just walking past him.

"Can't be too careful, mate," said Terry. "Been all sorts of pricks out there tonight."

"Like who?" asked Kett, shivering as he walked in. Even though it was chilly outside, the building had no right to be this cold. The air conditioning had to be on, and cranked to its lowest setting.

"Usual suspects," he said, wiping his nose with his gloved hand. "Stupid little boys playing hard men. See how hard they are when they've had a whack."

"Yeah, I saw the truncheon," said Kett.

"Not illegal," said Terry. "Read your rulebook, mate."

"I'm not here about that. You saw some lads, right? When was this?"

"An hour ago, maybe?" said Terry. "Running past like silly buggers, laughing their heads off."

"Three of them?"

"Two," he said. "Heading from the estate."

"They weren't with anyone else?"

"Could've been. I wasn't watching them."

"You didn't see where they went?"

"Like I said, I wasn't watching. Got better things to be doing."

It really was freezing in here, cold enough to make Kett feel like his clothes were damp. He could barely stop his teeth from chattering.

"You got the air on?" he asked.

Terry looked around, then shrugged.

"Nothing to do with me," he said. "Place does its own thing."

From somewhere upstairs came a clang of metal, something falling. Terry didn't react.

"You on your own in here?" asked Kett.

Terry lifted his free hand, wiping his rubbery lips. His glove was so caked in filth that it left black smears on his skin.

"What does that have to do with you?" he said.

"You didn't hear the news?"

"About the woman in the park?" said Terry. "I heard. Her own bloody fault, if you ask me, wandering about in the night by herself. Women shouldn't be out on their own. They should be escorted."

Kett didn't even know where to start with that.

"That's why I do this job," said Terry, slurring the end of the sentence. "Keep all the women safe. World's full of dragons, but lucky for them it's full of knights, too."

"I can't tell you how reassured that makes me, as the father of three girls," said Kett.

Terry nodded with satisfaction, missing the sarcasm altogether. He scratched his nose again, those tattoos peeking past the end of his gloves. Kett saw the sharp angles of a square.

Or a Swastika, maybe.

"You find the person who did that to her?" said Terry.

"Not yet," said Kett.

"Sometimes these things happen for a reason. Reminds people the world ain't what it used to be. One person dies to encourage the rest of 'em to be a little bit more sensible. You get what I'm saying?"

"No," said Kett. "Not really. Why the gloves, Terry?"

The security guard stared at them like he'd forgotten he was wearing them.

"Because it's cold," he said, his dull eyes meeting Kett's. "And, again, why is it any of your business?"

More rattling sounds were coming from somewhere in the building, but it might have been the rig of scaffolding. The wind had picked up.

"You mind if I have a look around?" he asked.

Terry thought about it for a moment.

"I don't," he said, licking his lips. "But the owners might, if you haven't got a warrant. You want me to call 'em?"

Kett shook his head as he hauled the front door open. The air that rushed in was warmer than the air in the lobby.

"Always a pleasure, Mr Prince."

"You know, I'm not sure whether to say this or not," the man said. "Because I don't like you much, and I don't think you deserve it. But I saw that man again."

"What man?"

"What man do you think? The one I saw on Friday night. The one in the mask."

Kett took a step towards him.

"You saw the same man?"

"Wasn't a mask, though," said Terry. "I think it was a helmet. Looked like a robot."

The man laughed to himself. Kett felt like slapping the smile off his face.

"This is the same guy you saw on Friday night, right after a woman was murdered? Am I right?"

Terry shrugged, still swaying.

"And you didn't think to call the police? When was this?"

"I don't know. About an hour ago. Two, maybe. He was heading up the road right there. All in black, with this black helmet."

Kett turned to the road, feeling breathless, like he was drowning in the night.

"You're sure?"

"Maybe. Maybe not. Maybe it was just a hood. It was dark, and I was upstairs, and there's all this fucking scaffolding, and I can't see—"

"Can't see for shit anymore," Kett finished for him. "Yeah, I remember."

He nodded up the street.

"Going that way?"

Terry nodded.

"Gliding," he said, moving his hand smoothly through the air. "Like a ghost."

"Stay here," said Kett. "I'm sending somebody else to talk to you."

"Why?" said Terry. "Fuck have I done?"

Kett didn't answer, fishing his phone from his pocket as he walked back to the road. He called Clare, who answered after the first ring.

"You found them?" he asked.

"No," said Kett. "But I found something else. The security guard at Norvic House says he might have seen our man in the mask heading out of the city an hour ago. Same direction as the lads."

"The same guy?" said Clare. "On foot? What the hell does that mean?"

The answer was obvious, and the Superintendent must have known it. But Kett said it anyway.

"It means he's going to kill again, sir."

CHAPTER NINETEEN

Savage couldn't remember the last time she'd woken up without something else's tongue in her mouth.

She stirred, stretching in the soft, empty bed. She must have left the curtains open a crack last night because a beam of pure sunlight had found its way into the room, curled up on the duvet like a cat. It was pure bliss for the five or so seconds it took her to realise Colin the dog wasn't in the room, waking her up with the usual combination of fishy breath and dripping slobber.

Duke wasn't here either. Not that he ever woke her up with a snog.

She slid her phone off the nightstand, seeing that it had just gone seven. She had two missed calls from Clare, the last one from a minute ago. It must have woken her. She sat on the edge of the bed to call him back, midway through a yawn, when he answered.

"Oh, I'm sorry, Kate," he said. "You sound tired. Why don't you just go back to sleep for a while, snuggle in with your new friend, enjoy some sweet, sleepover dreams?"

"Sorry, sir, I—"

"Or better yet, get your arse out of bed and *get to work!*"

She sprang to her feet, grabbing the bedpost as a head rush threatened to bring her down again.

"I need you in Earlham," Clare said. "The primary school. *Now*, Kate."

She heard him suck in a breath that she might have mistaken for a sob if it had been anybody else.

"They've found another one."

"Not a child, sir?" she said, but it was to an empty line.

She hurled the phone onto the bed and ran into the hallway, knocking on the door of the second bedroom.

"Steph," she said, easing it open. "You awake?"

Cafferty wasn't there to answer her. The bed was empty, the sheets pulled up over the pillows in a sloppy attempt to make it. The sergeant's bag was under the window, but her clothes had gone.

Savage headed into the kitchen. Colin was nowhere to be seen, and when she peeked down the stairs, she saw that the dog's lead had disappeared as well.

"What?" she said, her stomach sinking like a stone in the sea. "Colin? Where are you, girl?"

She ran back to her room, picking up her phone and finding Cafferty's number. It had only just started to ring when she heard a key in the lock of the front door, followed by a soft, familiar bark that chased away the worst of her anxiety.

She headed back to the stairs, expecting to see Duke, but it was Cafferty who was struggling to get inside, tripping over the excited dog. They both looked knackered, and there was a smudge of blood on the woman's tracksuit trousers.

"Sorry," said Cafferty when she saw Savage watching

her. "Did I wake you? I borrowed your keys, and your dog. I hope you don't mind."

The visiting sergeant winced.

"Oh God, you mind, don't you? You were spark out of it, and I couldn't sleep, and I usually go for a run in the morning, but Colin was getting excited, and I didn't want her to wake you up, so I told her she could come. I didn't realise she was allergic to actually moving, it took us about half an hour to get around the block. I was jogging on the spot for most of it. Then she spotted a squirrel and she turned into Seabiscuit, pulled me over a wall into somebody's garden. Cut my leg on a rock, and I nearly bloody lost her."

She wore such a nervous smile that Savage felt sorry for her.

"Are you alright?" she said.

"Well, it's put me off exercise, that's for sure. Are *you* alright?"

"I'm fine. It's just Colin's my alarm clock, I didn't realise how late it was."

Cafferty unclipped the dog's collar, and the staffie galloped up the stairs as fast as her legs could carry her. She was getting older, bless her. It had been almost five years since Kett had rescued her from the breeder, only his second case in the county. It could have been a million years ago. She still kissed like a young thing, though, slobbering over Savage's face when she hefted her up, full of pure love and excitement the way only dogs could be.

"Easy," said Savage, managing a smile for the moment or two it took her to remember the news she needed to pass on. "The Superintendent has asked for us, Steph. They've found another body."

Cafferty was halfway up the stairs, and her face fell.

"Shit," she said.

"Yep," said Savage, putting down the dog. "Shit."

THE PRIMARY SCHOOL in Earlham was pretty much unchanged since it had been built in the Victorian times. The red-brick building sat behind a wrought-iron fence that would have been better suited to a prison. Separate gates marked Boys and Girls led into the wide playground, and Savage broke the rules by going through the former. She was surprised to see that only one constable stood by the open door, fanning herself with her hat as the temperature started to climb.

"Going to be another hot one," she said as Savage and Cafferty walked up. "Straight through, take a left."

Savage crossed the deserted reception area into a hallway lined with enormous windows. She could hear somebody sobbing, and she followed the sound past empty rooms until she spotted another constable ahead. Even though he had his back to her, it was immediately obvious who it was. Nobody else's shoulders would have spanned so much of the corridor.

"Aaron?" she said.

Duke turned around, exhaustion written in the lines of his forehead. He gave her a tired smile, opening his arms instinctively for a hug, before slapping them to his sides when he saw that Cafferty was there too.

"Kate," he said, and she could hear the same relief in his voice at seeing her that she always felt when she saw him. "I mean, Sarge. Sarg*es*."

"Morning, Duke," said Cafferty, sniffing the air. "How do all schools smell the same as they did when I was a kid?"

The sobbing was coming from the door that Duke was

standing next to, and when Savage peeked through, she saw a classroom bedecked in colourful posters and children's artwork. A woman sat behind a desk, her head in her hands, the sobs ripping through her. A female constable knelt at her feet, one hand on her leg, whispering quiet words of reassurance. Neither of them looked up.

"It's not a child, is it?" Savage asked in a whisper.

Duke shook his head, leaning in.

"Teacher," he said. "Down the end of the hall, I think. I haven't seen the body. Clare's there, and Hay's just arrived."

"Kett?"

"Nobody can get hold of him," said Duke. "He didn't make it home last night, after the pub thing."

"Really?" said Savage.

She remembered the man who'd been at the tournament yesterday morning, the odd Scotsman. Kett had stormed out of the gymnasium when he'd seen him, and he'd come back looking more shaken than he'd been since everything that had happened with Hollenbeck last year. Harrison Baird, he'd called him. In all the chaos of yesterday, she hadn't had a chance to do any digging.

"He'll be fine," said Duke. "Probably sleeping in his car. It was a late one."

It didn't give her much reassurance, and she fired a text to Kett as she continued down the hallway.

You okay?

She turned left at the end of the corridor, passing through a large, cool assembly hall that was full of cardboard scenery, including a monstrous, bug-eyed whale that could have given Stephen King nightmares. Another constable steered them into a shorter corridor lined with empty coat pegs. This one ended at an open door. She hesitated outside it, listening to the soft voice of Cara Hay while she prepared herself for what she might find on the other side.

Not that *anything* could have prepared her for this.

The classroom could have belonged to any primary school in the country. Big windows let in a wave of morning light that splashed past the clay sculptures on the sill and washed over the artwork on the walls. Miniature tables and chairs sat in formation on the carpeted floor, pots of pens and pencils waiting patiently for a class that wouldn't arrive tomorrow morning, or any day soon.

It could have been any school, except for the desk on the far side of the room, where a dead woman now lay.

The desk had been swept clear, a chaos of stationery and books and even a laptop discarded on the floor. The woman's head rested at one end, her legs hanging over the other. Her hands jutted out to her sides, her fingers curled into talons. Her clothes suggested an older woman, a thick, green cardigan and a knee-length tweed skirt over dark tights. There was no sign of her shoes.

Her eyes were open, and even from the door, Savage could see the metallic sheen in them, that same awful semblance of life that every victim had shown, as if she had just woken here.

Lying on the floor beneath her head, crumpled and forgotten, was a white napkin stained with two red circles.

Clare and Hay stood with their backs to the door, but they must have heard Savage's arrival because they both turned to greet her. The Superintendent looked like a dead man walking, his eyes crimson, his skin grey. He snapped his mouth open as if to launch into his usual tirade of abuse, but closed it again without saying a word. When he stepped back to make room for her, he stumbled, almost falling.

"Kate," said Hay. "Sergeant Cafferty. Please, join us."

Savage approached the table, holding her breath—partly from the anticipation, and partly because the air was thick with the stench of blood and metal, as well as something sweet that almost overpowered it all.

The woman who lay on the desk was younger than her wardrobe had suggested. Her face put her in her late twenties, although it was hard to be sure because of the damage that had been done to the tissue around her eyes. The lids had been butchered, ringed with dried blood, the tissue swollen. Her cheeks were sunken, her lips parted slightly as if she wanted to whisper the name of her killer. Her slim neck was mottled with bruises, the skin broken in places from the severity of the attack.

Savage managed to hold the corpse's gaze for thirty seconds before she had to look away. She met Clare's eyes, seeing the same quiet horror there.

"Poor lamb," said Cafferty. "Does anyone know her name?"

"Miss Bartlett?" Savage guessed, reading the bright, rainbow-coloured letters that had been fixed along the top of the whiteboard.

"Judy Bartlett," said Clare, his voice like kicked gravel. "Her colleague discovered her this morning. The woman down the hall. She arrived at the school just before seven and found a window broken. Did a quick search, and..."

"Why was she here so early on a Sunday, sir?" asked Savage when he didn't finish.

"I wondered the same thing," said Clare. "I'm waiting for her to calm down before I start asking questions."

He rubbed his eyes.

"Before *you* start asking questions, I mean," he said when he'd looked up. "This one needs a woman's touch."

Savage nodded, but she didn't head off straight away.

"Same MO?" she said.

"Exactly," answered Hay. "She was strangled, then her eyes were removed. The killer was rushing, almost as much as with our first victim."

She waved her own words away.

"Our *second* victim, I mean. Chronologically. Helen Coulter. Something made him careless."

"Do you know when it happened?" Savage asked.

"Recently," said Hay. "Franklin will be able to tell you with more accuracy, but it's within a couple of hours. She's still warm."

That made it so much worse, thought Savage.

"The good news is that the killer seems to have climbed in through the window, and he may have cut himself. There's blood on the glass."

"That's good," said Savage, although she knew it wouldn't help them. Even if they got a match, it could take days, or weeks.

She made for the door, her heart heavy enough to slow her down. She glanced at Cafferty as she went.

"I'm going to stay here, Kate, if that's okay?" said the sergeant. "I'd like to take a closer look."

Savage had left the room before she thought to turn back.

"Have you heard from Kett, sir?" she asked Clare.

"I'm not his husband, Kate," the Super replied. "As much as the filthy pervert would like me to be. Why?"

"No reason," she said, thinking again of the man at the Sportspark, of the unseen conflict that had been waged outside the gymnasium doors.

Trying not to picture what might have happened to Kett if the man had turned up again.

She made her way back through the warren of the

school, finding the classroom. The crying inside had ebbed a little, the sobs replaced by quiet sniffs. Duke stood a little way along the corridor, looking out of the window onto a little garden area that blazed with flowers. He turned when he sensed her, and this time, seeing that she was alone, he opened his arms. She fell into them, letting him squeeze her so hard she heard her back pop. She took a long breath before she pulled free.

"How bad is it?" he asked.

"As bad as you're imagining," she replied. "Only worse. You alright? You didn't come home."

His reply became a yawn that he had to stifle with both hands, but he managed a nod. The bruise on his face seemed bigger, but she couldn't tell if it was a new one.

Savage walked to the door, seeing the same two women in the classroom. The teacher sat with her elbows on the desk, her face resting on the pillow of her hands, her glasses hanging on a string of beads. She was older than the murdered woman by a couple of decades. She'd been crying so much that her eyes were puffy, and the knot in Savage's stomach tightened further as she thought about the body in the other room, her ruined face. The constable was up on her feet, flustered, and she looked infinitely grateful when Savage walked through the door.

"You can get some air, if you like," Savage told her.

"I might just go and find a kettle," the PC replied. "Get a brew on. Will you be okay, Lisa?"

The teacher nodded as well as her hands would let her. The constable trotted out of the door, and Savage closed it behind her. The teacher sat back, scrubbing her lips, still sniffing.

"Hi, Lisa?" said Savage, crossing the room.

"Yes, that's right," said Lisa, a subtle touch of Scottish in her accent. She put on her glasses to better see Savage, her eyes huge through the greasy lenses. "Unless you want to call me Mrs Graham, like all the other kids."

Savage managed a smile, but it didn't last.

"I just want to say how sorry I am about your colleague."

"Friend," said Lisa. "Not a colleague. Jude was my friend."

The seats were too small to sit on, so Savage stood by the desk. There were a couple of framed photographs on it, stuck to her computer monitor. In one, Lisa stood in a huddle of people, all dressed in climbing gear—hard hats and ropes—with a wall behind them. Everyone was wearing a Christmas jumper. One of the other women in the shot was the same one who now lay dead in the other room.

The picture was too small for Savage to tell what colour her eyes had once been.

"Is that Judy?" she asked, nodding.

Lisa studied the picture for a moment, her face threatening to crumple under a fresh wave of emotion. She peeled the photograph from her monitor, looking at it through her glasses.

"They won't tell me anything," she said. "They won't tell me what happened to her. She's dead?"

Savage nodded.

"I knew she was, I checked for a pulse, I did all the things you're supposed to do." She remembered to breathe, almost choking on her own spit. "What happened to her eyes? They were... They were *metal*. I don't..."

She put down the photograph and took off her glasses, pushing her face into her trembling hand.

"Can you walk me through what happened?" asked Savage. "Why were you both here so early on a Sunday?"

"The play," said Lisa, her face still covered. "This stupid

play, and I shouldn't say that, because it was Jude's idea. She's wanted to do it since she got here, a whole school production. *Pinocchio*. We've still got five donkey heads to stitch together and half a set to paint."

She dropped her hand to the desk, staring at it.

"It's supposed to be on Tuesday, and the kids have worked so hard. I don't know what we're going to tell them."

She started crying again, tears rolling down the soft folds of her face.

"What do we tell them about Jude? They all loved her so much."

Savage pulled a tissue from the box on her desk, passing it over.

"What time did you arrive?"

"I can't remember. I left the house at six-thirty. I'm an early riser, even at the weekends." Lisa blew her nose, balling the tissue in a clenched fist. "It's only a ten-minute drive. The side door was open, so I knew Judy was here. Kettle was boiled. I came right to my class, thought I'd get ahead for a bit, check some emails."

"You didn't look for Judy?"

"I just figured she was busy in the hall, or in her classroom. I thought she'd stop by eventually."

"When did you find her?" said Savage. Lisa screwed up her face, shaking her head. "I know this is hard, but it's important."

"I can't remember," she said, nodding to the clock over the door. "Clock's broken, needs a new battery. I've been asking Ash for one for weeks. I was only in here fifteen minutes, though, and I started..."

She sat back, putting a hand on her stomach.

"I just had this feeling. I can't explain it. You know when you just *know* that something's not right?"

Savage nodded.

"Now that I think about it, maybe it was the breeze. It's usually stifling in here, especially when the weather's like this. But there was this wind. I didn't really notice it, just that something was wrong. I'm not explaining it very well, sorry. Call myself an English teacher."

"You're doing great," said Savage. "Go on."

"I went out there," Lisa said, speaking to the door. "Checked Holly's class next door, then Geoff's, the next one down. That's when I saw the window. Somebody had smashed it, glass all over the floor. Just assumed it was kids. Wouldn't be the first time they've put a brick through the window. You get a fair bit of trouble around here."

"Did you try to clean it up?" asked Savage. "You didn't cut yourself, did you?"

"No. That's Ash's job, I won't do it. I hate glass. But I started wondering if maybe Judy had broken it, if she'd had an accident. So I went to her... I went to her class."

The teacher lifted her head, holding back the tears like somebody trying to hold back a moving car.

"I thought she was having a rest, on her desk. So stupid. I was... was talking to her, I walked right up, laughing, and... She had this cloth over her face, with paint on it, and even when I took it off, I just thought she was pulling my leg. I thought she had some kind of props, for the play. Silver contact lenses. And..."

She gestured to her own face.

"Makeup. I thought it was makeup."

Savage saw her horror as she experienced it again, the same way she would every single hour of every single day for the rest of her life.

"I did try to bring her back. She was, she didn't feel dead, she wasn't cold. I *tried*."

"Nothing would have helped her," said Savage. "She was long gone before you got here."

She didn't know that for sure, of course, but she didn't want the woman living with what might have been.

"Did you hear anything? See anything? Smell anything? Especially in Judy's room."

"No," said Lisa. "Just the broken window, and... there *was* a smell, something metallic. And..."

She sniffed the air as she tried to remember.

"A man's smell, old and... I don't know, unpleasant."

"Sweat?" asked Savage. "BO?"

"More like dirty clothes," she said. "Some of the children here have the same smell, when their parents maybe don't wash their clothes as much as they should. And something else, almost like a perfume. Floral."

She shook her head, struggling.

"I'm not helping much, sorry."

There was a knock on the door, and the constable let herself in, three mugs of tea gripped in one hand.

"Sorry," she said. "Thought these might help."

She set them down on the desk, spilling more than a little.

"Shoot, sorry."

Savage picked up a framed photo before it could drown, waiting for the PC to mop up the mess with a wad of tissues.

"Lisa, do you have any idea why somebody would do this to Judy?"

"Goodness, no," said the teacher. "She was a ray of sunlight, Jude, as good as they come. She brought a new lease of life to the whole school when she arrived, pulled us all out of the muck of a bad Ofsted, gave us hope."

"When did she start here?"

"Half term," she said. "Just a couple of months ago. It

was only supposed to be maternity cover for Maggie, but everyone loved her so much they gave her a permanent position."

"Do you know where she moved here from? Another teaching job?"

"Yes. A primary school in the city. Bignold."

Savage leaned in just to make sure she'd heard her right.

"Bignold? The school next to the park, right next to Chapelfield Gardens? You're sure?"

Lisa nodded.

"Do you know if she lived around there?"

"I know she used to," she said. "She moved to this side of the city with the job. She's only renting."

"Was there a reason she left Bignold?" Savage asked. "Any unwanted admirers, anyone on the staff who made her feel uncomfortable? A boyfriend? Anything at all."

Lisa was crying again, hollowed out by the tears.

"I think she wanted a change. I got the feeling things were hard there. Bad memories. She never really talked about it."

Savage pulled a business card from her pocket and laid it next to the woman's mug.

"If you think of anything else, anything that might help, call me. We're going to find the person who did this to Judy."

To all of them, she added silently, thinking of Helen, and of Idris. She pushed herself away from the desk, heading for the door, only turning back when Lisa started to speak again.

"I hope you *don't* find him," the woman said.

"What?" asked Savage, surprised. "Why?"

The woman studied her with those sad, swollen eyes.

"Because then he might do this to you, too."

CHAPTER TWENTY

The sound of gunshots pulled Kett out of a dream of dodgeballs and Scotsmen.

He lurched upright, his knees cracking into something, his back spasming in protest. He couldn't work out where he was until he'd rubbed the sleep from his eyes. Then he saw the steering wheel, the empty passenger seat, and the face that was glaring at him through the fogged-up window.

A hand smacked itself against the glass again, that same crack of gunfire, and the door handle rattled.

"Can you hear me?" said a voice. "You can't be here."

Kett had to turn the key to get the electrics working, and when he wound the window down, he saw a uniformed PC standing there. Two more were positioned behind him, alert. They all stood down when they recognised his face.

"Sorry, sir," said the first copper. "Didn't know it was you. You alright? Do you need some help?"

"Help?" said Kett.

The PC looked at the other men, as if looking for reassurance. When he turned back to Kett, he had a nervous smile on his face. He recognised him as one of the officers he'd tasked last night with keeping an eye on the office block by the park, and on Terry Prince, the security guard.

"Nothing, sir," he said. "We're around if you need us. Did you hear?"

"Hear?" said Kett, who was still incapable of more than one word at a time.

"They've found another body," said the man. "Another woman. A teacher."

"Shit," muttered Kett, his brain finally awake.

He collected his phone from the central console, greeted by a low battery warning and ten text messages from Clare. They began fairly innocuously with 'Where are you?', then worked their way through a colourful spectrum of swear words and physical threats, ending with, 'And then I'll turn your tailbone into a fork and use it to eat your bollocks, you insufferable wank!' That one came in closer to four, which was—he checked the time—a little over three hours ago.

"Shit," he said again.

There was one message from Savage, asking if he was okay, and another from Porter, which he must have sent by mistake.

I love you, can't wait to curl up with you, big hugs and lots of kisses.

At least, he *hoped* it had been sent by mistake.

"Office?" he grunted to the copper in the window.

"No movement all night," said the PC. "In or out. Body's over in Earlham. The primary school."

"Thanks."

It took Kett a moment to get his bearings, because he couldn't for the life of him remember going to sleep. After speaking with Terry Prince, the arsehole security guard from Norvic House, he'd roamed the streets for a while looking for the men who'd attacked Porter, or the guy in the mask—if they were different people, of course. When the search had proved fruitless, he'd walked to his car, fully intending to head back to HQ. He must have closed his eyes for a moment, and sleep had ambushed him.

"You're getting old," he said as he navigated through the quiet city. "Too old for this, anyway."

The street that led up to the primary school was mobbed with emergency vehicles, and he parked behind them. When he flipped the mirror down to make sure he was presentable, he almost screamed. No wonder the PC who'd woken him had asked if he was okay. There was a trail of drool running from his chapped lips to his stubbled chin, and his eyes were red-raw from exhaustion. The grey patches around his temples were spreading like mould on bread, and in the unforgiving morning light, the number of wrinkles around his eyes seemed to have doubled.

"Too old," he said again. "Go home, Robbie. Get a better job."

Before this one kills you.

He found Savage sitting on a picnic bench in the playground, DS Cafferty perched on the edge of the table. Both had their eyes closed as they soaked up the sun that had climbed over the pitched roof of the old school building.

"Morning," he said as he walked up. "Do we know who she is?"

"Sir," said Savage, opening her eyes. She looked relieved to see him. "Yeah, her name's Judith Bartlett. Judy. She's thirty-one, worked here as a Year 3 teacher. Started in September after moving from another school. Bignold."

"Bignold?" said Kett.

This was a little too close to home. His own girls had been students there until they'd moved into their new house three years ago, after the King Rat case. He searched his memory, trying to recall if there had been a teacher called Miss Bartlett, but he came up blank.

"She was after your time," said Savage, reading his mind. "Started there in 2022."

"That's weird, though," said Kett. "Because we're miles away from the other victims here, the other side of the city. But Bignold's right next to where we found Helen and Idris. A stone's throw."

"Right," said Savage. "Doesn't feel like a coincidence."

The main door of the school opened, and what looked like a cartoon vampire staggered out, long arms waving at the sky as if he was trying to attack the sun. The Superintendent's head swivelled around, red eyes finding Kett. He crossed the playground towards them at speed, grunting.

"Just to warn you," said Savage, "he's in a foul mood."

"When isn't he?" said Kett.

"I'll tell you when," said Clare, who seemed to have the hearing of a bat. "When Fiona and I are enjoying our string bikinis and string cheese nights. That's when. You're the only bowl of monkey toss who makes me angry, because you're the only one who makes stuff like this happen."

"Wow," said Cafferty. "Rude."

Clare loomed over them. It might have been Kett's imagination, but he thought he saw steam coming out of the Superintendent's nose.

"Just putting it on record that I didn't make *this* happen," grumbled Kett.

"Where did you disappear to?" said Clare. "I thought we'd got lucky, and you'd fallen down a hole. Did you find anyone? Our drug dealers, perhaps?"

"No, sir," said Kett.

"Did you do anything useful, other than toss yourself in your car?"

"Wasn't tossing my—"

"And why do you look like an old shoe fished out of the canal?"

Kett didn't even know how to answer this one.

"You heard about the teacher?" said Clare, dropping onto another picnic bench.

"Yeah," said Kett. "Kate filled me in. We were just saying, we're a long way from his last two victims here, but she used to work at Bignold. That's a geographical link."

"Exactly," said Savage. "We thought the victims might be random. A white woman in her sixties who worked as a nurse, then a black kid in his twenties who might have links to the dealers. Helen and Idris live five minutes from each other. Judy works here, and she's got a house right over the road. No connection at all. Random. Except..."

"Except she used to live and work in the same neighbourhood," said Cafferty, taking over. "Until last year, she rented a room on, uh, Newmarket Street, was it? Right around the corner from the Walpole, and she taught in the school on the estate."

"So the killer came all the way over here to target her," said Kett. "He could have picked anyone from that side of town, but he chose Judy, and he had to travel across the city in order to find her. Did you get my messages, sir, about the security guard?"

Clare seemed to have shut down, fixed on something in the middle distance. It sounded a little like he was snoring.

"Sir?" said Kett.

Clare snorted, his eyes swimming back into focus.

"Were you *asleep*?" asked Kett.

"I'll put you to sleep," the man growled back, wiping his mouth. "Like a sick dog. What are you blabbing about?"

"The security guard at the tower said he'd seen a man in

a mask walking down Chapelfield Road, about an hour before we all got there. One, maybe. Same guy he'd seen on Friday, right after Helen was killed. Trouble is, he admits he can't see very well, and both times I've talked to him he's been drunk."

"Bit suspicious that he's looking out of the window at the precise time our killer has walked past," said Cafferty. "*Twice.* It's a big building."

"Right," said Kett, nodding.

"You think it's him?" asked Savage. "He works nights. There's every chance he could have slipped out and come here."

"I put a car outside the tower," said Kett. "Nobody saw him leave, although they can't have had eyes on every door. Terry Prince is a nasty piece of work, but I'm not sure if he fits the profile you guys made up for our serial killer."

"It's just a profile," said Cafferty. "We could be wrong."

"Let's say, for the moment, that Prince is telling the truth," said Kett. "He happened to see a masked man walk out of the underpass right after Helen was killed. Let's say this guy in the mask is the killer. He saw him again in the middle of the night, walking down the street with the same mask on. Why? Why would he risk being caught? There were police everywhere in the city last night, and any one of them would have stopped him when they saw the mask. What's he thinking?"

Savage and Cafferty glanced at each other, but Cafferty took the lead.

"It could be part of his ritual, sir. He needs to wear the mask for some reason, not just to kill, but for the whole process. It's part of his identity. Without it, he's human. With it, he's something more, somebody who is capable of anything. It will make him reckless, like he was last night. It will make him easier to catch."

She pulled out her pocket square and immediately began to fold it again.

"Maybe," she added, suddenly unsure.

"No, that's good," said Savage. "That makes sense."

"But?" said Kett, seeing the doubt on her face.

"I'm not sure, but it could be that he *wants* to get caught. He wants somebody to stop him. I mean, he's covering his victims' faces. The white cloths, the tarpaulin in the pub. Maybe he's ashamed. This is a compulsion, something he knows is wrong, but he can't control, and he can't stop. It's a... Like a cry for help."

Cafferty nodded respectfully.

"That's clever, Kate," she said.

"I mean, not as clever as yours," Savage told her. "But thanks."

"Good team," said Cafferty.

"Good team," Savage echoed, and they knocked their knuckles together.

"Stop fisting each other," said Clare.

"Oh, God, sir," said Savage. "We weren't—"

"This is all speculation, and it's useless," the Superintendent went on, standing up. "If we want to find the killer, we have to work out why he's targeting these specific people."

He lobbed a set of keys at Kett far too hard for him to stand any chance of catching them. Cafferty jumped off the table to fetch them.

"I want you lot inside Judy's house, see if there are any answers there."

"Yes, sir," said Kett. "Where are you going?"

"Somewhere dark and quiet," said Clare, slouching off. "So I can curl up and die."

JUDY BARTLETT'S house was another narrow terrace, this one built sometime in the last twenty years. Despite its youth, it seemed to be falling apart, the porch light hanging off the wall, the step cracked in two, and one of the numbers missing from the front door. The door itself did everything it could to resist them, even though they had the key. It had warped in the heat, grinding across a scar on the floor.

There was nothing in the hall except for a slim console and a mirror. Two coats hung from cat-shaped pegs on the wall, and Kett felt the same rush of vertigo he always did when he visited the homes of the dead, knowing that the young woman would never wear those articles of clothing again.

Judy had done her best to make the place feel homely, but it was obvious that she'd rented it, rather than bought. The walls were all magnolia, riddled with hairline cracks, the floors in the hallway and kitchen were cheap lino, the carpets everywhere else cheaper still. The living room had a single sofa that looked like it had been rescued from a skip, and Kett was surprised to see a ginger cat lying on it. The thing was so ancient it looked mummified, watching him with rheumy eyes.

"Hi," he said, letting it sniff his gloved fingers. It butted his hand, its purr louder than a diesel generator. "Sorry," he added. "About your mum."

There were a couple of books on the coffee table, and a stack of loose photos next to the TV. He picked them up, shuffling through them to see the young woman with her friends, her parents, her co-workers, the children she'd worked with. One was taken in the hall at Bignold, the same hall he'd gone to watch dozens of assemblies and Nativities when his girls had been there, and which he'd performed in himself when he was a child. It felt far too close to home.

He put the photos back, spotting an empty frame leaning against the low window ledge. It was the kind that let you add an assortment of photos, and Kett wondered how long Judy had been planning to add these pictures to it. It was one of those jobs people always seemed to put off. He'd done it himself, so many times. You waited weeks, months, years.

And sometimes, you ran out of time.

He sighed, feeling impossibly heavy as he trudged out of the room. Savage was in the kitchen, going through the drawers, and she shook her head as he passed the door. He made his way upstairs instead, finding a spare room that had been done up like a crafting space. One table held an abundance of colour—craft paper, pipe cleaners, pompoms, hundreds of pens and pencils, and pots of glitter. A smaller desk boasted two parakeets made up of toilet rolls and feathers, seashells for beaks.

Judy hadn't got as far as adding the eyes yet, and the vacant spaces turned Kett's stomach.

He rifled through a couple of drawers, finding some more photos, these in albums. They were much older pictures, many of Judy when she was a child. He could look at only a handful before he had to set them down.

He left the spare room, almost tripping on another cat that was creeping out of the bedroom. This one was younger, but it looked in bad shape. Half the fur on its back was missing, the skin red and flaking. He bent down to give it a scratch, but it darted for the stairs, clattering down at speed.

Kett pushed into the bedroom, seeing what he expected to see: a perfectly made bed, floral curtains tied back on hooks, two small bookcases overflowing with paperbacks, one topped with a vase of dried flowers. The wardrobe held a handful of outfits, all of them bright and cheery, as well as a pair of pastel pink Jimmy Choos still in their box. They looked like they'd never been worn.

He stopped at the chest of drawers, finding a stack of notes on the top. They had been written by children, clumsy words and bad spellings and crude drawings. Each one was a letter of love to a teacher who had obviously been adored by everyone she'd ever had in her class.

We will miss you so much.

Please take me with you, Miss Bartlett.

You have to come back and visit us every day or we'll be too sad :(

He put the letters back where he'd found them, taking a moment to let the tears come. He was scrubbing them away when he heard somebody climbing the stairs.

"Sir?" said Savage.

She stood in the doorway, finding this just as hard as he did. He'd known Savage for long enough to see the silent question in her expression—*are you okay?*—and he shook his head.

"Why would anyone go after a woman like Judy?" he asked.

"Because some people are monsters," she said.

"You find anything downstairs?"

"No, sir. She rented, paid everything on time. Both cats are rescues, she's been covering their medical treatment for years.

Her laptop is on the kitchen table, no password. I've had a glance through her texts and emails, and there's nothing. No apparent partner, no arguments, she's in touch with her parents—they're up in Manchester. Friends all seem to love her."

She shrugged.

"Everyone seems to love her."

Kett looked at the letters again, then at the neat little bedroom.

"Everyone seemed to love Helen, too," he said. "She was a nurse, and when she wasn't on the clock she was volunteering. The kid in the pub, as well. Idris. His parents said he helped in the food banks, and he worked with the local kids, ran football clubs for them. Is that what this is?"

He turned to Savage.

"Is that what connects them? Their selflessness? Their kindness?"

"I hope not, sir," she replied, frowning. "Because a killer who picks their victims—who strangles them, who pulls their eyes out—just because they're good people. I mean, that's..."

She didn't have a word for it.

And even with all those years on the job—all those cases, all those killers and all their dead, all the madness and the murder and the mourning—neither did he.

CHAPTER TWENTY-ONE

Porter sat in the passenger seat of the IRV, stifling a yawn with his hand as he watched the city roll past. He had a munter of a headache, partly because he hadn't slept in twenty-six hours, and partly thanks to the little scrote who'd pushed him down the stairs in the pub.

He'd made it to the hospital at around half-four, for a once-over, but he'd walked out again after three hours, still unseen. For all he knew, he had a massive concussion and would keel over dead by the end of the day, but that was infinitely better than spending any more time in A&E with the drunks and the druggies and the endless parade of weirdos.

And Duke, of course.

The big PC was driving, humming a tune beneath his breath as he navigated the empty roads. He looked like he'd just woken from a fourteen-hour nap, eaten a hearty breakfast, then enjoyed some kind of rejuvenating face massage, which was even more annoying given he'd had just as little sleep as Porter.

"Bastard," he grumbled, catching a glimpse of his own haggard, dark-eyed face in the side mirror.

"What, sir?" said Duke.

"Nothing."

He checked his phone, but Allie still hadn't replied to his text. She'd be in a grump with him because he hadn't made it home last night. The sad truth was she'd have been in a grump with him even if he *had* made it home. She'd have been in a grump with him if he'd let her have a fourteen-hour nap, cooked her a hearty breakfast, and then paid for her to enjoy a rejuvenating face massage. He didn't seem to be able to do anything right these days.

It wasn't unusual, of course. Kids put a strain on even the most loving marriages. And it wasn't like his and Allie's relationship had ever fit that description.

I sense a terrible coldness between you and the boy's mother, that crazy old bat had told him yesterday. Bullshit, of course, but through sheer luck, she'd managed to hit the nail right on the head. Things had been cold between them for a long time now, not just since Bobby had been born. Porter thought back, trying to remember a time in the last few years when Allie had ever been warm to him.

It broke his heart that he couldn't think of a single one.

But this severance can be mended. Find your warmth, or lose it forever.

The trouble was, they'd been out in the cold for so long, Porter couldn't remember how to be warm either. The two of them were stranded on ice floes, drifting further apart, and he wasn't sure if even Bobby's golden glow could stop them from freezing to death in the dark.

He started a sigh that became another yawn.

"You sure you don't want me to drop you home, sir?" said Duke. "You look knackered."

"I'm fine," he said. "*You* look bloody knackered."

As if to confirm it, Duke yawned too, his gaping mouth unhinging like a python's, sucking all of the air out of the car. It seemed to go on forever.

"You know, Aaron, it's customary for people to cover their mouths when they yawn," he said.

"Sorry, sir," said Duke. "I can't. Hands are on the wheeeeee—"

The last word stretched into another yawn, this one even longer.

"Besides," he said when he'd finished. "It is covered. That's what a beard is for."

"That's a beard?" said Porter, his temper like a fraying rope. "I thought you had a fetish for Victorian merkins."

"What?"

"Thought you'd superglued a dead weasel to your face."

Porter squinted at the constable.

"Maybe a live one."

"You know, jealousy isn't a good look on you," said Duke. "It's not your fault you can't grow a beard."

"Bloody can," said Porter. "Be twice as big as that dusty fart on your face."

"It's all in the genetics," Duke went on, fluffing his beard with one hand.

"Yeah? What are you related to? A grizzly bear's arsehole?"

"Least my chin doesn't look like a soft-boiled egg," said Duke. "Don't blame yourself, testosterone levels decrease when you're getting on a bit."

"What are you saying, Constable?" said Porter, the heat rising in his face.

"Just stating facts, sir," he said, a smile twitching

beneath his beard. "You can get supplements. Few pills and you'll grow a bit of bumfluff in no time."

Porter glared at him so hard he was surprised that the PC's beard didn't shrivel. He was about to hammer home the difference in their rank again when Duke turned the corner and slammed on the brakes.

A crowd of people stood in the middle of the street that led onto the estate, maybe fifty of them, a sea of angry faces. Most were adults, but kids ran back and forth from pavement to pavement, their laughter even louder than the shouts. A handful of uniformed coppers were doing their best to encourage everyone off the road, but they weren't having much luck.

"Changed my mind," said Porter. "Take me home."

"Really?" said Duke.

Porter didn't dignify this with an answer. He opened his door, the heat flooding in even though it was still early. The air was full of shouts, and more people were spilling from the neighbouring buildings, gathering at the back of the mob.

"Hell's going on?" Porter yelled at the closest constable as he walked over.

"Word's got out about the boy in the pub," she answered, her eyes never leaving the crowd. "They're pretty pissed."

"Wait until they hear about the next one," he muttered. "Got any more Uniforms?"

"I've asked, sir, but there's not many of us about."

She gave him an apologetic shrug.

"Alright, let them do what they're doing," he said. "Just try and keep it to this street. Get Duke to move his car, will you? Block the junction, make sure nobody gets flattened."

He walked towards the crowd, his hands up.

"Can I have your attention?" he called out, his voice swallowed by the wave of noise. "Just for a second. Hello?"

He hammered on the bonnet of an IRV, the sound of it like a gong. If anything, it seemed to rile his audience even more. One woman, somewhere in her thirties and the size of a small car, pushed to the front of the group.

"What are you doing to keep us safe, eh?" she said. "Our kids? When are you going to catch him?"

This earned a cheer of approval.

"He's killing us," said another woman. "Two dead, when's he going to do it again? We want answers!"

Porter spotted a couple of reporters jogging this way from the far end of the street, one of them carrying a camera on his shoulder. The noise of the crowd was swelling.

"Look," he yelled. "We're doing everything we can to find the person responsible for this, but for now, I need you all off the road."

This hit the crowd like a cup of lighter fluid hitting a fire. They surged forward a few feet, all shouting at once.

"Typical cop," somebody yelled. "More worried about us than a fucking serial killer."

"Wanker!" screamed somebody else.

Duke appeared next to him, one hand on his canister of PAVA. His eyes were like gimlets as he surveyed the mob.

"What are you going to do?" boomed one man. "Arrest us? Why don't you try?"

"For your safety," Porter started, and he stopped when a plastic bottle of Fanta sailed over the heads of the people, hitting the ground a few feet away from where he was standing. It split, orange liquid spraying everywhere, the bottle spinning.

A mighty cheer rose from the crowd.

"Oi!" Porter roared. "Pack it in!"

He was only making things worse, so he backed off, earning another cheer as he tripped on the kerb. His head was pounding, and he felt sick, too. He rubbed his mouth, seeing more people arriving by the second. There were some familiar faces here, people he'd spoken to when they went door-to-door yesterday. He spotted one: a short guy with a shock of white hair.

"Aaron, call Clare," he said. "Tell him we've got a situation developing."

As if to confirm it, a chant had broken out.

"We want justice, we want safety."

A handful of people were trying to get a 'Fuck the police!' started too, although it didn't seem to be catching on. Porter kept an eye on them, making a mental note of the ringleaders, then he cut around the edge of the crowd, heading for the man.

"Hey," he said, clicking his fingers. "Uh... Junior?"

It had been a guess, but he'd got it right. The guy squinted through the heaving bodies, frowning until he recognised Porter's face. He weaved his way over, offering a wary smile. He was wearing Christmas pyjamas, Porter saw, little elves pulling crackers, and he had his phone in his hand.

"Alright," said Junior, fighting to make himself heard. "I've forgotten your name, sorry."

"Pete. Porter. What's going on, mate?"

Junior studied the crowd for a moment, taking a photograph on his phone. He glanced back to where the children were playing. There were more of them now, celebrating like this was a street party, not a protest. He waved at one of the lads, who was too busy shooting a water pistol at a couple of girls to notice. A good thirty seconds had passed before he turned back to Porter.

"People are saying someone else is dead?" he said. "A kid?"

There was no point in denying it.

"Yeah. Local lad, a teenager. We're still trying to work out an ID, and figuring out what—"

"Iddy, right?" said Junior. "The Mellor kid."

"We don't know that for—"

"That's why we're angry," said Junior. He held his hands up to show he didn't want to start a fight, but the expression on his face said otherwise. "Just saying, mate. What are you doing? First that nurse, then Iddy? And then you come here and try to start something with *us*?"

"We're not starting anything, Junior," said Porter.

With almost perfect timing, a siren bleeped from the far end of the road. Two IRVs were rolling up, the fierce sun subduing their lights, bleaching the windscreens. Junior took a couple of photographs of them, then he spun the camera around and took one of Porter, too.

"We're not," Porter insisted. "We're here to find whoever did this. We're here to make sure they never do it again. But we can't do our jobs if you lot are in the way."

"In the way?" said Junior, a little more of his friendliness ebbing. "We're not in the way of anything. We're here making sure nothing else happens, you get me? I said it to you yesterday, if you don't do something about the violence, somebody else will."

He stepped closer, looking up at Porter.

"I promised Emma I'd keep them safe. She didn't even want to leave them here this morning. And look, look what's going on right outside my bloody window."

The unrest was growing, people shouting at the police officers as they climbed out of their cars. More bottles flew, and one of them was glass.

"Maybe you should get your kids inside," said Porter. "Till things simmer down."

"I fucking knew Iddy," said Junior, ignoring him. "We all did. He was proper decent, he wouldn't have hurt a fly. They did this, I'm telling you."

"They?" said Porter.

"You know who I mean. Those little shits. The Iron Dickheads. This was them."

"We don't know that for sure," said Porter, although his words were drowned out by another wave of noise. The coppers were forming a line, and there was more than one hand on a baton. "Have you seen them? The lads? Since last night?"

"They never go away," he said. "They never leave. Night after night. How many folk have to die before you take them up to the roof and drop them off?"

He nodded to the top of his tower block.

"Five seconds, mate, and they'd never bother anyone again."

There was a cry from where the kids were playing, a little girl on the ground.

"Fuck's sake," said Junior, setting off at a jog. "Just think about it, yeah? Make everyone's life a little easier."

"Not how it works," Porter muttered, although after last night, he was happy to consider it.

He watched Junior for long enough to see him help the girl to her feet, a hand to her head. Then he found his phone, calling the Superintendent. When Clare didn't answer, he left a message.

"It's going to kick off on the estate, sir. I think we're just making it worse. I'm going to pull everyone back to cool things down, but can you get..."

Another roar of angry voices, but this time it was

coming from the other end of the street. People were moving, a dozen of them breaking off as though they were scared of something. Porter couldn't see what because there were too many bodies in the way.

"Just get over here," he finished, ending the call.

He set off after the mob, the pain thudding inside his skull with every heavy footstep. More people had joined the flow, maybe thirty of them now. They weren't scattering the way they would if they'd seen somebody with a knife, they were all charging in the same direction, pelting past the entrance to one block of flats.

"The hell?" he said.

He turned back again, seeing Duke doing crowd control a little way off.

"Aaron!"

The PC heard him, sprinting over. The entire back half of the crowd seemed to have broken free, a stampede of people surging down the street. The sound of their footsteps was like thunder, but the cry of their voices reminded Porter of monkeys—the wild howl of a hunt.

"What's going on?" said Duke as he caught up.

"Nothing good," said Porter. "Get some Uniforms up here."

The torrent of people was spilling into the next street, heading right. The ones at the front were mostly men, and they were yelling like the crowd at a football match.

Porter cleared the corner, finding himself on a smaller road, flats on the right, houses on the left. The crowd was heading for an alleyway a little further along. Another man stood there, waving them on, screaming something.

They've found another body, thought Porter, because what else would rile them up like this?

There were too many people to fit in the small space, a

bottleneck at the end of the alley. Porter pushed into the back of them, forcing his way through.

"Move!" he roared.

"Get out of the way!" Duke added.

The PC shunted past him, almost knocking him over. He ploughed through the assembled people like a demolition ball, clearing a path. Porter followed, hearing shouts up ahead and then a scream of pain.

"Oi! Stop that!" Duke yelled.

Porter pushed out of the front of the crowd, seeing a small courtyard lined with garages. Halfway down, six or seven men were clustered around a shape on the ground, kicking and punching it with unreserved fury. Duke reached them in a heartbeat, siezing one by the back of his T-shirt and flinging him to the ground.

"Hey!" Porter shouted.

He started towards the group only for somebody to grab the sleeve of his jacket—a woman, her eyes boiling.

"Don't," she said. "Let them do it."

He shook free of her, only for a guy to take hold of his collar. Somebody else moved in front of him, pushing him back into the crowd. The noise was unbelievable, loud enough to crush him. He staggered, almost tripping on a foot, staying upright through sheer force of will. There were people all around him now, hands in his hair, snatching fistfuls of his clothes.

"Get the fuck off me!"

He drove his hands into the chest of the man in front of him, sending him skittering backwards. There were too many people holding onto his jacket, so he shrugged it off, wrenching free. One woman came after him only to be flattened by a constable who was charging through the mob. More followed, thank God, breaking them apart.

Porter turned back to the smaller group of men. Duke had taken out two of them, but he was struggling. One guy was throwing punches into the big constable's back, and Porter charged at him, driving his shoe into the man's knee. He folded like a sapling, hitting the street face-first.

"Enough!" Porter bellowed.

The men were still attacking whoever was on the ground—a skinny body in a tracksuit, curled into a ball, his arms wrapped around his head. Kicks thumped into his ribs, into his face.

He wasn't moving.

"I said enough!" Porter shouted, shoving one of the guys. He fell over the body, taking out another man on the way down.

One of the attackers turned his anger on Porter, lunging at him. Duke thwacked his baton into the man's arm and he screamed, falling back. The big PC positioned himself between Porter and the mob, barking orders at them. More constables were arriving, a flood of dark water that doused the flames of the angry crowd.

Three of the attackers bolted, heading for the wire fence at the far end of the alleyway. Duke sprinted after them like some kind of Viking berserker, more constables in pursuit.

Porter was too knackered to do anything but stay where he was. He swallowed a throatful of bile, his pulse thrashing. He felt like somebody had used a chainsaw to take off the top of his skull. He dropped onto his knees next to the motionless body on the street, pulling an arm away to see who lay there.

It was a teenage boy, his face swollen, his mouth bloody.

He wasn't dead, at least. He wasn't even unconscious. The look he gave Porter was the same look a mouse gives a cat when it's tired of being toyed with, when it just wants to die. He couldn't have been older than sixteen, and there was barely anything to him. One of his trainers had come off, his foot bare. He tried to sit up, groaning through bloodied teeth.

"You're alright," said Porter. "Stay there for a second, help is coming."

But that wasn't all that was coming. Despite the fact there were police everywhere, the heat of the crowd was starting to pick up again. Porter could hear shouts of "It's him!" and "Don't let him go!" from more than one person.

"Can you walk?" he asked the kid.

The boy nodded, turning his pale eyes to the sea of people.

Porter grabbed him under the arms and hauled him up. There was no way he could take him back towards the flats, they'd both be lynched. Duke and a couple of other PCs had vanished over the fence, chasing the attackers. The only other exit was a gap between two garages, and he set off towards it, dragging the kid after him.

Something smashed beside him, a spray of broken glass. More objects followed, bottles detonating against the garage doors, a brick rolling down the street.

"Jesus Christ," said Porter, picking up speed. The kid could barely walk, crying out in pain every time he put weight on his right leg. "The hell did you do?"

He squeezed between the garages, the space barely big enough for him. It was full of crap—literally—the stench making his nausea infinitely worse. His eyes were watering so much that when he reached the end of the garage, he couldn't see a thing. He scrubbed at them, finding a narrow gap between the back of the structure and a wooden fence.

"This way," he said, giving the kid's arm a tug.

He glanced back to see that a constable had plugged the

gap, fending off the crowd. But he still hurried, hearing the swell of noise over the roof of the garages, feeling the heat of their anger. They were so agitated that he half expected them to come teeming over the top of the buildings, like zombies.

The fence was halfway to coming down, and he gave it some encouragement with his shoulder. He clambered over the fallen panel into a neat little garden, heading along the side of a house and back onto the street. It was quieter here, although he could still hear the carnage from the other side of the houses. A scattering of people watched from the pavements, but none of them had murder in their eyes.

Porter took a second to find his bearings, then hauled the kid up the road. He tried to pull free, but he barely had the strength to stay upright. He was sobbing, bubbles of pink foam exploding from his swollen lips. His face was puffy, a nasty cut over his eye.

"What's your name?" said Porter, checking to make sure nobody was coming after them.

No reply, just those wretched sobs. Ahead, a couple of PCs walked out from the footpath that led around the flats. As soon as they saw Porter, they started running.

"Car!" he yelled. "We need a car."

One doubled back, the other clattered over, out of breath by the time she arrived.

"You alright, sir?" she said. "All hell broke loose."

"Don't let him out of your sight," said Porter, handing her the kid.

He found his phone, seeing that he'd missed four calls from Clare. He rang him back, and this time the Superintendent answered.

"What's going on, Pete?" he said, a rare note of concern in his voice. "You alright?"

"I don't know the answer to either of those, sir," he said. "They were trying to kill some kid. I've got him, I'm bringing him in."

"What kid?"

An engine revved, an IRV turning the corner. It gunned up the street, stopping next to Porter. He opened the back door.

"You want him restrained, sir?" said the constable.

He almost shook his head, then he remembered the fury of the crowd, and he nodded. The kid didn't resist as the woman snapped a pair of handcuffs onto his wrists, letting her guide him into the car.

"What tossing kid, Pete?" said Clare.

Porter slammed the back door and opened the passenger one. He glanced down the street to see a handful of people running out of the same driveway. They stopped when they saw the IRV, watching him like hawks. Even from here, he could feel their anger.

"I'm not sure," he said, climbing into the car. "But the locals seem to think he's our killer."

CHAPTER TWENTY-TWO

Kett opened the door of the hospital room expecting to find Porter inside, but the only copper there was PC Felicity 'Flick' Niven. She welcomed him with a wave as he closed the door behind him, then put a finger to her lips.

The other occupant of the room was a teenage boy, who lay in the bed. He was a wreck, his face purple, a thick bandage over his forehead. The bruises stretched into the brace around his neck and peeked from the sleeves of his pyjamas. One of his hands was wrapped in a bandage, the fingers splinted.

He was so still that Kett wondered if he was asleep, but he tilted his head to the door when he heard Kett enter. His eyes were so swollen he couldn't have seen who it was. He began to squirm, grimacing with the pain of it.

"You're alright," said Kett, keeping his voice low so as not to scare him. "I'm a friend."

"He's not said much, sir," said Flick. "Just his name. Ronin."

"Like the samurai?" said Kett. "Nice. Where's Pete?"

"Wasn't feeling too good. He went to get himself checked out."

"Duke with him?"

"No, they're all at HQ. They brought in about two dozen people in the riot vans, they needed help processing them all. It was carnage."

Kett walked to the bed, and the boy pushed himself back, as blind and helpless as a newborn kitten. Clare had passed on Porter's message, that the crowd had gone after him because they'd thought he was the man who'd murdered Helen and Idris. But this kid didn't look like he could get his shoes on without help.

"Ronin," he said. "My name's Robbie. I'm a policeman. Can you hear me alright?"

He only asked because there was a trail of dried blood running from one ear. The kid grunted something, trying to shape his battered lips around a word.

"He's asking for his mum," said Flick. "We're still trying to reach her, Ronin. She'll be here soon."

"Can you tell me what happened?" asked Kett. "Why did everyone come after you like that?"

The kid angled his head away, swallowing noisily past the tight collar. He said something else that even Flick couldn't make sense of.

"I know it's hard," said Kett. "But we need to know what happened so we can punish the people who did this to you."

He leaned in.

"So we can stop it from happening again."

He hadn't meant it to be a threat, but the kid turned back to him like it had been. There was a sliver of a gap between the bruised lids of his left eye, and he studied Kett through it.

"Nuffin," he said, or something like it.

"Nothing? You mean you didn't do anything?"

He tried to nod, but the collar wouldn't let him.

"That was some crowd," said Kett. "They were riled up, but still, there must have been a trigger. Where were you when it started?"

Porter hadn't been able to say much at all, other than it had happened outside the garages that belonged to the flats. Kett hadn't had a chance to speak to any of the other constables who'd been present.

"It's okay," said Flick, patting Ronin gently on the arm. "We're on your side. You can tell us."

"Nuffin," said Ronin, his voice cracked, slow. "I didn't do anything. I was out the back... This man started... shouting at me. He was calling me something. Grabbed me."

He had to stop to collect his breath.

"Then there were hundreds... of them. Tried to fucking kill me. Didn't do nuffin, wasn't doing nuffin."

"You're local?" said Kett. "You live around there?"

Another not-quite nod.

"How old are you, Ronin?"

"Seventeen," answered Flick. "Sorry, I forgot he'd already said."

"Can you tell me what you were doing by the garages?"

"Nuffin."

"You were out back, on your own, doing absolutely nothing?"

"Yeah," he said, a dry wheeze.

The door opened and a nurse walked in, eyeing Kett warily before bustling past. She clipped a heart monitor to the boy's finger, studying it.

"How are you feeling, Ronin?" she asked.

He didn't answer, trying to adjust his position in the

bed. He winced as the nurse pushed a thermometer into his ear.

"If these guys are bothering you, just let me know," she said when she'd finished.

"We only want to find out what happened to him," said Kett.

"What happened is they fractured four of his ribs, his orbital socket, and his wrist. They broke his finger, left bruises on every part of him, and gave him a severe concussion. So maybe let him have a bit of peace and quiet, yeah?"

She left the room, closing the door abruptly behind her. In the silence that followed, Kett tried not to picture it—the kid on the ground, kicks and punches raining in hard enough to break bones. There was nothing to the lad, he'd have snapped like a twig.

If he'd had any doubts before, he didn't now.

They'd been trying to kill him.

"What was he shouting at you?" he asked. "The man who grabbed you?"

"Called me a... killer," said Ronin, swallowing again. "They were all screaming it. Said I killed that boy."

He squinted up at Kett again.

"I didn't. I don't even know who they mean. Didn't kill nobody."

He gagged, like he was about to throw up. He was crying, too, the tears struggling to escape the pouches of his eyes. He looked seven, not seventeen.

"It hurts," he said.

"We're nearly done," said Flick. "Just answer Robbie's questions, then I'll go find out when your painkillers are coming. Deal?"

"I just need to get it clear in my head," said Kett. "You were standing by the garages, minding your own business.

Some man grabs you, shouts for help, and everyone comes running. Did I get that right?"

The tiniest of nods, but the kid wasn't looking at him anymore.

"Because it feels to me like there's a step missing," Kett went on. "Somewhere between you standing there, and the man grabbing you. Do you know him?"

No response.

"You've got beef?"

Ronin furrowed his brow in confusion.

"You've argued with him?"

"No," the boy croaked.

"You were wearing a tracksuit, right, when they brought you in? Was that for comfort, or is it a uniform?"

Another frown.

"Are you part of the gang? The Iron Soldiers?"

"No," he said, far too quickly. "Never heard of them."

"Were you dealing?" said Kett. "Out back, by the garages. It's quiet, good place to do it."

"No," he said, glaring up. "Don't do that shit. Not for them."

"For who, then?" asked Kett, closing in.

"No one," he spat, baring his teeth. One of his top ones had been snapped in half. "I just said, I don't do that shit. Won't."

"But you were doing something?" said Kett.

The kid stared at the sheet, picking at his bandaged wrist with his good hand.

"Something you shouldn't have been doing?"

Nothing.

"Then this has obviously all been some kind of misunderstanding," said Kett. "I'll have Flick here drop you back on the estate."

Ronin looked up so quickly that something in his neck popped. He arched his back in pain, crying out. Flick moved in, giving Kett a hard stare that made him feel even guiltier than he already did. He'd opened his mouth to apologise, but Ronin spoke first.

"Liftin'," he said. "All I was doing."

"Lifting? You mean stealing?"

"Yeah. Nothing fucking in 'em anyway."

"You were breaking into the garages?" Kett said.

"Just shit," Ronin went on, speaking through his tears. "Just weird shit, fucking nuffin."

The door opened again, the nurse returning. This time, she had an older woman with her, a doctor. They both gave Kett the same look, like he was responsible for putting the boy here.

"I'm done," said Kett. "Almost. Ronin, the guy who grabbed you, do you know his name?"

The lad shook his head.

"What did he look like?"

"Bald," he said, adding a shrug.

"Tattoos?" said Kett.

He didn't answer. The two women walked to the bed before he could ask anything else, the slit of Ronin's eye burning into Kett until the doctor had tugged the curtain closed.

"HIS NAME'S RONIN FRY," said Savage, before he was even out of the car. She was waiting for him at the end of the street where the boy had been attacked, fanning herself with a brown envelope. The sun was at its apex, like it had climbed higher for a better view. The heat was trapped between the buildings, turning the entire estate into a greenhouse, making the streets shimmer.

"He's seventeen, lives in the Winchester, second floor. He's on social services' register as a vulnerable child, his mum's known to us."

"Drugs?" asked Kett.

"How did you guess, sir? She's had a couple of B&Es in the last twelve months, one common assault against a former partner. No mention of the dad. Flat's empty. Nobody can get hold of her."

She looked into the car, then back at Kett.

"Where's Porter?"

"Hospital," said Kett, who had completely forgotten to check in on the DI before he'd left. "Where's Cafferty?"

"Back at HQ, working on the profile. She's trying to figure out what kind of serial killer would target nice people. Good people. I mean, if that's the thing that he's hunting for, the thing that connects our victims, it's unheard of."

She frowned.

"What's up?" he asked.

"I don't know. It's just... Steph seems to be a little too into it, you know what I mean? She thinks we can get some kind of recognition for the case. She's even given him a name."

"The suspect?"

"Yeah." She leaned in. "The Saint Killer."

Kett pulled a face.

"Yeah, it's not great. And it's pretty distasteful. But she's good, sir. She understands what makes these people tick. I think. We were talking about it, about why somebody would kill a person just because they were good, because they were kind. It could be somebody with a pathological self-loathing, a profound hatred of himself. He's so far gone that he views any attempt to help him as a deep affront, an insult. All goodness, all purity, must be eliminated, or this portrait he has of himself shatters. And a view of the self, even a negative one, is hugely important. It's what keeps us sane. We cling to it."

"That's a pretty good analysis," said Kett. "That was Steph?"

"Actually, sir, that was me. But I wouldn't have got there without her. Might be way off the mark, though."

"Better than anything I've got," he said. "Where are the garages?"

Savage nodded down the street.

"Right around the corner. Cara's there now. I've spoken to a handful of witnesses, but they're all reluctant to talk. They're tight here, they don't want to throw their neighbours under the bus."

"Everyone wants to throw their neighbours under a bus," said Kett.

He set off, the sun blistering the top of his head through his hair, making him feel like his brain was coming to a boil. He felt like checking the calendar to make sure it was still Spring, because this was ridiculous.

"Kid said the man who grabbed him was bald," he said. "Couldn't tell me anything else. Did anyone speak with the guy?"

"Not that I know of," said Savage. "He vanished when the mob split up. But a bodycam will have caught it. Did Ronin say what had happened?"

"Mistaken identity, I think," said Kett. "They wanted to blame somebody for the murders, and Ronin was in the wrong place at the wrong time, doing something... wrong."

They rounded the corner, and a constable lifted a ribbon of police tape. Twelve garages sat around a barren courtyard, their peeling red doors making them look sunburnt. More police tape hung across the road, limp enough for Kett to step over. Cara Hay, dressed in white overalls, as always, was taking photographs of a slick of dark blood on the asphalt. Five constables circled her, keeping a wary eye on the flats overhead. Kett wasn't sure why until he glanced up, seeing dark-eyed faces through the sun-bright windows.

"How is he?" said Hay.

"Porter?" said Kett.

"The child."

"Oh, right. Yeah, he's not great, but he's out of the woods. They did a real number on him."

He saw her question, and answered it.

"We don't know why. I thought he was dealing, but he claims he was breaking into the garages, trying to find stuff to steal. Sounds like everyone on the estate was on the other side of the flats, he saw his chance and took it. Somebody spotted him, started yelling."

Kett shrugged. Savage took over.

"And an angry mob did what angry mobs do."

"They thought he was the killer," said Kett. "They're mad about Idris, the boy in the pub. He was loved around here."

"How could he be the killer?" said Savage. "Aaron said he was about five-foot-tall and a hundred pounds, soaking wet. And he's *seventeen*."

"Bloodlust," Kett said, looking at the blood. There was so much of it he didn't understand how the boy had any left inside him. "I don't think anyone was stopping to ask questions. They would have killed him if Pete and Aaron hadn't got here. That kid owes them his life."

He turned to the row of garages on the left.

"You know which one he broke into?"

"Three have had their padlocks snipped," said Hay. "That one right there, and two on the other side."

Kett walked to the closest garage, seeing the padlock on the floor, cut clean through. It was open a crack, and he got his fingers underneath and lifted. The squeal it made when it slid open echoed off the flats like an angry dragon. He peeked inside to see a couple of cardboard boxes, an ancient bike, and a lawnmower—even though there weren't any lawns here to mow.

"Did he have cutters?" he asked.

"Not that we've found," said Hay.

"What about the owners of the garages, anyone spoken to them?"

She didn't have an answer for this, returning to her work.

"Not much worth stealing in here," said Savage, wandering inside. She lifted the lid of a box. "Unless you like old paint."

"That's what Ronin told me," said Kett as they crossed the courtyard together. "There was nothing worth stealing. Just shit, in his words. Weird shit."

He found the padlock on the ground and opened the garage door. This one had been oiled, rising smoothly. A car filled the small space, covered with a dust sheet. Kett lifted the corner, finding a Triumph, the green paint rusted, the tyres flat. He peeked through the window, but the vehicle didn't even have any seats.

"Vitesse," said Savage. "Lovely motor. My folks used to have one, back when they were together. Not that I remember it."

She squeezed past the back end before returning to the door.

"Empty."

The last of the garages was the one next door, the remains of the padlock still hanging from the bracket.

"He can't have got inside," said Kett, kicking it free.

"Or somebody's tried to secure it again," said Savage.

She did the honours this time, pulling the door up to reveal another mostly empty space. Black shelves lined the far wall, and they walked over together to see that they were stacked with records. There had to have been hundreds of them.

"Bloody Nora," said Savage, sliding one out. "Rolling Stones, Forty Licks. I thought he said there was nothing worth stealing."

"Is that worth stealing?" asked Kett.

"I mean, in good condition, yeah," said Savage, sliding out the record. "Probably not if some idiot has kept them in the garage. Few hundred for this, I'm guessing. Ronin should have paid more attention in his music lessons."

Kett felt an unexpected pang of sympathy for the kid. There'd been a fortune here, and he'd walked right past it.

They searched a few of the shelves before making their way back into the sun. Kett explored the line of garages, but the rest were still locked tight.

"What's up, sir?" said Savage, watching him.

"I don't know, Kate. Ronin said there was weird shit here, and none of this seems very weird to me."

"I bet vinyl seems weird to a kid who was born in 2007."

He headed the other way, reaching the end of the courtyard to find that the road continued to the left and right, leading to more garages on either side. They sat in the shadow of a line of sickly blackthorn trees that seemed ridiculously out of place here, but the shade was welcome enough.

"Check over there, would you, Kate?" he said, pointing right.

He went left, scouring the locks that secured the doors. By the time he was heading back, Savage was calling to him.

"Got one, sir."

She was standing over a butchered padlock, and when Kett gave her a nod, she lifted the door. It was stubborn enough that she had to hook her shoulder beneath it, driving it upwards. They ducked under together.

The smell hit him like a hammer to the nose: the acrid, chemical stench of something burnt to a crisp. He reeled back, cracking his head on the low door.

"Ow," he said, pinching his nose. "What is that?"

He couldn't see inside the garage because the sunlight was struggling to get under the door. There was just that smell, as stomach-churning as a kick to the bollocks. He took a few steps back, sucking down warm, Spring-scented air.

"Careful," he said to Savage. "That smells poisonous."

She clicked on the light.

"Oh my God," she said.

The last thing he wanted to do was get close to the garage again, but he locked in a lungful of breath as he stooped beneath the door.

Then breathed it all out again in a gasp of shock.

"Shit," he wheezed. "Is that?"

Savage turned to him, both hands over her mouth, her eyes liquid.

"Yeah," she said. "I think it is."

CHAPTER TWENTY-THREE

It wasn't a garage. It was a workshop.

Kett waited just outside the door, which they'd managed to crank fully open. Savage stood beside him, while Cara Hay made her way carefully through the cramped interior, fresh gloves on her hands and a cloth held over her mouth.

A trio of sturdy benches took up most of the space, one against each wall. Two were wooden, and held an assortment of books and equipment. The last was metal, and sitting right in the middle of its scarred, pitted surface was what looked like a portable camping stove topped with a metal pot. It was black with use, as were the tools and dishes that surrounded it: several sets of tongs, stacks of heavy cups, a pair of gloves that could have belonged to a giant, and plenty of stuff Kett couldn't make any sense of. A couple of hefty propane canisters had been tucked into the corner, tubes coiled around them.

"Tell me we got lucky, Cara," said Kett, trying not to breathe in.

She didn't answer straight away, studying the equipment on the middle bench. She used a gloved hand to lift the lid of the pot, jerking her head backwards as more of the same stench wafted out. She reached in, pulling out what looked like the world's smallest saucepan with the world's longest handle.

"That's a crucible," said Savage.

Cara still didn't answer, studying the item in her hand. She tilted it to the light, squinting.

"Used for smelting," Savage went on. "It's like the one Granddad had. He had a proper forge, but he used to make stuff out of steel. You need serious heat for that. This looks like the kind of setup you'd need for..."

She stopped, like she didn't want to jinx it.

"Tin," said Hay, finally speaking.

She walked over and held out the crucible. There was a sheen inside that was instantly recognisable, the same lifeless colour Kett had seen in the eyes of Helen, and Idris, and Judy.

"No doubt about it," she went on. "Somebody has been melting tin in here. See the residue? They're using a propane stove and a stainless-steel saucepan."

She returned to the workbench, picking up one mould, then the next. She carried it over, snapping a clip and opening it like a ring box. The indentation on each side was circular, and when it was closed, it would have made a perfect sphere.

"This is him," said Kett, feeling his pulse quicken.

Cara moved away again, and Kett had to retreat to clear his lungs. The stench had brought on a headache, like somebody was smelting molten metal inside his skull. He sucked in a couple of breaths, the pain ebbing for a couple of seconds before he heard footsteps thumping towards him. He didn't even have to turn around to recognise the lumbering gait of the Superintendent, and the thought of it made the ache in his temples even worse.

"This better be good, Kett," he grunted. "They woke me up from a nap for this."

Clare marched to the garage door, bracing his hands on his hips and inhaling deeply, like he was smelling a fine cheese and not scorched chemicals.

"Shit on me," he said. "This is his workshop?"

"We think so, sir," said Savage. "He's got everything he needs here, and the mould's the perfect shape for the prosthetic eyes."

"Indeed," said Hay. "The stove and the pan are all you need to smelt tin, it's got a low melting point. It's a metal caster's toolkit. He's even got an infrared thermometer, and that, for the fumes."

She nodded to one of the canisters in the corner, and Kett saw that it wasn't propane at all, it was oxygen. The tube was connected to a plastic breathing mask that lay on the wooden desk to the right.

"Gauntlets, a leather apron, everything," said Hay.

"Not everything," said Kett. "Where's his mask, or his helmet? You need one for this kind of work, right, like a welder?"

He scanned the garage, but it wasn't there.

"He took it with him," said Savage. "We already know he wears it when he's hunting a victim. Your security guard spotted him walking down the road in it last night. He uses it here, to forge the eyes, then he keeps hold of it."

"To make the kill," said Kett, nodding.

"There's something else missing," said Hay. "The raw material. The tin."

"How do you mean?" said Kett.

Hay walked out of the garage, pulling her mask away

from her face. She was sweating buckets in her overalls, and she doubled over, her hands on her knees. It took her a few seconds to find her breath.

"He's melting tin to make the balls that he puts inside his victims. But where's he getting the tin from?"

Nobody had an answer for her.

"It's not common," she said. "You can buy tin bars from specialist websites, but that would leave a trail. It would be easy enough to find who ordered them, where they were sent. Besides, the balls were an alloy, there was lead in them. It's harder to get hold of because it's toxic, which means it's unlikely he's adding it to the tin inside the crucible."

"You mean whatever he's melting already has lead inside it?" said Savage.

"That would be my guess. It's something old. Pewter cutlery, maybe. Tableware. They used to make everything out of it, before they realised lead would kill you. Cups, plates, teapots. It's highly likely he's melting down something like that."

"Why?" barked Clare. "Why would you do that? Kett?"

"I didn't do it, sir," said Kett.

"I mean use your brain, you toss-eyed cock muppet. Why would somebody go to the trouble of melting down old metal items to make eyes for their victims?"

"Uh..." said Kett, turning to Savage.

"Steph and I had a theory about that, sir," she said.

"Who?" snapped Clare.

"Steph. Cafferty. The sergeant who... It doesn't matter. She was saying that pewter was used in the olden days to make things that looked expensive but weren't. All the stuff Cara just mentioned, people bought pewter because it looked so much like silver."

"So?" said the Superintendent.

"So it's symbolic," said Savage, struggling. "It looks valuable, but it's not. It's fake."

"So?"

"I mean..." Savage paused, her eyes scrolling. "I'm thinking aloud, sir, but we think the killer's going after people because they're nice, don't we?"

"Do we?" said Clare.

"Because of their kindness," she went on. "Some inherent goodness. Helen working at the hospital. Idris and all the stuff he did with the food banks and the football club. Judy because... well, everyone loved her. They shine bright, like precious metals."

Clare yawned, like he'd grown tired of the whole affair. He wheeled his hand through the air to encourage Savage to keep going.

"So the killer's obsessed with these people. He's not using silver to replace the eyes, he's not even using pure tin. He's using a cheap, toxic alloy. It looks the part, but it's fake. What if he's saying these people seem good, but aren't? What if he thinks there's a... I don't know, a darkness to them, a hidden evil?"

She blew a sigh through her lips that became a raspberry.

"He might be saying that no matter how good people seem on the surface, they're toxic underneath," she went on. "And the whole eye thing is telling us that he's the only one who can see it."

"Bloody hell, Kate," said Kett. "You're very good at this."

"You are," added Clare, and for some reason, he reached out and ruffled Savage's hair like she was a poodle. "Good job."

He barged past Kett, yelling as he walked away.

"But it's all toss, because the only thing we need to do to find our killer is work out who owns this garage."

"Already thought of that," Kett shouted after him, adding a muttered, "obviously."

His first call, while they'd waited for Cara Hay to run over from the courtyard, had been to DS Spalding, asking her to look into it. He checked his phone to make sure he hadn't missed her, then met Savage in the shade of the blackthorn.

"What do you think happened?" he asked, then proceeded to answer himself. "Ronin's taking advantage of the fact there's nobody around, breaking into some garages, hoping to earn some cash. He targets the ones with a cheap padlock, cuts his way in, has a look. This..."

He pointed through the open door of the garage.

"Is weird shit. If you're seventeen, anyway. The smell, the equipment, he wouldn't have a clue what it was. He leaves it, heads to the courtyard, tries a couple more. Then somebody sees him."

"He said the man who grabbed him was bald?" asked Savage.

Kett nodded.

"Bald like your security guard?"

"That's a bit of a leap, Kate," he said, even though he'd thought it himself. "Plenty of bald folk around."

"And we're all beautiful," called Hay from the garage.

"Whoever the killer is, what if he caught Ronin inside the garage?" said Kett.

"This guy?" said Savage, shaking her head. "If he caught the kid inside, he'd have pulled down the door and killed him. He's already executed one teenage boy, I don't think he'd risk letting another one go."

"Right. Then he doesn't catch him inside the garage, but

he sees Ronin in the courtyard, realises he's been inside. He can't kill him out there, it's too public, too many people. So he grabs him, starts shouting."

"Lets the mob do his dirty work for him," said Savage. She didn't look sure. "That's some coincidence, though, isn't it? The killer arrives at the exact moment Ronin's inside his garage. He'd have to have been watching it."

"Cameras," said Kett. "Cara, is there any CCTV in there?"

"No," she called back.

Kett scanned the parade of colourful doors, but there were no cameras on any of them. The only thing on the other side of the narrow alley was a six-foot wall and the overhanging trees, and past them, the back of another block of flats. Dozens of dark windows stared back at him.

He walked to the end of the lane, which was sealed off by a wire fence that had drooped in the middle, presumably from people clambering over it. Past that was a strip of scrubland mined with dog shit, then the ugly brick flank of another building.

He'd turned around and started back before he realised he'd seen something else, something that had been almost invisible against the blue sky.

"Wait a minute," he said, spinning on his heels. He reached the fence, angling his head so that he could see through the crooked branches of the trees. "Kate, come here a second."

She joined him, following his finger through the thick canopy of the last tree in the row.

"Oh," she said. "That's something."

The something was Norvic House, the bright blue office building that sat a stone's throw from the underpass where Helen Coulter had been murdered. Kett could only see the top two floors from here, and the roof, the azure-glazed panels revealing nothing of what was inside. An army of killers could have been hiding there right now, watching him.

An army, or one man.

"You think somebody could see us from up there?" Kett asked.

"Yeah," Savage replied, moving to the garage door. "I mean, kind of. I can't really see the tower past the trees, but it's possible."

"It fits, though," said Kett. "Ronin breaks into the garage. Terry Prince is up there. We know he spends his time looking out the windows, he told us. He said he saw the killer in his mask, twice."

"Which was a weird coincidence in itself," said Savage.

"Right. For all we know, he's got a bloody telescope up there. He sees the kid breaking into his garage, and he runs down to intercept him."

"But by the time he gets here, Ronin's moved on, he's in the courtyard," said Savage. "So he rolls with plan B, shouts for the crowd, hopes they kick him to death."

"Terry's bald," said Kett.

"He's right in the middle of all of this," she said, turning her eyes upwards again. "The prince in his tower."

Kett's leg vibrated, the sound of the *Mexican Hat Dance* reverberating off the garage doors. He saw Spalding's name on the screen, and he didn't give her the chance to speak.

"Tell me it's Prince," he said.

"What?" came her reply. "Prince, sir? You mean the artist formerly known as what the hell are you going on about?"

"The garage," said Kett. "Is it owned by a man called Terrence Prince?"

"No," she spat back. "It's owned by a guy called Nolan O'Brien."

Kett spluttered out his disappointment.

"Who?" he said.

"I don't know anything else about him, except he lives in the Winchester. I'll ping you the address."

"You think O'Brien's an alias for Prince?"

"I don't know, sir. I'll just ping you the address."

"You think he's friends with Prince?"

"I don't know."

"Roommates?"

Silence.

"Fine," said Kett. "Just ping me the address."

CHAPTER TWENTY-FOUR

He didn't want to wait for tactical, but he didn't want to go alone.

Luckily, a good chunk of Norfolk Constabulary's uniformed officers were on hand. Seven constables crushed into the lift with him and Savage, their collective weight putting so much strain on the old gears that Kett didn't think they were going to make it to the ninth floor. There was barely any room for him to hold his phone to his ear, and not much signal either, but somehow he managed to speak with Clare to tell him what they were doing.

"Oh, and sir," he said as the doors opened. "Check in with the constables outside Norvic, would you? See if anyone has eyes on Terry Prince."

"Who?" said Clare, just as Kett was ending the call.

Security guard, he texted.

He pocketed the phone, following the directions on the wall towards the western corner of the building, where Nolan O'Brien's flat was located. He didn't really need them, because as he turned the corner, he caught a whiff of something deeply unpleasant and instantly recognisable.

He glanced at Savage, seeing in her expression that she'd caught it too.

"Shit," they said together.

The flat was the last one in the cramped corridor, and Kett got to it first. The coppers crowded behind him in two lines, the first couple with their Tasers out, one holding an enforcer ram.

Kett had lifted his hand to knock when he heard a bolt being drawn. It wasn't O'Brien's door that opened, though, it was the next flat down. A young woman leaned into the corridor, studying the collection of police officers. She had her arm wrapped around a girl who was maybe Moira's age, the kid's hair an explosion of ginger curls. Neither of them seemed particularly alarmed.

"You here about *him*?" the woman asked, nodding to the door Kett was standing next to.

"Nolan?" said Kett. "You know him?"

"He's a pain in the... you *know*," she said.

"Arse," added the kid. Her mum gave her a little shake.

"Hey! What did I tell you about that?"

The kid shrugged, reaching for the baton on the belt of the closest copper.

"Hey!" said her mum, pulling her back through the door. "Don't really know him, not like a friend or anything. He's not a bother, but whatever he's been smoking in there smells like..."

"Arse," the kid said again. This time, the woman nodded.

"It really does. You get it right in the face as soon as you come out of the lift. It's not fair, I got kids here."

"When was the last time you saw him?" said Kett.

She shrugged.

"Weeks ago. Hear him often enough, though, him and those birds."

She retreated inside, then emerged again.

"He's not what they were all shouting about outside, is he? That bloke who... you know..."

"Arse," said the kid, earning another shake.

"We don't know," said Kett. "Close the door, and lock it, until we tell you it's okay."

She vanished, the bolt sliding into place. Kett drummed his fist on O'Brien's door, calling out.

"Nolan? It's the police. Can you open up?"

The only reply was a scuff of movement, so faint that he wasn't sure if it had even come from inside the flat. He put his eye to the peephole, trying to make sense of the distorted view. Someone was moving on the other side of the door, running from one side of the room to the other.

"Last chance, Nolan," he yelled, stepping back.

He counted to five in his head, then nodded to the PC with the enforcer. The man actually took a run-up, swinging the ram into the lock with so much gusto that he put a hole through the flimsy wood.

"Whoops," he said, struggling to pull it out.

"Move," Kett told him.

The man stepped back, and Kett drove his boot into the door, right beneath the jammed enforcer. The damage had already been done, the door splintering open, the handle clanging to the floor. The two constables with Tasers charged through, swallowed by the dark corridor, and by the awful smell of the place.

"Armed police!" they yelled together, then one of them screamed wetly, like he'd run into the sharp end of a knife.

"What's going on?" said Kett, running through the door only to feel a sharp scratch across his scalp. He screamed too, grabbing his head to find something caught in his hair—something *alive*.

When he'd cupped it in his hands, he realised it was a little white and yellow bird of some kind. It stared at him through his fingers, wild-eyed, its beak open in terror.

"Tit," said Savage, leaning in.

"This, or him?" said Kett, nodding to the PC inside the flat, who was still screaming.

He didn't know what to do with the creature, so he opened his hands and set it free. The bird flitted onto the hat of another constable, preening itself. Kett clicked a switch, seeing that the corridor was dressed up like a boudoir: tie-dye blankets over the walls and across the ceiling, beads hanging over the doors. A solitary cabinet held a mug that was stuffed with incense sticks, all burnt to the metal quick.

More birds fluttered against the ceiling, some darting through the open door in search of freedom. Others were chasing the flies that buzzed around the hallway, giant bluebottles that could only mean one thing.

"Keep going," he told the two constables. The panicked one had calmed down, but he still looked terrified as he advanced into the dark flat.

"Police armed with Tasers!" they called as they went.

Kett opened the cabinet door, finding a stack of mail—all except one bearing Nolan O'Brien's name. The last was a letter from HMRC addressed to a company called Cousin Soul. He opened it as he walked through a curtain of wooden beads into the kitchen, praying that he'd find the source of the smell here—old meat left to rot, or an overflowing bin.

No such luck. The kitchen was cluttered but clean, the dishes stacked neatly by the sink and not so much as a crumb on the counters. The décor was much the same, floral patterns on the tablecloth and the curtains, more skeletal joss sticks sitting in their own ash. A couple of hardback books sat on top of the toaster, next to a vase of dead flowers.

Kett checked the letter, which was a request for unpaid tax. Cousin Soul seemed to be a small business, with O'Brien as the listed owner.

Another scream from deeper in the flat. Kett fought his way through one set of beads and then another as he pushed into the living room. Both constables were doing battle with a platoon of pigeons that had gathered there. The one who was screaming had lost his hat, and was waving his Taser so much that he was in danger of shooting the other guy.

"Oi!" Kett yelled at him. "Pack it in!"

"Bloody hate them, sir," said the PC, hopping on one foot as a pigeon waddled past him. "Rats with wings."

It wasn't just the pigeons. There were more songbirds in here, and even a crow sitting on the back of the sofa, holding out its enormous wings like it owned the place. It was easy enough to see how they'd got in, the window wide open. A giant bag of birdseed had been ripped to shreds, its contents practically devoured. A couple of flies bopped against the walls, quickly gobbled up.

This was what he'd seen through the peephole, he realised. Not somebody running, but the movement of the birds.

"Bedroom's empty, sir," said Savage from the corridor. She nodded to the only other door. "Smell's coming from in there, I think."

It was the bathroom, and it was locked. Kett patted his pockets looking for a coin, but Savage was way ahead of him, using a twenty pence piece to twist the safety lock.

They looked at each other for a moment, bracing themselves for the inevitable. Then Kett turned the handle again.

A wave of death rolled through the door as it opened, so thick that Kett felt like he couldn't breathe. Flies swatted him, landing on his face, exploring his ears and his mouth. He waved them away, staring into the room to see a toilet, a sink, and a bath full of black water. A body floated in it, swollen and monstrous, the face a bloated mess.

The eyes were missing, of course, but nothing had been left in their place, the sockets gaping.

Kett retreated, the gorge rising from his stomach, gathering at the back of his throat. He wanted to tell Savage not to look, but he knew that if he opened his mouth, he was going to unload. She was already at the bathroom door, anyway, one hand to her face at the smell, at the horror of what waited there.

"Flat's clear," somebody said. "You need us to call in forensics?"

Kett nodded.

"And Franklin," he croaked. "And warn her it's..."

The smell wrapped itself around his head, visions of the eyeless man filling his skull.

A bad one, he finished, but he was too busy running for the kitchen sink to say it out loud.

"IN THE SINK?" said Franklin.

The young pathologist stood in the bathroom of Nolan O'Brien's flat, dressed in white overalls and seemingly unfazed by the gruesome contents of the bath. Savage loitered in the open door, pinching her nose shut with one hand and holding onto the frame with the other, like she might have to haul herself to safety. The air in here was hot and heavy enough to drown in, although thankfully the flies had evacuated.

"Mostly in the sink," she said. "He didn't *quite* make it."

"Not like Robbie to be so queasy," said Franklin, snapping on a glove. "Probably the heat."

It had nothing to do with the heat, Savage knew, and Franklin was right, it wasn't like Kett to react so badly to a crime scene, even one as ghastly as this. He'd vomited in the kitchen, then legged it out of the flat, muttering something about calling the Superintendent. That had been an hour ago, and he still hadn't come back.

"Been a while since we've had soup," said Franklin, leaning over the bath.

"Soup?" said Savage.

"Yeah, body in the bathtub, and one that's been there a while."

"How long?" said Savage.

Franklin clucked her tongue, studying the butchered mess of the victim's face. She pulled a metal implement from her bag and gave the body a delicate poke. Something bubbled in the water, a flatulent sound that almost sent Savage running after Kett. The smell was unbelievably bad. She didn't think she'd ever get it out of her sinuses.

"I'm going to say two weeks," said Franklin. "Although, given the weather, it may be a couple of days less. It's a man, if you're wondering. Forties, maybe early fifties, pretty chunky, hasn't cut his nails in a while. I'm guessing that when we drain the tub, we'll find some jewellery, because the skin of his nipple has torn away. I think it was pierced."

"Right," said Savage, a choked whisper.

"Couple of tattoos on his arms, can't figure out what they are, sorry. Maybe an 88. Bit of facial hair, probably a goatee, but it's hard to see because the flies have been at him. It's just a good job the door was closed, and the window, or the birds would have eaten him down to the bone."

Savage closed her eyes, the world spinning.

"Can you see how he died?" she asked. "Strangled?"

Franklin prodded a little more, the body playing a bubbling tune.

"I'm going to need to get him out of the water," she said. "His head's at the wrong angle, I can't see his throat. You noticed the eyes were missing, yeah?"

"Yeah, Emily, I noticed the eyes were missing."

Franklin leaned closer, her knuckles on the edge of the bath to stop her from joining the dead man.

"Sockets are empty. The eyes have been completely removed, I can see where the nerve has been cut. Killer used a knife, or a pair of scissors. It's going to take me a while to be sure, but I think I can see the curve of the tool they employed for the task. Looks like the same thing that was used on our other victims."

"The sharpened spoon?" said Savage.

"That's the one."

"No tin prosthetics?" said Savage.

"I can't see any, although you're welcome to dunk for them?"

Franklin glanced back in time to see the look on Savage's face.

"I'll empty it now," she said. "Can you radio for some buckets, Kate?"

"Sure," said Savage, more than happy to be excused.

She walked away, hearing the sound of a hand in water as she went. As hard as her job was at times, there was no way in hell she'd have the stomach to do what Emily Franklin did.

Two constables remained outside the front door of the flat, and she asked them to call for some forensic containers. Then she made her way back into the living room. It had, thanks to the stampede of people and the open window, been largely emptied out. Only the songbirds remained, four of them lined up on a sturdy perch that looked like it had been designed for something much larger. There was a bell-shaped metal cage in the corner, the hatch open, and the walls were lined with feeders of all shapes and sizes.

The floor was so caked in white bird droppings that she could barely tell if there was a carpet or not.

"Who are you, Nolan?" she asked, and only the birds answered her.

It was a small room, and with the ornithological clutter, there was barely space for a two-seater sofa and an Eames chair that had lost its footstool. A teardrop-shaped wooden table separated them, with several half-burned candles and yet more incense sticks. A low bookcase beneath the window held hardback books, almost all of which were about the supernatural. Savage scanned the titles, then pulled one from the middle shelf.

"Messengers of the Dead," she said quietly, reading the title. "Psychopomps and their role in the lore and legend of death."

The cover showed a huge, black bird that wasn't too different from the crow that had been here when they'd arrived—so similar, in fact, that she felt an unpleasant shiver run through her. She held the book gently, letting it open where it wanted, but the dense text inside would take all day to read. She knew what they were, of course.

Psychopomps. She'd spoken to Kett about them when Aggie Clegg had been kidnapped, nearly two years ago.

Spirits tasked with transporting the souls of the dead to the afterlife.

She put the book back, then wrestled out another from the shelf above. This didn't have anything on the spine or the cover, and when she opened it, she saw that it was a notebook. The writing inside was small and haphazard, some of the letters joined up, others in blocky capitals—sometimes both in the same word. The book appeared to be some kind of ledger, with a column for dates, followed by one for initials, and a third for a name. Beneath each of these were a few lines of text.

The first entry was dated three years ago, on April 14th. The initials were PA, and the name after that was Alison. She struggled to read the lunatic scribbles.

"Visibility, poor... Fog, moderate. Channel, dry, cutting, scratch."

"Is that the shipping forecast?" came a voice from behind her.

She grinned as she turned around, almost laughing with the relief of seeing Duke in the living room door. It took all her restraint not to run to him, and the only reason she didn't was because DS Cafferty appeared beside him, the back of her hand over her mouth. She'd changed her pocket square to an orange one.

"Crikey," said Cafferty. "That's an awful pong."

"You okay?" said Duke. He looked exhausted, his head resting against the doorframe, his shoulders sagging. Savage wasn't sure if it was the light in the room, but his face looked yellow from the bruises.

She didn't really know how to answer, so she nodded down the corridor.

"Body in the bath. I wouldn't look."

Duke stayed where he was. Cafferty, on the other hand, made a beeline for the bathroom door.

"Same killer?" she shouted back.

"Yeah," said Savage. "Has to be."

Duke stood there, still waiting for her to answer his question.

"Not really," she told him. "This case. All these dead. This guy, Nolan O'Brien, he's been lying in that bath for two weeks, while we've all been..."

She shrugged, unable to find the words.

"You can't imagine it," she said. "Can you?"

Duke glanced back to make sure they were alone, then he walked into the room, wrapping his bear-like arms around her. The hug only lasted a couple of seconds, but it recharged her batteries, the familiar smell of him clearing her mind.

"What have you got there?" he asked, looking at the notebook.

"Not sure," she told him. "A diary of some kind. All this stuff, Nolan was seriously into the paranormal."

She flicked to the back page of the journal, finding the last entry. It was dated three weeks ago.

"RS-C," she said, reading it out. "Then 'like', maybe? I can't read it. It's the same gibberish underneath. 'Visibility, bright, zero fog, clear horizon, strong voice.' It's the shipping forecast, like you said. Goes on to say, 'Four lines: time of crossing, four, reason for crossing, involuntary, reluctant crossing, unaware of crossing.'"

"No idea," said Duke. "Crossing through, maybe death?"

"Maybe," said Savage, closing the book and tucking it under her arm.

She scanned the rest of the shelf, finding a stack of boxes at the bottom. She pulled out the top one, taking off the lid to see a set of large, beautifully decorated cards.

"Tarot," she said, showing Duke.

Cafferty walked back from the bathroom, one hand over her mouth. Despite her enthusiasm, she was looking a little green around the gills.

"God," was all she managed.

"Tarot," said Duke. "That's weird. Maybe that's what all the stuff in the book is. Maybe Nolan was a fortune teller. You think this guy knows your mate?"

"Enid?" said Savage. "There's a chance, I guess. I mean, it's not a big estate, there can't be that many fortune tellers living here."

"And the cards you picked," said Cafferty, recovering a little. "The tower, with the eye."

She gestured to the room, and then towards the bath.

"Tower. Eyes."

It was weird, Savage thought. She'd assumed it had been a coincidence when the old woman had walked up to her yesterday near the underpass, but what if it wasn't?

"Not much more we can do here until Emily and Cara have finished," she said to Duke. "How do you fancy getting your cards read again?"

CHAPTER TWENTY-FIVE

No matter how far he walked, Kett couldn't get the smell of the dead man out of his nose.

After emptying his guts in Nolan O'Brien's kitchen sink in front of a gaggle of wide-eyed constables, he'd taken the stairs out of Winchester Tower. Once he'd started, he'd found he couldn't stop, his legs carrying him down the street like they wanted to save him from the horrors of what they'd discovered inside the flat.

And no matter how far he walked, he couldn't get away. Every time he turned back, he saw the tower there, peeking over the roofs of the smaller buildings, the windows of the ninth floor watching him.

He pinched the bridge of his nose, sipping air through his mouth, the thick stench of death still there. There were officers around, patrolling in pairs or sitting in IRVs. The locals seemed to have retreated, but the heat was still climbing, and he knew the flats and houses here wouldn't contain the community's anger for long. He was close to the school where Judy had worked before she'd moved over to Earlham, and he headed past the park to the little corner shop.

He was paying for a bottle of water and a packet of Smints when he felt his phone buzz.

"Alison," he said when he answered, pinching the phone between his cheek and his shoulder as he unwrapped the mints. He tipped about a dozen of them onto his tongue, crunching them until a wave of spearmint blasted the residue from his sinuses.

"You having your lunch, sir?" said Spalding.

"Honestly, I don't think I'm ever going to eat again," he said, pocketing the pack. "Any luck with O'Brien?"

"There wasn't much to find. He's fifty-two, no immediate family. He's lived in the Winchester for eighteen years. Council flat. The garage is rented privately, but it's in his name. He runs a company from his flat. Cousin Soul. No real information about it, and no website. Listed as professional service not otherwise classified, which is where they dump all the crazy stuff. Uh..."

Kett heard the clack of a keyboard.

"Nothing much about him online at all. He's got some outstanding debts, couple of credit cards. But he is known to us."

"Yeah?" said Kett. "He's got a record?"

"He was arrested six years ago at a protest in the city. Anti-immigration, by the look of it. Bunch of them were brought in for slinging insults at foreigners. He was de-arrested and released on the same day."

"Doesn't really fit the pattern of a nice guy, then?"

"No," said Spalding. "I've got his mugshots here. There's a pretty big 88 on his upper right arm. 88, HH, as in..."

"As in he's a fan of Hitler," said Kett, thinking of the tattoos he'd seen on the man in the bath. He was a little less upset to have found him dead.

The mention of a tattoo made him think of something else. He swivelled, catching a glimpse of the bright blue Norvic building in the opposite direction.

"Did you ever pull anything on Terry Prince?" he said. "The security guard? He seemed like the kind of guy who'd happily join an anti-immigration protest, and he had tattoos as well. I thought I saw a Swastika."

"Prince," said Spalding, speaking through something in her mouth—a pen, most likely. "No, no record, no arrests. He's squeaky clean, believe it or not. Married, two grown-up kids."

"You spoken to his employer?"

"No," said Spalding. "No reason, is there? He's a witness, not a suspect."

"Can you do it?" said Kett. "I'm just feeling it."

"I don't want to know what you're feeling, sir," said Spalding. "I'll give them a call."

He thanked her and hung up, downing half the bottle of water as he made his way back along the street. He called Porter as he went, but the DI wasn't answering.

"Hey, Pete," he said after the tone. "You okay? Call me back."

He tried Clare next, who answered straight away.

"Don't," said the Super.

"Don't what?" asked Kett.

"Just don't," Clare barked, and the line went dead.

Kett kept the Norvic building in his line of sight as he made his way back up Vauxhall Street, reaching the main road a couple of minutes later. It was busier now, a line of traffic stretching back from the entrance to the Chapelfield Mall car park all the way to the roundabout. Shoppers, oblivious to the horror of what was going on here. The air was choked with fumes.

It was still better than what he'd been inhaling in the flat, though.

There was still an IRV parked in the slip road that led to the main door of the office block, and the solitary constable inside wound down her window when Kett appeared.

"Any sign of Prince?"

"No," she replied. "All quiet. I don't even know if there's anyone in there."

Kett stared up at the azure wall of the building, seeing nothing past the mirrored glass.

"Any more riots?" asked the PC. "That was scary."

"It was," he told her. "They're calmer now, but they'll burn the whole city down if we don't catch this guy."

Although, at the rate the killer was going through victims, there wouldn't be anyone left to see it.

He felt his phone buzz again, and he leaned against the side of the car as he answered it.

"Plot twist," said Spalding. "Where are you now?"

"Chapelfield," he said. "Why?"

"I just got off the phone to Royal Security, Terry Prince's employer. Or rather, his *ex*-employer. They got rid of him six months ago."

"What?" said Kett, pushing himself off the IRV.

"They wouldn't tell me why, just that he wasn't fit for purpose anymore. It was serious enough that they made sure he was unemployable."

"So he's not a security guard?"

"Nope," said Spalding. "They had no idea he was even in the Norvic. Whatever he's doing in there, it's not work."

"Shit," said Kett. "Can you let Clare know?"

"No," she said. "He'll only shout at—"

Kett hung up, turning back to the car.

"Radio for some backup, will you?" he told the constable. "As many as you can."

"Sir?" she said.

He ran to the front door of the tower, trying the handle. It was locked, and there was no sign of life in the dark interior. He jogged along the face of the building, seeing the constable get out of her car.

"Don't take your eyes off the door," he said. "You see him, you call. Send the others around the back."

He turned the corner, pushing through a barricade of vegetation as he cut between Norvic House and the block of flats next door. He emerged in a car park that held a single vehicle: a filthy white panel van with a 2002 plate. Kett stopped beside it, seeing a sticker on the back door: a glaring eye above the words 'I see you'.

The back of the building was sealed tight, but a fire escape led to a large terrace on the third floor. Kett ran up it, the steps clanging out a warning. The door at the top was open, wedged by a bucket of sand that had become a graveyard of cigarette butts.

Kett peeked into a short corridor that was surprisingly bright despite the heavily tinted windows. There was faint music coming from somewhere, a jaunty tune that would have suited a children's TV show.

He ducked back out of the door, hearing the ring of feet on the stairs. Two constables ran onto the terrace, one of them armed with a Taser.

"This it?" said Kett.

"More on the way, sir," the armed PC replied.

"It'll have to do," said Kett. "Stay close, and stay alert. We're looking for a man called Terry Prince. Looks like a gammon joint in a uniform. Bald. Tattoos."

"Sounds like my dad," said the PC with the Taser.

"He's not your dad," said Kett. "But he could be our killer."

At this, the two officers hesitated.

"The eye guy?" said the one who wasn't armed.

"Yeah," said Kett. "The eye guy."

The stairs clanged, and three more constables appeared. More were running through the car park below, their shouts echoing off the surrounding buildings.

Kett entered the tower, kicking open the heavy internal fire door to find himself in a stairwell. The music was louder here, and it was definitely from a kids' show. The squeaks and toots and chuckles would have been innocent anywhere else, but they sounded remarkably sinister here, echoing down the stairs. It was coming from overhead, and Kett set off, leading a line of constables behind him. The volume of the music grew with every flight of steps, and when he opened the door onto the top floor, it became a wall of sound.

The corridor here was darker, the lights on but dimmed. Somebody had painted crude animals on the whitewashed walls, rabbits and squirrels and other things he couldn't make sense of, all with long arms and grinning faces. Their eyes were wild spirals, their teeth sharp. Scrawled over their heads in blood-red paint were the words:

WELCOME TO FUNTOWN!

The music roared down the corridor, far too loud: a cartoonish voice singing about putting on your wellies and heading to the farm. Kett moved forward, his heart drumming in time to the fast-paced song.

Two doors, one on either side of the corridor, both open. He approached the left, peering through into an enormous space that had once been an open-plan office. Hundreds of thick ropes stretched between the internal columns and the walls, making it look like a forest of cobwebs. Colourful balls and pool noodles were scattered over the floor beneath them.

There was nobody here.

Kett was almost at the second door when the song ended. He stopped moving, and so did everyone behind him, as a deep, tuneless voice carried on singing.

"Bring your boots and fill your chutes, we're going to the farm."

A clatter of something being thrown across a room.

"We're going, you fuck, aren't we?"

If there was a reply, it was lost in the deafening volume of another track, this one about Noah's Ark. Kett took advantage of the noise, peeking through the door.

The office space here was identical in size, the windows darkened by sheets of newspaper. It, too, had been done up to look like a play area. An enormous, deflated bouncy castle sat against the left-hand wall, looking like the rotting corpse of a dragon. On the other side was a pit of cardboard boxes, filled with more plastic balls.

In the middle of the room, positioned between the four pillars, was a cage of metal fence panels.

Terry Prince stood in front of it, wearing his security guard's jacket and his shoes. What he'd forgotten to put on were his trousers, his filthy white briefs barely covering the saggy domes of his backside. In one hand, he held a bottle of alcohol. In the other was a pink teddy bear. He was shouting at somebody, but the music was too loud to make out what he was saying.

Kett glanced back to make sure the police officers were ready, then he walked into the room.

"Terry!" he yelled.

The man couldn't hear him. He was screaming at the

cage, but Kett couldn't make sense of the shadows inside it. There was definitely somebody in there, though, a short, skinny, motionless silhouette.

A *child*.

Kett spotted a set of speakers next to the ball pit, and he jogged over to find a CD player. When he pressed the pause button, the silence cut through the room like a guillotine blade.

"Terry," he said.

The security guard spun around, swaying so much he almost fell over. Liquid sloshed out of the bottle he was holding. He stared at the row of coppers like they'd materialised from thin air.

"The fuck?" he squeaked.

"On your knees," said Kett. "Now."

Terry's shock lasted another three seconds, then he pulled back his arm and lobbed the bottle at Kett. It was a good shot, hitting the wall a foot or so away from his head and raining glass and whisky. By the time Kett had uncovered his face, Terry was on the run, heading for the back of the office, still clutching his teddy bear. The coppers chased after him, a crashing wave of sound and fury.

"Fuck's sake," said Kett.

He jogged to the cage of metal panels, but there was no way in. It was maybe fifteen foot squared, and the interior was crammed with dozens of pieces of cut-out scenery that could have come from a theatre.

"Hello?" he said. "Who's in there?"

The skinny shape he'd seen before was right in the middle of the cage, and he had to switch on the torch on his phone to see it. It was a furry mascot suit of some kind, the body limp, the head angled far too sharply for there to be anyone inside.

"Hello?" he said again, giving the bars a rattle.

Nothing.

A clang, another shout. Terry and the coppers had piled out of a fire door on the far side of the room, but it sounded like they were coming around. Kett made his way back in time to see Terry barrel past, still in his jacket and his pants, as he ran into the office space with the ropes. The PCs were right behind him, smashing through the door, all hollering for him to stop.

By the time Kett had entered the office, Terry was halfway through the maze of cables. He was expertly weaving between them, ducking and vaulting like he'd done it a million times before. The police weren't having as much luck, two of them already snared by the webs, one upside down, his hat on the floor beneath him.

"Christ," said Kett, seeing past the ropes and the coppers and Terry Prince to the fire escape at the far end of the office.

He left the room the way he'd come in, heading through a double door a little further down. The corridor bent left, and he jogged along it, turning the corner at the far end just as Terry burst through the fire door. The bald man lumbered up, the sweat rolling off his knuckled scalp, his face beet red. The pink bear was still clutched in his hand. He was so knackered that he didn't see Kett until he'd almost run into him.

"There's nowhere to go, mate," said Kett. "Get on the floor."

Terry was done, wheezing accordion breaths as he came to a standstill. He seemed to think about turning around, but the door crashed open behind him, a PC staggering out—just as exhausted, and just as sweaty.

"Bugger it," barked Terry, collapsing against the wall. "Bugger, bugger, bugger."

"You calm?" said Kett, as more coppers poured into the corridor.

Terry nodded, his chins bulging beneath his scowling face. Kett could smell the whisky on him from here. The PC walked up like he was approaching a lion, but Terry was happy enough to let him fix the cuffs to his wrists. He'd dropped the bear by his feet, but didn't seem to care.

"I'm sorry," said the security guard, slurring his words. "I know I shouldn't have done it, I just couldn't help myself."

"Done what, Terry?" asked Kett.

"All this shit," said Terry, looking up. "I fucking killed them."

"Them?" said Kett. "You're talking about Helen Coulter? Idris Mellor? Judy Bartlett, and Nolan O'Brien, too?"

Terry looked at Kett, his red eyes swimming with tears, his face full of guilt.

"Yeah," he said.

Then he frowned, swaying like a metronome. He was absolutely off his face.

"Wait, what?"

"You killed those people?" Kett asked.

"No," he said, looking at the dropped bear. "I killed *them*. My dreams."

"What?"

Terry tried to take a step towards Kett, but the PC held onto his arm, rooting him in place.

"My dreams. Funland. Never gonna happen now."

He hung his head, sobbing. Kett looked at the PCs to see if any of them had any idea what was going on, but they were as confused as he was. The lack of air in the corridor was getting to him, as well as the overpowering reek of whisky.

"Get him outside," he said. "Put him in a car. You gonna go nicely, Terry?"

The man nodded, snorting a sob and staring at his stained pants.

"Just let me put my trousers on first, will you?"

CHAPTER TWENTY-SIX

For the second time that day, Porter made his way out of A&E. At least they'd managed to see him this time, although it hadn't done a lot of good. The nurse had shone a light in his eyes, flexed his neck a bit, made him stand on one leg, then told him he should probably just go home.

"Come back in if you start actually throwing up, if you have a seizure or pass out, or if you pop your clogs," she'd told him. "Although considering you're a police officer, you'll probably choose to keep working even when you're dead."

"You haven't met my Superintendent," he told her. "We don't get a choice."

She'd passed him a piece of paper with her personal number on it, too, in case he couldn't get through to the ward. This, more than the painkillers she'd given him, made him smile as he walked out the door—if only because it had been so long since anyone had shown the slightest bit of interest. It wasn't just the weight he'd packed on since

Bobby had been born, he knew, it was that life had just been so hard, and he'd been exhausted, and every time he looked at himself in the mirror, he'd died a little more behind the eyes.

Even so, he put the piece of paper in the bin as he walked back into the car park, feeling guilty for having it. He'd been dropped off by an IRV, so he hailed a taxi and promptly fell asleep in the back as they idled in the queues leaving the hospital. The driver woke him twenty minutes later with a blare of the horn, one that almost sent him through the roof.

"Bloody hell," he grumbled, paying with his phone. "Ever heard of a bit of compassion?"

He got out, letting himself into the house. Bobby was crying about something, and when he walked into the kitchen, he saw Allie trying to wrestle him into his shoes.

"Alright?" he said, standing in the doorway. He'd learned not to move straight in with a hug because most of the time she seemed repulsed by him, especially if he'd been at work.

Allie glanced back, and he could tell by the lines on her forehead that she was already furious. Bobby hadn't even noticed he was there, too busy trying to kick off his shoes.

"We *were* alright, Pete," she said. "Because we'd just got to sleep, hadn't we? Then somebody woke him up with the horn."

"Oh," said Porter. "Right. Sorry."

"So we're going out," said Allie, lobbing Bobby's shoe across the kitchen. "Without our shoes, apparently."

She stood up, folding her arms over her chest.

"Unless you want to do it? You finished?"

"No," he said. "Sorry. Just came to get changed. We haven't caught him yet."

He gave her a shrug, and she continued to glare at him until he turned away.

"I was in the hospital," he said. "Got pushed down the stairs."

"You seem fine to me, Pete," she said.

"I am, I guess," he told her. He was starting to feel sick again, although he didn't think it had anything to do with what had happened in the pub. "I can take him round the block. You want to go for a walk with Daddy, Bobs?"

Bobby looked up from his socks, finally seeing him. He slipped off his chair and ran over, and Porter lifted him up for a cuddle. He was a proper tank, as solid as they came, and the effort of holding him kicked off the ache in his back again. He pulled him close, blowing raspberries under the boy's double chin, making him chortle with laughter.

"Little walk with your old man?" he said. "Give mummy a rest?"

He felt Allie's hand slide across his chest, and for a blissful second he thought she was coming in for a cuddle too. But she was just reclaiming Bobby, pulling the kid away and heading out of the kitchen into the hall. She dumped him into his buggy like he was a sack of potatoes.

"We're fine," she said. "We're going out, and if he doesn't want to put his shoes on, then he doesn't have to, but he's not running around the park in his socks. Hear that, Robert?"

Bobby held his chubby hands to Porter, his face collapsing into a sob. Allie clipped him in before he could worm his way out, then she wheeled the buggy around to face the front door. Porter ducked back into the kitchen to collect the boy's shoes, throwing them into the buggy's cargo tray just as Allie was pushing it outside. Bobby screamed as she pushed him down the driveway, the buggy rocking with the force of his escape attempts.

"I could come too?" Porter called after them.

Allie shot a look over her shoulder, one that actually stung him—a physical pain right in the middle of his chest.

"You do whatever you need to do, Pete," she said. "We'll be fine. We always are."

HE HAD a shower and changed his clothes, grabbing a jacket to replace the one he'd lost in the riot. He managed less than five minutes on the sofa before the house felt too big and too quiet, so he walked down the road to HQ instead. When he reached the MIT bullpen, he found a handful of officers inside, including DS Spalding.

"You heard, sir?" she asked. "They're bringing in Terry Prince."

"Oh," he said, although he couldn't for the life of him remember who that was. "For the eyeball murders?"

Spalding didn't confirm it one way or another, sliding her well-chewed pencil back between her teeth. Porter glanced into the Incident Room to find it empty, although the photograph of the bald, wrinkle-headed security guard pinned to the wall reminded him who Prince was. Then he headed back across the office.

"Clare left any instructions?" he asked Spalding as he passed her desk.

"He left plenty of instructions for how to turn your genitals inside out," she replied. "Other than that, I think he wants everyone back in the city."

He took his Mondeo, driving the long way back into Norwich in the hope that he might pass Allie and Bobby on their walk. There was no sign of them in the town, though, or on the Hethersett Road. The disappointment of it gnawed away at him, made him feel like there was a black hole in the middle of his chest, one that would never be full again, or warm. He'd refused to let himself see how awful things had got, and that was partly just the way he dealt with life. Better to ignore the problems, let them fix themselves, right?

But it wasn't like he was never there for Allie. Other than the big cases, like this one, he was almost always home in time for dinner. He took Bobby out pretty much every single day he had off, and he always made sure they had a babysitter a few times a month so that he and Allie could go out and reclaim their youth in the restaurants and the pubs—occasionally the clubs, too, stumbling home at two in the morning drunk on Bacardi and good memories. He'd never neglected her, even though parenting took up so much of their time, and so much of his brain.

Lately, though, he'd started to wonder what would happen if things didn't get better. He'd never end it—he didn't think it was physically possible for him to tell Allie how he truly felt, a mental block he'd had for most of his life—but sooner or later, he thought, *she* would. Then what? She was a former teacher, an assistant head who'd taken extended maternity leave to nurture their son. He was a copper in a unit that commonly made the papers for the extreme violence of its cases, one that often saw him in mortal danger. There was no competition.

Is that what it would be, then? Every other weekend? Half a birthday, half a Christmas? Who was going to look after his son when he wasn't there? Who was going to keep him safe?

It was enough to give him cold sweats, despite the heat,

and he forced the thoughts out of his head, focussing on the roads until he entered the city. It was mobbed, as always, even though it was starting to get dark. He got off the main road as soon as he could, because he was worried his fraying temper might get him into trouble, navigating the quiet, circuitous streets that led towards the estate. He called Clare as he went, but the Super wasn't answering. He tried Kett instead, with no more luck. The only one who picked up was Savage.

"Sir," she said. "I was starting to wonder what had happened to you."

"Nothing much," he said. "Went home to change. You've arrested Prince? The eyeball killer?"

"The Saint Killer," came a voice that he thought belonged to the visiting sergeant, Cafferty.

"Sorry, I'm on speaker," said Savage. "I don't think we can call him that anymore, Steph. You heard about the body in the flat, sir?"

"Yeah," he said. "Dead Nazi?"

"We think so. Nazi and fortune teller, apparently."

"Odd combo," he said.

"Not really, the Nazis were obsessed with all that stuff," said Cafferty.

"What does that have to do with Prince?"

"We're not sure," said Savage. "Maybe nothing. Kett arrested Prince, I haven't heard all the details yet. You at HQ?"

"No, in the city," he said. He could feel the case unwinding inside his head, like cooked spaghetti. It was the same feeling of being out of control he had when he thought about Allie and Bobby. "What are you doing?"

"Heading over to see Enid," she said. "Just in case she knew the dead guy."

"Enid the witch?" he asked, thinking of what she'd told him about Allie. "Tell her she might have been onto something."

"What, sir?"

"Nothing."

He was driving into the estate from the northwest, the enormous Winchester Tower filling his windscreen. Compared to earlier, there weren't many people around, which was probably the only reason Porter saw the kid.

He'd driven past the alleyway before it even registered, and he pumped the brakes, throwing the Mondeo into reverse.

"Sir?" said Savage.

He pulled level with the alley again, seeing a lad in a black and grey tracksuit, his hood up. He was tagging a wall with an aerosol can, and so engrossed in his work that he hadn't noticed he wasn't alone.

"Shit," said Porter. "Hang on, I'll call you back."

He cut off Savage's reply, opening his door as quietly as he could. He couldn't get a good look at the man's face, but he was definitely wearing the right uniform for the gang. His trainers were the brightest thing in sight. The sound of his hissing can reverberated down the alley.

Porter ducked back into the car, opening the glove box and pulling out the extendable baton he kept in there. It wasn't exactly legal, but after everything that had happened last year on the Cold Iron Kills case, he'd stopped taking chances. It was better for him to get a bollocking than for Bobby to grow up without a dad.

Besides, it was only a baton. It wasn't much better than a toothpick in most situations.

He slipped it into his pocket, clambered out of the car,

and—before he could think about what he was doing—slammed the door.

Fuck.

The kid snapped his head around, his bright blue eyes meeting Porter's over the roof of the Mondeo. The same guy from before, he realised, the one who'd pushed him down the stairs. For a few seconds, they stood like that, the kid like a rabbit frozen by headlights.

Then Porter yelled, "Don't!" and the boy *did*, spinning in a tight circle and legging it.

"Good job, you muppet," he told himself as he broke into a run.

By the time he'd crossed the pavement and entered the alleyway, the kid was out of sight, the drum of his footsteps echoing back. Porter sprinted past the wall where he'd been standing, seeing the same piece of graffiti that had been outside the door in the flats: the words Iron Soldiers, topped with a crown.

"Come back!" he yelled, slowing as he approached the end of the alley. He snapped the baton out to its full length, holding it next to his head as he rounded the corner.

There was a courtyard ahead, nothing there but a couple of industrial wheelie bins. Blocks of flats boxed him in, two roads leading out, plus an archway over a footpath.

"Where are you, you little shit?" Porter shouted, the words bouncing back off the buildings. "Why don't you come and show me how tough you are when you aren't creeping up behind my back?"

"Where's the fun in that, *pussio*?" came a reply from the direction of the arch.

Porter crossed the courtyard, keeping a wary eye on the space behind the bins in case the kid had his mates there. He should have called for backup, he knew, but he hadn't wanted the arsehole to get away, and he didn't want to do it now because he didn't want him to know he was on his own.

"Got half the Force on the way," he bluffed. "Armed police, mate, shoot to kill. Sound good?"

"Sounds great!" came the reply, followed by a hoot of wild laughter.

Porter jogged through the arch, following the narrow footpath around to the left past more bins. With the flats on one side and a high brick wall on the other, he felt like he was inside a labyrinth.

The kid was waiting for him up ahead, outside an open door that led into the apartment building. There was a giant grin plastered on his face.

"What you gonna do, big lad? You want me?"

Porter slowed to a walk, the baton still raised.

"Then come and get me," said the kid.

He stepped into the building, vanishing into the dark.

"Fuck's sake," said Porter.

He took out his phone, calling 999 as he crept towards the door.

"This is DI Porter, Norfolk Police," he said when the operator answered. "I need immediate assistance, uh..."

He looked around, seeing no landmarks.

"Some shithole off Vauxhall, lots of bins. Suspect has entered a four-storey building with a..."

He reached the entrance, peering inside. He was sweating so much he could barely see.

"Red door, stinks of piss."

"I'm going to need a bit more than that," said the woman on the phone.

"Cat," said Porter, seeing one slink out of the door and leap effortlessly onto the wall. "Black, white feet. Look, just get somebody over here, or we're going to lose him."

He slipped the phone into his pocket, leaving the call open. A door led into a small laundry, the washing machine running. Next to that was a concrete staircase leading up. Porter could hear the lad's footsteps as he ran, more laughter, like he was enjoying this. The sound of it lit a fuse inside him, and he gripped the baton hard as he started to climb.

"You are going to get such a battering," he grunted.

He reached the first floor, pushing through an unsecured door to see a couple of much younger kids playing outside a flat.

"Hey, you guys see a teenager run past?" he asked them.

A woman appeared, ushering the kids inside.

"Police," he told her, wiggling the baton as proof. "Little drug dealing twat in a tracksuit?"

He wondered for a moment if she didn't speak English, because she didn't seem to understand him. Then she pointed to the ceiling.

"Next floor?"

She nodded as she closed her door. Porter carried on, sliding out his phone as he went.

"You still there?" he said.

"I am. Do you know where you are yet?"

"No, but wherever it is, it's on the second floor."

He reached the next level, pocketing the phone so he could open the fire door. An identical corridor greeted him, the walls scarred with graffiti and even a scorch mark where something had been set on fire.

The blue-eyed lad stood outside a door halfway down, a fist raised like he was holding an invisible weapon. He was still grinning like a village idiot at the fair.

Porter stopped, trying to catch his breath so he could shout. The kid beat him to it.

"Sorry about your face, innit," he said. "You was in the way, big man. Nothing personal."

"Yeah?" said Porter, taking a step towards him. "If you're sorry, get on the floor."

"Nah," he said. "Got something else for you, though."

"On the floor," Porter said again. He took a step, then hesitated. Every base instinct was telling him to get the hell out of there.

Everything was telling him he'd walked right into a trap.

"You got to remember something," said the kid, pulling a black scarf over his mouth. "This ting about to happen, you deserve it."

"What?" said Porter.

The kid pounded his fist on the door, the sound filling the corridor like gunshots. He took a couple of steps back, bouncing on the balls of his feet like he was gearing up for a fight.

"Iron Soldiers, *pussio*!" he shouted.

The door of the flat ripped open and a man looked out. He was in his forties, bearded, his flabby torso barely covered by a vest. He looked at the kid and shouted something.

"Oi!" yelled Porter.

The man turned to him, his face contorted by rage.

"Police!" Porter roared. "Get on the floor!"

The man vanished into the flat, yelling to somebody. Before Porter could take a step, he'd reappeared.

This time, he had a machete in his hand.

"Big mistake," said the guy, his voice thick with an accent.

He started caning it down the corridor towards him.

"Fuck," said Porter.

Another man burst from the flat, then a third, all of

them charging his way. Behind them, the kid howled with laughter.

"Nope," said Porter.

He wheeled around, crunching through the door into the stairwell, the sound of death following him like rolling thunder.

CHAPTER TWENTY-SEVEN

"IT WAS THAT ONE, WASN'T IT?"

Duke nudged his hairy chin towards a row of terraces on the other side of the road, their top windows basking in the fierce glow of the sinking sun, their ground floors mired in shadow. Savage squinted in the direction he was pointing his beard, trying to remember which one was Enid Heathen's house. They'd walked here from Winchester Tower, but so far nobody had been able to place it.

"The one with the flamingo," Duke went on. "I'm sure it had a flamingo. It had some kind of bird thing."

The plastic flamingo watched them as they walked by, looking relieved when they'd passed.

"That's it," said Cafferty, who was lagging behind. She must have hit a wall, Savage thought, because she'd been quiet ever since they'd left Nolan O'Brien's flat. "Horseshoe."

There it was, sure enough, a silver horseshoe mounted over the door. It was still the wrong way round, the legs pointing down, and Savage had to resist the urge to turn it over as they walked through the gate.

"Told you," said Duke, smearing a sleeve over his forehead, wincing as it touched the bruise on his face. "Bird thing."

Savage looked at him, wondering if he was suffering some kind of heat stroke.

"The horseshoe?" she asked.

"Bird, horse," said Duke, shrugging those giant shoulders. "Same thing."

"They're really not," said Cafferty.

The visiting sergeant rapped her knuckles on the door, standing back.

"They're both animals, is what I mean," said Duke. "I was thinking about an animal thing."

"Course you were," said Savage, giving his arm a squeeze.

She pulled out her phone to see if Porter had rung back, but there were no missed calls. Cafferty knocked again, and this time she ducked down to push open the letterbox.

"Enid? It's the police. Can you open up?"

"She's probably in there with Porter," said Duke. "Reading his cards, telling him what a loser he is."

"Give him a break, Aaron," said Savage. "He's going through a hard time, I think."

"Sorry," said Duke.

She gave him the look again.

"*Sarge*," he added, trying and failing not to roll his eyes.

She kept the look going, and he lifted his hands in defence.

"I'm sorry!"

She finally turned away.

"I really don't like this," he muttered.

"You'd better run for sergeant, then," said Savage.

A shape appeared in the glass panel of the door, a quavering voice.

"Hello?"

"Enid?" shouted Savage, taking over. "It's Kate, the police officer. We spoke yesterday."

"Police?" said the voice, clearer now. It wasn't Enid.

"Can you open the door?" said Savage. "Just for a second."

"You need a warrant," said the woman, although she didn't sound sure.

"Not to talk, we don't," said Savage. "Please just open the door, nobody is in any trouble."

A key turned, and the door shifted a crack—just enough for a dark eye to appear in the gap. Cafferty stepped up, giving it a gentle but insistent push until it swung all the way open.

"That's better," said Cafferty. "Nothing to be scared of out here."

The woman on the other side would have fallen over if the wall hadn't been there to hold her up. She was in her teens or early twenties, stick thin, her lank hair plastered to her face. At first, Savage thought she was the girl who'd been here yesterday, Enid's granddaughter, but it wasn't. She was wearing a *Top Gun* T-shirt that hung down to her thighs, and that was it. Savage didn't like to judge anyone until she'd got to know them, but everything about her hollow cheeks and her chapped lips made it clear she was using.

"What's your name?" asked Savage.

"Lily," she said, her haunted eyes taking them all in. She scratched her arm, the track marks clearly visible.

"Why are you here, Lily?" said Savage.

"Live here," she said.

"With Enid?"

The girl didn't answer, peering past Savage's shoulder to where Duke stood. She looked terrified of him.

"Is Enid looking after you?" said Savage.

"I don't know," said the girl.

"Is she here?"

"I don't..." Lily shook her head, still scratching her arm. "I don't think so?"

Savage stepped through the door, squeezing past Lily.

"Hey," said the girl. "You can't—"

"Can, and are," said Cafferty, following her into the house.

"Enid?" called Savage.

Any doubts that she was in the wrong house were scrubbed away when she entered the kitchen. It looked exactly the same. She could even see the mugs they'd used yesterday, sitting by the sink, unwashed.

There was nobody else here, or in the living room. The only other person in the house was upstairs in the master bedroom, another young woman lying on one of the six single mattresses that had been arranged over the floor. Even with the curtains closed and the lights off, Savage could see that she was off her face, a litter of drug paraphernalia scattered around her. This wasn't the granddaughter either.

She made her way back down to see Lily squatting in the front hall, shivering.

"What is this place?" she asked. "Where's Enid?"

Lily shook her head, looking like she was about to be sick.

"What about her granddaughter?" said Savage, thinking of the girl who'd been in the kitchen with them. "Dascha, was it? Is she here?"

"Garden's empty," said Cafferty, appearing through the open side door. "I think your mate played us."

"That doesn't make any sense," said Savage. "We were right here. Why would she invite us in yesterday if she was hiding something?"

Outside, Duke's radio bleeped, the sound of it making Lily flinch.

"Any available units," came the operator's voice. "Proceed to Vauxhall Street. Vauxhall Street. Officer in distress."

"Shit," said Duke, thumbing the radio. "This is PC Duke. I'm, like, a minute away. Where am I going?"

"Block of flats, red door, bins and... uh, a black cat," said the woman. "That's all I've got."

"Who is it?" yelled Savage, stepping over Lily to get out of the house. Duke relayed the question, and the answer was spat out a second later.

"DI Peter Porter."

"Shit," Duke said again.

He set off at a run, and so did Savage—in the other direction.

"It's this way, Aaron," she yelled.

He spun around, pounding after her. Cafferty joined them, and they bolted down the street together, swinging right at the bottom. There were a dozen blocks of flats visible from here, and none of them had red doors.

"I can't see a cat?" yelled Duke, a dozen yards ahead. "Can anyone see a cat?"

"There!" yelled Cafferty, pointing past a chain-link fence.

"Cat?" said Duke, skidding to a halt.

"No! *Porter*!"

They all turned to see the DI exploding through the

door of a four-storey building on the far side of a pedestrian walkway. He was maybe fifty yards away, but Savage could hear his bellowing breaths from here. He tripped on his own feet, landing hard on his hands and knees.

"Sir!" Savage called, running for the fence. "What's—"

Her question was answered when the door swung open again, and something ran out behind him. It was either a man or a bear, but whatever it was, it was holding a huge machete. Two more men followed, none of them wearing any trousers or socks or shoes, but all of them armed.

"Oi!" bellowed Duke, tearing down the street. "Get away from him!"

Porter was back on his feet and careening towards them. There was no break in the fence, but Duke had found a weak section, and he hauled himself over the sagging top, landing on his feet. He was running again in no time, his Taser out.

"Armed police!" he roared.

Savage clambered over the fence, scratching her arm on the wire. By the time she'd helped Cafferty down, Duke had reached Porter—and so had the men.

Duke fired his Taser, the barbs hitting the first guy in the neck. He almost took off, the machete spinning out of his hand as he crashed to the dirt. There was no time for another shot, the second guy swinging a hammer at the back of Porter's head.

Savage charged into him, planting her shoulder right in his solar plexus with a sickening crunch. He fell back, and she landed on top of him, hitting the same target with her knee. He tried to lift the hammer, but she snatched it away, holding it over her head.

"Don't move," she said, her throat full of acid.

He wasn't going to move. He could barely breathe, both

hands on his stomach as he tried to suck in air. His bloodshot eyes boiled with rage, his teeth red.

Savage glanced back to see that the third guy was bolting, his bare feet leaving a trail of bloody footprints. He still had a knife clenched in his fist. Duke was in pursuit, his baton out.

"Aaron!" she called out. "Leave him! It's not worth it."

If he heard her, he didn't stop. The man vanished through the door into the flats, and Duke followed, both of them swallowed up.

Savage looked at Porter, who was standing with his hands on his knees, wheezing almost as much as the man she was sitting on.

"Sir?" she said.

"I'm fine," he croaked. "Just knackered."

"Duke!" she said, pointing the hammer at the block of flats.

"Oh, shit, yeah," said Porter, starting a lumbering jog.

"I'll go," said Cafferty.

She broke away, sprinting so fast that she lost her pocket square. She flew into the building, her voice drifting back.

"Duke? Where are you?"

Porter walked to Savage, snapping a set of cuffs on the guy underneath her. She clambered off him, and the man arched his back, still struggling to breathe. He'd gone a little blue.

Savage swore, reaching for her phone only to realise it had fallen out of her pocket somewhere.

"Can you call for an ambulance, sir?"

Porter nodded, his phone to his ear.

"Maybe two?" said Savage, turning her attention to the man who'd been armed with the machete. He was out cold, his mouth frothing. The Taser barbs were still lodged in his neck. She probably should have checked for a pulse, but she didn't want to get close. Judging by the smell, he'd shit himself.

Besides, there was no time.

"You got this, sir?" she said, heading towards the building.

She didn't wait for Porter to answer, because a couple of IRVs had pulled up on the other side of the fence, coppers scrambling out. Savage waved to get their attention, then pelted towards the door—only to stop when Cafferty came staggering out of it, her face twisted into a mask of horror.

There was blood all over her hands.

"Steph?" said Savage. "What happened? Where's Aaron?"

"He needs help," said Cafferty. "We need help."

Savage froze. It was like somebody had hurled her into the sea at night, the cold enough to paralyse her.

"Aaron?"

Then Duke appeared in the door, a streak of blood on his face. He was talking into his radio.

"And hurry, he's bleeding out."

He looked at Savage.

"He fell," he said. "Fell right on his knife. I need help."

Savage managed a couple of steps, her head reeling. Then two constables overtook her, stampeding into the building.

She put her hands in her hair, her heart fizzing, her stomach trying to chew itself out of her like a wild animal. Cafferty walked over, looking at her blood-slick fingers, her eyes wide with shock.

"I tried," she said. "I tried, but it was his neck... There was nothing we could do."

"Don't," said Savage. "Don't blame yourself, Steph."

Cafferty nodded, but she never took her eyes off her hands. Savage spotted her pocket square lying in the dirt, and she picked it up. She took the visiting sergeant's arm and led her to a low wall, helping her sit down.

"Just wait here," she said. "There's an ambulance coming, they can check you over."

"I'll be okay," said Cafferty, although she didn't sound sure. She still had her hands out in front of her, like she was carrying an invisible tray. "Just... there was so much blood."

Savage shook out the pocket square ready to fold it up again, only to stop when she spotted an insignia in the corner. It was maybe the size of her thumbnail, stitched neatly in white thread, and there was no mistaking what it was.

An eye. Open, and watching.

Cafferty saw what she was looking at, and she finally dropped her bloodied hands.

"Thanks," she said. "Can you just pop it back in for me, Kate? I don't want to touch it."

"Sure," said Savage.

She folded the fabric neatly, and tucked it into the pocket of Cafferty's suit, feeling the woman's eyes on her.

"No problem."

CHAPTER TWENTY-EIGHT

Of all the places in the world that could have been described as Funland, the interview room at Police HQ was not one of them.

Superintendent Clare had picked the worst of the bunch, a cupboard-sized space at the back of the building that had been used as a toilet by far too many suspects over the years. In this weather, with the door shut, the smell was enough to reduce a grown man to tears.

Kett wasn't sure if it was the aroma that was making Terry Prince cry, though. The security guard sat on the other side of the interview table, his bald, meaty head resting in his hands. His face was a mess of tears and snot as he sobbed freely.

The whisky smell was almost enough to overpower the stench of the room, although Kett had realised on the drive over that most of it was coming from him, after Terry had thrown the bottle.

The only good news was that the security guard had put on some trousers before leaving Norvic House.

Terry hadn't asked for representation, and he'd turned

down the duty solicitor, which weren't exactly the actions of a guilty man—unless he'd wanted to get caught, of course, like Savage had predicted. The only thing he'd said since they'd loaded him into an IRV and driven him here was 'they're dead,' and he'd said that about a hundred times.

"Terrence Prince," said Clare, leaning over the table. "I've got to say, you don't seem very princely right now."

Terry didn't respond, still crying into his hands.

"You look more like a suppurating bollock," Clare went on. He clicked his fingers in the security guard's face. "Pull yourself together, man."

Terry peeked through his fingers, his eyes bloodshot and bulging. He clamped his lips around the sobs, managing to calm himself a little.

"Better," said Clare. "You know why you're here?"

Terry sat back, resting his forearms on the edge of the table. His head balanced uneasily on his accumulation of chins, his bottom lip vibrating. He took a long breath.

"I want to get this out first," he said, his voice thick with emotion and laced with fumes. "I haven't hurt anyone. You said I killed some folks, but I didn't touch them. Wouldn't. I'm not like that."

"You mean Helen Coulter, Idris Mellor, Judy Bartlett and..."

Clare stopped, grasping for the final name.

"Nolan O'Brien," said Kett.

"Never touched them," said Terry. "I know you're not gonna believe me now, but it's true."

"Let's start with the office building we found you in, then," said Clare. "You haven't been employed by Royal Security since last year. What were you doing in Norvic House? What in the name of Godfrey's toss is Funland?"

"*Whose* toss?" Terry asked, struggling.

"Because I'll tell you what it looked like," Clare went on. "It looked like a serial killer's wank palace. Cages, mirrors, blood-red letters on the walls, animals that look like they want to skin you alive and wear you."

"What?" said Terry, a flash of anger passing across his face. "Those animals are the Fun Brigade, they're supposed to be for the kids."

"The kids you were planning to keep in the cages?" said Clare. He jabbed a finger at Terry, and half a dozen peas flew out of his sleeve, rolling across the table. Terry stared at them like they were some kind of intimidation technique. "Or that infernal maze we found downstairs."

They'd discovered a labyrinth of mirrors and glass on the third floor, lit by crimson lightbulbs. It had to have taken months to put together.

"No!" he squeaked. "Just kids, the ones who come to Funland, for *fun*."

He threw his hands up.

"Come on," he said. "You guys must have kids. They love all that. Bouncy castles, rope mazes, ball pits."

"Men running around in their underwear, swigging whisky," said Kett.

"The filthy mattress you've been tossing about on," said Clare.

"Don't forget the bucket of piss we found in the corridor," said Kett. "Wholesome entertainment for all the family."

"I—" started Terry, but Clare slammed a hand on the table to silence him. More peas tumbled out, the security guard's eyes boggling as he watched them roll off the table.

"I wouldn't send my kids there, and most of the time I hate them," he said.

"It's not open yet," whined Terry. "It's not finished. You weren't supposed to be there. When it's done, it's going to be..."

He tailed off, sniffing.

"Was supposed to be *fun*," he said, talking to the table. "Supposed to take people's minds off all the shit, you know? That was only a prototype, only a, what do you call it, a proof of..."

"Life?" said Clare. "Like a kidnapping?"

"No, proof of *concept*," said Terry. "To show the council what it could be. That building's been empty for years, nobody wants it. Why not use it for the community, eh? For the kids?"

"Hang on," said Kett. "You were building Funland out of the goodness of your heart?"

"Yeah," said Terry. "Kind of. I mean, people would pay to come in. Not doing it for free, it's cost me a fortune. But it would be worth it. Day out right in the middle of the city, plenty of parking. Took me weeks to get all that stuff in there, couldn't let anyone know, could I? Not until it was ready. Figured once the council saw it, they'd say it was great, they'd agree to let me have it."

He wiped the snot from his upper lip.

"Put everything I had into it, every fucking penny. And now it's dead."

"But you didn't have permission to use the building?" said Kett. "Unless I'm missing something?"

Terry shook his head.

"So you broke in? How long have you been living there?"

"Since Christmas," he said. "I've been looking after it. No other fucker has, I can tell you that. Royal were supposed to have a guard on duty, but they're too tight, they never bothered."

He spluttered out another sigh.

"I thought if I made it, then they'd let me keep it. It was a gift to the city. To the estate. Those kids haven't got much, have they? I thought, why not give them something to cheer themselves up?"

"Why did your employer let you go last summer, Terrence?" Clare asked. "What happened?"

Terry sat back, his face growing even redder.

"That was bullshit," he said. "I never touched them."

"Touched who?"

"The kids!" roared Terry, his voice filling the room. "I was *playing* with them."

"What kids?" said Clare.

"At the school fete," said Terry, his eyeballs bulging. "I was working, but I'm not all business. I'm friendly, I just said I'd play with them a bit. It was hot, and I didn't want to wear my jacket on the bouncy castle, and they asked to see my tattoos, so I had my shirt undone."

"Your tattoos?" said Kett, leaning back in his chair.

"Yeah! My tattoos. Fuck's wrong with showing some children a bit of artwork? I got them for my kids when they were little."

Kett could still see the thick black lines of whatever had been inked on Terry's wrists, more shapes peeking up past the collar of his shirt.

"What are they?" he asked. "Your tattoos?"

"You wanna see 'em?"

Terry stood up so fast his chair clattered over behind him. Kett flinched, waiting for the bear of a man to throw himself over the table. But he was just unzipping his jacket, hurling it to the floor to reveal a filthy shirt with piss-yellow pits. He didn't bother with the buttons, he just pulled it over his head, revealing a bloated torso that was almost completely covered in ink.

Kett opened his mouth, but nothing came out.

The security guard looked like a walking advert for classic Children's TV. About thirty characters from various kids' shows had been inked—badly—across his body. The Flowerpot Men sat on one side of his quivering chest, a hairy nipple forming the shocked mouth of either Bill or Ben. A collection of Wombles clung to his other corpulent tit, hugging each other in apparent terror. There was a grinning Noddy on one shoulder, and Big Ears on the other, their stringy hands reaching for each other over Terry's collarbone, far too many fingers. A distinctly phallic Thomas the Tank Engine pulled a line of carriages down his right arm, ending at the wrist.

Taking pride of place across his stomach were Sooty, Sweep and Sue, lined up like a parade of dead-eyed suspects in a murder investigation. They were bookended by George and Zippy from Rainbow, the latter of whom resembled a gimp from a German fetish club. Kett wasn't sure, but he thought it was Bungle's ears he saw poking up over the man's belt.

"Jesus Christ," he said, finding his voice. "I think Swastikas would have been less scary."

"Swastikas?" said Terry, picking up his chair and slumping into it. "I don't have none of them. I'm not one of those guys. I love all the kids. All races. I'm not fussy."

He leaned forward, the faces of his tattoos gurning in protest.

"Look, they did an internal investigation and said it wasn't serious enough to call the police. Nobody complained, really. Nobody was... touched. We were just having a bounce. I didn't tell them all to take their tops off, did I? It was hot! And it's hard to keep your balance in there, which is why we were rolling about."

He put his hands to his face again.

"Okay," said Kett, drawing the word out. "You think you've seen it all, then you meet Terry Prince."

"After looking at that, I never want to see anything again," said Clare. "I'd happily gouge out my own..."

The Superintendent blanched, swallowing hard, an awkward silence falling across the room. He was saved by his phone, which rang inside his pocket.

"Finish this, Robert," he said, standing up to answer the call and leaving a puddle of peas behind him. "What is it, Kate?"

He walked to the door, wrenching it open.

"You bloody what?" he roared. "Tell that useless donkey to get his arse in here *now*, he's going to get the fisting of his short, tragic life!"

Clare slammed the door shut behind him hard enough to make Kett's ears ring.

"Fisting?" said Terry, alarmed.

"Doesn't mean what he thinks it does," said Kett. "Listen, Terry, I'm honestly going to need some time to process all..."

He studied the man's torso again, seeing Danger Mouse poking out from beneath a roll of fat like he was stuck under a boulder.

"All of *this*. But I need to ask you about the man in the mask. You're sure you saw him? On Friday, and again last night?"

Terry nodded.

"I know you were drunk, so I need you to think very carefully."

"I saw him," said Terry. "You don't forget something like that. There are good people and bad people in this world. I'm one of the good ones, obviously."

"Still open to debate, I think," said Kett.

"But *he's* not. You don't even need to see a man's face to know that."

Kett opened his phone, scrolling down to the images he'd found on Google earlier.

"You said the man was wearing a helmet, right? Was it like any of these?"

Terry dutifully took the phone, flicking his thumb over the screen.

"I told you, I don't remember," he said. "Don't see so well. Didn't go all the way around his head, I don't think. Had a kind of white hood underneath."

Kett pulled the phone back, searching Google for welding masks that didn't cover the whole head. He passed it over again.

"Like these?"

Terry pored over the images with his red eyes.

"No," he said. "Wasn't as new. More old-fashioned, with round eyes."

"I'm going to send someone in with some paper and a pen," he said. "You think you can draw it for me?"

For the first time since the interview had started, Terry brightened.

"Sure," he said. "Drawing's my thing. It's what I wanted to do, before the security stuff took over. Did all these myself."

He sat back, the characters on his body howling silently in their eternal torment.

"Good to know," said Kett.

He stood up, heading for the door.

"I'm not in trouble, am I?" said Terry. "I know it's hard to believe, but I only ever wanted to do something good. I'm not guilty of anything. Nothing serious, anyway."

"You're definitely guilty of ruining *Rainbow* for me," said Kett, feeling a sudden wash of sympathy for the man. "Just sit tight, somebody will be with you soon."

CHAPTER TWENTY-NINE

Kett could hear Clare bellowing from the corridor that led to the MIT bullpen, and he took a detour to the kitchen so he didn't have to be a part of it. By the time he'd made a few mugs of tea and carried them back, though, the tirade had grown even worse.

He pushed through the door to see the Superintendent standing in the middle of the open-plan office like a bug-eyed evangelical. He was gesticulating so much that he was in danger of taking off, the spit exploding from his lips.

His congregation consisted of Porter, Savage, Duke and Cafferty, as well as a huddle of terrified constables. They all sat in a semi-circle in front of him, not on chairs but on the floor, their legs crossed. Everyone looked exhausted.

"Because if you want to have your arses spanked," Clare roared. "If this is some twisted fetish that you've developed, then please don't bother breaking into a drug dealer's flat, don't go to the trouble of getting chased down the street by men with big knives, don't find yourself in the middle of a sweaty ten-copper pile up. Just come to me, pull down your trousers, and I'll give you the spanking of your life!"

Kett froze. The hot mugs were burning his hand, but he didn't want to draw any attention to himself.

"And don't think you can hide back there, Robert," said Clare. The Super's head twisted around slowly, like he was a possessed owl. "On the carpet. Now."

"The carpet, sir?" he said, dumping the tea on the nearest desk.

"Yes, Detective, the carpet, with all the other disobedient children."

Kett did as he was told, finding a space next to Porter. It took him a good few seconds to get on the floor, every joint in his body cracking. He noticed that Porter's suit was torn, and he had a couple of nasty scratches on his neck. His hands were red raw, like they'd been washed in bleach.

"You alright, Pete?"

"No, he's not alright," said Clare. "He's been a very naughty boy, and he's about to get his punishment. Isn't that right, Peter?"

"I just followed my—"

"Get over here," Clare went on, pointing to the floor in front of him. "All fours. Trousers down. Kate, fetch my favourite paddle from the office."

"*What*?" said Porter and Savage at the same time.

"This really isn't normal," muttered Cafferty.

"Can somebody please tell me what I missed?" said Kett, trying to stretch his legs so his back wouldn't cramp.

Clare threw his arms up in resignation, stomping to the desk with the tea and collecting a mug. Slowly, as if wary of angering him, everybody else got to their feet. Porter walked to the nearest chair like a dog with its tail between its legs, collapsing into it.

"It was my fault," he said. "I was driving back into the

city, and I spotted that blue-eyed Iron Soldier tagging a wall. Went after him."

"Stupid," muttered Clare, taking a sip of tea and choking with the heat of it. He slammed the mug onto the desk, outraged. "This is *hot*!"

"It's... tea, sir?" said Kett.

"It's a hundred bloody degrees in here, Kett, nobody wants a cup of your hot toss burning into their intestines!"

He stormed into his office.

"Uh," said Porter. "So the kid ran into one of the blocks of flats, and I followed."

Clare appeared again, another pack of frozen peas in his hands. He placed it delicately on a chair, then perched on it.

"Go on then!" he yelled.

"I chased him up to a flat," said Porter. "He knocked on the door, and some people came out, came after me."

"Not *some people*, Pete," said Clare. "Three armed men. One of them had a machete. And they didn't *come after you*, they tried to hack you to pieces."

"Seriously?" said Kett, collecting two mugs from the desk and passing one to Porter. "You're okay, though?"

"Luckily for him, Savage and Duke showed up," said Clare. "Or we'd be adding his name to the very, very long list of dead people we've found this weekend."

"To be fair, sir," said Porter. "I could have taken them."

"Taken them where? To the hospital, after they'd cut off your head?" said the Superintendent.

"You were running so fast you'd have lost them eventually," said Duke, trying and failing to hide a smirk.

"I wasn't running," said Porter. "I was manoeuvring them exactly where I wanted them."

"Out in the open," said Duke, nodding sagely. "Where they could surround you."

"I'm going to surround you in a minute, Constable," growled Porter.

Before Duke could ask the DI what he meant, Savage jumped in.

"One of the men died."

"Died?" said Kett. "How?"

"Fell on his knife," said Cafferty. "Slipped, went right in."

She pointed to her throat and stuck out her tongue.

"He bled out before we could save him."

"Shit," said Kett. "You were all there?"

"Nope," said Cafferty. "Aaron was up ahead, nobody else was in the building. It was just lucky old me."

Savage was staring at the visiting sergeant, but Kett couldn't read the expression on her face. After a second or two, she turned back to him.

"The good news is that the flat they were in seems to be a hub for most of the dealing that's going on in the estate. As well as the three arrests, we found a tonne of product, and a lot of cash. This is going to make a massive dent in their operation."

"And this place wasn't on our radar?" said Kett.

"Not at all," Savage told him. "Which is weird, right?"

It took him a few seconds to work out what she was getting at.

"Weird that this kid led us right to his drugs," he said. "Rather than away from them. I mean, these guys aren't exactly the brightest tools in the shed, he probably didn't even think about what he was doing."

"Yeah," said Savage. "Either that, or he's not working with the men in the flat. He's from a rival gang."

"He leads us to the enemy," said Kett, nodding. "That's good thinking, Kate. Smart. You caught the kid, too?"

"No," said Porter. "He vanished when the door opened and his mates ran out. Little prick didn't even have the balls to come after me himself."

He cricked his neck.

"Obviously took one look at me and shat himself," he said.

Duke opened his mouth to comment, but once again Savage jumped in.

"Something else is odd. We went to see Enid Heathen again, the woman who said she knew my grandparents."

"The one who read your palms?" said Kett, taking a welcome sip of tea.

"Cards, sir. But yeah, her. We went to the house she was in yesterday to see if she knew Nolan O'Brien. He was a fortune teller too. She wasn't there, just a couple of kids who were using. I don't think Enid lives there at all. I think she's in on this."

"In on the drugs?" said Kett. "Isn't she a hundred years old?"

Savage nodded.

"We know she's got a criminal past, she admitted it to me herself. Told me Granddad arrested her back in the day. What if she's part of the gang?"

"What if she's *running* it?" said Cafferty, who had claimed the last mug of tea. Kett didn't miss the way that Savage looked at the visiting sergeant again, a wariness in her expression.

"Enid's in charge of the Iron Soldiers?" said Clare, dubious.

"We didn't have time to ask any more questions," said Savage. "The call came in about Porter being in trouble, and—"

"Wasn't in trouble," said Porter. "Was handling it."

"And I went back to the house afterwards, but the kids had gone. None of the neighbours knew anything about it. Or wanted to talk, anyway."

"This is all toss," said Clare. "None of it helps us find our killer."

"Unless the deaths are all connected to the drugs, sir," said Savage. "We spoke with the men who chased Porter. Well, the *man*. The only one who wasn't stabbed. Or Tasered. He didn't know anything about our victims, but he did say that his outfit had been using the locals to try to sell their product."

"Teenagers?" said Kett. "Like the Iron Soldiers?"

"No," she said. "Well, yes to teenagers. They were using kids like Idris, same way the County Lines gangs do. But not just kids. He said they'd been recruiting more widely. Adults and professionals. Including nurses and teachers."

"Wait a minute," said Clare, slamming his empty mug on the desk. "You think Helen and Judy might have been working with the gangs? That's ridiculous."

"Is it, though?" said Cafferty. "Everything's so expensive now, people are struggling. I'd bloody do it if I could get away with it."

"That's exactly what he said," Savage added. "He told us people are desperate for a bit of extra cash. It makes the dealers' jobs so much easier, because somebody else takes the fall. Nobody's going to suspect a nurse in her sixties or a young teacher of selling drugs."

"Especially if they're good people," said Kett.

"We'll know more in a bit," said Savage. "Spalding's interviewing the guy now."

"But if our three dead people were dealing, what went wrong?" said Kett. "Why were they killed?"

"Kate just said it," grunted Clare. "Rival gangs. If we've

got two outfits tearing chunks out of each other in the city, then they're going to go after each other's weakest points."

"The dealers," said Kett, nodding. "So our three victims were all selling gear for one of the gangs. The other outfit finds out who they are, kills them all in the most brutal way they can."

"To send a message," said Porter.

"To send a message," Kett echoed. "That's cartel-level butchery, though. Feels a bit out of place here. Did you get anything else out of the dealer?"

"No," said Savage. "He clammed up pretty quickly."

"What about the man we arrested outside the pub? Craig, uh..."

"Capper," said Clare. "Believe me, if he'd known anything, he'd have spilled his guts when I threatened to perform penile surgery with a baton."

"It's always the way," said Savage. "The people at the bottom don't know anything. They get their orders, and they're the ones who are caught if something goes wrong."

"So this isn't a serial killer, then?" said Kett. "I mean, in the traditional sense. What about the profiles you guys put together? They sounded pretty convincing."

Cafferty stared into her mug.

"Honestly, sir," the visiting sergeant said, looking a little disappointed, "it's Ockham's Razor. We can come up with as many amazing theories as you like, and believe me, you've got a proper genius working here."

She threw a smile at Savage.

"As smart as they come. But a profile is only ever going to be a profile, and when you've got a bagful of evidence pointing to a simpler solution, that's what you need to go with. As much as I'd love for this to be a psychopath playing games, something for the textbooks, a Netflix deal and early retirement for me, the drug explanation makes more sense."

"Kate?" said Kett.

Savage chewed on it, her eyes on the floor.

"Go with your gut," he told her.

"My gut is telling me we're still looking for somebody else," she said, looking up. "There's a pattern that doesn't fit with the drug narrative. The good person thing."

"Except it does fit," said Clare. "If you'd been listening. Nobody is going to suspect a good person of being a drug dealer."

"I get that, sir. But... I don't know. Nolan O'Brien is our killer's first victim, right? The first one that we know about, anyway. Emily thinks the body's been in the bath for two weeks or so."

"Her report just came in," said Clare. "O'Brien had his throat crushed. His eyes were removed with the same tool as the others."

"So this is our killer," Savage went on. "He goes after Nolan first. But Nolan isn't a good guy. He's got priors for violent protest, anti-immigration stuff, fascist tattoos. We found some pretty hardcore right-wing material in his flat, and a lot of Nazi themed esoteric stuff. He's—"

"An arsehole," said Duke.

"Right. To put it bluntly, he's an arsehole. And I think that's why the killer didn't replace his eyes after he'd taken them."

She glanced at Cafferty.

"I mean, that's why *we* think it. Me and Steph."

"No, Kate, this is all you," said Cafferty. "Go on."

"I think the tin in the eyes reflects how the killer sees his victims. Literally, maybe. It reflects their goodness, it shines. Nolan wasn't worthy of it, so he didn't get the prosthetics.

He was simply blinded, in this life and—in the killer's mind—the next one, too. The metal eyes are right at the heart of this, and I don't think they're a punishment. I think they're a kind of reward."

"Some reward," said Porter.

"He's giving them something that he feels is a blessing," Savage went on. "A gift for their goodness, something they can take with them to the next life, maybe."

She puffed out a breath, lifting her hands to signal she was done.

"So Nolan O'Brien wasn't a victim like the others," said Kett. "He was practice."

"A trial run for the surgery," said Cafferty.

"Exactly," said Savage. "Once the killer knew he could do it, he targeted the people he really wanted. The good ones."

"And he used O'Brien's garage," said Clare. "After he'd killed him."

"The smelting stuff was O'Brien's?" said Kett.

"There's no record of him buying it," said Savage. "I think the killer brought it, stored it there."

"But they knew each other?" said Kett. "O'Brien and the killer? They must have done, because the killer left the body in the bath and used the garage. He wouldn't have done that if he hadn't been certain O'Brien didn't have friends and family stopping by. What's the connection? How did they meet?"

"Nolan was a palm reader too, or something along those lines," said Savage. "He had a company, Cousin Soul. I think he was reading people's fortunes. We found a ledger, but it's all in some kind of code. If we can crack it, we might find the killer. Chances are, he was a client."

"That's good, Kate," said Kett. "That's great. The ledger's here?"

"On my desk," said Savage.

She covered a yawn with her hand, and it spread around the room, ending with a gargantuan roar of exhaustion from Clare.

"Right," said the Superintendent twenty seconds later, when he'd finally finished. "I know you're all exhausted, but I need you here. Drink coffee, suck it up. We keep working until we catch this tosser. Kate, I want you on the ledger. Robbie, Pete, follow up the drug leads. Duke, get me an ice cream."

"Ice cream!" said Duke, pumping a fist.

"What about me, sir?" said Cafferty.

Clare stared at her blankly.

"Cafferty," she told him.

It didn't seem to register in the Superintendent's bloodshot eyes.

"I'll just help Kate, then," she said, fuming quietly as she walked off.

"You might want to hold up," came a voice from the door that led to the interview rooms. Spalding was trotting through it, and she looked like she'd been running. She reached the group, stopping beside the Superintendent. "So much for snitches get stitches. The guy who attacked Porter will not stop talking."

"Baton, penis," said Clare. "I gave him the talk when he came in."

Spalding pulled a notepad from the inside pocket of her jacket.

"He doubled down on what he told you, Kate, that they're using civilians to push product. Gave me a few first names, which isn't a lot of help—except for the fact we know one of them."

She held up the notepad, but her writing was too small for Kett to read. Savage spotted it immediately.

"Roger. You don't think he means Helen's boyfriend?"

"Sex Man?" said Clare.

"Sexton. Did he say anything about him?"

"Only that he's old," said Spalding. "And that he's been dealing at the hospital."

"Holy shit," said Kett. "Sexton's a porter, isn't he?"

"Yeah," said Savage. "And... hang on."

She tore away, running to her desk and collecting a thick, leather-bound journal. By the time she'd got back, she'd opened it, putting it on the desk and pointing to a clump of text.

"This is the last entry in Nolan O'Brien's journal," she said. "The date's from two weeks ago, right around when he died. We're assuming this is his client list, right? Look at the initials."

"RS-C," said Kett. "The RS is clear enough, if this is Roger Sexton, but what about the C?"

"Cauliflower?" said Duke, leaning over.

Nobody answered him.

"Somebody interviewed Roger when he came in, right?" said Kett.

"I did," said Clare. "I told you already, multiple CCTV feeds show him cycling home minutes after saying goodbye to Helen in the park, the Ring cam has him arriving. The security camera from the flat shows that he doesn't go back inside the underpass."

"So you let him go?" said Kett.

"I let him go," Clare replied. "I've been doing this job a

long time, Robert. I can tell when somebody's guilty. I can smell it."

"Well you might want to trim those nose hairs, sir," said Kett. "Because there are three links between Roger and the bodies. He would have been with Helen minutes before she died. He might have been dealing for the gangs. And that could be his name in O'Brien's journal."

"Woulda, coulda, *putta* up your tosshole, Kett," said Clare.

"Rude!" said Cafferty, who had wandered back over.

"It's all circumstantial," Clare went on.

There was a knock on the door, and they all turned to see a constable standing there. She looked like she'd been asked to enter a lion's den while wearing bacon underpants.

"What?" bellowed Clare. "Have your shoes been nailed to the floor? Have you had knee surgery and require assistance? Have you walked into quick-setting cement? Do you need a charging cable in your—"

"What is it?" Kett interrupted, beckoning the constable in.

"I've got this for you, sir," she said, holding up a piece of paper.

She walked over, skirting around Clare like she was worried he was going to attack her. She passed the paper to Kett, who had to turn it upside down, and then sideways, before he could make any sense of the haphazard squiggles.

"It's from the suspect in the interview room," she said. "The sweaty one with the tattoos."

The quality of the artwork wasn't much better than the ink on Terry Prince's body, but he could just about see a skinny man dressed in dark overalls and heavy boots, a mask over his face. The mask was long enough to hang down over his throat, and it had two perfectly round holes that reminded Kett of a spider's eyes. Terry had drawn straps on either side, and a circular hood that rose above the top of the mask, which he'd left white.

The only thing he couldn't figure out was the scrawl of lines and circles between the man's legs, dangling all the way to the floor.

"What is that?" he asked.

"Penis," said Clare. "I'd recognise one anywhere."

"He had his knob out?" said Duke.

The constable who'd delivered the illustration leaned in.

"That thing?" she said. "Oh, yeah, he told me to tell you. He said it might have been the dark, or the scaffolding over the building, or the fact he can't see very well anymore, but he was pretty sure the man in the mask was either gliding, like a ghost..."

She shrugged.

"Or riding a bike."

CHAPTER THIRTY

Evening had moved in while they'd been looking the other way, a quiet gloom settling over the city, shadows softening all the hard edges.

Savage drove, Kett in the passenger seat, Porter and DS Cafferty in the back. They were following Clare's ancient Mercedes, Duke occasionally waving to them through the rear window like a kid in the back seat of a school bus. Clare, in turn, was chasing the tactical van, Ed Proctor at the wheel.

They weren't taking any chances this time.

It felt weird to be driving away from the estate where they'd found their dead, Kett thought. Roger Sexton's house was to the northwest of the city, miles from the underpass where Helen had been found, miles from Nolan O'Brien's flat and the school where Judy Bartlett once worked, miles from the epicentre of almost everything that had happened since Friday evening. It made sense that a killer wouldn't commit their atrocities in their own back garden, of course. But still, as they cut through the streets on a wave of blue light, something felt very wrong.

At least Norwich was quiet, even for a Sunday night. News of the case had broken quickly, and escalated fast. Nobody wanted to be walking the streets when a killer could drag them into the bushes and scoop out their eyes. Just twenty-nine minutes after leaving HQ, the tactical van rumbled onto Roger's street, the brakes squealing as it came to a stop.

Proctor was out in a heartbeat, his officers erupting from the back doors. Kett took his time, partly because he didn't want to get in the way, and partly because he was well and truly knackered. In the seat next to him, Porter looked like a corpse. The DI was quiet, his face serious. The job would do that to anyone, but this seemed like something else, something more.

"You doing okay, Pete?" he asked.

"Yeah," said Porter, opening his door. "Dandy."

They exited the IRV into the growing dark, meeting Clare and Duke by the Mercedes. Sexton's compact house sat in the middle of a neat garden. There was an attached garage, no car in the driveway. The curtains in every window were drawn, even though it wasn't fully dark yet.

Proctor was already at the front door, his rifle ready. He glanced at Clare.

"Are you sure about this, Kett?" the Superintendent asked. "Because if you're wrong, I'm going to..."

He didn't seem to have the energy to finish, using his hands to demonstrate what looked like somebody tying a balloon animal in knots.

"Not sure, sir," said Kett. "Not at all. But we're here now."

Clare breathed out a long sigh, then nodded to Proctor.

The team moved into action immediately, one member thumping an enforcer ram into the door hard enough to shatter the glass panel. He had to do it twice more before the lock exploded from the wall. Proctor piled in, his voice filling the street.

"Armed police! On the floor!"

The rest of the unit crashed into the house, echoing his cry like warriors on a battlefield. The shock and awe must have worked, because it was less than thirty seconds later that Proctor reappeared, pulling off his helmet.

"Suspect secure," he said, heading back to the street. "And crying his eyes out. No weapons. Did you really need us for this?"

"Oh, sorry, Ed," Clare spat back, flushed from the heat. "I didn't realise you had better things to be doing."

It looked for a second like they were going to start trading blows, then Proctor returned to his van, and Clare stomped towards the house. Kett let him get a head start, wondering whether anyone would notice if he just went home and never came back.

"Can you guys search the house?" Kett told the rest of the task force. "I'll handle Roger."

Handling Roger wasn't going to be a problem, he discovered when he'd walked into the surprisingly spacious front room. The man sat on the edge of his sofa in the shadow of the Superintendent, still wearing tight-fitting Lycra shorts and a yellow cycling T-shirt. He was bent double, his hands cuffed behind him and his head pushed forward, almost between his knees. He wasn't just crying, he was sobbing, his body wracked with emotion. He was making such an awful sound that the remaining members of the firearms team were staring awkwardly at him, not quite sure what to do with themselves.

"We'll be okay," said Kett, ushering them out of the living room and closing the door.

He took a closer look at the room, finding himself surrounded by birds. They were real, he saw, but unlike those in Nolan O'Brien's flat, they were stuffed and preserved, their artificial eyes bright. Beneath the reek of an air freshener that was plugged into the wall, Kett could smell something musty and unpleasant that might have been formaldehyde.

"You know why we're here, Roger?" said Clare, looming over the man.

"No, I don't," Roger replied, coughing the words out in his Newcastle accent. "I told you everything, I did everything you asked. I didn't hurt Helen."

"You lied to me," said Clare. "Didn't you, Roger?"

"I didn't," he said, sitting up straight so he could look the Superintendent in the eye. "I didn't hurt her. I wouldn't have. I—"

"What about the drugs?" said Kett.

Roger snapped his mouth shut so urgently that his teeth clacked. He shook his head in denial, but he seemed to have lost the ability to speak.

"Can't imagine there's a lot of demand for heroin up at the hospital," Kett went on. "Other than pain relief, I guess. What were you selling? Cocaine? Ket? Amphetamines?"

Roger continued to shake his head.

"Long hours, when you're a doctor or a nurse," Kett said. "And we all need a little pick-me-up every now and again. Who was supplying the drugs, and who were you sending the money to?"

"I wasn't—"

"Listen," said Kett, moving across the room fast enough to frighten Roger back into the sofa. "I am too tired for any bullshit. I'm going to give you one chance to tell me the truth. Then I'm going to bring back the men with guns. Understood?"

Roger's head stopped swaying from side to side.

"Who gave you the drugs?"

"I don't know," he croaked. "I never met them. Knew a fella who knew them, one of the cleaners. He told me I could make some decent scran. I get a text telling me where to pick up, then I text them back when I've got the money."

"Same location?"

"No, it's different every time. I've got the phone, I can show you. But I never hurt anyone, it was just a bit of dope, it—"

"You never met them? Never saw them? Never caught a glimpse of anyone at any of the drop-off locations? Never had a conversation on the phone?"

"I'm sorry," he said. "I never should have done it, it was so stupid. It's just the money, it was only ever for the money."

"Did these people ever say anything else?" Kett asked. "Did they ever threaten you? Threaten to hurt you, or anyone close to you?"

"No!" said Roger. "I told you, I..."

Something happened to the man's face, a crack in his expression.

"Wait," he said. "Is that why... Is that what happened to Helen? Did they hurt her because of me?"

He looked from Kett to Clare and back again, his eyes wild. His voice was rising in pitch, a lunatic's scream.

"Did *I* do that to her?"

"That's what we want to know," said Kett. "Tell me again what happened on Friday evening, when you walked Helen home."

"I told you already! I left her in the park, I came straight back here. You said... You told me you'd found cameras. I was telling the truth."

"You didn't cycle back later in the evening?" said Kett. "To finish what you'd started?"

"What? No!"

"Do you know a man called Nolan O'Brien, Roger?"

"No!"

"Idris Mellor? Judy Bartlett?"

"No!"

His face was twisted into an insane mask of panic, his teeth bared, his jaw bulging.

"Because it's all connected," said Kett. "All of those victims, the drugs, the gangs, and right now, you're the only link between them."

"Go fuck yourself," spat Roger. "Both of you. Let me go, or I'll make sure you never fucking work again."

"Sounds like a threat," said Kett, the heat of the room making his skin prickle. "Makes me wonder if you did anything else for the gangs, other than sell drugs. Did you ever threaten anyone? Did you ever hurt anyone?"

"Fuck you," he growled.

"Nice birds," said Clare, studying their feathered audience. "You make these yourself?"

"Fuck you."

"You like playing with dead things, Roger?" Clare went on. "Those aren't their real eyes, are they? You can't preserve the eyes, they collapse. Too much fluid. I remember seeing that on a documentary once. You have to use fake ones."

"Helen had a bag of fake eyes in her flat," said Kett. "All shapes and sizes. Did you give them to her?"

"Fuck. You."

A knock on the door, Savage peeking through.

"Sir," she said. "You need to see this."

"What?" said Roger. "What is she talking about? See what?"

The man struggled to get up, but Clare planted a hand on his balding head and gave him a solid push back down again.

"You go," the Superintendent said, nodding to Kett. "I've got him."

"What?" roared Roger. "Just leave it alone, you fuck! Get out of my house!"

Kett walked into the hall, taking a breath to try to steady his pulse. Savage had disappeared through the side door into the garage, and he dutifully went after her. Six bikes hung on brackets on the walls, sleek and expensive, a mountain of equipment scattered over the floor. There were propane bottles here, two of them, as well as a shelf full of saucepans. The back of the garage was open, and Savage led the way outside to where Duke and DS Cafferty were standing by a couple of wheelie bins, the lids open.

"What is it?" Kett asked.

"In there, sir," said Savage, nodding to the black bin.

He peered inside, doing his best to ignore the reek of old food and rot. The plastic bag on the top had been ripped open, and sitting on a mound of waste was a child's wallet. It was bright red, the Marvel logo splashed across the front.

"Who found it?" he asked.

"Cafferty did, sir," said Savage.

"Just luck," said the sergeant. "Aaron didn't want to touch the bins."

"Icky," said Duke.

"Get it out," Kett said.

Savage plucked the wallet from the bin with a gloved hand, peeling open the Velcro.

"Two fivers, one card," she said. "That's all."

She teased the card free, holding it up. All Kett could see without his glasses was the NatWest logo and a whole lot of blurred writing.

"What does it say, Kate?" he asked, trying to keep his cool.

"It's a bank card, sir," she replied. "It's Idris Mellor's wallet."

"Holy shit," was all he could think to say.

KETT AND PORTER sat on the low wall outside the house, watching as Roger Sexton was led out of the door and down the drive. Clare helped him into the back of an IRV with a less-than-gentle shove, slamming the door hard enough for the sound of it to echo down the street. The Superintendent rubbed his face like he was trying to pull off a mask, and when he looked up, his skin was so loose and his eyes so dark, Kett could have sworn he was wearing one.

"You want me to handle the interview this time?" Kett asked.

"No," said Clare, walking over to them. "This bastard's all mine. Fool me once, that's a shame. Fool me twice, uh..."

His brow concertinaed like he was doing a maths test, then he gave up.

"I am too tired. This is our man. It has to be. He's admitted to working with the gangs that have been terrorising the estate. His garage is full of the same kind of equipment we found in O'Brien's garage, and there's a bloody taxidermy lab in his spare bedroom, a bunch of fake eyes that are almost identical to the ones we found in Helen's flat. *And* he had our victim's wallet in his bin. It's him."

"Not to mention he's bald," said Kett. "Bald*ing*, anyway. Like the guy who tried to get the mob to attack the kid outside the garages."

"Exactly," said Clare, heading for his car, tapping his nose. "Don't doubt me again, either of you. I can smell guilt. I told you it was him."

"You absolutely did not," Kett said quietly.

He watched the IRV pull away, Roger glaring at him through the window. Clare's Mercedes followed, both turning left at the end of the road.

"What do you reckon, Pete?" said Kett. "Is this him?"

Porter didn't reply. He was staring at the pavement.

"Pete?" said Kett, and when he still didn't answer, he put a hand on the DI's arm. Porter looked up like he'd forgotten where he was.

"Huh?" was all he managed.

"Why don't you go home?" said Kett. "You haven't slept, and you've been through the wringer. We can handle it from here."

The DI spluttered out a sigh, scuffing his shoe on the pavement.

"It's okay, sir," he said. "I want to see this through."

There was something he wasn't saying, and Kett gave him all the time he needed.

"And home's the last place I want to be."

"What's going on?" Kett asked. "You and Allie?"

Porter nodded, chewing on his thumbnail.

"Mate, you've been here before, a hundred times," said Kett. "You'll get through it. You always do."

"That's just it, though. That's exactly it. We fix it, then it breaks again, over and over and over. Things are shit, so we slap a plaster on it, pretend it's better. But it's not, Robbie. It's never better. I don't know why we can't see it."

A couple of constables climbed into another IRV, heading off.

"Because it's hard when you've got kids," said Kett when they'd gone. "It's impossible. You give so much to them that you lose everything else. You lose yourself, you lose each other."

"So it doesn't get any better," said Porter, a statement rather than a question. "What happens, then? We split up, and what about Bobby? Best case, he bounces between us for the rest of his life. Worst case..."

He took a breath like a drowning man.

"Worst case, she gets full custody, and I never see him. He grows up with Allie, and some other dad. I can't do that. I can't say goodbye to him."

"It's not goodbye, Pete," said Kett. "No matter what happens. You're an amazing dad, and Allie's never going to use him against you, she'll never stop you seeing him. She loves you."

Porter breathed out a bitter laugh, shaking his head. When he spoke again, it was quieter still.

"It's just messed me up," he said. "The thought of not being with him, of not being there to look after him. How can I make sure he's safe if I'm not even in the same house?"

He groaned into his hands.

"Rather die than lose him like that."

"Come on, Pete," said Kett.

"Sorry. I'm just knackered."

"Then go home," said Kett. "If not for you, then for Bobby. Put him to bed, read him a story. Then talk to Allie. Tell her how you're feeling. She'll understand."

Porter glanced at Kett, one eyebrow arched, and it was Kett's turn to laugh.

"Maybe she'll surprise you," he said. "Oh, I forgot to say, you texted me earlier, and I think it was meant for her."

He pulled out his phone and showed the message to Porter.

I love you, can't wait to curl up with you, big hugs and lots of kisses.

"I'm assuming you didn't want to hug me?"

"I kind of do now, sir," he said, brightening. "I was wondering why she never replied."

Porter nodded his thanks, heading to the huddle of constables on the side of the road.

"Who wants to take me home?"

"Sir," came a voice from behind him.

Kett turned to see Savage appearing from the ruined front door. She glanced behind her as she walked up.

"That was a good find, Kate," he said. "The wallet."

"It wasn't me, sir," she said, sitting on the wall. "That's what I wanted to talk to you about."

She looked back at the house again, wary.

"Steph found the wallet. She said it was right there when she tore open the binbag, sitting on top of the rubbish."

"And?"

"It's just... odd, sir. She was the only one who saw the man fall on his knife earlier, too. Aaron ran into the building, but he lost the target. The guy had run into the cellar. By the time he'd found them, it was too late. Steph was already there. He said..."

Another look back.

"He said she was just kneeling over him, watching him bleed out."

"Didn't sound like there was much she could have done," said Kett. "Where are you going with this, Kate?"

"Nowhere, sir. But we don't know her, do we? We don't know anything about her. Those pocket squares she wears, they're not too different to the napkin we found on Helen's face, and in Judy's classroom. I saw one when she dropped it, there's an eye stitched into—"

"What are you guys gossiping about?" someone shouted from the house. It was Cafferty, watching them from the shadows along the side of the garage.

"Nothing," said Savage, jumping up like she'd had an electric shock. "The case, you know? The wallet."

Cafferty crossed the garden, trampling the flowers that Roger was growing. She ran her hands through her short hair, studying Kett before turning to Savage.

"Careless," she said.

"What is?" said Savage.

"Leaving the wallet there, where anyone could find it. He must have known the police would be coming. All that stuff in his garage, the propane tanks, the burners. All those creepy dead birds. He could have incinerated the whole lot, and nobody would have known. Why risk it?"

"Maybe he wanted to be caught," said Kett. "You said it before, Kate, some killers make it easy for the police, deliberately. They know they need help, they know they can't stop."

Neither Cafferty nor Savage answered him. They were both watching each other.

"Anyway," said Kett. "Whatever he was planning, we caught him. It was good police work. Clare's taken him for an interview, and Hay's on her way. I'm going to give you guys a choice. You can go back to HQ, get started on the paperwork, or you can go home, take a breather."

"HQ," said Savage, at the exact same time Cafferty said, "Home."

This, at least, drew a small smile from Savage.

"Home sounds good," she said. "You heading back to Boston, Steph?"

Cafferty checked her watch.

"Bit late," she replied. "And if it's all the same to you, I'd like to hang around for another day or two. See where this goes."

The smile slid off Savage's face, and Cafferty saw it.

"I can totally get a hotel, though," said the sergeant. "Or bunk at HQ. I really don't want to be a bother."

"No, it's fine," said Savage, although she didn't look like she meant it.

"Plenty of room at HQ, and you're more than welcome there," said Kett, getting off the wall. "Hey, Steph, you mind if I borrow that handkerchief of yours?"

"This?" said Cafferty, pointing to her pocket square. Kett nodded.

She pulled it out, holding onto it for a second or two before reluctantly handing it over. Kett unfolded it, searching the corners until he saw it: a small, white insignia stitched into the fabric. Even without his glasses on, he could tell that it was a heart.

He turned the pocket square to show Savage, then he used it to brush the dirt and lichen from his backside.

"Thanks," he said, offering it back to a grimacing Cafferty.

"You know what, sir, why don't you go ahead and keep that one?" she said. "I've got hundreds."

Kett looked at Savage, who seemed a little less tense than she had been a moment before. She smiled her gratitude, then turned to Cafferty.

"Don't worry about a bunk, Steph. You can stay with me another night."

"That's great!" said the visiting sergeant. "For a second there, I thought you'd gone off me."

The two women walked off down the street together. Kett watched them go, then turned to the house, thinking of Roger, thinking of the wallet, thinking of four dead people without their eyes, and wondering why that same word kept pushing into his head, unwelcome and uninvited.

Careless.

CHAPTER THIRTY-ONE

WITH NOTHING ELSE TO DO AT ROGER'S HOUSE, AND Clare handling the interview with their new prime suspect, Kett made his way home.

It was less than a couple of miles to his place, so he decided to walk. The last of the day bled out as he trudged through the empty streets, the cold creeping back in—merciful at first, after the smothering heat, but quickly finding its way into his sweat-damp clothes, dead men's fingers probing his skin.

He had plenty of time to think as he walked. It seemed perfectly clear they'd caught their killer. Roger Sexton knew at least one of the victims, he was practically in a relationship with Helen Coulter. He'd certainly gifted her the glass eyes they'd found in her flat, because they'd discovered a bag of identical ones upstairs in his house. He'd admitted to running drugs for the gang, too, which meant he could have crossed paths with Idris Mellor. Judy, too, if she'd been part of the same operation.

This was all circumstantial, though, as were the items they'd found inside his garage. Propane tanks were common, so were camping stoves and saucepans. They hadn't found any tin, or moulds, or any of the other equipment they'd discovered inside O'Brien's garage. And as creepy as the birds were, stuffing animals was a long way from killing people.

The only clincher was the wallet. Somehow, it had gone from being inside the pocket of a dead teenage boy in a derelict city centre pub, to Roger Sexton's wheelie bin. His years on the job had told him that the simplest solution was most often the right one, which meant Roger himself had disposed of it there. Yes, it was careless. But either he'd been arrogant enough to assume nobody would look, or part of him just wanted the entire affair to be over.

He wanted to be caught.

If the latter was the reason, though, then why hadn't he confessed? Roger hadn't acted like a guilty man when they'd spoken with him, even when he'd started to get angry. Kett had read enough books to know that when they were caught, serial murderers tended to gloat about their killings, they wouldn't shut up about them. The relief of capture was close to euphoria, in some cases. This wasn't a man who took pride in his dead.

But if it wasn't Roger, if they'd got the wrong guy, then who was responsible for the deaths? The gangs, acting like cartels? Or somebody new, somebody who wasn't even on their radar yet?

He saw his house from the other end of the street, lit up like a football stadium. He unlocked the mortice and then tried the Yale, but the door still wouldn't open. He had to knock, the way he always did, before somebody came to slide the bolts back.

"Hey," said Billie when she'd opened the door. "Sorry."

She was already in her pyjamas, her honey-coloured

hair framing her face. She smiled at him, and it felt like he'd drunk a glass of cool water after a five-mile run. She leaned into him and he kissed her, tasting chocolate on her lips. She must have tasted something else on his, because she recoiled, pulling a face.

"Sorry," he said, his turn to apologise. "Long day."

He walked into the house, feeling like he was shedding a tonne of weight as he took off his jacket. Evie came running out of the living room when she heard the door close, a set of plastic cuffs in her hands.

"Daddy's home!" she screamed.

"Daddy's home!" echoed Moira from the sofa. She was lying along the full length of it, her hands on her chest. "I can't move, I'm in prison."

"Oh dear," said Kett. "I guess that was kind of inevitable, given how naughty you are."

Moira gasped.

Kett gave Evie a hug, then walked to Moira and kissed her on the forehead. The way she was lying, with her arms crossed over her chest, was far too close to the position Helen Coulter had been in when they'd found her. He took her little hand, pulling it away, holding it.

"Did Evie arrest you?" he asked.

"I did," Evie replied. "She wouldn't let me have her *Gabby's Dollhouse* cats, so I'm punishing her."

"Not sure that's a crime," said Kett. "As her senior officer, Moira, I'm going to release you without charge. Because it's bedtime."

The two girls groaned in perfect harmony.

"Five more minutes, then," he said. "No more arrests."

"But I need to put her in prison because she won't stop farting!" said Evie, and they burst into giggles.

Kett followed the sound of a boiling kettle into the kitchen, catching Billie mid-yawn.

"Knackered?" he asked, and she nodded. "Sorry I didn't make it home. This case..."

"I saw it on the news," she told him, speaking in a whisper. "He really took their *eyes*?"

Kett nodded, fetching a couple of mugs from the cupboard.

"You caught him?" said Billie.

"I think so," he answered, and she didn't look reassured. "We'll know by the morning. And Billie, this doesn't have anything to do with us, okay? This isn't Hollenbeck, this isn't personal."

She didn't believe him, the way she never would. This time, though, she had a good reason.

"He told me that's what he'd do," she said, her hand on the switch for the kettle so that she could flick it before it came to a boil. "The... Pig Man. He said that's what he'd do to you and the kids if I ever tried to escape. If you ever came after me. *One* of the things he'd do."

This was new. Just when Kett thought he'd heard the worst details of Billie's kidnapping, another ugly truth surfaced.

"He said lots of things, though," she said, snapping the kettle off. "He was just full of shit."

"Mummy said a rude word!" cried Evie, who was walking through the door. "Arrest her!"

"She said *ship*," said Kett. "He was full of ships. She was talking about a giant whale."

"Can I lock Moira in the cupboard tonight?" Evie asked. "As her prison?"

"No!" said Kett and Billie together.

Evie stomped off in a huff.

"It's not a bad idea, though," said Kett. "We could lock them all in the cupboard, have some quiet time."

Billie smiled, kissing him again. The joy of it was killed instantly when he felt the buzz of his phone in his pocket. He ignored it, but when it rang again, he pulled it out, seeing the Superintendent's name on the screen.

"Maybe I should get Evie to put *me* in the cupboard," he said. "So I don't have to deal with this."

He answered, hearing Clare's deep, throaty breaths rasping down the line like a sex pest.

"Sir? Everything okay?"

"No," said Clare, his voice crinkly with static. "Would you like me to give you a list of everything that's definitely not okay, Kett? Starting with my monstrous haemorrhoids? Would that make you a happy man?"

"No, sir," he said, wishing he'd left his phone where it was. "I meant with Roger."

"Refusing to talk," said Clare. "He's lawyering up, so we're going to let him stew overnight. That isn't why I was calling."

Evie came back into the room, wearing Kett's shoes. She marched over, deadly serious.

"My name's Robbie Kett!" she said in her booming dad voice.

"What?" said Clare. "I can barely hear you."

"I hate my job!" Evie said. "I'm tired! My back hurts!"

"Well what do you want me to do about it, Robert?" Clare barked. "Suck it up, you big baby."

"No, sir, that's not me," said Kett, waving a hand at Evie to try to shut her up. "Why are you calling?"

Moira shuffled into the room wearing Kett's trainers, yelling at the top of her voice.

"My name is Robert, and I pooped myself!"

"What?" roared Clare.

"No, I—"

"There's no shame in it, Robbie," the Superintendent went on. "It happens to the best of us, as we get older."

"God, no, it—" Kett pushed past his girls. "Look, sir, can you please get to the point?"

"Cara Hay just called. She thinks she's figured out where the killer got the tin for his prosthetic eyes."

Kett locked himself in the toilet under the stairs, resting his forehead against the cool door.

"The letters on the metal ball we found in Helen Coulter, they weren't letters, they were numbers. She matched them to a set of toy soldiers she found online."

"What?" said Kett. "Soldiers?"

"Tin soldiers," said Clare. "Toys. Old ones, because they contain lead. She thinks they were Victorian, or earlier. She found a similar set online, on eBay, marked Herbu, numbered 180. The numbers must have survived the smelting process."

"Hang on, you're saying the killer melted antique toy soldiers into balls, and put them into his victims' eyes?"

"It seems that way," said Clare. "That's why I was calling. Did you see anything like that at Roger's house? Old toys? War memorabilia? Ornaments?"

"No," said Kett. "Nothing. Just the stuffed birds."

"Me neither," said Clare, huffing with impatience.

"It doesn't mean it's not him, sir," said Kett.

But the Superintendent had already gone.

KETT AND BILLIE lay in bed once the girls were asleep, nursing fresh cups of tea. The window was open, the cool evening air carrying in the smell of the flowers Billie had planted by the front door: jasmine and primrose and other things he couldn't name.

It wasn't even ten, but he could barely keep his eyes open, the exhaustion playing tricks in the corners of his vision: flashing lights, and looming shadows that might have been people. Every now and again he'd start to drift, the hallucinations morphing into dreams for a second or two before he startled himself awake. The third or fourth time it happened, he managed to slosh tea all over the duvet.

"Give up," Billie told him, taking his half-finished cup and putting it on her bedside table. "Just let it happen."

"In a second," he said. "I feel like I've hardly seen you."

She tucked herself under his arm, and for a little while they talked—not about the case, of course, because the horrors weren't allowed through the front door. Billie told him about their day, about the argument she'd had with the neighbour because he'd parked over their drive again, about the fact the milk had been out of date so she couldn't make pancakes, about Maureen from the shop and her imminent divorce. All things that belonged here in the real world. Safe things.

"I think Pete might be heading the same way," said Kett, stroking Billie's hair.

"Divorce?" she said. "No way. He'd never leave Allie. He's besotted, especially now they've got Bobby."

"Bobby's the only reason they're holding it together. Pete's terrified of being forced out of his son's life. He told me he'd rather die than not be able to spend time with him."

Billie was quiet for a moment.

"I get that," she said.

She sat up, withdrawing from him the way she often did when she fell into the past, as if she was right back there in

Schofield's basement. She folded her arms over her chest, tightening, contracting, shrinking.

"Hey," said Kett. "We don't have to talk about it. You're right, we should get some sleep."

She didn't answer, her head shaking softly.

"Come back," said Kett, knowing that she wouldn't.

"I thought it too," she said. "Back when *he* took me."

The Pig Man. Schofield. When he'd targeted Billie, he'd told her if she didn't go along with it, if she didn't go willingly with him, he'd come after the girls instead. He'd given her time to think about it before the day he'd ripped her out of their lives, and she'd made the only decision she could. The same one anybody would make.

"I couldn't face it, the idea of not being with them," she went on. "I thought it would be better to die than to lose them. But..."

She hitched in a breath through gritted teeth.

"But I thought maybe it was better if it wasn't just me," she said, struggling to find the words. "If I couldn't be with them, then maybe I should..."

She put her hands to her face, still shaking her head.

"Billie, it's over, you don't have to—"

"It's not over," she said. "Not for me. Not ever. Because I thought it, Robbie, I honestly thought it would be better if they were dead too, if I... I thought about doing it. Me and them. They were so little, so... It was better that I was there with them, wherever they went, better we were all together, so I could still look after them."

Something flashed at the back of Kett's head, a dull explosion that he couldn't make any sense of.

"God," she said, wiping away tears. "I'm sorry. I'm so stupid."

He took her hand, held it tight as she tried to pull away.

"You're not stupid," he said. "You're human. It's not a bad thing, it's a good one. It's what any of us would do. You care for them so much you'd do anything to keep them safe."

There it was again, a flash of dark light, something trying to surface.

"Sure," said Billie, her voice bitter with disbelief.

"No, I mean it," he said. "All you did was love them. That's all you're guilty of. And you didn't do it, you never hurt them, never even came close."

She stared at the crumpled duvet, swallowing hard.

"Right?" he said, his own voice a whisper.

Billie pulled free, turning her back to him, curling her legs up as tight as she could. She was a rock now, he knew. She wouldn't say another word until the morning, no matter what he did.

"You didn't do anything wrong," he said, pulling the covers up to her neck, smoothing a hand over them. "I love you. We all love you."

He shuffled down into the bed, feeling cold now despite the heat. It had been so long since the Pig Man had taken Billie, so many years since Schofield had died, but he was still right here in the room.

He always would be.

Kett clicked off his light and closed his eyes, attempting to find his way back to whatever his mind had been trying to tell him.

Better we were all together, so I could still look after them.

But the exhaustion and the emotion were too much, a wave of grief that washed over his head, drowning him in the quiet and the dark of sleep.

CHAPTER THIRTY-TWO

Porter sat at a desk in the Incident Room, staring at his phone. The small hit of elation he'd felt earlier when he realised he'd messaged Kett instead of Allie had long since faded. He'd sent the text again when he'd left Roger Sexton's house, copied and pasted—*I love you, can't wait to curl up with you, big hugs and lots of kisses*—and now, even though the little tick told him Allie had read the bloody thing hours ago, she still hadn't replied.

He sat back, rubbing his eyes until fireworks went off. He was about as tired as he'd been in a long time, probably since the whole Hollenbeck thing last year. It had taken him a while to sleep through the night after that. For a few weeks, he'd woken screaming from nightmares of being hunted through the old sugar factory, something only a mix of melatonin, wine and the benzodiazepines he'd stolen from Allie's bottomless stash had cured. It had been so bad that he'd been relegated to the spare room for a couple of nights.

A couple of nights that had turned into six months.

"You've fucked it, Pete," he told himself, putting his arms on the desk and resting his head in them.

Sleep was right there, and it would have had him if the Incident Room door hadn't crashed open, the noise of it like the building was coming down. He jerked up, seeing Duke striding in like a giant teddy from a children's book, his yawning mouth big enough to fit a chair into.

"Bloody hell, Aaron," he said. "Why don't you just come through the wall next time?"

Duke tried to reply while he was still yawning, turning the words into nonsense.

"What?" said Porter.

"I said, what are you still doing here, sir?" Duke repeated, pulling a chair to the other side of Porter's desk and dropping into it like he was riding a horse. He stared at Porter over his steepled fingers.

"Apparently, I'm about to have a job interview," said Porter. "What are *you* doing here?"

"Was helping the Super," said Duke, checking his watch. "It's nearly eleven, sir, shouldn't you be in bed?"

"You're not my mum, mate," said Porter. "I'm not even tired. Shouldn't *you* be in bed?"

"I'm not tired either," said Duke, and the annoying thing was he looked like he was telling the truth. The phrase bright-eyed and bushy-tailed came to Porter's mind. "Besides, Kate's gone back with Steph, I figured I'd leave them to it. You really should get some rest, sir, you've been up since yesterday morning."

"I'm fine, *Constable*," snapped Porter. "I'd be better still if you let me have a bit of peace and quiet."

Duke stretched his arms out, his back cracking.

"What's the suspect doing?" said Porter.

"Not much. He's in his cell, won't talk without a brief. He's pretty dodgy, though. He's got a vibe. And those birds."

The PC shuddered.

"Anyone who can do that to a cute little tweeter. Stuff them, whip out their eyes and sew glass ones in their place. It's just grim."

Porter closed his eyes, trying to tune out his voice.

"Been an insane weekend," Duke prattled on. "Can you believe it was only yesterday we were playing dodgeball? Feels like a million years ago."

"Duke," said Porter, his eyes still closed. "Please stop talking. Or better still, go home."

"I told you, sir, I'm fine. *You* go home."

"It would be better for everyone if *you* went home," said Porter. "Because you need some sleep. Like a baby."

"You're old, sir, *you* need more sleep."

"I'm going to put you both to sleep in a minute!" came a roar from the open door. "Permanently, with a tossing injection. Believe me, it will be a mercy killing. Why are you still here, Pete?"

"I'm fine, sir," said Porter. "I'm literally not tired. *He's* tired."

"You know, this reminds me of a case I once worked," said Clare, entering the room and dropping a folder onto a desk. "Older man, I can't remember his name. He saved a couple of kids from a house fire."

"Oh," said Porter, who had been expecting far worse.

"Yeah, real hero he was. He jumped out of bed when he smelled the smoke, put on a pair of slippers and a dressing gown, legged it into the next-door neighbour's house without the slightest bit of concern for himself. Pulled out the kids, and the dog, if I remember right."

"And we remind you of him, sir?" said Duke, his chin held high.

"Christ, no," said Clare. "I just remember seeing him right after, before he got carted to the hospital. He was still wearing his slippers. Furry things, with faces. Hedgehogs, I think. Crumpled to toss, burned, flattened, filthy, and utterly useless. I remember them staring up at me with their sad little eyes."

He smiled at the memory.

"You two remind me of them."

"The slippers, sir?" said Porter.

Clare nodded.

"But since you're still here, I've got a job for you. Roger Sexman is almost certainly our killer, but if it's not him, then it's the gangs. Agreed?"

Nobody replied, but Clare didn't seem to notice.

"I don't know what their reaction will be to us finding their safe house earlier, but the chances are they'll be on high alert. If they've got other bases of operations on the estate, they'll want to clear them out, move product. I've got coppers on the streets, as many as I can spare, but I want you two back over there to help."

Porter groaned.

"Cool, sir," said Duke, standing up. "Happy to help."

"Happy to help," echoed Porter in a falsetto.

"Good," said Clare. "Now that Terry Prince is out of Norvic House, it's the best place to keep an eye on things. I want you on a stakeout, in Funland."

"Together?" said Porter, with another groan.

"It's not a date, Pete," said Clare. "You don't have to sit on his lap."

"He'd sit on *my* lap, sir!" Porter protested. "Obviously."

Clare gurned at him.

"Fine," said Porter, using what felt like the last of his energy to get out of his chair. He checked his phone before putting it into his pocket. Still no reply from Allie. As awful as a night with Duke sounded, it was still better than having to go home to find out why she wasn't talking to him.

"Any sign of the gangs, you call for backup," said Clare. "If you go charging after them again, gung-ho, then I'm going to use a paring knife to remove your gung and your ho. Is that clear?"

"Not at all, sir," said Porter.

"Take it in shifts. One of you watches, the other sleeps."

"He can sleep," said Porter and Duke together.

Porter glared at the constable, and Duke grinned right back.

"Just toss off, both of you," said Clare, waving them away like a bad smell. "The keys are on my desk."

SAVAGE OPENED the door to her flat as quietly as she could, trying not to alert Colin the dog to the fact that she was home. The staffie spent the day with the downstairs neighbours when she was at work, and they usually dropped her off at eight or so when their kids went to bed. They loved everything about Colin, except for the noise she made when Savage came home late at night.

She tiptoed into the microscopic hall, holding her breath—only to hear DS Cafferty stomp in behind her in her Doc Martens. Upstairs, Colin launched into a round of growling barks that were loud enough to wake the entire street.

"Hey!" Savage called up. "It's just me, you plank."

"And me," said Cafferty, which made the dog's greeting even more furious.

Savage let Cafferty past so she could close the door, then she raced the visiting sergeant up the stairs. As soon as she opened the living room door, Colin bundled out, ignoring her completely in order to investigate the other woman. She seemed unsure, until Cafferty gave her a scratch on the head.

"You know me!" she said. "I literally took you for a walk this morning. You tried to kill me when you saw the squirrel. Remember?"

Colin lifted her head at the mention of squirrels, running into the living room and standing on her back feet by the window. She barked again, snorting like a pig.

"Enough!" said Savage, closing the curtains. "Pack it in. They're all in bed."

She turned to see Cafferty loitering in the living room door, watching her. That sense of unease was back, and she ducked down to pat Colin's flank so that Cafferty wouldn't see it. She wished Duke was here, but he'd been doped up on caffeine and sugar when she'd left HQ. Knowing him, he'd work all night. Again.

"Speaking of bed," she said. "That's where I'm going."

Cafferty checked her watch, frowning.

"Not even midnight yet, Kate," she said. "You're six years younger than me, what's your excuse?"

"You're not tired?" said Savage, standing up. The dog returned to Cafferty, sniffing her shoes. The DS ignored her.

"Tired, but wired," she replied. "Do you mind if I head out for a run? Helps me wind down. I won't sleep without it."

"No," said Savage, even though she *did* mind. "I mean, if it helps?"

"It won't be a long one," she said. "Quick 5k. Well, as quick as I ever am. This giant body isn't built for running. Or, you know, anything really. I'll be as quiet as a mouse when I come back, I promise."

Savage nodded.

"I'll leave the door unlocked."

Cafferty beamed, vanishing into the hall. Savage waited in the living room until she heard the woman bound down the stairs, then the front door opening.

"I'll be as quiet as a mouse!" she yelled again.

The door slammed shut with enough force to rattle the windows.

"Sure," said Savage.

She peeked through the curtains to see Cafferty jogging up the street, still in her work suit but now with her trainers on. She rounded the corner into the night, her long, snake-like shadow slithering after her.

Only then did she move, heading for the spare room and switching on the light. Cafferty's suitcase lay on its side in the corner, the top closed but unzipped. Her rucksack sat next to it.

She hesitated, unsure. Cafferty was a police officer, a detective. The sergeant had been nothing but kind to her since she'd arrived, and her insights into the case had been invaluable. They'd clicked so well that Savage felt like she'd made a new friend.

But that gaping eye on her pocket square was haunting her. Of all the symbols she could have had, why that one? Even if every one of those squares of fabric had a different symbol, *why that one?* Cafferty had been the only one to see the suspect slip and stab himself in the neck inside the flats.

She was just squatting over him, Duke had said. *Watching him bleed out.*

And now that Savage was thinking about it, Cafferty had gone for a run that morning, hadn't she? How long had she been out of the house? Long enough to get to the school in Earlham?

Long enough to attack Judy Bartlett?

Kett had always told her to trust her gut, and right now her gut was churning.

She knelt by the suitcase, lifting the lid. Cafferty's clothes had been bundled inside in a haphazard fashion, and everything else had been carelessly tossed in with them. Savage saw a torch, a hairbrush, a bottle of shampoo that was leaking everywhere, half a dozen charging cables and a black cycling helmet.

"Weird," she said.

She lifted a jumper, probing into the mountain of fabric until she found a canvas tote bag. It was full of pocket squares, she saw when she opened it, a rainbow of colours, all neatly folded. She had to pull one out to see what was embroidered in the corner: a flower. The next had a knife, for some reason, stitched in white on a bright yellow background. She'd pulled out ten, with no sign of another eye, before she gave up.

She folded them as well as she could, stuffing them back into the bag and leaving it where she'd found it. As she did, though, she uncovered the bottom of the case, discovering more random items rattling around there: three loose batteries, another phone, a tape measure, a screwdriver.

She ran her hand down the back of the suitcase, stopping when her fingers came into contact with a solid lump. Whatever it was, it was being kept inside a sock.

Again, she hesitated, looking back.

What are you doing, Kate? she asked herself.

She picked up the sock, feeling something heavy.

Something round.

She held the sock over the clothes in the case, and let the object roll out onto a crumpled jumper.

"Oh shit," she said.

It was a glass eye, perfectly spherical, the iris a dazzling shade of blue.

"Oh shit is right," said a voice behind her.

Savage spun around, seeing Cafferty in the doorway.

Quiet as a mouse.

"What are you doing, Kate?" said the sergeant.

"Nothing," said Savage, standing up. "Sorry, Steph, I..."

Cafferty walked into the room, and gently closed the door behind her. She wore a smile, but when she turned her eyes to Savage, they looked as lifeless as the one in the suitcase.

"No, Kate, I'm the one who's sorry," she said, starting across the room, one hand in her pocket. "I really didn't want it to end like this."

CHAPTER THIRTY-THREE

Porter had been on stakeout duty with Duke for exactly seventeen minutes and forty-six seconds, and he was already mentally rehearsing his resignation letter to Norfolk Constabulary.

They'd let themselves in through the front door of Norvic House and made their way up seven flights of steps, by torchlight, to the top floor. It was the best place to look for the gangs, but instead of positioning himself by a window and keeping an eye on the city, Duke had been exploring Terry Prince's Funland. Right now, the giant PC was spinning back and forth on a rope swing that had been fixed into the ceiling, *wheeeeing* like a four-year-old drunk on Coke. The entire building seemed to be creaking with the effort of holding him up.

"You do realise that's probably a sex swing," said Porter, walking to the western side of the building, his Maglite lighting the way. "Terry's had his naked pink arse on there a hundred times, probably while wanking off to the Sooty Show."

The creaking stopped, and Duke hopped off.

"You really know how to spoil a party," said the constable.

"Yeah, that's what Sooty said."

"You've got to admit, this place is pretty cool," said Duke, heading off to explore the room. "I can't believe he built it all by himself."

"It's not cool, Aaron, it's creepy," said Porter, opening the bag he'd brought in with him and pulling out a pair of binoculars. "And gross. I caught diphtheria, rabies and probably chlamydia just by walking past that ball pit."

He heard the hollow rumble of plastic, and turned to see Duke wading into the cardboard pool of colourful balls. The big constable was giggling.

"Jesus Christ," said Porter, turning to the window. "Don't blame me when your knob falls off."

The view from up here wouldn't have been bad if it had been daytime. But in the dead of night, past the scaffolding, he couldn't see much at all. To make matters worse, the gangs—at least he assumed it was the gangs—had taken out a lot of the streetlights, turning the roads into black holes. A parade of elephants could walk past down there and he wouldn't see it.

He tried with the binoculars, but it wasn't much better. The only consolation was that he could see the IRV, which sat on the main road, and the two constables hunkered inside it. It was one of four that they'd passed on their way to the tower. Clare had been right to send them. It wasn't just the gangs that stalked the streets tonight. The people on the estate were still angry, and still afraid. He'd spotted two small groups of local men standing outside the buildings, hatchet-eyed and probably armed. He'd called it in, of course, but the Superintendent's advice had been to leave them to it.

Better that than another riot.

He heard a clatter behind him and turned to see what idiocy Duke was up to now, but the big PC had dropped into one of Prince's folding chairs. The exhaustion seemed to have finally caught up with him, his eyes dark and heavy. He muted his radio and left it on the floor beside his chair. When he yawned into his sleeve, Porter gave him a smug look.

"Not tired," mumbled Duke, still mid-yawn. "Sugar crash."

"Sure," said Porter. He handed Duke the binoculars. "You keep watch, I'll see if I can find a better viewpoint."

"You bring any snacks, sir?" said Duke, looking at the bag.

"I did not," said Porter, waiting until he'd reached the door before pulling out one of the four Snickers he had in his jacket pocket. "Don't fall asleep, mate."

He ate the chocolate bar while he patrolled the top floor, almost dropping the torch as he tried to check his phone. Allie still hadn't replied. She would be asleep now, Bobby curled up beside her, and the cold pressure he felt inside him when he thought of them made him want to cry. It was grief, he knew. Even though it hadn't happened yet, the end was coming. It felt like a wave, a million tonnes of dark water crashing towards him, and there was nothing he could do to stop it.

"You've fucked it," he told himself again.

The view from the other three sides of the building was no better, so he made his way back. He shouldered open the stairwell door as he passed it, wondering whether to check the rest of the tower, or at least the rest of Funland on the floor below. He aimed the torch into the deep well of shadow, hearing a distant metallic clang that probably came from the street, but which sounded far too close.

"Nope," he said, heading back onto the top floor.

He pulled out his phone as he went, texting the same message to Savage and then Kett.

I'm on a stakeout with Aaron in Funland, please kill me now.

He gave them a few seconds to reply, but neither did.

He heard snoring as he retreated along the corridor, and he laughed quietly to himself as he walked into the giant office space. Duke was fast asleep on his tiny chair, his back arched, his face pointing at the ceiling. His gulping mouth really was huge, and Porter spent a couple of minutes searching the room for something to dunk in it. In the end, partly because he didn't want to touch anything that had belonged to Terry Prince, and partly because he didn't actually have the heart to wake the constable, he decided not to. Instead, he pulled a blanket from the bag he'd brought, draping it over Duke's torso and tucking it beneath the chair.

"Sweet dreams, you dope," he said quietly.

He took a twenty-second video of him, his snores like a bass speaker at a music festival, and texted it to Savage.

How do you put up with this???

Then he pulled another chair up to the window, put his binoculars to his eyes, and settled down for a long, *long* night.

AS TIRED AS HE WAS, Kett couldn't sleep.

He'd lain motionless in the bed for almost an hour, listening to Billie's tight, guarded breaths gradually loosen into the more regular rhythm of sleep. Even then, he'd been reluctant to move, for fear of waking her. Sleep was the one place where his wife found peace, where the horrors of the past couldn't reach her.

Except in the dreams, of course.

They started as midnight crept closer, nightmares that made Billie murmur, and then cry out. Every time her body jerked, he put his hand on her shoulder, squeezing just hard enough to settle her.

"You're okay," he told her, just a whisper. "You're safe."

Billie wasn't the reason he couldn't drift off, though. Not the *only* reason, anyway. Her confession to him was still sinking in, the horrific truth of it—that she'd considered taking not just her own life, but the lives of their daughters, too.

Better we were all together, so I could still look after them.

He had to keep telling himself that it hadn't happened, that it *never* would have happened. But he couldn't help putting himself there, in the middle of that nightmare. Walking through the door of their old house in London, finding Billie.

Finding the girls.

It was like there was a hurricane inside him, the roar of a thousand storms tearing through his skull. The panic was overwhelming, and he had to keep telling himself not to think it in case thinking it somehow changed the past, somehow made it real.

But he *couldn't* stop thinking about it, because Billie's words had triggered something else inside him, that tentative, cobweb-thin feeling that he was missing something in the case.

Something important.

Better we were all together, so I could still look after them.

As hard as it was, he tried to put himself in Billie's shoes. Knowing that somebody was coming for you, that they were going to abduct you, take you away from everyone you loved and probably kill you. It was no wonder the thought had crossed her mind. Nobody knew what happened after this life, not for sure. But whatever it was, it was better not to be alone. Wasn't it?

Would *he* have had the same thought in the same situation? If death was inevitable, would part of him have considered taking his children too?

No. He couldn't even bring himself to think it. But he *wasn't* in the same situation.

It brought some small sense of comfort, though: the idea that if his worst nightmare had come true, if the girls had passed, Billie would be there to look after them. As horrific as it was to imagine losing them all, at least they wouldn't be on their own.

That same idea exploded inside his head, not a dark light this time but a supernova.

"Shit," he said, sitting up fast enough to stir Billie from her slumber. "Shit, shit, shit."

He climbed out of the bed, his hands in his hair like he could physically stop the thought from escaping.

Better we were all together, so I could still look after them.

Savage had spoken about this, back at HQ, about the killer staking some kind of claim to his victims in the afterlife, punishing them after death. Or rewarding them.

Maybe, though, this wasn't a punishment or a reward.

Better we were all together, so I could still look after them.

Maybe it was a *duty*.

He grabbed his trousers from the back of the chair, finding his phone and calling Savage as he left the room.

Good people. That was what three of their victims had in common, alongside the metal in their eyes. Helen, the nurse who volunteered on the children's ward. Idris, the friendly teenager who ran football clubs for local kids. And Judy, the teacher. All good, kind people. All loved. It didn't make any sense to target them, unless that's what the killer was looking for.

The phone rang, then cut off. Savage would be asleep.

He tried again, peeking into Evie's room to find her buried beneath her quilts. He snuck in, pulling them away from her sweaty face so she could breathe. He checked on Moira next, who lay on top of her covers wearing nothing but her pants, her cheeks blazing. Then Alice, swaddled in a nest of duvets. They looked so helpless, so small. If, God forbid, anything happened to them, if they moved on to the next life together, all he'd ask was for somebody to be there with them, a friendly face.

A good person.

"Holy shit," he said again.

His phone clicked, a soft groan as Savage answered.

"Kate?" he said, jogging down the stairs.

The line went dead.

"Come on," he said.

He called her again, but this time it went straight to voicemail. He waited for the beep.

"It's Robbie. Listen, I think I've got something. Call me back. It can't wait until the morning."

He put his phone on the table so that he could pull on his trousers, grabbing a T-shirt from the basket in the laundry room. Then he dialled Clare's number. It rang four times before it was answered by something that sounded like a constipated stegosaurus.

"Urgh."

"Sir?" said Kett. "You at HQ?"

"I'm in bed, you great, flapping scrotum," came the reply. "I've managed... Oh, look, twenty minutes of rest. That will do me, won't it? Twenty minutes, I'll be right as rain after that. I'm wide awake, I'm as fresh as a bunch of tossing daisies, I'm bright and breezy, I'm—"

Kett hung up, putting on his shoes and grabbing his jacket. He closed the door as quietly as he could behind him, locking it. He'd made it out onto the driveway before he remembered he'd left his car at work.

"Fuck's sake," he grumbled.

He set off anyway, ringing for a cab as he walked and telling it to meet him at the end of the street. By the time he'd got there, Clare was calling back.

"What is it?" the Super barked.

"Roger Sexton. He had a daughter, right?"

"Yes. In her forties. Lives in Auckland. That's who he was talking to after Helen was killed."

"Does he have grandkids?"

"No," said Clare. He sounded like he was chugging a glass of water. "Why?"

"What about Terry Prince? He has kids, right? I remember him mentioning them."

"Yes," said Clare. "Grown up. *Why*, Robert?"

Kett stood on the corner of the street, the chill creeping up his sleeves and down his collar, chasing away the last of his exhaustion.

"The killer's going after good people," he said. "It doesn't make any sense, unless he's... Unless he's recruiting."

"What in the name of Godfrey's toss are you going on about, Kett?"

"I'm not sure. Not a hundred per cent. Kate said one of the reasons the killer might have been replacing the eyes of his victims was because they wanted to reward them in the afterlife. The eyes were a gift. But what if they weren't a gift, what if they were a tool?"

"You're a bloody tool, Kett. Get to the point."

"I don't know what the point is, sir," he said. "I haven't got there yet. I just think this is what the killer is doing, they're creating a..."

He stumbled as another thought entered his head.

"Hang on, you said the killer was using tin soldiers for the eyes, right?"

"That's what Hay tells me."

"Tin soldiers. *Toy* soldiers. It fits."

"The only thing that's going to fit is my foot up your—"

"What if the killer has lost somebody?" Kett went on. "A child. Recently. They're mourning, they're insane with grief. Anyone would be, right? They're desperate to do something to help, desperate for their child not to be on their own, wherever they are. So they... They send somebody to look after them."

Saying it aloud made it sound too crazy to be real.

"Go on," said Clare.

"I think the people they're sending are people they know, people their child knew. A nurse, a neighbour, a teacher."

There was a set of headlights making its way up the road, slowing down as it reached him.

"I think we need to look for a kid who died after being ill, somebody who spent time in the hospital. Somebody who went to Bignold when Judy worked there. Somebody who did one of Idris' football things, or who knew him from the community. That's the link, sir. The child is the link."

The taxi pulled up, and Kett got into the back.

"Wymondham," he said. "Police HQ, and hurry."

He put the phone back to his ear.

"Roger isn't our killer, sir," he said as the driver pulled away. "He's still out there."

CHAPTER THIRTY-FOUR

Monday

Porter's pony wasn't behaving itself. For a start, it was the smallest horse in the race, its legs half the size of everyone else's. It was also bright pink, which didn't make any sense.

"Come on!" he yelled, digging his heels into the animal's chunky flanks, tugging on the reins. "We're going to lose!"

Every other horse was galloping like the wind. Duke's was in the lead, a majestic black stallion with a golden mane. The constable kept looking back at Porter, that stupid grin on his stupid bearded face. He wasn't even holding onto the reins because his horse had wheels, tearing towards the finish line with a roar of exhaust and flames from its boosters.

"That's cheating, you massive twat!" Porter yelled, his voice so loud that his pony bucked, and—

He felt himself toppling out of the dream just in time to stop himself falling off his chair. He staggered to his feet, hearing the echo of horse's hooves, the cheer of the crowd, fast fading into the quiet of the building.

"Shit a brick," he muttered, bracing his hands on his knees.

He couldn't even remember falling asleep. By the light of their torches, he saw that Duke was still unconscious in his chair, the blanket halfway off him. He was practising the mating song of an elephant seal with gusto, the air trembling with the volume of his snores. He hadn't seen a thing, thank God.

Porter checked his watch to see that he'd been dozing for almost an hour. Midnight had come and gone.

"Shit. A. Brick."

He picked up the binoculars from where he'd dropped them, walking to the window and scanning the street below. It looked deserted, no sign of traffic. He found the IRV on the main road, both coppers inside nursing cups of coffee.

"Where did you get them from?" he asked, his voice steaming up the glass.

He dropped the binoculars onto his chair, cracking his back as he stretched. He pulled out another Snickers, wondering if he could pop the entire thing into Duke's snoring mouth without the PC waking up. It would serve him right for riding a rocket-powered horse in a pony race.

It would be a waste of a good Snickers, he decided as he unwrapped it. He gloated instead, standing in front of Duke and taking a massive bite.

"Mmmmm. Are you hungry, Aaron? Because this is delicious. I bet you'd love one of these smooth, silky, choco—"

He almost choked on a peanut, coughing hard to dislodge it.

"That was your fault," he wheezed at Duke, scrubbing tears from his eyes. "You knob."

He was halfway through another bite when he heard a noise. It sounded like hooves, he thought, and he realised that it was the same sound that had woken him from his dream. He stopped chewing, cocking his head, trying to work out if he was imagining it—or if he'd maybe fallen asleep again.

There it was, a drum of sound that could have been footsteps, or maybe something being dragged over the floor. He couldn't place it.

But it was coming from inside the building.

He carefully folded the wrapper over his Snickers, putting it back in his pocket. He walked to his bag again, finding the extendable baton he'd brought with him and flicking it to its full length. He grabbed his torch and gave Duke's foot a kick.

"Oi," he said. "Aaron, wake up."

Duke snorted, then fell back into the same rhythm. Porter kicked him again, harder.

"Duke!"

Still nothing.

He poked the tip of the baton into Duke's mouth, making him gag like a chicken getting its neck wrung. But even that didn't wake him.

"Jesus Christ," he said.

He gave up, taking pity on the man and tucking the blanket back under his bushy chin. He took a photo, then called control asking for one of the PCs outside the building to ring him. He headed out of the room, using the torch to light his way.

He pushed open the stairwell door, listening to the echo of his breath whisper down into the bottomless dark. He couldn't hear anything else, so he set off, taking the steps slowly. The shadows leaped like wild things, dancing around the light of his torch, mocking him all the way to the ground floor. He was pushing through the door when his phone rang, and he had to tuck the baton beneath his arm before he could answer it.

"What?" he said.

"Got asked to call you, sir," said a man's voice. "It's PC Knapp."

"I thought PC *Nap* was upstairs," he said, laughing at his own joke. "You the ones parked outside the Norvic?"

"Yeah," said the constable.

"Can you see the front door?"

"Yeah."

"Any sign of anything odd?"

"Nope," said Knapp. "Been a few folk around, a couple of locals. No sign of the gangs or anything like that."

Porter walked into the corridor, aiming his torch one way and then the other. Even with the police right outside, even though he could have a dozen officers here in less than a minute, the quiet tower was doing a number on him. There was nothing quite as scary as exploring an abandoned building by torchlight. He'd seen far too many horror films for that.

"You doing okay in there, sir?" said the PC.

"I'm fine," he snapped. "Why wouldn't I be fine? Not scared at all, mate. Just keep an eye out, and be ready to roll."

He hung up, his feet crunching on a carpet of crisp packets and old paper as he made his way down the corridor. His heart was throwing a fit behind his ribs, his throat dry. He pulled out the Snickers and took another bite, just to take his mind off things.

"You're a grown man, Pete," he told himself through a mouthful of chocolate. "No need to be—"

Something crashed behind him, and he shrieked. He dropped the Snickers as he spun around, his torch revealing the long, empty corridor.

"What?" he said.

It had sounded like something falling over, or maybe an object being thrown at a window. It was towards the back of the building, and he struggled to remember if anyone had eyes on that side. He gripped the baton in one hand and the torch in the other, moving purposefully forward. The door at the end of the corridor was unlocked, and he opened it slowly, peering into the dark space beyond.

"Hello?" he said, the building squashing his voice into a whisper. "Police."

He was in a smaller office, perforated by slim columns. Through the windows, and past the scaffolding, he could see the car park at the rear of the Norvic, barely lit by a single security light. It looked empty.

He entered the office, unpicking the dark corners with his torch and finding absolutely nothing. He was doubling back towards the corridor when he heard another noise, a muffled shout of anger from somewhere outside. He crossed the threadbare carpet, heading around the corner into the second half of the office. This wing lay along the southeast flank of the building. He could make out the block of flats next door, on the other side of a narrow alley of overgrown scrubland.

Something was moving in the dark vegetation between the buildings, a flurry of motion. Another cry, this one full of pain.

Porter clicked off his torch and approached the window, trying to make sense of the shapes in the bushes. There was a web of scaffolding in the way, and the night was just too heavy. He glanced left, then right, but there was no fire exit on this side of the block, no way of getting out.

He found his phone, calling Knapp's number.

"Yeah, can you guys get around the side of the building? See all that green shit? I think somebody's in there."

"Yes, sir," said Knapp.

Porter hung up, heading back to the window. He cupped his hand to the tinted glass, squinting. It took his eyes a moment to get used to the dark, but when they did, he spotted the outline of two hooded men on the edge of the wasteland. One was standing there, not doing anything. The other looked like he was kicking at something on the ground.

He had to adjust the angle of his head, pushing his cheek against the cold glass, before he made out the third man lying in the dirt, the kicks raining in. He wasn't moving.

"Shit," he said.

He rapped the baton on the window, yelling.

"Oi! Stop that!"

The two men looked up. Even though their faces weren't visible in the darkness of their hoods, he could feel their gaze on him. The second kicked the guy on the ground again, like he was a goalkeeper sending the ball upfield. The thud was perfectly audible even from inside.

"Oi! Get away from him! Police!"

He thwacked the baton against the window, hard enough to crack it. He walloped it again, and this time it shattered. Without the tinted glass, he got a better view of the two men. Both were wearing grey and black tracksuits, bumbags strapped over their shoulders, white trainers on their feet.

"I said get the fuck away from him!" roared Porter. "Now!"

He didn't think they were going to move, but there was another shout as the PCs from the car tore down the road. The second kid got in one more kick to his victim's head, then he legged it, his pounding footsteps echoing off the tall buildings.

The first guy, though, didn't run. He cocked his head like a curious dog, staring at Porter from the shadows of his hoodie.

"Stay where you are!" called the closest PC.

The kid reached up and pulled back his hood. Porter already knew what he was going to see: dark skin, fierce blue eyes, a shit-eating grin stretching off the sides of his face.

"This is for you," the kid said, and he actually blew Porter a kiss.

Then he bolted like an Olympic sprinter, sucked into the dark.

Porter used the baton to knock away the last few shards of glass before clambering out of the window. It was a bigger drop than he'd been expecting, and he landed badly, his ankle twisting beneath him. He dropped onto his knees, the baton flying.

"Fucktwatshitballs!" he growled, using the building to get back to his feet—just in time, as the two PCs burst through the wall of overgrown shrubs.

"Get down!" yelled the closest one, shining his torch in Porter's face. "Get on the... Oh, sorry, sir."

The light was pulled away. Porter screwed his eyes shut, seeing glowing flowers blossom across the dark.

"They went that way," he said, hoping that he was pointing in the right direction. "Towards Walpole Street. Call for a bloody ambulance."

He shook the strobing lights from his head, kneeling beside the man on the ground. He was in his forties, although it was hard to tell for sure because his face was so swollen, his dark beard soaked with blood. He wore a pair of filthy jeans and a leather jacket over a black T-shirt. On his feet were a pair of brown shoes, and clutched in his hand was a rucksack.

"Hey," said Porter. The man groaned, squirming in the dirt. He tried to pull his rucksack closer, but Porter grabbed it, rooting it in place. "You're alright, just stay still."

More police were arriving, one crashing through the bushes, another two jogging down the street.

"Make sure he's okay," said Porter. "There's two scrotes in tracksuits somewhere. They were laying into him."

He unzipped the rucksack, shining his torch inside to find two packages the size of bricks, wrapped tight in brown tape, and an old Nokia phone.

Beneath them was a long and very sharp knife, the blade stained with rust.

Or maybe blood.

"I'll take that," he said, tugging the bag out of the injured man's grip. "On second thoughts, secure this twat, and get tactical out here."

"Where are you going, sir?" said a constable as he removed his handcuffs.

Porter carried the bag out of the wasteland and onto the road. There was no sign of the lads who'd attacked the man, but the estate wasn't that big, and Porter was fast running out of patience.

"I'm going to find those pricks, and end this."

CHAPTER THIRTY-FIVE

KETT SAT AT HIS COMPUTER, THE SCREEN A BLUR EVEN through his glasses. He took them off so that he could scrub the exhaustion from his eyes, but if anything, it made it worse.

Sitting a few desks behind him was DS Spalding. Even though he wasn't facing her, he could feel her stare on the back of his neck, as cold as an ice pick. He didn't blame her, or any of the other detectives who'd been dragged into work as a result of his call to Superintendent Clare. This wasn't exactly anybody's top choice of location for Sunday night—or Monday morning, as it now was.

But nobody was complaining, outwardly, that was, because they all wanted the same thing.

They all wanted to catch this arsehole.

"Right," said Spalding. "I've got enrolment lists for Bignold School. What are we looking for?"

Kett spun his chair around.

"My guess is it's somebody who's lost a child. Recently, but far back enough to give him time to plan and prepare his attacks.

I'm guessing two to six months. The kid would have had Judy Bartlett as a teacher at Bignold, so it's before she moved across town. Can you cross-reference that with any known deaths?"

Spalding looked like she wanted to reply with something scathing, but she swallowed it down, nodding. Kett turned back to his screen, scouring the reports from the children's department at the hospital. The number of kids who had been ill there in recent months, and those who had never made it home, broke his heart.

"Has anyone managed to wake Savage up yet?" yelled Clare as he appeared from his office. He'd buttoned his shirt up wrong, and his fly was undone, but nobody had been brave enough to tell him. "She's not picking up."

Kett checked his phone to see if Savage had called him back, but there was nothing.

"Not like her," he said. "Have you tried Steph?"

"Who?" barked Clare, looming over Kett's desk.

"Cafferty," he went on. "The sergeant. From Lincolnshire. She's staying with Kate."

Clare stared at Kett like he thought he'd gone mad.

"Nobody's heard from her at all?" said Kett, a flicker of panic rising inside him. Clare leaned closer.

"What, Robert?"

"It's probably nothing," he said. "But Kate was worried about Cafferty. She was saying something about her pocket square, that it had an eye on it. I didn't think it was anything, but... Maybe it's worth sending a couple of uniforms over to her flat?"

"You think *Cafferty's* our killer?" said Clare.

"No, sir, but..."

He put a hand to his stomach.

"Something just feels off. I don't know what."

"Fine!" barked Clare, spinning around and heading into his office. "Not like I've got anything else to be doing, is it?"

Kett turned to the screen, trying to make sense of the names that swam against the too-bright glow.

"I don't really get why we're doing this," said Spalding. "Given we found Idris' wallet in Roger Sexton's bin. It has to be him, surely."

"With any luck, you're right," said Kett. "But it's not clicking. I was thinking about the wallet, how it got there. This is personal for our suspect, right? The killer knows his victims. He's chosen them because they're good people, he thinks they'll look after his kid in the next life."

"I mean, yeah, sir, if you believe that theory," said Spalding. "Which is a big if. Because it's insane."

"It's not insane," he said, looking back again. "It makes perfect sense. You love someone that much, you'd do anything for them, in this life or the next one."

Spalding chewed her pencil, her expression hard to read.

"What I'm saying is that the killer knew Helen," Kett went on. "He'd researched where she worked, how she got to work, which way she walked home. He must have, if he was waiting for her in the park on Friday night. And if he knew everything there was to know about her, then—"

"He'd have known about Roger, too," said Spalding, nodding. "So he planted the wallet in Sexton's bin, knowing we'd find it, knowing we'd arrest Roger instead."

"He doesn't want to get caught," said Kett.

He leaned back, frowning.

"What?" barked Clare as he returned to the bullpen. "You've got that look on your face again, like an old man who's forgotten where he's put his underpants."

Kett shook his head, doubting himself again.

"There's one thing I don't get, sir. The killer is creating an army of good people for the next life, right? To look after his kid. But why wouldn't he just, you know... do it himself?"

"Suicide?" said Clare.

"Yeah. If he's that worried, why wouldn't he end his own life to take care of the child?"

"Because he's a coward," said Clare.

"Or because he has another kid," Kett replied, the truth of it suddenly hitting him. "Maybe more than one. That's why he can't go. He can't leave *them*. We're looking for a child with siblings."

"This might help," said a voice. Kett turned to see PC Niven running across the bullpen, a sheet of paper in her hand. She slapped it onto his desk like she was playing snap. "The sign-up sheets for Idris Mellor's football club, going back the last couple of years."

"Good job, Flick," said Kett.

There were a lot of names, over a hundred of them, but two struck him like a double tap from a pistol.

"Wait," he said, tapping his finger on the paper. "Short. Luke and Cora Short."

"Short?" said Clare, leaning in beside him.

"I know the name," said Kett.

He did, but he was struggling to place it. He turned to his computer, typing the names of the two children into Google. The result was instantaneous, the page full of tributes from the local papers. He clicked on the top link to see a grinning boy aged ten or eleven, wearing pyjamas and an elf hat. He was sitting in a hospital bed with a young girl beside him, both holding perfectly wrapped presents.

"Luke Short," he said. "Passed away just after Christmas, from Leukaemia. He was in the N&N. He lived on the estate."

"How do you know?" said Clare.

"Because I met his dad," said Kett, finally remembering where he'd heard the name. "Yesterday. Junior Short. He lives in the flats right by where Helen was killed. He was the one who gave us the security camera that overlooked the underpass."

He typed Junior Short into the search engine, but this time there wasn't much to go on. He had to scroll halfway down the page before he found what he was looking for: an announcement on the local St John's Ambulance website. The page loaded to show Junior, standing in a green uniform, a smile on his face. The date was less than a year ago, but even with his silver hair, he looked a decade younger.

"'*We are sad to announce that beloved volunteer Junior is leaving us for personal reasons,*'" he read aloud. "'*A former paramedic and father of two, Reece Junior Short has been a part of St John's for nearly seven years, providing invaluable expertise and a caring touch for countless public events. He will be sorely missed.*'"

Kett clicked back to the article about Luke, the boy who'd passed away, scrolling down until he found it.

"Luke's father is called Reece. Junior is his middle name."

"Reece Short," said Spalding, walking over. "RS. Nolan O'Brien's journal."

"What if O'Brien wasn't a fortune teller?" said Kett, feeling another part of the puzzle click into place. "What if he was a medium? What if that's how they met? Short's son died, and he was trying to find a way of reaching him. If you believe enough to try to speak to the dead, then you believe there are other ways of helping them."

"Like sending an army of good people to protect him," said Clare. "But the initials in O'Brien's diary were RS-C, weren't they? What's the C for?"

"Child?" said Spalding.

"That's it," said Kett. "And Junior's a paramedic. He knows how to save a life, he knows how to take one. It's him. It has to be. When I met Junior, he talked about both his kids as if they were alive. Luke and Cora. He was throwing us off the scent. He..."

Kett closed his eyes, trying to remember the conversation. Junior had said something, a passing comment that Kett hadn't even picked up on at the time, but which might have been the key to everything.

Nothing worse than feeling like you're on your own.

In this life, or the next.

"It's him," he said, scooting his chair back and almost taking out the Superintendent. "It's Junior. Get somebody over there, *now!*"

PORTER WAS MAKING his way along the dark street, hunting for dickheads, when Kett's call came through.

"Sir," he said as he answered. "You heard? The Iron Sausages are out, they were beating someone up right outside the—"

"Forget about them for a second," said Kett. He sounded out of breath, like he was running. "You're still there? The Norvic?"

Porter looked back down the road, seeing the towering

blue building fifty yards behind him. The wind had picked up, the scaffolding rattling like old bones. A dozen or so coppers patrolled the surrounding streets, just shadows in the night.

"Yeah," he said. "Why?"

"Look, Pete, I think the guy we met yesterday—Saturday—the one in the flats, is the killer. Junior. You remember him?"

"Short guy, white hair?" said Porter. "The killer? Why?"

"Long story. I need you up at his flat. You've got Uniforms there?"

"About a million of them," said Porter, heading back the way he'd come. "The block next door to the Norvic, wasn't it?"

"Yeah, up the stairs."

Porter put his fingers in his mouth, whistling to the PCs up ahead.

"Over here!" he yelled. "And bring a ram!"

He reached the main door of the apartment building, pushing it open. The lobby looked the same as it had yesterday, the bikes chained up in the corner, the air full of the sweet smell of incense, children's pictures tacked to the windows. He held the door for the first of the constables, then made for the stairs.

"I saw him again yesterday, sir," he said, climbing. "Junior. He was at the riot, taking photos."

"Yeah?" said Kett. "You spoke to him?"

"Not for long. He had to run off, his kids were fighting or something."

"Kids? Plural?"

"I don't know," said Porter, reaching the third floor. "Yeah, kids, I'm sure that's what he said. Why?"

"You saw them?"

"I saw kids," he said. "I don't know who they belonged to."

Porter heard a door slam, realising it was on the phone. An engine growled to life.

"We're on our way," said Kett. "Just make sure he's in, and don't let him leave."

"Understood," said Porter, walking into the corridor that led to Junior's flat.

"And Pete, do *not* go in there alone, okay?"

Going in alone wasn't going to be an issue. Six constables were right behind him, one armed with an enforcer. Porter hammered a fist on the door and stood back.

"Junior?" he shouted, his voice echoing off the walls. "Open the door, mate. It's the police."

He locked his breath in his lungs as he listened for a reply, but the entire block was silent. He didn't bother knocking again, he just stood to the side and nodded to the constable. The man didn't seem to put much effort into it, but the ram knocked the flimsy door clean out of its frame, the wood splintering.

"Police!" yelled Porter, storming inside. "Stay right where you are!"

The entrance hall was empty, the lights off. He snapped on the switches as he went, poking his head into the deserted kitchen.

"Upstairs," he barked at the constables.

The living room was empty too, as were the cupboards, and the microscopic toilet.

"Up here, sir!"

Porter jogged up the creaking steps, almost tripping over a toy ambulance that had been left on the landing. Figures spilled out of it, and he hopped over them, seeing two PCs standing outside a bedroom. He couldn't make out anything past their shoulders, but when he squeezed between them, he saw the same prison cell-sized room where Junior had handed them the security camera. There was barely enough space for the third constable, who stood beside the bunk beds.

"What is it?" he asked her.

She lifted the covers off the top bunk with such a look of fear on her face that he half expected to find a body there. Instead, he saw a green cardboard folder lying on the immaculately ironed sheet.

Taped to the front of it was a photograph of a young boy, a giant smile on his face.

"Move," he said.

He picked up the heavy folder and sat on the bottom bunk to open it. It was rammed with paper, literally hundreds of pages. He knew, deep down, what he'd find inside, but it still took his breath away when he pulled out the first sheet and saw Helen Coulter's face smiling back at him, the same picture from the NHS website that they'd already seen. He set it on the bed and pulled out the next one, a stapled collection of bills with Helen's name and address, as well as a payslip from the hospital.

Beneath that was another photograph, Helen again, this time in her nursing scrubs. She sat next to the same boy whose picture was taped to the front of the folder, in the canteen at the hospital, her arm around his shoulders.

"Shit a brick," he muttered.

He emptied the entire folder onto the duvet, pushing the documents apart to see more photos: Helen, Idris, Judy, and a whole bunch of people he didn't recognise. He pulled out his phone, calling Kett.

"You got him?" said the DCI.

"No, sir. He's not here. But you were right, it's him.

He's got a tonne of stuff on his victims, Helen and the others. It was right here in the bedroom. We literally walked past it."

"You're sure?" said Kett.

"I'm looking at them now. All of them, and more."

"More victims?" said Kett.

"More *targets*, I think. He isn't finished yet. He might have gone after them tonight, but their information is here, addresses, everything. We can intercept him."

"If it's not too late," said Kett. "Text it all to me, we're almost in the city."

Porter dropped the phone onto the bed, frantically sorting through the paperwork in search of the identities of the people in the photographs. There were at least ten of them, though, and he'd managed to jumble everything up when he'd tipped it out of the folder. He picked the one that had been next in line behind Judy: a doctor, his address over in Hethersett.

"Sir," said a constable, peering through the door. "We've found something."

"Well bring it here, then," he snapped back.

"Probably better if you see it for yourself," said the PC.

Porter grabbed his phone, putting it to his ear.

"You there, sir?"

"Yeah," said Kett.

"You should probably head to Hethersett," he said. "One of the kid's doctors lives out there, Sandeep Sabhar. Might be on Junior's hit list. I'll text the address. But honestly, there are loads of them."

He followed the constable onto the landing, his foot crunching one of the figures that had tumbled out of the toy ambulance. It was a small metal man, he saw, his rifle bent out of shape where his foot had crushed it.

A tin soldier, he thought, as if they needed any more confirmation.

The PC was in the front bedroom, standing beside a desk in the corner. Porter had to squeeze between the bed and the open doors of the wardrobe to get to him. He spotted a laptop, which was closed, and next to that, an inkjet printer. There were documents sitting in the paper tray.

"There, sir," said the PC, gesturing.

"You couldn't have carried them through?" he said, giving him a hard stare.

He laid the phone on the desk to free up his hands, picking up what turned out to be a collection of photographs badly printed on cheap paper. They were all from the riot yesterday, he realised, shots of angry locals and flustered coppers. He flicked through the top three, then froze when he found himself in one, looking right at the camera and about four stone heavier than he was in real life.

"You bastard," he said, remembering Junior taking the shot.

He turned to the next image, seeing the stampede when everyone had gone after the kid. Then the next, taken in the garages, a bad shot snapped over the top of a lot of heads. The bald guy who'd caught Ronin was here. It wasn't Roger, or Terry. It wasn't anyone they knew, and he wasn't even really bald.

"Pete?" said Kett from the desk, the line still open.

Junior had obviously moved to the front of the crowd, because the next photo showed Duke standing over the kid on the floor, fighting off the mob. The one after that was Duke again, a close-up of his serious face. So was the one after that, although the constable was smiling here.

The next printed sheet held an article from a couple of

years ago, when Duke had been awarded the title of Britain's Bravest Copper.

The last, and Porter had no idea how Junior had got it, was a copy of the PC's driving licence, including his address.

"Oh, shit a brick," said Porter, suddenly cold.

He grabbed the phone.

"Sir, why did you think it was Junior?"

"Like I said, Pete, it's a long story," said Kett, his voice fading in and out. "His son died. We think he's sending good people after him. He's making an army to watch over his kid."

An army of good people, thought Porter.

"Forget the doctor," he said, running for the door. "He's going after Duke."

CHAPTER THIRTY-SIX

Duke's first thought on waking, as was often the case these days, was of Savage.

I love you, Kate, he thought, yawning his way up from oblivion and expecting to see her lying next to him in the dimly lit bedroom.

When he grunted upright, though, he found that he wasn't in his bed after all, but sitting in a folding chair in the huge office that had doubled as Terry Prince's Funland. The light wasn't coming from his bedside lamp, it was coming from a torch on the floor.

The memories re-entered his head like a collapsing building, in disordered chunks and lost in a cloud of dust. He got up, the folding chair sticking to his backside for a few seconds before he jiggled it loose. He picked up the torch and used it to search the room, remembering that Porter was supposed to be here. There was no sign of him, but he'd left his bag open by the window.

"Porter?" he called out, his voice reverberating around the space.

The DI was probably asleep somewhere, because he'd *definitely* been tired.

Duke peered through the window, but he couldn't see much past the scaffolding. He turned to the room instead, yawning again as he admired the collection of activities and attractions that had been built here. Whatever you said about Terry, he'd done a bang-up job of this place. If he and Kate ever had kids—*when* they had kids, he corrected himself, because he couldn't imagine anything better than that—he'd love to bring them here.

That thought gave him an idea for the wedding: a Funland ceremony. They could even have it in a theme park somewhere, with rides and ball pits and a mirror maze, like the one they'd found downstairs. The priest could dress up as a furry mascot, and maybe he and Savage could wear costumes as well.

"You're a genius, Aaron," he told himself as he walked to the door. "Kate is going to love that."

He needed to tell Savage before he forgot, so he pulled out his phone and called her. He cancelled it after a couple of rings, because it suddenly occurred to him that she'd probably be asleep. He texted her instead.

Sorry, still on steakout. How'd you fancy a Funland wedding?!

He added a heart emoji, then a roller coaster one, then a bug-eyed squirrel that resembled the creatures that had been painted on the walls of the corridor, before sending it. He'd suggested so many wedding ideas to Savage over the last two years, he'd filled entire albums with photos and magazine cut-outs and seating plans and colour themes. She hadn't seemed particularly excited about any of them, which he totally respected. You only got married once. It had to be perfect.

Funland could be perfect.

He walked into the corridor, beaming his torch back and forth, humming as he went. He was trying to remember what he'd had for dinner, because there was a funny taste in his mouth. Greasy, and a little metallic. He scraped his tongue on his teeth as he headed past the stairwell.

"Yo, Porter! Where are you?"

He opened the door of the next section of Funland, illuminating those endless tangles of rope with his torch.

"Porter?" he called. "You get stuck in there?"

No reply, other than a whistle of wind somewhere to the right. He made his way into the office, skirting along the front of the obstacle course so he didn't get tangled up in it. When he aimed the torch along the wall of glass, he saw that one of the windows had been broken.

"Pete?"

He leaned out into the cool evening, feeling the brush of the wind on his face. The ledge of scaffolding was right there, the wooden boards rattling softly.

"Sir? You out there?"

No sign of him. Duke retreated into the office, finding Porter's number on his phone. Before he could call it, though, his ringtone blared: *Wannabe* by the Spice Girls. Savage's face appeared on the screen, and he kissed her nose before he answered it.

"Sorry if I woke you," he said. "You okay?"

A hiss of static, then what sounded like a whimper.

"Kate?"

"I'm fine, Aaron," she said after a moment or two. "Just stretching. Are you? You called?"

"Yeah, I'm cool," he said.

"Yeah, I'm cool..." she said, drawing the last word out expectantly.

"*Sarge*," he added, and it was worth it to hear Savage laugh. "I'm still on the stakeout."

"Eating steak?"

"Huh?" he said, frowning. "No. Catching criminals."

"Caught any?"

Duke walked back into the corridor, heading for the stairwell.

"Not yet," he said.

"Well it's pretty hard to catch them when you're asleep."

"Asleep?" he spluttered. "No chance."

"So it wasn't you in the video Porter sent me? Sitting in a chair, snoring like a tuba full of angry ducks?"

"What?" he said. "No! And on an unrelated note, I am going to kill that man when I find him."

He opened the stairwell door, aiming his torch into the dark.

"Porter?" he called. "Where are you?"

"Bit weird of him to walk off," said Savage.

"Probably eating something in a dark corner," said Duke. "What have you been up to, anyway?"

"You wouldn't believe me if I told you," she said.

He heard a door close on the other end of the line, Savage speaking more quietly.

"God, what a night, Aaron. I made a complete tit of myself."

"Don't see how that's possible," he said, still standing in the open door of the stairwell. There was a hell of a breeze blowing past him.

"Steph—DS Cafferty—she went out for a run, and I... I searched her bags while she was out."

"What?" said Duke. "Why?"

"I don't know. A feeling. I found an eye."

"A *real* one?"

"No, you dope. A glass one. Exactly the same as the prosthetic eyes we found in Helen Coulter's flat. I panicked, thought she might be the killer, but before I could call anyone, she came back, caught me in her room, red-handed. I thought she was going to attack me or something."

"Are you okay?" said Duke. "*Steph's* the killer?"

"No. She's harmless. Well, kind of. Turns out she's a magpie; she likes taking things from cases. Evidence. She nabbed the eye from Helen's flat, didn't think anyone would notice as there were loads of them. You should have seen her, Aaron, she was so upset. Said she didn't want our new friendship to end like this. I felt terrible."

"*You* don't have anything to feel terrible about," said Duke. "She's the one who messed up. Stealing evidence is a massive red flag."

"Yeah, I know," said Savage. "But... Oh, hang on, Aaron, Kett's calling."

"At this hour?" said Duke, but Savage had already gone.

He mentally kicked himself. He hadn't even remembered to ask her about the Funland wedding. He tried Porter's number, but nobody answered. He yelled his name instead, listening to it echo down the stairs. If the DI was here, he wasn't replying.

Duke had no idea whether to go back to his post or search the rest of the building. Knowing Porter, he'd tried to chew his way through a vending machine and the bloody thing had fallen on him.

He was letting the stairwell door close when he finally heard a reply.

"Aaron?"

Porter's shout came from somewhere below, and it sounded groggy, as if he'd just woken up. Duke laughed to himself as he started down the stairs. His first assumption had been right. Porter had curled up in a corner somewhere and fallen asleep.

"Aaron?" the DI shouted again.

"I'm coming," he yelled back. "Give me a second."

He pushed through the door onto the sixth floor.

"Sir?"

"Through here," came the reply, the voice louder.

Duke walked into the nearest room, seeing the maze of glass that stretched from one side to the other. He swept the torch over the mirrored walls, the light refracting at odd angles. How perfect would something like this be on their big day? A church full of mirrors.

"Aaron?"

The voice was closer, barely a whisper.

"What are you even doing in there, sir?" said Duke. "I thought looking into one mirror would be bad enough for you."

He sniggered at his own joke as he entered the labyrinth, surrounded by twisted versions of himself—too tall, too short, too fat, too thin. Their crooked faces and dark eyes made him feel a little uneasy as he made his way, and he called out again.

"Where the hell are you?"

No reply. If Porter was playing a prank, if he suddenly jumped out and tried to scare him, then Duke wouldn't be responsible for what happened. Porter would need a porter to carry him out of here, straight to A&E.

His phone began to ring again, and when he pulled it out he saw Porter's name on the screen. He stopped walking, confused, the mirror-Dukes freezing alongside him.

All except for one.

Duke turned to see a reflection come to life, peeling

itself from the dark. But it wasn't him, it was a monster with no face, just two round, soulless eyes, lunging towards him.

Oh no, thought Duke.

He didn't have time to speak the words aloud. The monster's mask cracked into his face like a battering ram, and the world went black.

CHAPTER THIRTY-SEVEN

"Yeah, I've got a message," yelled Porter, when Duke's voicemail beeped. "Answer your bloody phone!"

He wrenched open the front door of Norvic House and ran into the lobby, hearing a clatter of feet behind him as the constables followed. With no need to be stealthy anymore, he flicked on the lights, the fluorescents waking slowly before burning blindingly bright. He covered his eyes with a hand as he shouldered through the interior door, heading for the stairs.

"You got him on his radio yet?" he said.

"No, sir," said PC Knapp, right behind him. "He's not responding."

He'd muted it, Porter remembered, so he could sleep. With any luck, he was still snoring in his chair. Even if Junior was coming after him, he would be targeting Duke's house, which was where most of the PCs from the estate had been sent in the hope of catching him. There was no way the killer could know Duke was here, inside the Norvic.

Right?

Unless Junior had seen them arrive earlier that night, of course. Unless he'd been watching from his bedroom window as they'd delivered his next victim on a platter.

"Aaron!" he roared up the stairs. "Where are you?"

He started climbing, two of the constables quickly overtaking him. They were both armed with Tasers, but it wasn't particularly reassuring.

"Top floor," he told them. "Duke's in the room on the right. Be careful!"

He tried Duke's phone again as he followed the constables out of the stairwell, counting the rings. The PCs ran through the door into the office on the right, their shouts echoing back.

"Come on, mate," Porter said beneath his breath, trying to ignore the lunatic painted figures that grinned at him from the walls. "Be okay."

The call cut off, unanswered, just as one of the constables reappeared.

"He's not in here, sir," he said.

"Then find him!" yelled Porter. "Check the fire exits out the back, and the roof."

He pushed into the rope room, turning on the lights to reveal the spiderweb of cables that ran from one side to the other. It was bright enough for him to see that the office was empty, and it was impossible to miss the window that had been smashed.

He ran over, seeing the scaffolding outside the shattered pane, and the ladders that led down to the street. His shoes crunched broken glass into the carpet, and he realised that nobody had fallen out.

Somebody had broken *in*.

"Duke!" he yelled, running for the door. "Fuck's sake, where are you?"

He called his phone when he was out in the corridor, and this time he heard faint music. He followed it to the stairwell, pushing through the door just as the tune ended.

When he dialled Duke's number again, he realised it was coming from somewhere downstairs.

His god-awful ringtone.

"Hey!" he shouted down the corridor. "I need you back here!"

No answer. The PCs had moved to the other side of the building, out of earshot. The rest of his backup had got lost on their way up, or were searching the lower levels.

"Fuck's sake," Porter said, racing down the steps.

He stopped at the next floor down, dialling Duke again and hearing the Spice Girls. The tune grew louder as he walked into the corridor, coming from a room on the left. He vaguely remembered that this was Terry's mirror maze.

"Aaron?" he said, jogging over.

The call cut off, plunging the building into silence.

Almost silence.

He could hear a noise on the other side of the door, the clatter of something falling, a smash.

Then a soft, muted cry.

"Sixth floor!" he yelled to anyone who might be listening. "Hurry!"

He called Kett as he shunted through the door, the DCI answering immediately.

"Sixth floor," he said. "Mirror maze. I think Junior's in the building."

He hung up so he could focus on the lights. They blinked on infuriatingly slowly, the bulbs not white but red, turning the enormous room into a sea of blood. A wall of Porters stared back at him from the maze, all as shocked as he was.

"Aaron?" he called out. "You in here?"

That noise again, a grunting voice.

"Oi!" Porter yelled, running towards the front line of mirrors and glass, looking for the way in. He pulled out the baton as he went, extending it with a flick of his wrist.

Another clattering thud. Porter pushed into the maze, surrounded by warped bodies and demonic faces, no sign of anyone except himself.

"Aaron?"

He turned right, trying to make sense of anything in the crimson light. He headed down another twisted aisle of mirrors, moving as fast as they would let him. He had no idea where he was, the maze seeming to shift around him like a nest of coiling snakes. He could still hear a voice, a whisper choked with sobs.

"Thank you," it was saying. "Thank you. Thank you."

A wet sound. Something like a blade in flesh.

"Aaron, answer me!"

Porter spun around a corner and saw him. Duke. Lying on the ground a few yards away, his face hidden from view by a figure in black who kneeled beside him. The man was doing something, his hand working back and forth.

"Get the fuck away from him!" Porter screamed, lifting the baton and breaking into a run—making it halfway there before crunching into an invisible wall of clear plastic.

He bounced off, hard, the pain radiating from his nose. He staggered for a second, stunned. He'd dropped the baton, no sign of it in the blood-coloured shadows.

The man looked back and saw him. His face was something from a nightmare: solid black, with two perfectly round insect eyes. It wasn't a white hood he was wearing underneath, it was his hair—perfectly silver.

"Get away from him, Junior," Porter said again,

hammering on the plastic wall, feeling it tremble in its frame. "I swear to God, this is your last fucking chance."

The man turned slowly back, carrying on with whatever he'd been doing. Porter still couldn't see Duke's face.

"Aaron!" he roared. "Help! I need help in here!"

Porter drove his foot into the clear panel of plastic, then again. On the third try, it collapsed out of the frame and he fell through, landing on his hands and knees.

He got up, throwing himself on the back of the masked man before he could turn around again.

They tumbled over Duke, crashing into a mirror in a hail of broken glass. Porter pinned him, but the man threw his head back, a flash of silver hair then an explosion of pain as his skull connected with Porter's injured nose. He was freakishly strong, rolling Porter off him onto a carpet of razor-sharp shards. They cut through his suit, slicing the skin of his hands as he tried to get up. The man was back on his feet, protected by his gloves. He vanished into the forest of mirrors.

Duke lay perfectly still. There was blood on his face.

Around his eyes.

"Fuck," said Porter, hobbling over to the constable. "Fuck, fuck—*fuck!*"

Junior lunged out of the shadows, and Porter punched him—only for his fist to connect with a mirror.

Something sliced across the back of his neck. He spun, seeing a dozen masked men vanish into the maze, running in every direction. He didn't know which one was real. He put his hand to the wound, feeling blood on his fingers, as hot as boiling water.

He stood over Duke, turning in slow circles, trying to make sense of the kaleidoscope of light and shadow in the endless mirrors. He went for his phone, but his hand was slick with blood and it tumbled from his fingers. There was no sign of the baton anywhere, and Duke didn't have his. The Taser and the PAVA spray were gone as well.

"In here!" he screamed, praying that somebody would hear him. "Sixth floor! The maze!"

A pad of feet from nearby, Junior circling him, trying to find his way back to Duke.

"If you want him, you're going to have to go through me, you prick," said Porter.

A rush of movement in the mirror to his right.

He turned *left* just in time, weaving out of the way of Junior's blade as the man pounced from between two mirrors. Porter grabbed his arm, wrenching it down hard enough to make him cry out in pain. Then he threw an elbow into his face.

The mask absorbed the worst of it, Junior fighting back, trying to drive his weapon into Porter's stomach. He clung on to the man's wrist with everything he had.

"It's over, Junior!" he said. "Just drop it!"

The killer wasn't giving up, his face snapping forward in another headbutt, then again. Porter couldn't get a shot in because he didn't dare let go of his arm. He tried a kick instead, driving his foot into Junior's knee only for it to miss.

He lost his balance, dragging the man down on top of him as he fell.

"You can both go," said Junior behind his mask, pinning Porter to the floor. "You can both go to him."

Porter struggled, but Junior was straddling him, trapping his arms. He lifted the weapon, ready to drive it down into the jelly of his eye.

"Thank you," he said.

"No!" cried Porter.

Something bright red cracked into Junior's face with a

dull clang—hard enough to snap his head back and rip the mask away. He managed to keep his balance until it crunched into him a second time, then his limp body rolled to the floor.

Porter looked up, seeing a fire extinguisher, and past that the kid who held it. He was wearing a grey and black tracksuit, and even though he had his hood up, Porter could see a flash of blue eyes.

"You?" he groaned, trying to sit up.

"Looked like you needed a little help, big man," said the kid, hurling the fire extinguisher to the floor.

Voices spilled into the room, police officers shouting. The kid glanced through the labyrinth of mirrors, then turned back to Porter.

"Iron Soldiers," he said, tapping his head. "You ever think maybe we ain't the bad guys?"

"What?" said Porter. "Why?"

"Enid told me to watch over you. Said you were a good spirit. Said she wasn't done with you yet."

He vanished between the mirrors, then snuck back, flashing Porter a bright grin.

"Pussio."

Then he was gone again, chased by his reflections.

"Wait," said Porter, but the kid was a ghost.

He sat up like he'd been knocked down by a car, the pain rolling through him. He checked Junior first, in case he was still awake. But the man had a crater in his forehead where he'd been struck, his eyes already swollen shut.

"Fucker," Porter growled.

He crawled over the minefield of glass to where Duke lay, still motionless. The giant PC wore a mask of blood, looking like Zorro.

"Aaron?" he said, putting his hand on the constable's face. "Aaron, you okay?"

He moved his fingers to Duke's throat, working them beneath his beard.

"We're over here!" he yelled to the constables across the room, feeling the stew of emotion climb his gullet. "Get an ambulance!"

He found a pulse and almost cried with the relief of it.

"You're going to be alright, mate," he said. "Just hang on. Help's coming."

"Pete?" yelled a voice, filling the room.

It was Kett.

"Get an ambulance, Robbie," Porter yelled again. "He's hurt!"

He ran his fingers along Duke's face, trying to find the damage.

"Come on," he said.

He'd been too late, he knew. Junior had carved him up. He'd taken his eyes.

He'd taken his fucking eyes.

"Come on, Aaron, look at me."

There was too much blood to see anything, but most of it looked like it was coming from a four-inch gash in Duke's forehead. Porter pushed his hand against it, trying to stem the flow, and Duke whimpered.

"Easy," Porter told him. "Don't move."

Slowly, Duke opened his left eye.

Then his right.

They were bloodshot, but other than that, they looked okay.

This time, Porter couldn't stop the tears from falling, the relief spilling through him like warm water. He crashed back, offering a quiet prayer to the ceiling.

"You crying, sir?" croaked Duke.

"No," said Porter, scrubbing his eyes with his bloodied hands. "Obviously. I'm just allergic. To your bullshit."

There was a series of crashes from across the room as somebody ploughed through the mirrors. Duke managed to prop himself up on his elbows, but he didn't seem capable of much more than that.

"Thanks, sir," he said. "For coming back for me."

"What did you expect me to do?" said Porter, studying his bleeding hands, seeing the sparkle of glass in his flesh. The pain was coming back now, and it was furious. "Couldn't let you get all the glory."

"You got him?" asked Duke.

Porter glanced back to see that Junior still hadn't moved. He wasn't even sure if he was breathing. The kid had vanished, although it wasn't clear where he was planning on going, given that the building was full of police.

"Yeah, Aaron. I got him."

A mirror further down the aisle toppled over, smashing on the floor. Kett stumbled through the gap, finding them in the crimson dark.

"Christ," he said, his boots crunching glass as he ran over. "You okay? What the hell happened?"

"I'll tell you," said Porter. "I just might need a second."

"Because he's tired," said Duke.

Porter laughed, and it chased away a little of the pain.

"For once in his stupid life, Duke's right," he said, closing his eyes. "I am very, very tired."

CHAPTER THIRTY-EIGHT

They tended to their wounded inside the maze of mirrors, watched over by a hundred twisted versions of themselves.

Kett stood to the side as the paramedics did their thing, one of them patching up Duke's battered face, putting temporary stitches over the ugly wound above his eye. Savage kneeled next to her fiancé, her arm looped around his shoulder, her mouth to his ear. She was talking to him, but Kett couldn't make out what she was saying.

The big PC was doing his best to smile, but he was rattled. He kept glancing into the forest of glass, his wide eyes bright against his blood-red skin as they searched for monsters. He could have been twelve years old.

The other paramedic worked on Junior Short, trying to assess the damage to his skull. The killer was out cold, and he didn't look like he'd be waking up anytime soon.

If at all.

Porter sat on the ground beside Kett, his back to a mirrored wall. He was in a bad way, a nasty cut on his neck and his hands torn to pieces, but he'd refused to leave the room until he knew Duke was okay. He'd told Kett what had happened, of course, but none of it made any sense.

"Honestly, Pete," Kett said. "You can go. Get one of the Uniforms to take you up to the hospital. Those hands need checked."

Porter stared at his palms, and Kett saw the twinkle of broken glass in his ravaged flesh.

"I mean it," said Kett. "Terry Prince was not a clean man. God knows what's on this floor."

"I'm okay, sir," Porter replied, his voice soft, his eyes distant.

There was a crash from the other end of the maze, then a shout.

"Where are you, you tossers?"

"Over here, sir," Kett called back.

"Where's here?"

Kett looked back and forth, seeing nothing but reflections.

"I'm not sure," he said.

Another crash, then a roar of fury.

"Whose bright idea was it to do this in a bastard mirror maze?" the Superintendent screamed. "I can't see a bloody thing!"

"You sure you don't want to go?" Kett asked Porter. "You've still got time to make a break for it. It'll take him all week to find us."

This, at least, got a quiet laugh from the DI.

"Get out of the way, you stupid arse!" roared Clare, presumably speaking to his own reflection.

There was a chorus of violent crashes, then the Super lurched around a corner. He looked positively demonic in the red light of the room, but when he marched over and saw Duke sitting on the floor, his fury seemed to fade a little.

"Dead?" he asked.

"Uh, no, sir," said Duke. "I'm alive."

"I meant Junior, you bollock."

"No," said the paramedic. "He's taken a brutal hit to the head. Two, actually. I think his neck might be broken. But there's a chance he'll recover."

"Shame," said Clare, although he didn't elaborate on which part of her report he was talking about. "Good work, Pete."

Porter spat out a laugh.

"I'd love to claim the credit, sir, but it wasn't me."

Clare looked at Kett, who shook his head.

"Who was it, then?"

"The kid," said Porter, still staring at his hands. "One of those little scrotes in tracksuits. We saw a couple of them beating up some guy outside the tower."

"I know," said Clare. "You rescued the guy they were attacking. And his bag of drugs. They were trying to steal it?"

Porter considered it for a moment.

"I don't think so. They could have grabbed the bag before they ran, but they didn't. I couldn't figure it out, why the kid—the same kid that saved my arse tonight—led us to the flat where they were keeping all the drugs. It didn't make any sense, even if the gangs are fighting over turf, it's still a risky move. These young men are running around the streets at night, they call themselves the Iron Soldiers, and they're beating the shit out of drug dealers, including the ones at the Walpole who came after me and Jonesy."

He finally looked up.

"I think they're trying to *help*," he went on. "They're some kind of... vigilante group."

"Now I've heard it all," said Clare. "Vigilantes in track-suits? Come off it, Pete."

"The kid must have hid in here when we chased him off," said Porter. "Or he came back. I don't know. I was on the floor. Junior..."

He swallowed, struggling.

"He had me. He was going to kill me. The kid flattened him with that fire extinguisher, then he told me they weren't the bad guys, or something like that."

"Vigilantes or not, they're *still* the bad guys," said Clare. "We caught him?"

Porter shook his head, putting his hand to the wound in his neck.

"It gets weirder," he said. "I asked him why he did it, why he saved me. He said Enid told him to."

"Enid?" said Savage. "Heathen?"

Porter shrugged.

"I don't know any other Enids. He said, uh... said something like she told him to watch over me. That I'm a good spirit, and she's not done with me yet."

"How the hell did she know you were here?" said Clare.

Porter didn't have an answer.

"Probably the cards," Duke suggested. "She's psychic."

"Shut up, Aaron," said the Superintendent, turning to the first paramedic. "I take it this one is going to be okay, since he's prattling on as usual?"

"He's going to have a pretty awesome scar," she replied. "But there's nothing fatal, and no brain damage."

"No *new* brain damage," muttered Porter.

"Thanks to you, sir," said Duke, wincing as the paramedic applied some tape to his forehead. "I'd be a dead man if you hadn't shown up. A dead man with no eyes."

He shuddered, and Savage held him tighter.

"Don't flatter yourself, Aaron," said Porter. "I wasn't trying to save you."

"I heard what you said to Junior," the constable went on. "When you were standing over me. 'If you want to get to him, you have to go through me.'"

Savage flashed Porter a grateful smile, and even in the hellish light, Kett saw the DI blush.

"What I actually said was, if you want him, it's fine with me," said Porter.

Duke laughed, and immediately groaned in pain.

"I know you love me, sir," he said.

"Loved you more when you were unconscious."

"Enough!" roared Clare. "If I wanted to spend time with a pair of annoying bollocks who cause me nothing but pain and embarrassment, I'd take off my trousers. Duke, get out of here. Porter, you too. And for God's sake, take them in separate ambulances."

He turned to Kett.

"Are you hurt?"

"No," Kett replied. "I was late to the party."

"Well that's one refreshing change, at least," the Superintendent said. "You're in charge of cleaning up this mess. I want a full report on my desk first thing in the morning."

Kett was too tired to argue with him. He took Porter's arm and helped him stand up, while the paramedic and Savage worked together to heft Duke off the floor. The PC wobbled a little, but there wasn't a hope in hell of getting a stretcher through the tight, mirrored aisles, so he didn't have much choice.

For a second, they all stood there in silence, watched by an audience of reflected faces. It might have been Kett's exhaustion, but each figure caught in those mirrored walls seemed to bear a different injury. Drenched in blood-coloured light, he had the uncanny feeling that they were surrounded by ghosts—the versions of themselves who hadn't made it to the end of a case, who hadn't survived the monsters and the madmen they'd faced over the last five years.

How much longer would they have to do it? How many more times would they need to face evil, and escape death?

Sooner or later, Kett knew, their luck would run out.

And the mirrors they'd broken tonight wouldn't help.

"Have you all popped your clogs?" barked Clare, making everyone jump. "Have you run out of power? Do you need me to wind you up? Have you tossed yourselves into a state of frothy biological paralysis? Shall I go fetch a charging cable and ram it up your—"

"We're going, sir!" said Porter, limping for the exit, meeting Savage and Duke there. "Jesus Christ, we're going."

They vanished into the myriad of shifting reflections, their shuffling footsteps gradually fading. Kett was about to follow when he heard a moan from Junior's direction. The man's head was writhing on its pillow of broken glass, his mouth open. The paramedic did her best to calm him.

Kett walked to where he lay, leaning over him. The man's face had swollen up so much that his eyes were fused shut.

No small irony.

"Junior," he said. "Can you hear me?"

The man's mouth flexed, his tongue pushing between his teeth. Somehow, he managed to gargle out a handful of words.

"Let... me... go."

"You're not going anywhere," said Clare. "Except prison."

"I don't think that's what he means, sir," said Kett. "He wants to go to his son. Right, Junior?"

The man tilted his head, trying to see, trying to move. And despite the horror of what he'd done, the pain he'd inflicted on his victims, Kett felt an overwhelming sadness for him. Junior had gone through something unimaginable, he'd lost his child, and somewhere in the boundless grief he thought he'd found a way to help him.

He crouched down and placed a hand on his arm.

"I'm sorry about Luke," he said. "Truly."

"Let me... go," Junior said. "Let me go to him."

"No," said Kett, his knees cracking as he stood up again. "You don't get to do that."

He backed away, heading for the exit. Then he stopped, looking back.

"One question, Junior. Why the eyes? If you wanted these people to help Luke in the afterlife, why take their eyes?"

The man twisted his head, the rest of his body motionless. The paramedic stroked his silver hair.

"So they could see him," said Junior. "They were Luke's favourite toys, the soldiers. They'd show his angels where to find him."

Kett didn't know what to say to that, so he didn't say anything. He set off after the others, passing the Superintendent on the way out.

"Mad," grunted Clare. "He's stark raving mad."

But he wasn't, thought Kett. He was just a dad who'd found himself walking through the worst kind of hell. The love for your children was so intense that it was its own kind of madness, and Kett wasn't sure, at the end of the day, that he wouldn't have done something similar himself for his own girls.

"Yeah," was all he managed to say.

And he walked away.

CHAPTER THIRTY-NINE

"I REALLY, REALLY DIDN'T WANT IT TO END LIKE THIS, Kate."

Sergeant Stephanie Melanie Cafferty stood in the atrium of the Norfolk and Norwich hospital, her rucksack slung over her shoulder. She was wearing a neatly folded purple pocket square in her suit jacket, but it was the only ordered thing about her. Her hair was unbrushed, her shirt untucked, and she looked like a shadow of the woman who'd arrived in Norwich just two days ago.

"Me neither, Steph," said Savage.

She felt genuinely gutted about the whole thing, because she really had found a kindred spirit in the visiting sergeant. It was hard enough to make friends in this job, because nobody really understood the pressure of it. The violence and the madness.

The horror.

She'd clicked with Cafferty instantly, and she felt genuinely sad that their friendship had shattered so quickly, and so profoundly. It wasn't just Cafferty's fault, of course.

She'd broken the rules by taking evidence, but Savage was the one who'd ruptured their trust by rooting through her bags. Whatever happened to Cafferty, whether she stayed in the job or not, there was no hope of rebuilding what had been lost.

"You'll stay in touch?" said Cafferty. "I mean, if there's another serial killer or something?"

"Yeah," said Savage. "Of course. We wouldn't have been able to catch Junior, if it wasn't for you."

Cafferty waved the words away with a bashful smile.

"I think I was wrong on most counts," she said. "But it sure was fun trying to figure it out together."

"It was," said Savage.

Cafferty laughed.

"I've just realised something. Enid's fortune telling, in the kitchen. The tower, the eye. I think maybe she was trying to tell *me* something."

"Yeah?" said Savage.

"Distress. Calamity. Disgrace. Ruin. It certainly fits."

Savage nodded.

"Good luck, Steph. I hope they go easy on you."

The sergeant shrugged her broad shoulders.

"Honestly, Kate, it's not my first offence. Something tells me they're not going to be so forgiving this time."

She sighed, then hoiked up her rucksack.

"You take care, Sergeant Savage," she said. "And can I give you some unwanted advice?"

"Sure," she said.

"That great big, hairy hunk of a man up there loves you more than I've ever seen anyone love anything. Whatever's holding you back, let it go."

Savage opened her mouth to reply, and found that she couldn't. Besides, Cafferty was walking away, heading through the sliding doors into the shimmering heat of the car park, vanishing around the corner.

"Let it go?" muttered Savage, a little indignantly.

She passed Porter on the way to the elevators, the DI sitting on a chair in the waiting area, looking about as miserable as she'd ever seen him. His hands were bandaged so heavily it looked like he was wearing oven mitts.

"You okay, sir?" she asked.

"Yeah," he said. "Just waiting for a ride."

"I can give you one, if you hang on for half an hour?"

He shook his head, staring at the doors.

"Well, text me if you change your mind," she said. She looked at his hands. "Or, you know, just come and find me."

She rode up in the lift, still fuming about Cafferty's comment.

"Let it *go*?"

When she got to Duke's room, she slammed the door behind her with a little more force than she'd intended. He was sitting up in bed, the top of his head bandaged like a sore thumb. He was one big bruise, but he still had a smile on his face.

He *always* had a smile on his face when he looked at her.

"Don't be sad, babe," he said, the words obviously causing him pain. "I've got something that will cheer you up."

She sat on the edge of his bed, taking his huge hand in both of hers. There were nicks and cuts all over him, and it hurt her heart to see them.

"I was thinking," he said, his words full of excitement, "about the wedding."

She felt a sudden, unpleasant rush of adrenaline, the way she always did when he mentioned it. She held his hand a little harder, in the hope it might make him stop, but he was on a roll.

"The whole Funland thing, Terry's place, in the tower. That would be such a good theme, right?"

"Funland?" she said, trying and failing to keep the shock from her expression. "As in the place where you almost died last night?"

"Yeah. Well, no, probably not the mirror maze, but everything else. Like, all the games and things, the ball pits. Bouncy castles. We could dress up. It would be so much fun. People would love it."

She blew a slow breath through her tight lips, and he petered out.

"Furry vicar?" he added.

"Probably not," she said. "Sorry."

"That's cool," said Duke, slumping a little in the bed. "It was just an idea, because you haven't really liked any of the other ones. But we'll get there. We'll find something you like. I want it to be perfect, Kate, because *you're* perfect. I want it to be a day we remember for the rest of our lives."

He put his other calloused hand to her cheek, and she leaned into it. She didn't know why she was so reluctant to move forward, to set a date, to actually marry him. She loved him, of course. There was absolutely no doubt about that. She'd never felt this way about anybody before, other than maybe the dog. She wanted him to be her husband, she wanted to commit, she wanted to grow old with him, the whole 'until death do us part' stuff.

She wanted it all.

So what was holding her back? Why couldn't she make the leap? If she'd spoken to a therapist, she knew there would be a tonne of stuff about her own parents, about the fact she'd never really known her dad, about her mum being so distant.

And deep down, she knew that she was afraid, because if they both stayed in the job, then at some point the job would kill them. The thought of it made her want to run away, because despite what everyone said, it was better to have *never* loved, than to love and lose it all.

"We'll get there, Kate," he said. "I love you."

She gave him the look, and he laughed.

"I love you, *Sarge*."

She laughed too, looking into Duke's eyes, so full of warmth, so full of affection, so full of care. Eyes that a killer had tried to take away from him. She'd come so close to losing him, again.

So why not do everything she could to keep him close?

Let it go.

"Let's do it," she said, a rush of joy and excitement rising inside her, washing away the panic and the fear. "Let's set a date."

"Yeah?" said Duke. "Seriously? A date? For the wedding?"

She nodded.

"Funland?"

"No, Aaron, not that. But let's get married. I want to get married. This year."

"Holy shit! This year? We're actually going to do it?"

He leaned forward and wrapped her in his tree-trunk arms. She pushed her face into his chest, laughing.

"Yeah," she said. "We're going to do it."

IT WAS ALMOST LUNCHTIME, and an hour later than she'd said she'd be, when Allie Porter walked through the doors of the hospital. She was pushing Bobby's stroller, the kid struggling against his straps, his face bright red and sweaty from the hot day. Allie looked just as flustered, snapping at him when he started to squeal, and just as angry at Porter when she saw him in the waiting area.

"Hi," he said, getting out of his chair and giving her a little wave with his padded hand. The meds were doing a good job of keeping the pain away, but he was still struggling. The flesh of his palms had been torn to ribbons.

There had been a time in his life when his heart had soared whenever Allie had entered a room. Literally, it had felt like it was straining to get out of his chest. Most of that feeling had probably been nerves, because Allie had always been beautiful, more so now than ever, and he'd always worried that one day she'd realise how far out of his league she was. He knew all too well how lucky he'd been that she'd chosen him to spend her days with, to have a baby with.

Today, though, as he watched her stomp towards him, jerking the buggy to try to keep Bobby quiet, her face twisted into a knot of irritation, he felt his heart plop right into his shoes.

"Why couldn't you get a taxi?" she said. Not so much as a hello or a how are you.

She stared at his hands like he was pulling a prank on her. Bobby strained to get to him, and it crushed Porter's soul that he wasn't able to pick the kid up.

"Hey," he said. "Daddy's okay, just a few cuts."

"Come on, then," said Allie, turning the buggy around fast enough to give Bobby whiplash. "I'm parked on the road, I don't want a ticket."

Porter followed her through the door, a pressure in his chest like he'd dived too deep into a cold, black lake. Even the sun couldn't chase away the chill. Allie's Mercedes was parked right outside, in a bus stop, but fortunately, the car park wasn't too busy. He couldn't help her load a screaming Bobby back into his seat. He couldn't even fumble his own door open, even though he tried. He just watched her grow increasingly angry at the car, at his son, at him, until they were all inside and the doors were closed.

Here, at least, the breeze from the vents seemed to cool her fury a little. Bobby's screams became quiet sobs, then happy murmurs as he spotted the buses grumbling past.

Allie put her hands on the wheel, steadying herself.

"Alright," she said, turning to him. She managed a tight smile, a dim reflection of the one he'd fallen for all those years ago. "Home? We can put a film on, eat some popcorn. There's this new thing on Disney that Bobby's obsessed with."

He nodded through a yawn, and Allie breathed out a sigh of frustration.

"Or you could sleep, I guess," she snapped. "I'll take him out somewhere."

Porter thought again about how much he loved her, but he couldn't help asking how much of it was still real, and how much of it was a story he liked to tell himself.

Because all he felt right now was empty.

"Actually..." he started.

It was the hardest thing he'd ever had to say, but he took a breath and said it.

"I think we need to talk."

KETT STOOD ON THE ROAD, watching as a platoon of coppers tore apart a house on the edge of the estate. To his left, over the rooftops, the blue sentinel of Norvic House watched from inside its cage of scaffolding, a prisoner inside a cell. It still turned his blood to ice, how close they'd come to losing Duke in there last night.

He'd managed to sleep, at least. All of five hours, before the girls had woken him up with a breakfast in bed that consisted of two slices of unbuttered white bread and a shoe. He would have happily stayed in bed while Billie did the school run, but Clare had called and told him they'd managed to hack the phone that Porter had found in the dealer's bag. A long list of addresses for the gang that had been causing so much misery in the city.

If he'd had any doubts before about the Iron Soldiers being some sort of vigilante group, they were fading fast.

The Superintendent lurked next to him, dark-eyed and serious. Kett wasn't sure whether the man had got any sleep or not. His face looked like a hot water bottle that had been through an elephant's digestive system, but these days, he *always* looked like that.

"You think we can trust that lad?" said Clare, watching the PCs through the windows of the house.

"He did save Pete," said Kett. "He could have left him there, left him to Junior, left him to die. And it makes sense, you know? We've never seen these guys do anything other than go after the actual dealers. Even when they turned up at the Walpole, they weren't trying to sell Jonesy anything, they were trying to scare him off."

"Vigilantes in hoodies," said Clare, shaking his head. "I didn't have that on my bingo card for this year. But it seems like the kid was telling the truth. Remember the two young women we found in Enid's house?"

"The addicts?"

"We tracked them down this morning. They told us the place is for rehab. According to them, the Iron Soldiers rescued them from the gang, and Enid was looking after them. She's rescued a lot of people, including most of the Iron Soldiers themselves. Half of them are ex-County Lines."

"What?" said Kett. "So they *are* working together? Enid and the Soldiers?"

"It seems so," said Clare. "But there's no sign of the old bat. She's gone. Not only that, but there's nobody on record with that name. She's clever. She knew about us, the stuff with Savage's granddad, and Porter's home life. She did her research. Whoever she is, she was leading us on a merry goose chase. She's gone into hiding, and it looks like the lads have too."

One of the coppers walked out of the house, hauling a cuffed man alongside him.

"Something tells me that we'll see her again," said Kett.

"Bloody hope not," said Clare. "I'd quite like to flush this whole sorry mess down the toilet."

"Anything from Junior?" said Kett, watching the police haul another suspect out of the house.

"He's not said much," Clare told him. "But it doesn't matter. It's not like any jury will find him innocent. I'm more worried they'll rule him insane."

"Either way, he's never getting out," said Kett. "He's done."

"They found some books in Nolan O'Brien's flat," Clare said. "Paranormal stuff, all about the power of the eyes, all about how to find your way in the afterlife. Junior must have been inspired there. I don't know if we'll ever find out the whole truth of it."

For a few minutes, they watched as Cara Hay's forensic team filed into the house, carting their equipment with them.

"You believe in the afterlife, Robbie?" asked Clare.

The question was so unexpected that Kett didn't know how to reply.

"I do," Clare went on. "Paradise. No murders, no haemorrhoids, no Robert Kett. I can't bloody wait."

Kett laughed quietly.

"Not sure if I believe in it, sir," he said. "But I hope it's true. For all the people who didn't get much of a chance here, you know?"

He swallowed, thinking of Luke Short on his hospital bed, seeing his bright smile.

"All the kids," he went on, rubbing his eyes. "Be nice to think they go somewhere good. With good people."

"Yeah," said Clare.

The Superintendent clapped a hand on Kett's shoulder, squeezing, then set off towards the house.

"Go on, now," he said. "Get out of here."

"Home, sir?" said Kett, feeling a glimmer of hope.

"No, you cup of flaming toss, to HQ. You've got paperwork to finish."

"Right," said Kett.

He headed for the car, enjoying the sun on his face, feeling the sense of calm he often did when they'd closed a case. There would always be more monsters, of course. The world was full of them. But for now, at least, there was just the warm day and the chattering birds.

His phone buzzed as he opened the door of the Volvo, but he didn't recognise the number. He considered not answering it, but the more time he spent here, in the pleasant warmth of the afternoon, the less time he'd spend in the festering cesspit of the Extreme Crime Task Force's Incident Room.

He leaned on the roof of the car to answer it.

"This is DCI Kett."

A hoarse breath on the other end, then a dry sniff.

"Robert Kett?"

It was an old man's voice, full of quiet fury.

"Yeah," he said. "Who's this?"

"You can call me Nigel Topper," it said.

The name made Kett push himself off the car.

"Or, if you'd rather," the man went on, "Mad Dog."

A flash from Kett's past, a memory that he'd spent half his life trying to repress.

A gun. A river. A dead man.

"Shit," he said.

The old man on the end of the line laughed, as if Kett had just confirmed something for him. And Kett suddenly found himself back inside the Sportspark, speaking to Harrison Baird.

I think you kent my father, back in London. Dougie Baird. Used to work for a fella called Nigel Topper, back when you were under John Cooper in the Met. Ring any bells?

This bell was ringing so loudly he couldn't hear himself think.

"This is just a courtesy call, Robert," said the man on the phone. "This is just to make you aware that I know. After all these years, I know what you did."

There would always be more monsters.

The day was suddenly cold, the birds quiet. Kett lowered the phone, but he could still hear Mad Dog's voice.

"And now it's time to pay the reaper."

DCI KETT RETURNS IN...

UNTIL DEATH

The wedding of the year.
The crime of the century.

Summer 2026

PAPER GIRLS
ALEX SMITH
BAD DOG
ALEX SMITH
THREE LITTLE PIGS
ALEX SMITH
WHIP CRACK
ALEX SMITH
RUN RABBIT RUN
ALEX SMITH
STONE COLD DEAD
ALEX SMITH
EVERY MOTHER'S SON
ALEX SMITH
SWEET BRIAR ROSE
ALEX SMITH
JAW BREAKER
ALEX SMITH
KNOCK KNOCK
ALEX SMITH
KING RAT
ALEX SMITH
KNUCKLE BONES
ALEX SMITH
LUCKY NUMBER SEVEN
ALEX SMITH
UNHOLY SAINTS
ALEX SMITH
TRULY MADLY DEADLY
ALEX SMITH
EVERY LAST DEVIL
ALEX SMITH
RED LINE
ALEX SMITH
COLD IRON KILLS
ALEX SMITH
TIN SOLDIERS
ALEX SMITH
READ THE DCI KETT BOOKS NOW!

ABOUT THE AUTHOR

Alex Smith wrote his first book when he was six. It wasn't particularly good, but it did have some supernatural monsters in it. His latest books, the DCI Robert Kett and DI Harrison Baird thrillers, have monsters in them too, although these monsters are very human, and all the more terrifying for it. In between, he has published fourteen novels for children and teenagers under his full name, Alexander Gordon Smith—including the number one best-selling series Escape From Furnace, which is loved by millions of readers worldwide and which is soon to become a motion picture. He lives in Norwich with his wife and three young daughters.

Find out more at alexsmithbooks.com

RELENTLESS
MEDIA

Printed in Dunstable, United Kingdom

80278062R00262